FOR THE BIRDS

ROSE GARDNER INVESTIGATIONS #2

DENISE GROVER SWANK

FOR THE BIRDS

ROSE GARDNER INVESTIGATIONS #2

Book two in the New York Times and USA Today bestselling
Rose Gardner Investigations series.

Rose Gardner is trying to build a new normal. One that leaves
the Fenton County crime world—including James "Skeeter"
Malcom, the current king—behind. Her best friend and room-
mate is a big part of that effort, but Neely Kate is busy building
her own life anew. She disappeared for a few days, scaring the
spit out of Rose—which is why Rose finds it impossible to deny
her when she suggests they look for a missing parrot. Only this
time Neely Kate isn't interested in the reward money; she's set
them up to work with a cranky private investigator known as
Kermit the Hermit. Rose sees it for what it is: another bid for
them to become private investigators.

If nothing else, it's a good distraction...until one of James's neme-
ses, Buck Reynolds, comes calling for help. James's brother has
gone missing, and Wagner is number one on the crime king's
suspect list. Only, according to him, he's innocent.

Rose had promised herself she was through with the crime world, but she wants to see his James's brother safe. Besides, can she really say no when she might be the only one who can keep order in the county?

Cover design: Damonza

Developmental Editor: Angela Polidoro

Copy editor: Shannon Page

Proofreader: Carolina Miller-Schneider

ISBN: 978-1-939996-53-4

❀ Created with Vellum

CHAPTER 1

I hadn't intended to start off my day with a hostage negotiation, much less for it to happen at my landscaping company.

"Just put the gun down, and nobody gets hurt."

"But he took Mr. Bearington!" my niece Ashley said, pointing a water gun at her brother. Her cheeks were flushed and her eyes had filled with tears. "He's going to rip his head off!"

"No, he's not." I turned to her brother, then said with forced patience, "Mikey. Give the bear back to your sister."

"He's not just a bear, Aunt Rose!" Ashley protested, waving the pistol. Lord only knew where she'd gotten it . . . probably from my best friend Neely Kate's desk drawer. "He's Mr. Bearington, and Mommy gave him to me before she left."

Before my sister Violet left for Houston for chemo and a bone marrow transplant. She was finally coming home this afternoon, and everyone was on edge. The kids hadn't seen her in over three months. The last time they saw her, she'd just been through an aggressive round of chemo, and they'd had to wear masks and gowns whenever they were near her. Both kids had returned with nightmares.

I knelt down in front of my two-year-old nephew, who eyed me with distrust—not that I was surprised. I hadn't seen much of him or Ashley in the last six months, and six months had been a quarter of his life. Mike had asked me to keep my visits with them to a minimum. He'd claimed that seeing me reminded them that their mother was gone. I'd agreed to it in the beginning, but something felt off. His parents were out of town this week, which had made me the most logical person to watch the kids while he flew to Houston to bring Violet home, but he'd seemed reluctant to accept my offer.

"Ashley loves Mr. Bearington. Don't you want to give him back to her?"

His tiny brow furrowed and his lips puckered as he shook his head in defiance. *"No."*

I narrowed my eyes at him as I tried to figure out how to handle the situation. I could just reach out and take the bear from him, but I was hoping to reach a more diplomatic solution.

The jingling bell on the front door of my office alerted me that someone was walking in, but I was too invested in my battle of wills with a toddler to greet them.

"This looks like a standoff—and I would know." The voice unmistakably belonged to Joe, my best friend's brother.

I turned and saw him standing in the doorway in his sheriff's uniform, his broad shoulders filling the space. Though I was exasperated with my nephew, Joe's grin was contagious.

"What seems to be the problem here?" he asked, walking in and closing the door behind him.

"Uncle Joe," Ashley said as she ran for him and wrapped herself around his leg. "Mikey won't give me Mr. Bearington."

Uncle Joe. The name caught me off guard. Ashley had started calling him Uncle Joe last summer, while he and I were dating, and she'd kept it up because he'd lived next door to my sister for a while after our breakup.

He leaned over and cupped her tiny shoulder with his large

hand. "Let me see what I can do. I'm pretty good with negotiations." Joe grabbed my desk chair and rolled it in front of Mikey and took a seat, making him closer to the boy's height. "Hey, Mikey. Remember me?"

Mikey glared up at him and shook his head, clutching the bear tighter.

Joe grinned. "That's okay. It's been a while, but you and I go way back." Joe leaned closer and lowered his voice. "It just so happens that I know your favorite ice cream used to be strawberry. Is it still strawberry?"

Mikey's eyes widened in surprise, and he nodded.

"If you give Ashley back her bear, I'll take you over to Dena's cupcake shop and get you some ice cream. What do you say to that?"

"I'd say that's bribery," I said. "And it's only ten in the morning."

Joe glanced up at me, his eyes twinkling. "You're just sorry I thought of it first."

I tried to glare at him but couldn't quite pull it off. "Okay. Maybe."

Joe turned back to Mikey and gave him an intent look. "What do you say, big guy? Ice cream?"

Mikey nodded and shoved the bear at his sister, who clutched it to her chest and buried her face into it.

"I'm not sure I should ask," Joe said, "but how's babysitting going?"

I laughed. "Pretty much what you're seeing. Lots of crying and obstinance."

Joe grinned. "And how are the kids doin'?"

"Ha. Ha." I swatted his shoulder. "You think you're so funny."

Joe turned to Ashley. "I am funny, aren't I?"

She slowly shook her head. "No, Uncle Joe," she said, her tone solemn.

He laughed. *"No?* Then it's obvious you haven't spent enough time with me lately."

Just as obvious that they hadn't spent enough time with *me*. Or their mother. In any case, they were here now, and I was pretty sure they were acting out due to nerves.

Ashley's mouth tipped down. "My mommy's coming home today."

If Joe was surprised by her subdued tone, he didn't let on. "She's been gone a long time, huh?"

She nodded, then just as quickly gave Joe a pouty face. "Can I get ice cream too, Uncle Joe?"

Joe grabbed her and pulled her into a hug, tickling her belly. "You *could* have had ice cream if you'd said I was funny. Now . . ."

She squealed and giggled, and then Mikey felt left out and grabbed Joe's leg, and Joe scooped him up into his other arm.

A wave of nostalgia washed through me, and I caught Joe's equally subdued gaze. He'd always been amazing with my niece and nephew when we were together. But Joe had more cause to be melancholy than I did. As obvious as it was that he'd make a great father, over the past year and a half he'd lost two babies by two different women . . . and neither one of them had been me. My niece and nephew were no doubt a bitter reminder of what could have been.

But as quickly as his sadness appeared, he pushed it away and flashed a smile. "Aunt Rose," Joe said, "can you leave the office to go get ice cream?"

I grimaced. "Can you either take the kids or bring the ice cream back to them? I'd like to call Neely Kate. She's still not back yet."

Joe's jovial expression slid right off his face, concern filling his eyes. "Where'd she go?"

"She was going to talk to a potential client about a design, but she should have been back by now."

His eyes shuttered, and he was Chief Deputy Simmons now. "How long ago was she supposed to be back?"

After finding out that Neely Kate was his half sister in February, Joe had taken his new role as a brother to heart.

"An hour ago," I said, waving him off. "I'm sure it's nothin'."

"Not necessarily." He set both kids on the floor and stood, walking over to me. "That's why I'm here. To find out what you know about what's goin' on in the criminal world."

The hair on the back of my neck stood on end.

"I know you've had ties to Skeeter Malcolm," he added.

I crossed my arms over my chest. "That was in the past."

His eyebrows rose as his gaze pierced mine. "Rumor has it you had dealings in the criminal world only a few weeks ago."

My mouth dropped open. "And what do you know about that?"

"I know that you took a meeting with Malcolm, Wagner, and Reynolds at the Putnam Industrial Park."

I tried to hide my surprise. The only way he could know about that meeting was if someone had talked. I'd bet my farm that it hadn't been one of James Malcolm's men, but I didn't trust Buck Reynolds or Kip Wagner any farther than I could throw them. Still, if Joe knew about it, I saw no reason to hide it from him. "I did."

"As the Lady in Black." It wasn't a question.

"I was doing my part as a concerned citizen to keep peace in this county."

His lips pressed together in a tight line, and several seconds passed before he said, "You have to see that you're playin' with fire."

"I'm not playin' with anything anymore," I said with a hint of attitude. "I'm done with that world."

Joe didn't look convinced, not that I was surprised. My alter ego had wreaked havoc on my life, so I'd hung up my hat as Lady in February. But I couldn't pretend I hadn't liked pulling her out of mothballs weeks ago. Unfortunately, James Malcolm, king of the Fenton County crime world, had double-crossed me during that meeting, and I had neither seen nor heard from him since. I was starting to think I might *never* hear from him—a thought that had me vacillating between "good riddance" and a hopeless feeling of loss and regret.

He lowered his voice. "I know you were meeting over that damned missin' necklace."

"The only thing I'm gonna tell you is that the matter was resolved and peace was restored."

"You sure about that?" he asked in a dry tone.

"Uncle Joe," Ashley said, tugging on his arm. "You said we could get ice cream."

"I sure did," he said, bestowing his bright smile on her. "But Mikey's taken off his shoes. Why don't you help him get them back on so we can walk across the town square?"

I started to protest that Mikey had his shoes on—I'd put them on myself—when I saw his little bare feet. He'd tucked his shoes under my desk.

I resisted the urge to sigh. I'd been watching my niece and nephew for the past two days, and it had been nonstop action. Since Neely Kate lived with me in my farmhouse, I couldn't help wondering if she was staying away for longer than necessary to catch a few moments of peace.

As soon as the thought crept into my mind, I chased it away. Neely Kate had loved every minute of having Ashley and Mikey around, but she *had* seemed a little sad this morning.

Neely Kate and Joe had both lost babies before they were born. She had miscarried her twins last January, and the doctor had told her she'd probably never have more children. If there was ever a woman who was meant to be a mother, it was my best friend. Spending two days with my niece and nephew had likely broken her heart.

But at the moment, I was concerned that Joe was questioning peace in the county.

Ashley scrambled under the desk to get Mikey's shoes, and I took advantage of the few moments of reprieve. "What do you know that you're not telling me?"

"Seems like you're in a better position to know than me," he said.

I shook my head. "I wasn't lyin'. I haven't heard a peep about that world since that meeting."

He studied me as though deciphering whether I was telling the truth. Finally, he said, "There's some rumblings goin' round. Something about Skeeter Malcolm's brother."

"Scooter?" I asked in surprise, then shook my head. "He has nothing to do with that world. Bruce Wayne said James refuses to let him take part."

Joe looked surprised that I was talking about it so freely, but Joe knew the higher-up politics of the county criminal world. I saw no point in beating around the bush.

"Scooter's missin'."

"What?" I said louder than intended. "What happened?"

"Hell if I know." Then he cringed and glanced back to see if the kids had noticed his swear. They hadn't; Ashley had returned to playing with Mr. Bearington, and her brother was now playing with the Velcro straps rather than putting the shoes on. Joe leaned closer and lowered his voice even more. "It's not like Malcolm filed a missing person report."

"No, I guess not," I said with a frown, my imagination working overtime. "So how do *you* know about it? I take it you have some super-secret source since you knew about the parley from a few weeks ago."

"Parley?" he asked in surprise.

I gave him a smug look. "I guess you don't know *everything*." I looked up into his worried brown eyes. "I told you. I worked out a peace agreement over the necklace. James invoked parley to discuss it."

"Well, I'm not so sure it worked," Joe said, "because Scooter's missin', and word has it that one of Malcolm's rivals took him."

"Which one?" I asked.

He gave me a look of disgust. "Exactly. The man has more enemies than I can count." He eyed me with suspicion. "You really didn't know?"

"No." Nevertheless, I was worried. While I'd never met Scooter, he was a close friend of my business partner, Bruce Wayne. And James . . . he had to be beside himself with worry. Scooter was a simple man, not capable of the machinations that could help him escape a kidnapper's grasp—and everyone who knew him said he was as kind as he was uncomplicated.

But I couldn't concern myself with James. He'd made it clear he didn't want me to.

"With Neely Kate's and your connections to the underworld and Scooter missin' . . ."

My heart lodged in my throat. "I should be careful."

Ashley tugged on Joe's arm again, and Mikey, who'd finally stopped playing with the shoes and put them on, tugged on the other.

"Come on, Uncle Joe. You can talk to Aunt Rose later," Ashley said, trying to strong-arm him toward the door. "We have to get ice cream before Mommy comes home."

"Ice cream," Mikey said, pulling on his other hand.

I swallowed my worry and forced a smile. "You know Neely Kate—she's gotten distracted by something. I'm sure she's fine. Go ahead and take them to Dena's, and I'll call her and see what's keepin' her so long. I'll have an answer by the time you three get back."

"Okay," Joe said with a concerned look. Then he pretended to let the kids pull him to the door. "Call me if you find out anything alarming."

I grabbed my phone off my desk and pulled up Neely Kate's number. When she didn't answer, I told myself not to panic. There could be half a dozen reasonable explanations, but I was worried nonetheless. Joe was right. We'd inserted ourselves into the Fenton County crime world with that parley, and we hadn't even bothered with a disguise—we'd gone as ourselves. Yes, I'd attended as the Lady in Black, but this time I hadn't been wearing any kind of veil or mask.

Besides, Neely Kate hadn't been herself over the last few days. And after her disappearance last week, that had me worried.

CHAPTER 2

*N*eely Kate had run off to Ardmore, Oklahoma, where she'd lived with her mother before Jenny Lynn Rivers had dumped her, at age twelve, on her grandmother's doorstep in Fenton County and had never come back. After her high school graduation, Neely Kate had returned to Ardmore and stayed for nearly two years. She rarely talked about anything to do with her mother, who'd never contacted her after abandoning her, *or* Oklahoma. While I knew she was deeply ashamed of her previous life, I wasn't sure why. I knew beyond a shadow of a doubt that Neely Kate had been abused, but I didn't know any details. I'd respected her privacy, knowing how much it hurt her to discuss it, but now I wondered if that had been a mistake.

Kate Simmons, Neely Kate's newly discovered half sister, had been sending her letters in the mail, and although my best friend refused to tell me any details, I knew Kate was holding something over her head. So Neely Kate's sudden trip to Oklahoma hadn't come as a total surprise . . . but her companion had.

Jed Carlisle.

Jed was James "Skeeter" Malcolm's right-hand man. He'd acted as my bodyguard last winter, so I trusted him implicitly. I was grateful he'd been with her, but I couldn't help wondering how they had ended up together in the first place, and she refused to tell me. I could have asked James, but my pride insisted that *he* had to come to *me* first.

Neely Kate had returned after two days, apologizing for taking off and assuring me that everything was okay. She said she'd taken care of everything—and she'd left it at that. So why did she still seem distracted and on edge?

The bell on the office door jingled, and Neely Kate walked into the office. She was wearing her favorite blue dress, the one I'd told her made her eyes look like the summer sky.

I placed my hand on my chest and said, "Oh, thank God."

She shut the door behind her and moved closer. "Why do you look like that?" Fear filled her eyes. "Oh, my stars and garters. Did something happen?"

I closed the distance between us and pulled her into a hug. "No. I was just worried. I tried to call you and you didn't answer."

"I was at that landscaping appointment."

"I know . . ." Now that the initial relief had worn off, I was struck by her appearance—mussed hair, pink cheeks, and bright eyes . . . a look that seemed to seesaw between happy and sad. I hadn't thought much of her wearing the dress today since we were throwing Violet a welcome home party this afternoon, but now I wondered if there were other reasons.

"I didn't think I'd be gone so long." She pulled away and looked around the office. "Where are the kids?"

"Joe came by and took them to Dena's for ice cream."

"It's not even lunchtime."

I shook my head and grinned. "He bribed them to stop fighting."

She laughed. "So *that's* the key. Have you heard anything from Violet or Mike?"

"No. Not yet, but I don't think their plane has landed. The plan for the party hasn't changed, as far as I know."

Neely Kate shook her head. "I still can't believe Mike went to get her. Are they moving forward with the divorce?"

"I'm not sure. Vi said they've been talking on the phone after she talks to the kids. In fact, she's goin' home with them after the party."

"I'm surprised he's so willing to forgive her," Neely Kate said. "He seemed pretty pissed at her last fall."

"Thinkin' someone you love is gonna die probably changes things," I said absently, shocked when an image of James surfaced in my head. If Scooter had been snatched—or, worse yet, killed— the perpetrator had done it to hurt James. Which meant James wasn't just hurting; he could be in danger too.

Not my concern.

Then why did my heart seize up and make it difficult to breathe?

I sat in my chair. "I was concerned because Joe told me something worrisome when he came by."

Her eyes widened. "Oh?"

"Scooter Malcolm is missing."

"Oh." Her voice had lowered an octave as she walked over to her desk and set her purse in her drawer, avoiding eye contact with me.

"Wait. *You knew?*"

I wasn't necessarily surprised. Neely Kate knew just about everything that was going on in Fenton County, let alone Henryetta—a fact she was downright proud of, which made her behavior all the stranger. "I'd heard."

"Why in Sam Hill didn't you tell me?"

She looked up at me with contrition in her eyes. "Jed told me the day we came back from Oklahoma. That's why we returned so suddenly."

I gave myself a tiny shake, suddenly confused. "You told me you came back because you'd finished up your business."

She walked over and sat on the edge of my desk, her eyes

pleading with mine. "I did. But we also found out that Scooter was missing, and Jed was eager to get back."

"Why didn't you tell me?" I repeated, trying to keep the hurt out of my voice.

She grimaced. "Because of Skeeter. I know you and him . . ."

"Scooter's disappearance has nothing to do with my feelings for James Malcolm."

"Are you sure about that?" she asked quietly.

I wanted to say yes, but it would have been a lie. Still, this was far bigger than my fight with James. "How is Bruce Wayne taking this news?"

"I'm not sure he knows. In fact, I'm surprised Joe knows. Jed says Skeeter's keeping it quiet."

I blinked. "*Says?* As in you've talked to Jed about Scooter this week?"

Guilty surprise washed over her face, like she was a teenager who'd gotten caught sneaking out of the house. "Yeah."

I started to ask her why she hadn't told me that either when the front door opened and Joe walked in with Ashley next to him and Mikey on his hip. Each child had an ice cream cone.

Neely Kate hopped off my desk and spun around. "What are you thinkin' feedin' them ice cream practically for breakfast?" she asked with a laugh as she walked over to him and reached for Mikey. I knew a stalling tactic when I saw one, but I decided to allow it. If there was anything to tell, she certainly wasn't going to share it in front of Joe. "I don't think we should get ice cream on Aunt Rose's pretty clothes."

I was wearing a new outfit Neely Kate had persuaded me to buy—a full pink skirt with a large floral pattern, but it was the top that really pushed me out of my comfort zone, which was most likely the main reason she'd convinced me to get it. The white shirt had a slightly off-the-shoulder neckline that plunged into a deep V in both the front and back. It was completely impractical for work, but I didn't have any site visits planned for the day, and we were planning to close the office when we went to the nursery for Violet's welcome home party.

My nephew held out an arm and she scooped him into her arms as Joe said, "It held off World War III for a good half hour. I was just doin' my part to save humanity."

"Oh really?" she asked with a grin. "So why do I see some strawberry ice cream at the corner of your mouth?"

His eyes twinkling, he licked the corner of his mouth. "I was trying to save my uniform. It's hot out there."

"I can't believe Dena served them ice cream," Neely Kate said, shaking her head. "She's pretty strict with her no ice cream until after noon policy."

"She didn't want to give us any," Ashley said between licks of her chocolate cone. "She only agreed when Uncle Joe said he'd go to the carnival tonight."

"Why would Dena care if Joe went to the carnival tonight?" I asked and instantly regretted it. "Oh." She'd asked him to go with *her*.

Joe grimaced and used the napkin in his hand to wipe Mikey's face as he quickly changed the subject. "Is Maeve still expecting us all at the nursery at a quarter to one?"

"Yeah," I said, feeling awkward. The only woman Joe had been with after our breakup was his long-time, on-and-off-again girl-friend, Hilary, and even then, he'd been pressured into it. As far as I knew, this was the first time he'd agreed to go out with someone with actual girlfriend potential.

I hadn't thought much about Joe not dating. He'd been through a lot over the last year and a half. In February, he'd killed his father (to save me), his sister had been arrested for killing Hilary and their unborn baby, and he'd found out that Neely Kate was his half sister. One of those things would have been enough to throw a man for a serious loop, let alone three.

Maybe he was finally ready to move on, which was a good thing. I wanted Joe to be happy. Still, there was no denying the thought of seeing him with someone new made me feel slightly uncomfortable.

"Then maybe we'll see you there," Neely Kate said. "Rose and I are goin' too."

Joe looked a little uncomfortable too. It was obvious he'd like to be anywhere other than standing in my office talking about his date with his sister and ex-girlfriend.

"Well," he said, running his hand over his head. "I need to talk to the prosecutor and tie up some things before I see you at the nursery." He bolted out the door before we could say anything else.

"Hmm . . ." Neely Kate said, watching him jaywalk across the street. "What do you make of that?" But the tone in her voice suggested she knew exactly what to make of it.

"It's not any of my concern." And it wasn't. My biggest concern at the moment was breaking the news about Scooter to Bruce Wayne. He'd be joining us at the party, but I didn't want to wait. Which made me even more surprised that Neely Kate had held out on us for so long. I grabbed my purse and stood. "But there's something that is. I need to go see Bruce Wayne at the job site. Can you watch the kids?"

She caught my short tone. "Yeah." She set Mikey down on the floor and moved toward her desk. "Bruce Wayne doesn't have the altered plans for the Greens' backyard. He's not supposed to get to it until tomorrow, but would you drop them off just in case?"

"Of course."

She dug through a stack of documents on her desk, then handed me a paper. I reached for it, but she held on and looked me in the eyes.

"I'm sorry, Rose."

"You should have told me, Neely Kate."

"It wasn't for me to tell. Jed asked me to keep it quiet, so I did."

"Even from me?" I asked, the pain clear in my voice.

"And how many secrets have you kept from me?" she asked

without a hint of malice. "How many secrets have you shared with Skeeter Malcolm that you never once considered sharing with me?"

I sucked in a breath.

"And before you try to deny it," she said, her tone picking up some heat, "don't forget about those Tuesday night meetings you refused to tell me about."

I'd been meeting James every Tuesday night for months right up until our falling out three weeks ago. Neely Kate had known about the arrangement, but I'd never acknowledged it. "You're right. I'm sorry."

Her gaze still held mine. "I wanted to tell you about Scooter, but I couldn't. I kept my word. Just like I'm sure you kept yours."

She was right. About all of it. I'd kept more secrets from her than I could count. And they were all tied to James Malcolm. Why did it feel like everything tied back to James? "Well, we're not mixed up in the Fenton County crime world anymore, so no worries about keeping secrets."

I snatched the paper from her, kissed Ashley and Mikey good-bye, and headed out to my truck. It wasn't until I was halfway down the street that I realized Neely Kate hadn't agreed.

CHAPTER 3

*B*ruce Wayne was working on a yard in a neighborhood south of town, so the fifteen-minute drive gave me plenty of time to think.

It shamed me to think I'd let James get between Neely Kate and me. I'd kept his secrets and then some—unquestionably. What had he ever done for me?

Treated me with more respect than any other man in my life.

When he saw me, he didn't see the weak and naïve woman Joe had met over a year ago while working undercover. And he didn't see the woman I'd been with my boyfriend Mason, intelligent but in need of protecting. James was the first man who'd challenged me to think myself capable of so much more. He'd helped me create my alter ego, the Lady in Black, and then encouraged me to meld the strong, take-charge woman I became while wearing the veiled disguise with the woman I was to everyone else. In turn, I'd helped him see something in himself: the good man behind the criminal. He owned a diner that was losing money, but he kept it so he could continue to employ a kind woman from his childhood . . . and because he liked the pancakes. He was intolerant of violence against women and children and came down hard on anyone who disobeyed his decree. His legitimate businesses made him more than his illegal enterprises, but while part of him wanted to try the straight and narrow, he maintained his position to ensure none of the sociopaths waiting in the wings took over.

James Malcolm and I had become friends, and we'd both shared things with each other that we'd never shared with anyone else, so I'd believed our Tuesday night meetings—which had consisted of sitting on the back of my truck and talking about what was going on in our lives for an hour or more—had softened his heart.

All of which had made the pain of his betrayal so much worse.

The parley I'd set up had been between James and his adversaries, Buck Reynolds and Kip Wagner. Neely Kate and I had been looking for a necklace for her "friend," only to discover he'd stolen it from Buck Reynolds. No surprise, Reynolds had wanted it back. James had hoped to prevent that, suspecting that his challenger planned to sell the necklace to finance his bid to take over the county crime world. I'd set up the meeting to return the necklace in exchange for peace in the county. Except James had never intended to cooperate—his intention had been to use the meeting to force their surrender.

It wasn't actually his plan that had upset me—I might have even gone along with it. It was the fact that he hadn't trusted me enough to tell me the truth.

After everything we'd been through together.

A tiny voice in my head said he'd orchestrated this. That he'd wanted me to get pissed enough to write him out of my life. I'd suspected for some time that he had feelings for me, but at first it had been a moot point. I'd been happy with Mason. Then Mason had left, and I'd spent months recovering from our breakup. Several weeks ago, I'd finally admitted to myself that I was attracted to James, drawn to him like a moth to a flame. And while the one time we'd kissed had been hotter than any kiss I'd ever experienced in my life, James had pushed me away and declared it impossible. If his enemies caught word that he had feelings for me, I would become his greatest liability.

If he'd admitted his feelings for me and made them public, would I be missing now instead of Scooter?

I turned into the neighborhood where Bruce Wayne and his crew were working, then pulled my truck in behind my business partner's truck after I found the house. Bruce Wayne and his four-man crew were hard at work digging a trench to lay the foundation for a small wall at the edge of the front planting bed.

Bruce Wayne looked up when he saw me walking toward him and did a double take. I used to work on the job sites with him until we started getting more business. Now I focused more on creating designs and estimates, though I still liked to get my hands in the dirt.

"Rose," he said, shielding his eyes to watch me approach and taking in my outfit with a grin. My usual uniform was a lot less fancy: T-shirts and jeans or shorts. "I know you're not here to work. You checking up on me?"

I forced a smile. "You're too good to warrant checking on. I'm glad I had the foresight to make you a partner instead of an employee. Otherwise, you might have left and stolen all my business."

He grinned.

I handed him the paper. "Neely Kate said you needed the revised plans for the backyard."

He took the paper and scanned it before folding it up and stuffing it into his back pocket. "Shouldn't be a trouble." He paused and then said, "But I know you didn't come down here just to give me this. I'm not scheduled to get to their backyard until tomorrow. Is this about Violet?"

"No." I glanced at the guys working with him. "Can I borrow you for a moment?"

Worry filled his eyes. "Yeah. Sure."

He told the men something in Spanish, then followed me to the shade of a maple tree ten feet away. "What's up?" he asked.

"It's about Scooter Malcolm."

The blank expression on his face confirmed he hadn't heard. "What about him?"

"He's missing."

He swallowed and glanced over at his crew. "For how long?"

Why hadn't I pinned Neely Kate down and gotten more information? "I don't know. At least since late last week."

"What happened to him?"

"Honestly, Bruce Wayne, I'm not sure. Joe was the one who told me. He was surprised *I* didn't know."

"You're still havin' your spat with Skeeter?" he asked, his gaze still on his men.

"I'm not havin' a spat with Skeeter Malcolm," I protested, my voice rising a little. I took a breath to settle down. "This has nothing to do with me and everything to do with Scooter. Joe thinks someone snatched him."

Bruce Wayne didn't respond, but his eyes hardened and he gave a sharp nod.

"What do you think?" I asked. "Was he prone to running off?"

He shook his head. "No."

"When was the last time you saw him?"

That got his attention.

"Are you investigatin'?" he asked, lifting an eyebrow.

"What?" I asked in surprise. "I'm just askin'."

He gave me a sharp look.

"Why would I be investigatin' Scooter Malcolm's disappearance? I don't even know him, and James Malcolm and I are no longer friends or associates."

"Huh."

"What's that mean?"

He shook his head and gave me an ornery grin. "It's in your blood, Rose Gardner. You can't help yourself. Neely Kate wants to investigate something, and you dig in your heels and pretend you're not interested, and before you know it, you're takin' over the case."

"I do *not*."

He tilted his head. "Which part?"

Dang it. "Well, I'm not investigatin' Scooter Malcolm's disappearance. Sounds like a dangerous venture. Besides, I'm sure James Malcolm will manage just fine without my help. There can't be too many suspects."

While Joe had claimed James had more enemies than he could count, the truth was that most were too afraid of the judgment they'd face should their coup attempt fail. As far as I knew, there were only two men who had the guts, and they'd both sworn to me that they wouldn't try to take over James' kingdom. Still, words were cheap to some people—Wagner and Reynolds would be the first place I'd start.

If I was looking for Scooter . . . and I definitely wasn't.

"Just call me curious," I found myself saying. "When was the last time you talked to him?"

"A few weeks ago. At the pool hall." James' pool hall. "We got together to shoot some pool and catch up. He had a new girlfriend, and he wanted me and Anna to meet her."

"Scooter had a new girlfriend? Who was she?" Funny, I'd never heard anything about Scooter dating anyone—James still seemed to think of him as a kid—but he was in his thirties, so it stood to reason he'd have a significant other.

"A woman he met at Walmart. He's working there now." Bruce Wayne cracked a hint of a grin. "In the lawn and garden department. He jokes that he's our direct competition."

"Did he or his girlfriend have any connection to Rayna Dyer? She worked in housewares." Poor Rayna had been caught up in the necklace mess. Her ex had hidden the stolen necklace in with the rest of her jewelry, and her father-in-law had killed her while looking for it.

Bruce Wayne seemed caught off guard. "I don't know." He paused. "You think this might have something to do with that missing necklace?"

I shook my head. "No. I don't know. I don't see how it could, but it *is* a coincidence."

"True." Then he gave a little shake. "Jeanne. Jeanne Putnam is his girlfriend." He turned serious. "So you *are* investigatin'?"

"No. I guess I just can't help askin' questions. I think I'll leave it to the big boys to duke this out." James would have the same short list of suspects as I did, after all.

It was definitely time to change the subject. "If you want to talk or anything . . . just let me know. I know he and David were the only ones to stick with you during your arrest and trial."

He nodded, but his face was a blank slate. He hated any mention of his arrest for murder. He'd lost his family over it, even after I'd helped prove he was innocent, and the whole incident had hurt him deeply. He was part of my makeshift family now. The group I'd inadvertently cobbled together over the last year or so.

"I've got to get back to work," he said. "I'll try to make it to Violet's party as close to one as I can make it."

"Okay."

When he started to walk away, I reached out and pulled him into a hug. His body stiffened—he'd always been reluctant about hugs—but then his body relaxed and his arms wrapped around me. "Thanks for comin' by to tell me, Rose. It means more than you know."

"Of course, Bruce Wayne." I gave him a squeeze, but my head began to tingle just before I dropped my hold. Everything went black, and I knew I was about to have a vision.

The visions had been a part of my life for as long as I could remember. They were always glimpses of other people in the future, from inside their heads.

I was outside and I/Bruce Wayne lifted my hand to wipe my

brow. I scanned the horizon to study the brewing storm clouds. "Let's get this wrapped up before the storm hits."

Then, just as suddenly, I was back in the present saying, "You're gonna try to beat the storm."

I cringed. For most of my life, I'd hated my visions. They were unpredictable, often uncontrollable, and a huge invasion of other people's privacy. They'd also saved my life and the lives of some of my loved ones. My acceptance of them was a work in progress.

"A vision?" Bruce Wayne asked quietly, and I nodded.

He was one of only a handful of people who knew the truth. I could usually play the visions off, and if people noticed the visual cues that I was having one—like the dilated pupils and the fact I completely zoned out for a couple of seconds—they usually just wrote it off as strange or quirky behavior. The fact that I uncontrollably blurted out something about whatever I'd seen was a little harder to explain away, but I'd had plenty of practice. About a year ago, I'd started forcing visions, which had come in handy in investigations. I'd noticed a decrease in spontaneous ones since then, but some still slipped through.

"It was nothing important. Just that you were trying to finish up and pack up before a storm hit."

He gave me a warm smile. "Thanks for the heads-up."

With that, he went back to his crew and didn't waste any time before getting back to work. His crew respected him, partially because he was a level-headed boss, but also because he never asked them to do anything he wasn't willing to jump in and do himself. I was lucky to have him as a business partner, and I knew it.

I hopped into my truck to head back to the office, but it was just past eleven, so I decided to stop by Homer's Diner and pick up some lunch for Neely Kate and the kids. As I headed inside to order, it occurred to me that I was just half a mile from the Henryetta Animal Clinic.

I'd been on three dates with Levi Romano, the new veterinarian, in the past three weeks. Up until now, Levi had done all the pursuing, but maybe that should change. He was totally into me —and not afraid to let me know it—and better yet, he was about as far removed from the criminal element in Fenton County as I could get. Considering that my last two (and only ever) boyfriends had been a sheriff deputy and the county assistant D.A., and that James was the acting crime boss, a vet was a welcome change. Besides, I was looking good today. No need to let it go to waste.

I placed two separate orders—one for Levi and one for the rest of us—then headed to the animal clinic, my stomach a ball of nerves. Levi's receptionist, Mary, hadn't liked me from the start, but in fairness, she'd had to wade through a crush of women who were eager to get a date with the most eligible bachelor in Fenton County. I'd hoped Mary would become nicer once she realized that Levi and I had been on a few dates, but if anything, she'd gotten meaner.

I walked into the clinic, and while the waiting room was empty of both patients and their owners, I was greeted by the commingled smells of wet dog and perfume. Mary, who looked to be in her forties, was dousing the space around her desk with a spray bottle from Bath and Body Works. She took one look at me, and her resting bitch face turned into a full-blown scowl.

"You don't have an appointment."

"I know. I'm just here to bring Levi lunch."

"Dr. Romano," she corrected with a glint in her eye that suggested she'd fight me over it.

"Okay . . . Could you tell *Dr. Romano* I'm here to see him?"

"Noooo . . . You don't have an appointment."

I dug my phone out of my pocket and sent Levi a short text.

LOOK IN YOUR WAITING ROOM.

Seconds later, one of the exam room doors opened and Levi appeared in the doorway holding a kitten in his hand. His face lit up. "Rose!"

I smiled, feeling a little giddy at the sight of him. Levi Romano had earned his Most Eligible Bachelor status with little effort. He was very good-looking. His brown hair was just long enough to run your hands through—if I were tempted to do such a thing—and his warm brown eyes and dazzling smile made me feel like I was the center of the universe. It helped that he was tall and his shoulders filled out his lab coat quite nicely. It was no wonder every woman in Fenton County was interested in him.

Well, *almost* every woman in the county.

While I could appreciate the view and Levi was a very attentive, charming man, I didn't feel that spark . . . and I really, really wanted to. This moment of giddiness was the first time I'd had a physical reaction to him, which made me feel hopeful that it would come in time. Bringing him lunch had been the right decision.

"Hey, Levi. I hope I'm not interruptin' anything."

"Not at all. Ms. Jergins just dropped by so little Oscar could get his shots."

"I won't keep you," I said, lifting the bag with the Homer's Diner logo in my hand. "I was in the area, so I thought I'd bring you lunch."

His eyes lit up with happiness, but it faded slightly as he walked out into the waiting room, the kitten still in his hands. Goodness, the man belonged on a calendar. "You have no idea how thrilled I am to see you, but I can't get away for another hour."

"Oh, that's okay." I waved a hand in dismissal. "I can't stay. I'm just the delivery person."

He stopped in front of me, close enough for me to notice how good he smelled despite the fact that he'd been handling animals all day. His gaze dropped to my exposed chest, but it lifted to meet my eyes just as I was starting to feel self-conscious. "You have no idea how happy I am to see you," he said in a lowered voice. "After our last date, I was certain you were giving me the brush-off."

The date had gone well, but he'd leaned over to kiss me after parking next to my truck in front of the landscaping office. I'd panicked and turned my head at the last minute, then dashed out of his truck so quickly he was still leaning in for a kiss when I slammed the door.

I gave him an apologetic grin. "I know. I'm sorry. I told you I'm still workin' through some things from my previous relationship. Maybe this wasn't such a good idea after all."

The last thing I wanted to do was hurt him. He didn't need to be at the mercy of my issues.

"No." He put his hand on my arm, cupping it lightly while still holding the kitten in his other hand. "I knew what I was getting into. I told you that I was willing to take it slow." His brow lifted. "We've been taking it slow, right?"

"Yeah, but you just said—"

"What I just said doesn't matter."

"Of course it does! Why on earth would you want to keep seein' a woman you think is about to give you the brush-off?

He laughed. "Oh, Rose. You have no idea how refreshing you are. I like that you keep me on my toes."

I cringed. "You're makin' me sound cold."

"No!" He shook his head. "That's not it at all." He pressed his lips together, looking thoughtful, then finally said, "You know Mary fields off a few women who make appointments just to see me . . ."

Mary snorted from her desk. "A few?"

Levi rolled his eyes and glanced over his shoulder. "Isn't it your break time, Mary?"

"No," was her curt response.

"Take one anyway," he said good-naturedly. He grinned at me as she grumbled her way up out of the chair. "Here. Take Oscar back to the exam room, will you?" He handed the kitten to her, and if looks could kill, she would have committed a violent double homicide on the spot. I was a little worried about Oscar, truth be told.

After she disappeared into the back, Levi grabbed my hand and tugged me over to sit in one of the waiting room chairs. "Rose, I like you. A lot. You're different from the women I usually date. I know that we're taking this on a day-by-day basis, and I'm okay with that. Are you?"

"I am, but I want you to know that I didn't bring you lunch to string you along," I said, feeling guilty.

He took the bag from my hand and set it on the chair next to him. "No, I am thrilled you brought me lunch. Not only do I love Homer's Diner, but you took time out of your busy day and thought of me. That's enough for me right now."

That made me feel better.

"I want to go out with you again," he said. "What do you say? How about tonight?"

"Neely Kate and I are goin' to the carnival tonight. I'm not a huge fan, but I promised." It occurred to me that he might think it was another brush-off, so I added, "Would you like to come with us? I don't think she'd mind."

"To the carnival?"

"Yeah," I said trying to sound nonchalant. "You don't have—"

Levi leaned forward and gave me a soft kiss, then sat back and grinned. "I would *love* to go to the carnival with you and Neely Kate tonight."

I paused, completely caught off guard by his kiss. We'd been out three times and this was the first time he'd kissed me. I took a second to process my feelings. Something seemed off, and I realized what it was: I felt that I was cheating. But cheating on whom? Mason? We'd been broken up for nearly six months, and his mother had told me that he was dating a bit in Little Rock. Cheating on James? I nearly laughed. We'd never had anything approaching a relationship, so cheating would be impossible. The man in front of me was every woman's dream. I was crazy to think of giving that up. I just needed to get used to the idea was all.

I waited for Levi to acknowledge our first kiss, but he just sat there and grinned.

I needed to pull myself together.

"Are you sure you want to go?" I asked. "I'm sure the carnivals in Kansas City would make this one seem lame."

"You could ask me to a monster truck rally, and I'd jump at the chance." He leaned closer and whispered, "And I hate monster truck rallies."

"Don't feel like you have to say yes, Levi. We can go out another time."

"I want to spend time with you, Rose." He squeezed my hand. "The more time we spend together, the better we'll get to know each other . . . and the easier it will be for me to win you over." A huge grin spread across his face. "Besides, it will be good practice for me to get ready for the county fair next month. I've been asked to judge some of the 4-H animal entries. I'll feel better if I know what kind of crowd I'll be dealing with."

I laughed.

There was a feline screech in the open exam room, and little Oscar streaked out through the door.

Levi stood and flashed me a grin. "Duty calls."

His receptionist came running out of the room with a scratch mark on her cheek. "Come back here, you little devil!"

Levi pulled me to my feet and gave me a tiny push toward the door. "Go. Save yourself."

I laughed and was about to leave, but a brightly colored flyer on the bulletin board caught my eye. There was a photo of a vibrant green parrot against a white background, and huge black letters above and below him exclaimed:

Lost Parrot
$500 Reward

I moved closer to get a better look at the smaller text at the bottom of the flyer.

Talking parrot last seen on Saturday morning in Henryetta Park. Squawker loves carrots, Wheel of Fortune, *and long walks in the park.*

Was the owner looking to find the parrot or to get Squawker a date?

$500 reward for the safe return of my best friend.

Boomer T. Whipple

501-555-1453

At first, I was slightly disturbed that Boomer's best friend was a talking parrot, but who was I to judge? Until I'd befriended Neely Kate a year ago, my dog had been mine.

Dropping to his knees, Levi reached under the chair the kitten had chosen for its hiding place. "Come on," he said softly. "Come to Dr. Levi."

Oscar's owner, a twenty-something woman, stood in the exam room doorway, her gaze firmly on Levi's butt as she nodded her head and said, "Yes, Dr. Levi. I'll come—"

"Ms. Jergins," Mary snapped.

The woman had the good sense to look flustered.

"Got him," Levi said, cradling the kitten to his chest. "Although if there happens to be a next time, maybe we should try bribing him instead of terrorizing him." He glanced up at me with a look of surprise. "You're still here."

I grinned. "And miss the show? Enjoy your lunch."

I started to head out the door, but he called after me, "Text me the details for tonight."

But that good feeling fled as I drove back to the office in my truck. I felt unsettled again. Was I leading Levi on? I *did* like him, and surely it was too early in our relationship—if you could call it that—to be thinking about something serious. Was it too much to hope something would stir inside me?

Was it too much to hope I'd stop thinking about James?

CHAPTER 4

A small crowd had gathered inside Gardner Sisters Nursery. The afternoon was hot and muggy, and storm clouds were gathering on the horizon. Maeve and Anna, the two employees who'd run the nursery in my sister's absence, had set out water and lemonade on a serving table at the back of the shop. Ashley had helped me arrange the lettered cupcakes we'd ordered from Dena's bakery to spell out *Welcome Home, Violet*, which we'd encircled with cupcakes decorated with piped flowers.

I had to admit that I was nervous. My relationship with my sister had been a roller coaster over the last year. She'd roped Joe into becoming our business partner in the nursery after getting the business into serious money trouble . . . plus she'd used him to try to make me jealous while I was dating Mason. A part of me worried that the peace I'd finally found would be destroyed with her return; the rest of me felt guilty for even considering it. Violet had gone away to save her life, and now I was worried about her coming back.

What kind of monster did that make me?

Besides, my sister's health scare seemed to have mellowed her.

I hadn't seen her since April, when I'd gone to Houston to donate my bone marrow for her transplant, but I'd talked to her every week or so. I knew she was nervous too. Nervous we'd all moved on with our lives without her. Nervous her kids wouldn't remember or want her. Nervous she no longer had a place in my life.

"How much longer, Aunt Rose?" Ashley asked as we moved toward the front of the store.

The shop was filled with about twenty of Violet's friends from the garden club, high school, and church, and even a few customers had shown up to welcome her home.

I glanced down to make sure her face was still clean and her hair was held back in the braids Neely Kate had given her. I wanted both kids to look their absolute best when Violet arrived. "Soon. Your daddy sent a message that they should be here any time now."

Neely Kate bounced Mikey on her hip as she walked around the shop pointing out objects and asking him to tell her what they were. She looked over at me and smiled.

"Let's go see if Miss Maeve needs us to do anything," I said, tucking Ashley's hand in mine and walking over to the register.

Maeve stared out the window with an anxious look in her eyes.

"She's going to love her welcome home party, Maeve," I said. "I promise."

Maeve turned to face me. "I hope she doesn't think I was trying to take over or usurp her position."

"I know for a fact she doesn't," I reassured her. Maeve was Mason's mother, but she'd become more like a mother to me than my own momma had been. We'd agreed to stay in each other's lives after my breakup with Mason, but I think it was harder than either of us had expected. "Violet has told me time and again how much she appreciates you filling in while she's been gone." I reached over and grabbed her hand, making her look me in the eyes. "And she's so happy you're going to stay on, Maeve. She told me so herself. She won't be able to work more than a few hours a day at the most. She still needs to get her strength back."

"I just don't want to overstep my bounds."

"You aren't."

Ashley pulled free and ran to the door. "They're here!"

Mike's car was pulling into a parking space we'd purposely left open for him. It was close to the door so Violet wouldn't have as far to walk.

My stomach twisted into what felt like a pretzel, and I suddenly felt Neely Kate next to me, snagging my hand with her free one. I shot her a questioning glance, and she nodded—a silent way of telling me she was there for me, whatever I needed.

I squeezed back, feeling guilty about how this morning had unfolded. What with the kids, a client appointment at the office, and the excitement of the welcome home party, I hadn't had a chance to tell her about Levi coming with us tonight . . . or about the flyer, which had stuck with me. Bruce Wayne was right—I *did* like investigating—but maybe if I focused on finding Squawker, I'd be less tempted to get wrapped up in the situation with Scooter.

"We need to talk later, okay?" I said in a hopeful voice. "I'm sorry I've been keepin' things from you."

"You hush now," she scolded with a soft smile. "You've got nothing to be sorry for. I've done the same thing. Maybe we can start dolin' out our secrets little by little so we don't feel naked from sharing them."

I nodded. "That sounds like a good idea."

Her smile warmed my chest, and I realized how lucky I was to have two sisters—one by blood and one of my heart.

The door opened and Violet stepped into the opening, wearing white shorts and a red off-the-shoulder shirt covered with white flowers. She'd lost so much weight her shoulder blades stuck out and her cheekbones were more prominent than usual. A white scarf was tied around her head, and when she saw the crowd, she self-consciously lifted a hand to touch it.

Mike, who stood behind her, leaned in to whisper something into her ear as he put his hand on her shoulder. She reached up and covered his hand with her own.

"You take Mikey," Neely Kate said, handing over my nephew.

Ashley was already wrapped around her mother's legs as I walked over with my nephew in my arms.

"Welcome home, Violet," I said, tears filling my eyes. I couldn't believe how fragile she looked.

She gave me a hesitant look, and it was like something burst inside me. I reached for her, pulling her into an embrace with one arm as I held Mikey with the other. Ashley still clung to Violet's legs on the opposite side.

"I love you," I whispered as I held her tighter, trying to ignore a spike of fear—she felt like a bundle of bones.

"I love you too," she said in a tearful response. She broke loose, swiping a few tears away, and cupped her son's cheek and looked into his eyes. "Hey, Mikey. Momma's home."

He stared at her with big eyes, and for a moment, I wasn't sure how he would react. Then he reached for her.

I worried he'd be too heavy, but Violet put him on her hip as he buried his face into her neck.

Mike must have shared my concern because he was already making a beeline for the storage room behind the counter. "Maeve, you got a chair back here?"

"Yes," Maeve said, following him. "I should have thought of that . . ."

Violet held both of her children close—her son on her hip and her daughter at her side—as she scanned the group and released a chuckle. "The nursery's gotten a lot busier since I left."

Everyone laughed.

Tears swam in her eyes. "Y'all have no idea how much this means to me." Her voice broke. "I know what's important now."

Her gaze drifted to Mike, who had found a chair and was placing it next to the counter.

Seconds later, he was back at her side, lifting Mikey into his arms and ushering her over to the chair.

Everyone started talking at once, telling Violet how beautiful she looked in her scarf, how much they'd missed her, and how much she'd missed at home.

I moved to the back with Neely Kate, on the outside looking in. I'd always felt that way with Violet's friends. Truth be told, I'd felt that way my entire life until I'd finally decided to take charge of my fate.

The door opened and Joe walked in, giving me and Neely Kate a grimace when he saw that Violet had already arrived. He glanced at the crowd as he made his way back to us.

"I got held up, but there's so many people here, I suspect she hasn't noticed I'm late."

"She just got here no more than five minutes ago," Neely Kate said.

"Good turnout," he said. "That's good." Violet's behavior over the past year or so hadn't just alienated me—her affair with the married mayor had pushed away a lot of her friends, making Violet, who'd frequently dispensed gossip, the subject of plenty of flapping tongues. It was good to see that her illness had convinced many of them to let bygones be bygones. While I had forgiven her too, and loved her with all my heart, I couldn't totally forget the things she'd done to me. No matter how hard I tried.

"Your sister looks happy," Neely Kate said, watching her with a wistful look.

Mikey was on her lap, snuggling close, while Mike stood behind her with a hand on her shoulder, as though he was trying to pour strength and comfort into her with his touch.

Violet *did* look happy. I hoped she really had learned what was important. I'd always thought Mike was good for her.

Joe sidled up next to Neely Kate and slung an arm around her shoulders. "Hey, sis. You get a chance to look at the paint samples for my kitchen?"

"Sorry, Joe. Not yet."

"What's got you so busy lately?" he asked, sounding amused. As far as I knew, he had no idea Neely Kate had up and gone to Ardmore, which was a near-miracle considering how attentive he'd been to her these past few months.

"The landscapin' business is boomin'," she said. "And there's so much for me to learn." Neely Kate had learned quickly, and business had slowed down considerably the last couple of weeks.

Violet's gaze landed on Joe, and her face lit up.

"You should go say hi," I said, giving him a little push.

"I think there's room for me now." He grinned and headed over.

Since Neely Kate and I had a moment alone, I decided now was as good a time as any to bring up the invitation I'd issued to Levi.

"Since I was dressed up today, I picked up something for Levi when I got our lunch."

Neely Kate perked up. "You did?" Her excitement shifted to confusion. "But you ate with us."

"I didn't plan on staying, which was good since he didn't have time to eat with me. I was just fixin' to do something nice for him."

She bumped her shoulder into mine. "I'm sure he appreciated it."

"He was pleasantly surprised." I paused. "He asked me to go out with him tonight."

"Oh." Her grin softened. "See? I knew wearin' that outfit would pay off."

"I'm not canceling *our* plans," I said. "I told him you and I were going to the carnival, but I invited him to come along. Are you upset?"

"Upset? No! I'm excited for you. You know I wholeheartedly approve of Levi." Then she made a face. "But I don't want to be a third wheel."

"You're not. I only invited him because he thought I was giving him the brush-off after our last date. And when I told him no again . . . well, I didn't want him to think I really was avoiding him. I'm sorry." Neely Kate and I had been treading on shaky ground ever since her trip, and now I felt like I'd messed up again.

"Rose! No. Don't be sorry. I don't mind if Levi comes. I'm just sayin' I'll stay home so you two can have a real date."

I stared at her in disbelief. "But last week you were *dyin'* to go to the carnival."

She shrugged and then gave me a devious grin. "I'd rather let you and Dr. Levi have a romantic evening together."

"At the *carnival?*"

"Of course! Clinging to him at the top of the Ferris wheel—on top of the world . . . you can see half the town from up there."

I chuckled. "And who would want to see half of Henryetta?"

She laughed and shoved my arm. "You have no romantic imagination."

My smile wavered. I *did* have romantic imagination. I just had it with the wrong man, whom I was desperate to forget. "I'm gonna take your word on that, but I still feel bad because you were the whole reason we were goin' in the first place."

She lifted a shoulder into a half-shrug. "The kids have worn me out. I'll stay home with Muffy. She's probably lonely since we left her at the farm by herself today. I'll sit out on the front porch and watch her play while I read a book."

Everything she said sounded true, yet I couldn't help thinking there was something she wasn't telling me. "Are you *sure?*"

"Yes! Men don't get much better than Levi Romano. You can't

let him get away, because there are women lining up to go out with him."

"Literally," I said. "On his appointment books."

"Well then, that's settled. Let's get some cupcakes before Miss Mildred starts stuffing them into her purse."

A quick glance at the refreshments table proved she wasn't exaggerating. My eighty-three-year-old former neighbor was holding two cupcakes over her open purse. Miss Mildred was eccentric, but I never would have thought her capable of sneaking cupcakes.

"Hey, Miss Mildred," Neely Kate said. "Whatcha doin' with those cupcakes?"

She spun to face us, looking flustered. "Why, I'm gonna eat 'em, of course."

"Two of them?" Neely Kate leaned closer and peered into her purse. "And you're takin' two more home for later?"

"We have a box you can put those in so you don't muck up your purse," I said, trying not to laugh.

Irritation filled her eyes. "Are you the cupcake police?"

"Sorry, Miss Mildred," Neely Kate said. "I'm just worried you're gonna give yourself diabetes."

"I can manage my own daggum diabetes."

Miss Mildred wandered off, grumping about "meddlin' girls," but I didn't pay her any mind. Bruce Wayne had just walked in; he'd changed since this morning, and his hair was damp. I watched as Anna headed straight for him and gave him a welcoming kiss. Bruce Wayne smiled at her like she was the only woman alive, and my heart nearly burst with happiness for him. He'd had a rough childhood, devoid of the affection and regard he deserved, and while his friends, myself included, had helped him change his life with our love and friendship, Anna was the one who'd truly brought out the man he was today.

My traitorous mind was quick to turn to James. He was a different man today than the one I'd first met. Jed had once told me that I made James a better man and leader, and James himself had showed me time and again that he truly respected my opinions. He'd also trusted me enough to show me his vulnerable side, something he usually revealed to no one.

Fool that I was, I'd started falling for him. And even though I knew better, I couldn't seem to stop.

CHAPTER 5

A half hour later, Mike told me that he was going to take Violet and the kids home. "We'll help load the kids' things in your car," Neely Kate said.

"Thanks," Mike said. As she walked away, he said, "And thanks for putting this welcome home party together for Violet. I know we were all worried it might be too much, but it really meant a lot to her."

I pulled him into a hug. "She's loved. I wanted her to know how much people care about her. But I'd really like to spend some time alone with her. I was hopin' I could come by and maybe bring y'all some dinner."

"That's sweet," he said. "But the church has that covered. How about you call tomorrow and see if she's up to it?"

My heart hurt from his words. Had she told him to keep me away? *I will not cry.* "Oh. I hadn't heard anything about the dinners. I'm surprised Jonah didn't mention it."

"Not the New Living Hope Revival Church. The Baptist church. The one we went to before we were separated."

"Oh." But if they were making another go of being together, I guessed it made sense.

He leaned closer. "Can I ask your help with something else?"

"Of course. Anything I can do to help make her transition home easier."

"Since Violet's moving in with me, she wants to sell your mother's house, but she's still too weak to take care of it. Can you make the arrangements?"

I blinked. "What?" Then I shook my head as his words sank in. "Momma left it to Violet, not me."

A hard look filled his eyes. "Are you sayin' you won't help?"

"No, that's not it at all. But I think this is something *Violet* and I need to discuss." What had gotten into him? I'd known Mike since I was a teenager, and he'd never been unkind to me, let alone belligerent. "Have I done something to offend you, Mike?"

He gave me a long look. "It's been a draining day for Violet. I need to get her home. I'd appreciate it if you wouldn't mention this to her. She's tired enough as it is."

Then he turned around and announced to everyone that he was taking his family home.

After Violet and Mike left with the kids, Neely Kate and I helped Maeve and Anna clean up. I couldn't stop stewing about what Mike had said. I was probably making too much out of it, but I planned to talk to Violet about the house the first chance I got. I sent her a text.

Let me know when you're settled in. I love and miss you.

While we were packing up the leftover cupcakes, Neely Kate got a phone call. After taking a quick look at the screen, she said, "I'll be right back." Then she headed out the front door before answering.

This had happened several times since her trip last week. I had a feeling she was talking to Jed, that he was one of her secrets. It fit with the way she'd looked after her longer-than-usual absence this morning, plus the easy way she'd blown off the carnival. I kept waiting for her to tell me of her own volition, but it was starting to look like that wasn't going to happen. Was it because she didn't think I'd understand? Jed was amazing, and I couldn't have picked a better man for her. So why didn't she want to tell me?

She came back several minutes later, looking happier than she had all day, and I couldn't help feeling hurt. I wanted to share this with her.

After we got into my truck, I turned to Neely Kate, about to ask her about Jed. She beat me to it. "I have something to tell you."

I grabbed her hand. "Neely Kate, I want you to know I'm totally supportive."

Surprise filled her eyes, and then her face broke out into a beaming smile. "Really? Did you overhear my phone call?" She waved a hand in dismissal. "I don't care if you were eavesdropping. I just can't believe you're okay with this."

"Why wouldn't I be? I wish you'd trust me."

"It's just that you've been so resistant to starting something in the past."

Had I? Carter Hale, her divorce attorney, had made it clear that he was interested in her, and I'd hinted I didn't approve. Had I not made it clear enough that I just didn't approve of *him*? He wasn't a bad man, but he would have used her and spit her out. Jed, though . . . I'd literally trusted that man with my life, and I'd seen firsthand how much he cared about Neely Kate. He'd sooner cut off his own hand than hurt her. "I'm sorry if I've given you that impression," I said. "But if this makes you happy, how can I not support it?"

She shook her head in amazement. "I seriously can't believe this. Since we don't have any plans this afternoon, why don't we head over there now?"

"*To the pool hall?*"

"The pool hall? Why would we go to the pool hall? We're headin' to his office."

"He has his own office?" How come I'd never known that?

41

"Of course he has an office! Any legit P.I. does."

I blinked. "Wait, what?"

"Kermit Cooper. The P.I. we're workin' with."

That was the absolute last thing I had expected to hear.

"He said if we showed up this afternoon, he'd get us started on our first case."

"A case?"

"Of course a case. Why else would we be working with a private investigator?"

Why indeed . . . "How did you find Kimmel . . . ?"

"Kermit. And it was serendipity."

I didn't believe that for a hot minute. "So are you plannin' on quittin' the landscaping business to work on becomin' a P.I.?"

"Of course I'm not quittin'. But if we want to be P.I.s, we have to either go to school or shadow a real P.I. for two years. This is our start."

I was about to protest, but hadn't I intended to talk to her about the missing parrot? Bruce Wayne was right—I did like investigating. Why keep denying it? Plus, I could see Neely Kate was excited about this. After everything she'd been through—and I knew she'd faced some demons last week back in Oklahoma—I didn't want to disappoint her.

"Okay, let's check this out. But only if you agree that we're *not* callin' ourselves Sparkle Investigations."

She pursed her lips. "Well, of course we're not, silly."

I breathed a sigh of relief. This conversation had gone better than I'd feared.

"We'll be usin' Kermit Cooper's agency name. Moppet Investigations."

I almost argued with her, but she was right. If we were using his name, we wouldn't need one of our own.

Neely Kate chattered the whole way to his office, and I could tell she was nervous, which surprised me. Then again, this was what she'd wanted for months—she was bound to be anxious now that we were finally doing it.

Neely Kate had plugged the address into her phone and the automated voice guided us to our destination: a run-down, rusted mobile home surrounded by weeds and dirt. It was just outside the city limits.

"Um . . ." I said as I stared at it. "Are you sure this is it? There's no sign or anything."

"Yeah," she said, trying to stay upbeat. "I bet he just doesn't put much money or effort into his office because he's busy workin' cases. And he doesn't need a sign because his business is all word of mouth."

"Yeah . . . maybe." I parked the truck, and we walked up to the rickety front porch.

Neely Kate glanced up at the narrow stairs and porch, then down at my pink skirt and white top. "Maybe you should wait down there until he answers so you don't get anything on you."

"Okay."

She marched up the steps and knocked on the door.

"It's open," came a gruff voice from inside. "Come in."

Neely Kate gave me an excited grin and opened the door. I quickly climbed the stairs and followed her inside.

She had to be disappointed at what she found, but she hid it well. The place looked nothing like an office and every bit like a teenage boy's room—and it smelled like one too. A middle-aged man was sitting in the recliner watching the news.

"Mr. Cooper?" Neely Kate asked.

"You them girls I heard about?" he grunted, keeping his gaze on the TV.

"Yeah," she said, not sounding as confident. "That's us."

"I hear you wanna be P.I.s."

"That's right," she said. "Jed Carlisle said you'd train us."

Jed? I gaped at her in shock. Jed had set this up?

"Yep, I said I would." He put his hand on the arm of his chair and pushed himself up out of it. Once he was standing, he turned to get a look at us. I wasn't sure what to expect from a P.I., but Kermit Cooper wasn't it. He looked to be anywhere from his mid-forties to mid-fifties, and if he was agile enough to run from the criminal element, his physique didn't indicate it. His button-down white shirt was covered with multiple stains—enough to suggest he'd worked on collecting them. He had a couple days' growth of beard, and his partially balding head could have used some of the hair from his chin. His eyes narrowed as he took us in, and he pointed a finger at me. "You plannin' to wear fancy clothes like that all the time?"

"Actually, no," I said. "I'm usually dressed in—"

"Save it for someone who wants to hear it, sweetheart. I don't care if you show up wrapped in tin foil, not my business."

My mouth dropped open.

Neely Kate winced and gave me an apologetic look.

"Now, I don't get a ton of cases," he said. "But I just got one this afternoon. Right before Carlisle called me."

Well, *that* wasn't a coincidence . . . What was Jed up to?

"The info's still on the copy machine from when it was faxed in."

"Faxed in?" I asked. What decade was this?

Neely Kate shrugged her shoulders as she turned around and tried to find the copy machine. I spotted it on the floor, partially covered in empty takeout bags, and pointed it out to her.

She squatted in front of it and grabbed a single sheet of paper from the tray while I tried to hide my disgust at the pigsty where Kermit Cooper apparently lived *and* worked. The only thing of interest in the whole place was a circular map of the world on his wall by the kitchen table. The North Pole was in the middle, the continents were spread out around it in a circle, and a thick white circle bordered the entire thing.

"This is an interestin' map," I said, deciding that I might as well try to break the ice if we were going to be working together. "I've never seen one like it."

He released a loud grunt. "That ain't for you, Miss Fancy Pants."

So much for small talk.

Neely Kate looked up from the paper. "It's about a lost parrot."

How many lost parrots could there be in Henryetta? I started to tell her about the flyer in Levi's office, but another grunt from Kermit convinced me to wait until we left.

"So what happens next?" Neely Kate asked him as she lowered the paper to her side.

"Here's how it's gonna work," Kermit said, moving closer. I resisted the urge to pinch my nose to block the wave of BO coming my way. "You two are gonna go look for the damned parrot."

"Jed said you were gonna teach us," Neely Kate countered. "We're supposed to be apprenticing with you."

"Ever heard of the phrase *do one, get paid for none?*"

"Um," I said, pursing my lips. "I'm pretty sure it's *see one, do one, teach one.*" I'd learned that phrase during my *Grey's Anatomy* marathons.

"That be them doctors' motto when they train younger folk . . . This one's mine. You two will go out and find that bird, and then I'll collect the money."

Neely Kate's eyes widened. "*You'll* get the money?"

"You said you wanted to apprentice, and apprentices don't get paid."

This was sounding like the worst arrangement ever. "So let me get this straight," I said. "If we do all the work and you get paid, what do we get out of it?"

"I'll sign off on your hours, and you'll get to sit for the P.I. exam."

And there was the crux of it. Neely Kate was dying to be a real P.I., and unless she went to school, she had to apprentice with someone. But I found it hard to believe this guy was a legitimate investigator, even if the license I saw tacked to the wall said otherwise.

Neely Kate gave me a pleading look, and I couldn't bring myself to tell her no.

"So are you gonna give us *any* guidance?" I asked.

He rolled his eyes. "Looky here, Miss Fancy Pants, I don't see you lasting two hours, let alone two days, so I don't feel like wasting my time. If you solve this case, then we'll talk about me trainin' ya." He waved a hand in dismissal. "Y'all are just a couple of bored housewives who've seen too much *Cagney and Lacey*. You two chickies are on your own for this one."

I was about to tell him that we'd solved multiple cases and we didn't have to prove anything to him, but Neely Kate beat me to it.

"*Lacey?*" she asked. "You mean that girl from *The Bachelor?*"

I stared at her in disbelief. There was so much to take offense to in his statement, and *that* was what Neely Kate had picked up on?

His mouth dropped open; then he shut it and shook his head. "Never heard of *Cagney and Lacey*? What in the hell is the world comin' to?"

I was asking myself the same thing.

"You two get," he said, waving his hand toward the door. "Let me know when you find the bird."

I didn't waste any time exiting the trailer, and Neely Kate was right behind me with the paper in her hand. We hadn't even gotten to the truck when I spun around and confronted her.

"You better start doin' some fast talkin', Neely Kate."

"About which part?"

"All of it!" I took a breath, then said in a calmer tone, "Let's start with Jed."

She grimaced. "He found out that I want to be a P.I., so he set this up."

"That's all well and good," I said, "but that's not what I'm talkin' about, and you know it."

Her cheeks turned pink.

"Look," I said with a heavy sigh, "I know you two left town together. I was hopin' you'd tell me more, but you haven't said a word. Neely Kate, I want to know how it was you wound up together on your trip in the first place."

She glanced away toward the trailer. "Kate was sendin' me threatening letters."

"You said those stopped."

"I lied."

Tears stung my eyes. "Why?"

Her own tear-filled eyes turned to face me. "I was ashamed. I . . . did something in Oklahoma, when I went back there after high school, and Kate hinted that she knew about it. I went to see Skeeter last week, hopin' he'd been keepin' tabs on Kate."

I wrapped my arms over my chest, ignoring the stab of pain I felt at the mere mention of James' name. "He talked to you?"

"Yeah. He wasn't very happy that Merv and I had gotten into a disagreement."

"Over what?"

"Merv told me I wasn't welcome at the pool hall and tried to make me leave."

Something in her voice caught my attention. "What do you mean 'tried to make you leave'? Did he get physical with you?"

"Jed intervened."

"So he *did*?" I was going to march in there and give that man a piece of my mind.

"Rose," she said with a tiny smile. "Did you ever consider this might be why I didn't tell you? You're all riled up, and it happened a week ago."

"Justifiably."

"Okay, you're right, but it's done. I broke Merv's nose and messed up his hand, and all I got was a few stitches."

I gasped in horror and reached for her shoulders. *"You got stitches?* Where? How do I not know this?"

"On the back of my head. You couldn't see them, and I didn't want to worry you. We're gettin' off track. And, no, before you ask, Skeeter didn't hold what happened at the parley against me. He took my side in the disagreement and sent Jed with me to talk to Kate."

"James sent him as a bodyguard?" Somehow that relieved me.

"No. He sent Jed to ask Kate what she knew about an account. Of course, she refused to tell him anything, and she said we both had to come back this week or she was gonna spill my secrets. Since I didn't know what she *actually* knew, I decided to find out who she'd talked to in Ardmore."

"And James sent Jed with you?"

Her mouth twitched. "No, Rose. He insisted Jed come back, but Jed refused. Skeeter fired him."

I took a step back. *"What?"*

"Jed hinted this has happened before—Skeeter has a temper and fires him on occasion—but he'd decided he wasn't goin' back to work for Skeeter this time. That he was done."

I took several seconds to process what she'd just said. "But they both changed their minds, right?" I finally asked. "Because you said Jed came back as soon as he found out Scooter was missin'."

"No," she said quietly. "Jed's helpin' him find Scooter, but that's it. As soon as they find him, Jed says he's done."

I couldn't believe it. Jed had been James' best friend since they'd been kids. How could either of them throw away their friendship like that? "What's Jed gonna do now?"

"He doesn't know."

I studied her for a second. "So what did you find in Ardmore?"

Her blue eyes locked with mine, and she remained silent.

"You're really not gonna tell me?" The hurt crept into my voice.

She reached out and grabbed my hand and clung to it. "When you're lookin' at me now, what do you see?"

I tried to pull my hand free, but Neely Kate held it tight.

"What does that have to do with any of this?" I asked.

"Please, Rose. Just answer the question."

I took a breath and decided to give her a real answer. "I see a woman who's fearless. She sees what she wants and goes after it. She doesn't take crap from people—as evidenced by the damage you inflicted on Merv—and she stands up for the people she loves. She doesn't back down from anything."

She nodded, still holding on to my hand, but there was a new sadness in her eyes. "That's who I am *now*. But that's not who I was in Ardmore. I was weak and . . . I . . . was *so* far from strong. I want you to see the me *now*, Rose, not that weak, stupid girl."

"I won't think any less of you, Neely Kate."

"I know that on some level. Deep down, anyway." She dropped my hand and shrugged. "It's like you and Levi."

I jutted my head back in surprise. "What about me and Levi?"

"You still haven't told him about your visons, have you?"

I cringed. "No, but—"

"Do you really believe he'll think less of you?"

"I don't know . . ."

"Well, *he won't*, but you're still not ready to share that with him."

I could see where she was going with this, but I wasn't buying it. "That's like comparing apples and oranges. You and me are a heck of a lot closer than me and Levi. And whatever Kate claims to know scared the pee out of you. I want to help you."

After a moment of silence, she took a step closer. "I'll tell you one part of my past—a big part—and that's all I'll tell you for now, okay? I'll tell you the rest when I'm ready. Like we said earlier, we'll do it a little at a time."

I wanted her to feel safe telling me all of it, especially since I was pretty sure she'd told Jed. But I was thankful she was telling me anything at all. "Okay."

She took a breath and held it, her hands shaking.

I grabbed her hands and held them between my own. "There's absolutely *nothing* you can tell me that will change my opinion of you, Neely Kate."

She nodded, but the look in her eyes suggested she didn't believe me. Just when I feared she'd changed her mind, she whispered, "I killed a man."

I let the surprise wash over me, then offered her a shaky smile. "So have I."

"I'm not sure this one was self-defense, Rose."

I wasn't prepared for that, but I nodded. "I'm sure you had a good reason for doin' what you did. The police obviously let you off."

"The police don't know anything about it."

I let that roll around in my head for a moment. If the police didn't know about it, did that mean Neely Kate was still at risk? "They don't know how he died?"

"They never found his body."

I took several breaths, my imagination running wild, but she was watching me like a hawk with fear in her eyes. I pulled her into a hug. "I trust you, Neely Kate. I trust that you did what you had to do."

She hugged me back and started to cry.

"Did you really think I'd turn my back on you?" I whispered in her ear. "You've had a hard life. I suspected you'd been in some rough situations that required violence, just like with Merv." I grabbed her shoulders and stared into her eyes. "There won't be any judgment coming from me. We just need to worry about Kate."

"I don't think she knows the whole story. Just bits and pieces."

"And what does Jed say?"

"He thinks I'm safe."

I nodded. "Then we'll trust Jed."

She watched me for a second. "You're not gonna ask for more details?"

"Not unless you want to share them. I only need to know the names of the skeletons in your closet. I don't necessarily need to know how they got there or what they're wearin'." ·

She threw her arms around me and squeezed. "I love you, Rose."

"I love you too." I squeezed her back for several seconds, then pulled away and said, "Now tell me how in the Sam Hill we ended up at Kermit Cooper's trailer."

Her face flushed. "Jed."

I gave her a coy smile. "So you two . . . ?"

She gave me a hesitant look.

"If you're worried I'm upset and don't approve, put those concerns to rest. You'll never find a more loyal man than Jed Carlisle." I grinned. "And he's pretty cute too."

She flushed more.

"And if you're ever in a bind, Jed is the man you want on your side. I've seen him fight off three men and win . . . and that was after he started off tied to a chair. He was amazing to watch."

Her face fell slightly. "Do you . . . like Jed?"

My mouth tipped into a sad smile. "No. Not like that."

"Skeeter," she said in a resigned tone.

"I'm not sure whether to deny it or confirm it, but I'm trying to move on."

She nodded. "I'm just surprised you'd be romantically involved with the criminal leader of the county."

"First, we're not romantically involved. They're just feelings." And an amazingly hot kiss, but that was a moment of weakness on both our parts. "He shows me a different side of him," I said. "A side no one else sees. Not even Jed."

She nodded again, then put her hand on my arm. "But he's still a criminal."

My lips pressed together as I tilted my head in agreement. "So is Jed."

"Jed wants out," Neely Kate said. "He wants to do something legit."

And so did James, deep down in the part of him that he didn't let the world see. Jed was free to go and forge his own path, but James would be left with his thumb in the dike of the criminal world, trying to keep it contained. If he left, all hell could break loose.

What in the world was I doing standing here defending James Malcolm, even if it was only to myself?

"You're probably wondering why I'm so adamant you date Levi when I know you still have a thing for Skeeter. Especially since I'm seein' Jed now," Neely Kate said. "You must think I'm a hypocrite."

I didn't say anything.

She glanced away. "You and I are different." When she turned back, there was a new fire burning in her eyes. "You have a moral code that Skeeter Malcolm can never live up to."

I gasped. "Are you insultin' me?"

She laughed. "Only you would think bein' called moral would be an insult." Her merriment faded. "I'm sayin' he is firmly entrenched in a world you can never condone. Do you really want to subject yourself to that?"

She wasn't telling me anything I hadn't already told myself. "This isn't about me. This is about you and Jed. Have you figured out how to tell Joe? How do you think he's gonna handle you datin' Skeeter Malcolm's right-hand man, even if he is retired?"

"I'll deal with Joe when the time comes. For now, Jed doesn't want anyone to know . . . not that he's ashamed of me," she hastily added. "He's worried I'll be a target. Especially with Scooter missin'."

"He asked you to keep it from me?"

She made a face. "No. That was me. I'm really happy, and I was worried you wouldn't approve." Tears filled her eyes. "But it was hard bein' happy when I couldn't share it with my best friend."

"I know." I grinned. "And I suspected something, so you're not as good at keeping secrets as you might think. Just don't try to hide it from the world forever."

"We won't," she said. "Who knows, he might get tired of me."

"Not likely." She blushed. "Just be careful with your heart, Neely Kate," I said softly. "You've been hurt so many times. I know Jed would never purposely hurt you, but with his world . . ."

"I know," she said. "I'm willing to take my chances."

I wasn't, because at the end of the day, Neely Kate was right. I might be attracted to James Malcolm, but we could never be together. Not really. He'd been right to put a stop to our kiss before it got out of hand.

Maybe looking for a lost parrot was exactly what I needed. That and time.

"Is this how you investigate a case?" Kermit shouted from his front porch. "Who the heck taught you?"

Neely Kate shot him a glare, then turned to me. "Let's go find a parrot."

CHAPTER 6

*W*e got in the truck and drove to Chuck and Cluck to get a snack and discuss what was on the paper.

"Squawker is a twenty-year-old blue-fronted Amazon parrot and lives with Boomer T. Whipple," Neely Kate read.

"Twenty?" I asked in surprise. "I wonder how long they live."

"A long time, I think," she said, looking at the paper again. "This says he was last seen Saturday morning at the park."

I nodded. "Squawker loves the park. He also loves carrots and *Wheel of Fortune*."

Neely Kate did a double take. "Wait. How do you know that?"

"I saw a flyer at Levi's office this morning." I pulled in behind two cars in the drive-thru of the Chuck and Cluck. "It said there was a five-hundred-dollar reward. Does that sheet say anything about how much Kermit's getting paid?"

She looked it over. "No."

"You know, if you really want to investigate this case, we could just do it on our own and collect the reward money. Shoot, I saw the flyer in Levi's waiting room this morning, and I was gonna ask if you wanted to investigate."

"Really?"

"Yeah. We could probably find the parrot in time to collect the award money before the carnival tonight." I lifted an eyebrow. "*If you were going to the carnival instead of havin' your secret rendezvous with a certain someone . . .*"

She ignored my comment. "This doesn't say much. Mr. Whipple put up flyers and got a few calls, but his bird is still missing. That's why he hired a private detective to look for him. And sure, we could get the reward out from under Kermit, but what we really need is for a P.I. to sign off on the hours for us."

"And you think that man is gonna help us?" I asked in disbelief. "I'm pretty doggone sure we have to know things for that test, things he's supposed to teach us. What if we spend two years doing free work for him, only to find out it was a gigantic waste of time?"

"We'll handle this one case and see how it goes."

I had a feeling the next time wouldn't be any different, despite what Kermit had said about teaching us. Besides, I wasn't so sure there'd be a next time. He hardly seemed like he had a booming business.

I shrugged my shoulders in concession. "Let's focus on this case. How about you call Mr. Whipple and see if we can meet with him this afternoon?"

I checked my phone while she placed the call. Violet had sent a selfie of herself, Mike, and the kids all snuggled on the sofa watching a movie with a one-word text.

HOME.

She looked content. She looked happy. So why did I still feel like something wasn't right? I almost texted her back asking her to call me, but I wasn't going to steal this from her. My concerns could wait.

Levi had sent me a message reminding me to send him the details, so I texted him to pick me up at six from the office. That would give Neely Kate and me a couple of hours to start working our case.

Working *our* case. Neely Kate was rubbing off on me.

~

A HALF HOUR LATER, I parked my truck in front of Boomer T. Whipple's white bungalow-style house. It was in my old neighborhood, it turned out—three blocks from my childhood home, but I'd never met Boomer Whipple, let alone heard anything about him. The yard was pretty sparse, and the maple trees and yews in front of the windows needed trimming in the worst way. I shook my head. Since I'd started my new profession in earnest, I couldn't help noticing people's landscaping.

"I think I should warn you," Neely Kate said as we walked up to the front door. "Mr. Whipple thought I was Kermit's secretary when I called."

"Okay . . ."

She stood on his front porch, rang the doorbell, then glanced back at me. "He's not too happy we're girls."

"What?"

The front door opened, revealing an elderly man on the threshold. He curled his upper lip in disgust the moment he saw us. "*You two* are gonna find my bird?" His gaze lingered on me. "Or are you planning on takin' him on a date?"

In hindsight, I realized I probably should have changed, but he was being rude, so I gave him a hard stare. "We've nailed bank robbers, kidnappers, and murderers, Mr. Whipple. Finding a bird shouldn't be that hard, but if you find us lacking, then maybe you should get someone else. Come on, Neely Kate. He's wastin' our time."

She gave me a look of disbelief . . . but then the corners of her mouth lifted slightly. "You're right. I knew we should have taken that smuggling case instead."

We'd only made it a few steps from the house when Mr. Whipple called out, "Wait. Where are you goin'?"

I stopped and pivoted to face him. "To find a real case."

"Squawker *is* a real case!"

"And we're real detectives, so we expect you to treat us like we are. If you can't do that, there are plenty of clients who can."

His frown expressed his dissatisfaction at being put in this position, but he waved us toward his house. "Come on." It was the last thing he said before stepping inside and letting the storm door slam behind him.

Neely Kate shot me a mischievous grin.

I grinned back. "I can be devious when I want to be."

"I'll say."

We followed Mr. Whipple into the house and found him standing next to a large bird cage in his living room. He looked so sad I almost felt bad about what I'd just done.

"Is that Squawker's cage?" Neely Kate asked in a gentle voice.

He nodded, then glanced over his shoulder at us. "Is it true? Did you really do those things?"

I took a step closer. "It's all true and then some. I promise you that we'll do our best to find your parrot."

He nodded again and walked over to an armchair. Neely Kate and I moved to the sofa, and she pulled her pink sparkly note-book and pen out of her purse.

Mr. Whipple's eyes grew round, but he didn't say anything.

"I'm Neely Kate Rivers, and this is Rose Gardner. We're working with Kermit Cooper."

He nodded. "Okay."

I noticed that Neely Kate had given her maiden name but kept the observation to myself.

"Now, Mr. Whipple," Neely Kate said, glancing down at the list of questions we'd come up with. "The information we have says the last time Squawker was seen was last Saturday at the park. Was that by you or other people?"

"My neighbor said he saw him. He knew Squawker was missing. But I'm not sure I trust him."

"Why not?"

"He and I don't get along."

"When was the last time *you* saw him?" she asked.

"Last Thursday night."

"Did he escape?" I asked.

"No. Someone broke in and stole him."

I glanced at Neely Kate in surprise, then leaned forward. "Did you call the police?"

"Of course I called the police!" He flopped back in his chair. "But the responding officer didn't seem all that concerned. He was more interested in their attempt to steal the TV."

"Do you remember who the police officer was?" I asked. The city of Henryetta had hired the worst group of police officers in the state, but there were varying degrees of ineptitude and belligerence.

"Not his name. He was a tall, skinny guy with a chip on his shoulder."

"Officer Ernie," Neely Kate said.

Mr. Whipple looked up in surprise. "Maybe."

He was the worst one of all. If he'd investigated the robbery, I had no doubt he'd missed things. "Do you know what time the robber broke in?" I asked.

"It wasn't all that late. Maybe ten? I go to bed early, so I was asleep. Whoever did it came in through the back door."

"You heard the break-in?" I asked.

"I heard Squawker havin' a fit. I jumped up and ran into the livin' room, and the front door was wide open with my TV layin' in the grass."

"So the only thing they took was Squawker?"

His lips pinched into a tight line. "The officer said they didn't take him either. That he escaped out the open front door."

"But you still think he was stolen?"

"I believed him at first. But Squawker didn't come back."

"So he's gotten loose before?" Neely Kate asked.

"Yeah, and he always came home."

I shifted on the sagging sofa. "You said a neighbor claims to have seen him in the park?"

"Uh-huh. At first I wasn't surprised. I take him for walks in the park. He likes to fly into trees so he can watch the kids play. He's a people watcher. That's part of the reason he likes to go to the park.

"There was no sign of him when I went to look, so I made the flyers." He licked his bottom lip. "If he's loose, he's bound to be scared and hungry. I just want to bring him home."

I waited while Neely Kate made more notes. A moment later, she asked our next question. "Do know who might have taken Squawker?"

"No."

"You took him out in public," I said. "People saw him. A parrot is an unusual pet. Maybe someone liked him and decided they wanted him as *their* pet."

"Huh," he said as though considering it.

"Did anyone ever express an interest in him on your walks? Make comments that he was cute and they wanted a parrot like him?"

Mr. Whipple shook his head. "I don't remember anything like that happening."

"When was the last time you took him out?" I asked.

"It's been a couple of weeks since we went to the park, but I let him hang out in the backyard all day on Wednesday. He likes it out there."

"And he doesn't fly away?" Neely Kate asked.

"No. I built him a big cage. I'll show you." He got up from his chair and hobbled through his small kitchen to a back door.

As soon as I walked onto his patio, my mouth dropped open.

"Holy moly," Neely Kate said as she tilted her head to look up. The cage—about twenty feet wide and deep and over ten feet tall

—filled up most of the small backyard. There were multiple perches and swings and even a couple of small trees.

"Squawker is happier out here than inside. I had a couple of appointments on Wednesday, so I left him outside."

"Wasn't it too hot for him?" I asked, trying to remember what the weather had been like last Wednesday.

"He's a blue-fronted Amazon parrot. His ancestors were born in the heat. And besides, I have a mister I turn on for him." To prove his point, he turned a knob next to the cage, and a fine mist started spraying from a plastic tube and hitting me and Neely Kate in the face. If Mr. Whipple noticed, he didn't let on.

"You thought of everything," Neely Kate said, patting the moisture off her cheeks with a tissue she dug out of her purse.

"Not everything," Mr. Whipple said with a sad look. "I didn't get him a chip. Otherwise, I could track him."

"Um . . . I don't think they work like that," I said to ease his guilt.

He glared at me. "So what good are they?"

I started to answer, then thought better of it. Instead, I pointed to a lawn chair in the cage. "Is that for you?"

"We hang out together," he said defensively.

I held up my hand. "I'm sorry. I didn't mean anything offensive. It just proves you two are close."

His glare fell. "We are."

"So you let him out Wednesday, came home, and then what?" Neely Kate asked.

"He seemed anxious."

"Birds get anxious?"

"Squawker does. Just like people do."

"Do you know what made him anxious?" I asked.

"I wasn't sure, but he kept saying, 'Shut up, you stupid asshole, and clean up the blood.'"

My eyebrow shot up in alarm. "Does he usually talk like that?"

"No. But I let him watch a show he shouldn't have watched—

one of them *Law and Order*s—and I'm pretty sure that's what upset him."

"So he mimics what he hears?" I asked.

"Yeah. He doesn't say anything original. You can't ask him what he ate for lunch, 'cause he'd have to reason that out. He just repeats what he hears someone else sayin'. He's said worse than that from watchin' TV."

"But you didn't hear anything like that from him in the morning?" Neely Kate asked.

"No, not until I came back."

Neely Kate wrote something in her notebook, then asked, "Is there a Mrs. Whipple?"

"Not anymore," he said, looking longingly into the cage. "She died ten years ago."

"Any girlfriends?" she asked.

He shook his head. "No one can compare to my Angela. So I got Squawker."

"Where did you get him?" I asked. "There aren't any pet stores in Henryetta. Did you buy him from someone?"

He shook his head. "I got him from a breeder in Little Rock."

"Can you give us the name?" I asked.

Anger flashed in his eyes. "I'm not replacin' Squawker just like that! He's like my baby!"

I'd already figured that out. "That's not why I want it, Mr. Whipple. If you're certain someone stole Squawker, then we need to figure out why they took him. I want to call the breeder to ask if he's heard of any other birds being taken. It's a stretch, but we're coverin' all the bases."

"Oh." He looked down at a ball in the bird cage. "That's a good idea. Sorry, I—I just miss him." His voice broke, and Neely Kate walked over and gave him a hug.

"We'll do our very best to find him, Mr. Whipple. I know what it's like to lose someone you love."

He clung to her for several seconds, then cupped her cheek as a tear fell down his face. "God bless you."

She pulled a business card out of her pocket and placed it in his. "This has our numbers. If you think of anything else, don't hesitate to call."

He nodded. "Okay."

We let ourselves out and stood in his front yard.

"What do you think really happened to Mr. Whipple's parrot?" I asked.

"I think Mr. Whipple's right. I think he was stolen."

"Me too. We just need to figure out why."

CHAPTER 7

I checked the time on my phone. "We still have an hour and a half before I meet Levi. Want to talk to some neighbors to see if they saw or heard anything?"

"Sounds like a good idea to me."

We started with the house to his right and knocked on the door. A frazzled woman about my age answered the door. "I'm not buyin' whatever you're sellin'."

"Oh," Neely Kate said. "We're not sellin' anything."

"Well, I ain't goin' to church either. I done already accepted Jesus as my personal Lord and Savior eighteen years ago, then nine years ago, and then five. I don't know how many times y'all think it takes to make it stick."

"Uh . . ." I said. "We're not here about goin' to church either."

Her eyes widened. "Oh, Lord. This is about that contest I entered, ain't it? You're here to award my prize." She reached a hand up to her head. "Floyd! Get down here! I won!"

"Actually, Ms. . . . ?" I said.

"Smith. But you can call me Anita." She giggled. "But then you already know that." She leaned her head out the door and looked around. "I don't see the camera. Just hold tight." Then she slammed the door shut in our faces.

"Crappy doodles. What does she think she's won?" I asked, feeling guilty that we hadn't told her the truth.

"I don't know, but I think we should leave."

"We can't just leave!"

Neely Kate pointed to the door. "That woman thinks she won somethin', Rose. And now we have to tell her she didn't!"

"How do you think she's gonna feel if we just take off?"

"How long's she gonna be?" Neely Kate asked. "Maybe that was her way of givin' us the brush-off."

"Let's wait about ten more seconds before leavin'." But ten seconds came and went, and she still hadn't returned.

"Rose, I'm tellin' you, this is going to be bad. We need to go before she finally opens that door."

I was about to agree with her when the front door flung open and a woman appeared in the opening. At first I didn't recognize Anita because her hair, which had been up in a bun, was now long and full and obviously a wig. She'd changed into a cute skirt and top and three-inch heels, which explained why she was suddenly taller than us. There was, inexplicably, an umbrella in her hand.

She gave us an expectant look, then screamed and started dancing and stomping around.

"Oh, my stars and garters," Neely Kate said as she took a step backward. "What is *happening?*"

I wasn't sure, but I was starting to regret not making a run for it sooner.

"Uh . . . Anita . . ."

Neely Kate grabbed my arm and tugged. "I'm *beggin'* you, Rose. Let's just run."

"We can't." I took a deep breath and pushed it out. "Anita. We're not here because you won a contest," I said, all in one long rush of words.

She stopped hooting and hollering and gave me a blank look. Then she grinned. "That's a trick. It's part of it. I've seen 'em do it before. You're here to give me my plane ticket to Memphis."

I glanced back at Neely Kate, but she just grimaced and shrugged.

"No, Anita. We're not. I'm afraid there's been a misunderstandin'."

Her eyes narrowed. "No," she said, shaking her head. "I sent my audition tape, and you're here to give me a plane ticket to Memphis!"

"Why in the world would we be givin' you a plane ticket to Memphis?" Neely Kate asked. "There aren't any direct flights from Little Rock or Shreveport. By the time you land in Memphis, you could have driven there and back."

I had no idea how Neely Kate had that particular information stored in her head, but I was sure she was right.

"That's not the point!" Anita said, stomping her foot. "The point is that my lifelong dream is about to be fulfilled! I got on the show!" She looked around again. "Where's the camera?"

"Anita," I said. "There is no camera."

"Oh, I get it! There's a hidden camera." She walked out on her concrete porch with an umbrella in her hand. "Hit it, Floyd!"

I glanced up and saw a long-haired man leaning out the upstairs window, giving us a thumbs-up and a huge smile.

"Am I gonna be on TV too?" he asked.

"Just shut up and hit it!" Anita shouted up to him.

The music started mid-song and she immediately belted out the lyrics. *"You have my heart, and we'll never be worlds apart."* She took exaggerated steps down the stairs, stomping the concrete to the beat of her song.

Neely Kate and I took several steps back.

"Oh, my word," Neely Kate said. "This is her music video."

"What?"

Anita continued singing, gyrating her hips and arms to the

beat—only slightly off—as she made her way across her front lawn.

"She's singing Rihanna's 'Umbrella.'" Neely Kate's eyes widened. "It's because she thinks she's on that show!" she said, getting excited. "*Memphis Superstar*!"

I gave her a blank look.

"People send in audition tapes of their own live-action versions of popular music videos. Then they have to reenact everything when one of the producers shows up at their door. This must be hers."

Anita was singing and dancing her heart out, although *very* off-key. "*Now that it's raining more than ever.*" She turned on the garden hose and started spraying water into the air, only she'd forgotten to open her umbrella, which she hastily did now. She sang something about being under an umbrella while mascara ran down her cheeks.

"We *have* to stop her, Neely Kate," I whispered.

"Are you *kiddin'* me? This is amazin'!"

I let her move on to the next verse as she sidled up to a tree and spun her umbrella around in front of her, moving it up and down and side to side as though she was playing a complicated game of peekaboo.

"I have to stop this," I said to Neely Kate, then turned to face the spinning umbrella. "Anita."

Neely Kate lightly slapped my arm. "What are you doin'? She's almost done. You're gonna hurt her feelin's more if you stop her than if you let her go on."

"She's gonna be embarrassed when she finds out we aren't who she thinks we are."

"No, she won't." The song ended and Neely Kate gave me a serious look. "Let me handle this."

Better her than me. Anita was on the ground on her knees with the umbrella in both hands, her arms straight over her head.

Neely Kate gave Anita a slow clap. "That was amazing! Wasn't that amazing, Beth Ann?"

It was the alias she'd created for me while we were looking for the necklace weeks ago, so I decided to use hers. "I'll say, Nancy." What was she up to?

Neely Kate motioned for Anita to get up. "I'm not gonna lie to you, Anita. Competition's stiff, but you're definitely in the running."

Disappointment covered Anita's face. "You're not here to give me a plane ticket to Memphis?"

"Not yet. But we *would* like to do a personal interview while we're here . . . if that's okay."

She lifted a shoulder into a shrug. "Sure."

Neely Kate pulled out her phone and opened up the video app. "We're gonna record it with my phone for a more indie look."

"Okay," she said, her eyes glimmering with excitement.

"Where did you find the inspiration for your cover of 'Umbrella'?" Neely Kate asked.

Anita launched into a long story about her boyfriend Floyd and a crazy drunken night involving an umbrella and edible massage oil.

I was going to have to take a shower when I got home.

"Do you get inspiration from nature?" Neely Kate asked. "Parts of your performance seemed somewhat birdlike."

Anita blinked, looking confused. "Uh . . . yeah . . ."

"It's just that I heard Rihanna gets inspiration from her surroundings." Neely Kate waved her hands in a big circle. "Her immediate surroundings."

Anita nodded. "Yes. Of course."

"Are there any birds around here that might have served as inspiration?"

Anita looked at her like she was crazy. I could relate. I decided to take things into my own hands. I pointed at the giant cage in Mr. Whipple's backyard. "Oh! Is that an aviary?"

She spun around. "That's where Mr. Whipple keeps his crazy bird."

"Crazy bird?" I asked.

"That bird cusses like nobody's business. It's flat-out weird. I can't even go out in my backyard when that bird's outside because it catcalls and insults me."

"Insults you?"

"It calls me a liberal hippie." She shuddered. "I could get disowned for that."

"Wow," Neely Kate said. "You must *really* hate that parrot."

Anita put her hands on her hips, the umbrella jutting out to the side. "I don't think I ever said it was a parrot."

Uh-oh. "What else could be livin' in a big cage like that?" I hedged. "And most birds don't talk."

"Yeah. I guess." She shrugged it off. "That old man loves that bird, and he's a mess since it went missing."

Neely Kate gasped. "What happened to it?"

"Someone broke into his house and stole it."

"Oh, my goodness!" Neely Kate gushed. "Do you have any idea who would take it?"

Anita shook her head. "A lot of people in the neighborhood couldn't stand that bird, but I don't know anyone who would steal him." She frowned. "I hope he's okay. Mr. Whipple treats it like it's his baby. I'm not sure how he'll handle it if his parrot doesn't come home."

"Do people like Mr. Whipple?" I pressed.

She looked surprised. "He has his cranky moments, but he's usually a nice old man. I was raised in this house, so I remember him and his wife before she died. It's just so sad he's alone."

"So he gets along with *everyone*?" I asked.

"Well . . . there is that one guy."

"Who?" Neely Kate asked.

"He lives down on the corner, but he doesn't get along with anyone."

"Which corner?" I asked. "And what's his name?"

She pointed to the house across the street. "Harvey Milner. But why are you asking so many questions about Harvey and Mr. Whipple?"

Neely Kate put her phone into her pocket. "We're just tryin' to get a broader picture of you!" she said enthusiastically. She formed a square with her fingers and framed Anita's face, then widened her fingers as though widening the picture.

And Anita was buying every word of it.

We were in a handbasket getting carted off straight to hell.

Neely Kate turned to face me, pivoting on her feet with a dramatic flair. "Well, Beth Ann, I'm impressed. I think our work is done here."

I didn't say anything, feeling lower than worm dirt for tricking Anita.

"Really?" she squealed. "I'm on?"

My head started to tingle and my vision faded, and I only had a fraction of a second to wonder who would be the subject of my approaching vision.

I was at my farmhouse, sitting on the sofa in the living room. The lights were dim, but I was familiar enough with the room that I instantly recognized it. Someone was next to me, holding my hand, and based on the way his hand dwarfed mine, it was a man.

Feelings rose up inside me, longing—both sexual and the need for something emotionally deeper—and happiness tinged with sorrow.

"I don't want to hide it anymore," I said in Neely Kate's voice. "Rose knows. At least I can stop hiding it from her."

"Things are too dangerous right now," I heard Jed say. "We need to go to Little Rock again. We can take the whole day."

I turned to look up at him. The adoration in his eyes made my heart catch, but pain rippled behind it. "So you're doin' his biddin'."

He didn't answer.

"I don't have to see her anymore. She doesn't know anything."

"But you could string her along. She doesn't know we went to Ardmore."

The vision faded and I said, "You're gonna string her along."

Well, crap.

Anita's eyes flew wide open.

"Beth Ann," Neely Kate said, her exasperation thinly veiled. "You know this is the best we can do." She turned to Anita. "Look, Anita. It's between you and a guy in Biloxi. Our executive producer wants the guy, but Beth Ann and I decided to fight for you, so now we'll take our video back to him and let him decide. *Unfortunately*, if you don't hear back from us, you won't have made the cut, but don't let that get you down. You can tell all your friends and family that you were officially a semi-finalist on *Memphis Superstar*."

Anita gave me a wary glance. "Yeah. I guess . . ."

Neely Kate put a hand on Anita's arm. "Thank you for your time." She must have finally agreed it was time to escape, because she turned and headed for the truck. "Let's go, Beth Ann."

I had started to follow her when Anita called out, "Why are y'all in a landscaping truck?"

"We're incognito," Neely Kate hollered back. "We couldn't very well sneak up on you with *Memphis Superstar* plastered on the side of our vehicle!"

We didn't waste any time hopping into the truck.

"I can't believe that just happened. I feel so guilty," I said as soon as I pulled away from the curb.

"I'm sorry, but you and I both know she'll never even get close to bein' on *Memphis Superstar*. You heard her sing. And then her dancin' . . ."

She had a point. "Still . . ."

"Look, I would have preferred *not* to lie to her, but now she'll tell everyone that she got close to bein' on the show. This is a win-win situation. We got the information we needed, and we didn't have to embarrass her."

"I guess." It still felt wrong.

"You had a vision," she said. "Who was it for?"

I gave her a sheepish look. "You."

She was silent for a moment. Although it had been Neely Kate's idea for me to try more forced visions to reduce my spontaneous ones, we'd had an unspoken agreement over the past few weeks: I wouldn't force any visions of her until she stopped getting letters from her sister Kate.

"What did you see?"

I was silent for a moment. "You were at the farmhouse with Jed. You told him I knew about you two, and he said it was still too dangerous to let other people know. Then he said you needed to go to Little Rock with him and you could have the entire day together."

"What was the stringin' her along line about?" she asked in a wary tone.

"Jed said Kate doesn't know what you found out in Ardmore. He suggested you could turn the tables and string her along."

She was silent for a moment. "So he was definitely goin'?"

"It sounded like it. He wanted you to come so he could spend time with you."

"Hmm . . ." She didn't look happy, which confused me. She'd seemed plenty happy with him in her vision.

"Never mind all that." She did a little shimmy in her seat, then turned to face me. "We need to focus on finding Squawker."

"We have to figure out what to do next. We can't very well question Anita's other neighbors while she's home. She'll catch on."

"Yeah, the logo on the side of the truck's gonna be an issue. How about we just drive around and scope things out?"

"Okay."

I turned right and then turned again to drive down the street behind Mr. Whipple's house. It was quiet, although that wasn't too surprising on a hot summer's late afternoon. All the houses looked the same—old bungalows of various styles and upkeep— and nothing looked out of the ordinary. There was definitely no sign of a green parrot.

Since we were in my old neighborhood, I realized I could kill two birds with one stone, pun not intended. "Say, do you mind if we stop by my old house? Mike said something to me about selling it, and I thought it might be a good idea to stop by and take a peek. I haven't been around to check on it in a few weeks."

"Violet's selling the house? Doesn't she want to see if things work out with her and Mike first?"

"I don't know, but Mike asked me to help sell it."

"I thought Violet owned it."

"She does."

"That's weird . . ."

"I know."

"Hey," she said. "You only moved out of your momma's house last November, and Mr. Whipple's lived in his house for decades. How is it you didn't know him? Or Anita, for that matter?"

I frowned. "I told you I didn't socialize very much before last year."

"Even with your neighbors?"

"*Especially* with the neighbors," I said as I pulled into the driveway. "Momma didn't want to risk any of them finding out about my visions."

As I got out of the car, I appraised the house with a buyer's eye . The yard was freshly mowed, thanks to Bruce Wayne and his new yard care crew, and the bushes had been trimmed. The annuals I'd always planted were absent, but the few perennials like the black-eyed Susans and the rose bushes were blooming.

The house was in need of repainting, but the roof had been replaced about five years ago after a bad hail storm.

I unlocked the side door that led into the kitchen, and as soon as I stepped inside, old memories washed over me—good and bad—just as the wash of heat flushed my face. I glanced over my shoulder at the house Joe had lived in. It was hard to believe it had all only happened a year ago.

"Mercy, it's hot in here," Neely Kate said, fanning herself.

"Since no one was living here, I turned the air up to eighty-five."

"You've been paying the utility bills, haven't you?" Neely Kate asked.

"Violet couldn't do it." I stood in the doorway from the kitchen to the living room. I gasped at the orderly room I found. Every last personal belonging, whether from Violet or the kids, was gone. "Mike moved everything out. Why didn't Violet mention this sooner?"

"You two have been getting along lately," Neely Kate said. "Maybe she was worried about upsetting you."

"Maybe." I turned to my best friend. "Something strange is goin' on. Mike was borderline rude when he asked me about the house. I've never seen him act like that before."

"Do you think Violet said something bad about you? You know she spread some lies about you last fall."

I considered it for a moment. "No. She seems happy. I could always tell when she was up to something devious."

"Maybe Mike was just tired and cranky from all the people."

"Yeah," I said, but something told me there was more to it.

I still felt uneasy about the whole enterprise—what was the rush?—but we went through the house, making note of what would need to be updated before it was put on the market.

"It looks great, Rose," Neely Kate said when we'd reached the back bedroom. "It could use new windows, and the bathroom

73

and kitchen could do with an update, but you should ask a realtor how much difference it will make."

"Thanks, Neely Kate." I checked the time. Five thirty. "I have to meet Levi soon, so there's no time to do anything else tonight. We need to go back to Mr. Whipple's street tomorrow, but we can't take my truck in case Anita's around." I headed down the hall toward the kitchen.

"Maybe I can get my car running again. I'll have Witt look at it. He's got plenty of time."

I turned around to face her. "What? Why? I thought he was working at the garage."

"It closed. Witt's tryin' to find a place in town to rent so he can set up his own shop with a couple of friends."

"It closed?" That seemed strange. Last I heard, it was open, just a few weeks ago.

She shrugged. "Ted's business has really slacked off since several of his guys were part of that mess in February. Witt knew business was bad, but Ted didn't give them any notice. Witt's gonna try to buy some of his tools and equipment. In the meantime, though, he's got plenty of free time to work on my car. Then we'll be less conspicuous."

Neely Kate's car was an old clunker. The inconspicuous part was debatable.

We went out the side door, and she watched me lock the house back up. "If it's gonna take Witt a while to fix your car, maybe we can just park the truck around the corner and canvass the neighborhood."

"I'll call him and find out when he can come out."

"And let's follow up on who sold Mr. Whipple the parrot. He never gave us the name. And we should find out everything we can about any enemies he might have—from old jobs, from church . . . if he goes. After what Anita said about Squawker's disappearance hurting Mr. Whipple, it seems like it would be the perfect way for an enemy to get revenge."

I noticed a dark sedan I didn't recognize parked on the street in front of the house. There was a guy sitting behind the steering wheel, only he wasn't on the phone or anything.

Neely Kate stared at me, grinning.

"What?" I asked, watching the car. The driver looked right at me and didn't move, like he was challenging me to a stare-off.

"You're sounding just like a private detective."

The driver finally looked away, and the car started to drive down the street.

Neely Kate turned around. "What are you watching?"

"That car, but it took off. It was almost like he was watching the house." Or me. What if whoever took Scooter was coming after me next?

"Maybe I should mention it to Joe. He might be able to get the Henryetta police to do a couple of drive-bys of the house."

"Yeah." Then I gave her my full attention. "It was probably nothing. I'm just being paranoid."

It seemed like that was happening a lot lately. Too bad some of the paranoia was justified.

CHAPTER 8

*L*evi picked me up from the office promptly at six. He'd agreed to drop me off at the farm later that night so Neely Kate could take the truck home. His text message —I'd love to take you home—had raised gooseflesh on my arms.

This would be his first visit to my farm. In the past, I'd always had him drop me off at the office. Plus, he'd kissed me so casually earlier, which meant he was probably going to kiss me again.

I wasn't sure how I felt about that.

"I hope inviting me didn't mess up your plans with Neely Kate," he said as he watched me lock the door to the office.

"No, she said she'd rather go home and read a book." As if.

"Are you sure?" he asked.

I turned around to face him and grinned. "She's excited I'm going out with you. She jumped at the chance to leave us to our own devices."

"As long as she knew she was welcome . . ."

"She did. Trust me." I had a strong suspicion Neely Kate and Jed were going to take advantage of my absence. Maybe the vision I'd had earlier would take place tonight.

Levi gave me a long sideways glance as we started walking

toward his truck halfway down the block. "You look beautiful," he said, his voice deeper than before.

I felt a blush rising to my cheeks. I suddenly felt self-conscious in my fluffy pink skirt and white shirt—like my bared chest made me naked. But that was ridiculous, and I knew it. Maybe Kermit's comment about my clothes was making me paranoid about looking too dressed up. "Thank you."

"After you left this morning, I realized I never told you that. I was kicking myself all afternoon. It was just such a surprise to see you."

"That's okay." I glanced down at my clothes. "I didn't have time to go home and change." Not that Neely Kate would have let me.

"I love what you're wearing."

I blushed. "But I suspect I'm overdressed."

Neely Kate had assured me that I wasn't, but she liked dressing in flashy clothing and being the center of attention. In fact, knowing her, she'd convinced me to buy this outfit in the hopes I'd wear it for Levi. If I hadn't stopped by his office earlier, she probably would have wrangled something up.

"You would know better than me," he said. "I suspect things are different down here." He opened the passenger door and waited for me to get in.

"I have a confession to make," I said, looking up at him.

He paused and his smiled wavered. "Okay."

"I've never been to a carnival."

His eyebrows lifted. "But this morning . . ." He gave me a sheepish look. "I guess you never said you'd gone to one before."

"Is that weird?"

He laughed. "Why would it be weird? I've never been to a circus."

"Me neither."

His smile spread. "Then we have even more in common."

"Do you still want to go?" I asked. "We can do something else if you'd prefer."

He studied me for a moment. "Since neither of us have been to a Fenton County carnival, I think we should go to this one together."

It was the perfect response, and I found myself smiling back at him. "Okay."

The carnival was set up in a field west of town, about ten minutes away. One of the things I liked most about being with Levi was that it was rarely awkward. He knew how to carry a conversation, yet he always made sure to include the other person in it. But this time I decided to use his expertise to my advantage.

"What do you know about blue-fronted Amazon parrots?" I asked.

His eyebrows shot up. "Are you interested in getting a parrot?"

I could have lied to him, but if I was going to keep seeing him, I needed to start telling him things. Neely Kate was right. I'd paid the price of dishonesty in a relationship, and I didn't want to go there again. "No." How much did I tell him? That we were doing free labor for a P.I.? Or just that we were looking for the bird?

"I saw you eyeing that flyer this morning."

Bingo. "Yeah. Neely Kate has a thing for animals, so she wants to look for him. We talked to Mr. Whipple this afternoon."

"*You did?*"

I shrugged. "Nothing like takin' the bull by the horns and goin' straight to the source." I paused to gauge his reaction. Levi sounded surprised, but he didn't act like we'd done anything out of the ordinary. "Mr. Whipple says Squawker likes to fly into the trees in the park." I turned to face him. "I didn't think parrots could fly."

"They can naturally, but most owners clip their wings. I've only seen Squawker in my office once. He'd eaten something off the kitchen counter, so Mr. Whipple brought him in for a checkup. I suggested he clip Squawker's wings because that's the danger. If they can fly, they can get into things they shouldn't. Or get hurt flying into things inside a small house."

"Mr. Whipple thinks someone stole his bird. Is there a black market for birds?"

"Sure. With some species like a cockatoo, but not usually with blue-fronted Amazons. Mr. Whipple said he stopped a robbery mid-progress and the would-be robber dropped his TV in his yard. I suspect Squawker got loose during the robbery, got scared, and flew off. The fact he was seen in the park two days later only confirms my theory."

"Mr. Whipple says he doesn't trust the neighbor who saw him."

Levi looked surprised. "He thinks he's lying?"

"He didn't accuse him of lying, but his next-door neighbor said Mr. Whipple and his neighbor down the street don't get along."

"You talked to his next-door neighbor?" He came to a halt at a stoplight and gave me a long look. "Neely Kate either has a true soft spot for animals, in which case she could make a serious case for being Mary's replacement, or you all are desperate for the reward money." Concern filled his eyes. "Are you having financial issues?"

I shook my head. "Oh, no. Six months ago, I was in dire straits, but we're in the black. We're doing well."

"Then why are you two putting so much effort into looking for a lost bird?"

I debated how much to say, then decided there was little point in keeping any of it quiet. I'd just lay it all out and let him walk away of his own free will if he felt so inclined. That would decide this "relationship" once and for all. "The truth is we like to investigate things."

"You're private detectives?" he asked, not sounding all that surprised.

"No . . . more like amateur sleuths."

"So you've had cases before?"

"A few . . . like the dog we were lookin' for when Neely Kate and I brought the baby pig to your office. But that one was more like helpin' out a friend."

"Do you ever get into anything dangerous?"

"Uh . . . A time or two."

He pulled into the crowded parking lot and parked in the second to the back row, taking one of the few spaces left.

I saw a few people walking across the parking lot, and it was obvious that I was overdressed.

"Maybe we should just go to Little Italy for dinner," I said as a woman in denim short shorts and a sparkly pink tube top walked past our car.

"Rose," Levi said in a soft tone, and I turned to face him. "You are stunningly beautiful. That's nothing to be ashamed of. In fact, I'm pretty damn excited for half the county to see you're out with *me* tonight. Besides, you're not the only woman dressed up. Look at her." He pointed toward a woman wearing a pale yellow, spaghetti-strap sundress.

"Not even close," I said with a grin. "But you're sweet to try."

"There's nothing sweet about it," he said in a husky tone. Then he lowered his face to mine. His lips were soft and coaxing, but they turned more insistent when I didn't pull back.

Kissing Levi wasn't repulsive. He was a good kisser—and I'd had a few bad kisses to know the difference—but it just felt wrong. Would that change if I gave this thing between us more time? How many men had I kissed in the last year? Five? Maybe I was just channeling Miss Mildred and worrying I was acting like a hussy.

His face lit up as he pulled away and sat back. "Let's give it a go, and if we hate it or you feel uncomfortable, we'll leave."

"Okay."

I opened the door, but Levi was out in a flash and came around to take my hand as I got out. "I'm gonna leave my purse in the car if that's okay," I said. "I don't want to carry it around."

"Of course. I keep a bag in the back for when I'm on call, so I'll be locking it up."

I got a few odd looks but not as many as I'd feared. The carnival was one of the traveling kind and only had six rides, one of which happened to be a Ferris wheel. Levi bought a long string of tickets, and we headed toward the first ride, a tilt-a-whirl, joining the line of about twenty people.

I watched the ride in progress, then leaned into Levi and whispered, "Do people get sick on that thing with all the spinnin' around?"

He turned to me in surprise. "You've never been on one before?"

"I told you I've never been to a carnival."

He blinked in confusion. "What about a theme park?"

I didn't answer, feeling embarrassed. Up until now, I'd kept most of my childhood from him, not wanting him to know about the abuse I'd endured from my mother. How she'd kept me from every childhood normality.

His face softened and he placed a hand on my upper arm. "Rose, I'm sorry. I didn't mean to make you feel uncomfortable."

"No, it's nothing," I said, glancing back at the ride, which had now stopped.

"No," he said, cupping my face and gently turning me back to face him. "Clearly it's not." He paused, and I could tell he was carefully weighing his words. Finally, he said, "There's a lot I don't know about you. I feel like I've told you so much about me, yet I have so many questions about you. I've waited for you to feel comfortable enough to share with me—and I'm so appreciative for the little bit you shared in the car. I won't push you for more now, but I want you to know I'm eager to listen when you're ready to talk."

"Thank you, Levi. That means a lot."

"Would you rather do something else?"

Someone caught my attention out of the corner of my eye, and I saw one of James' men, Brett, standing by a ring toss game. He was watching me, but he quickly glanced away. I couldn't believe he was there by coincidence. Was James having me watched because his brother was missing? Or was it for his own personal curiosity?

But Levi was waiting for an answer. "No," I said, trying not to sound distracted. "I want to try it."

The line started to move, and Levi put an arm around my back and ushered me toward the ticket taker. I cast a glance over my shoulder, but Brett was gone.

The ride was fun, fun enough that I wanted to go on it again, much to Levi's amusement. After our third time, we moved on to the next ride, one with swings hanging from chains that spun around a base, and then on to an octopus ride. I couldn't believe how much I loved them, from the spike of adrenaline to the way my stomach dropped.

"The rest are pretty tame compared to what we just rode," Levi said with a huge grin. "So it's probably safe to get something to eat."

"Oh," I said, realizing it was close to eight. "You must be starving."

"I've been having too much fun with you."

We walked over to a food vendor and ordered pizza and fried Twinkies. Before we sat down at one of the picnic tables, Levi made sure the seat was clean for my skirt. We talked about all the times Levi had gone to carnivals as a kid and then as a teen, one time on a date that had ended in disaster on the tilt-a-whirl.

"Let's just say alcohol was involved," Levi said with a grin.

"Which one of you threw up?" I teased.

His eyes twinkled. "I plead the fifth." He offered me the last bite of his fried Twinkie, but I shook my head. "So what did you do on dates when you were a teen?" he asked before stuffing the last piece into his mouth.

The pizza and fried food twisted in my stomach. *This* was when I admitted that my life had been a lame waste of time until a year ago.

"Rose!" I heard a woman say. "Fancy seeing you here!"

I turned to face Dena, both grateful for the temporary reprieve and a little uneasy because she was with Joe. It helped that Joe looked every bit as uncomfortable with the situation.

"Hey, Dena."

"Who's your date?" she asked with a grin.

Levi was eyeing me closely, and then he shifted his attention to Joe. I needed to nip this in the bud before things became even *more* awkward.

I stood to make the introductions. "Dena, this is Dr. Levi Romano, the new vet in town. He took over the Henryetta Animal Clinic after Dr. Ritchie retired. Levi, this is Dena Breene, the owner of Dena's Bakery, and if you haven't tried one of her pastries, you don't know what you're missin'."

Levi stood and offered Dena his hand. "It's a pleasure to meet you, Dena. I'll be sure to stop by sometime and try one."

"I heard you were taking over," Dena said. "I also heard that the pet population doubled after you came to town."

Levi chuckled. "Well, pets *do* bring joy to people's lives." He turned to Joe, and his body posture changed slightly. "Who's your date?"

Dena glanced over at Joe and said, "This is—"

Joe stuck out his hand, using his no-nonsense voice. "Joe Simmons, Fenton County Chief Deputy Sheriff."

Levi clasped his hand and squeezed. "That's an impressive title, Chief Deputy."

Joe pulled his hand free and stared him in the eyes. "It's not as fancy as it sounds. I arrest criminals just like all the other deputies do."

My mouth dropped open, and Dena's eyes widened in surprise.

"Joe," I warned.

Joe held Levi's gaze for a second more; then his face relaxed . . . slightly. "Sorry. I'm a bit defensive about the title. I want my men to respect me, not the nameplate."

"Understandable," Levi said, still on edge.

Dena seemed to have bought Joe's story, but I sure didn't. Was he acting out of jealousy, or did he know something about Levi I didn't? That latter seemed unlikely, but—

My head began to tingle, and I shot a panicked look to Joe before everything faded, leaving me smack-dab in the middle of a vision.

I was in Dena's head, watching Joe as he pulled up in front of a dark house.

"You didn't leave any lights on?" Joe asked, sounding concerned.

"I left the bakery late and forgot to turn them on."

"Then I insist on coming in and makin' sure everything's okay."

I laughed. "Why, Sheriff Simmons, did you just invite yourself inside?"

His mouth dropped open. "Dena . . . I didn't mean—"

I leaned forward and kissed him on the lips, cutting him off. He was shocked at first, but then he eagerly kissed me back.

"So you still want to come in and check my house?" I asked. "Because I was thinkin' about one room in particular."

My vision ended and I blurted out, "You're gonna invite him to your room."

Horror instantly washed through me, and I gasped as Dena gave me a look of disbelief.

"I know I talked about it," Joe said, giving me a grin I knew from experience was forced.

"But Randy doesn't have time to come help me with the drywall until next week."

Dena released a nervous laugh. "That's right. You're remodeling your house."

"It's a rental," Joe said, then cast me a glance. "And I'm almost done. Next week I'm gonna look for something to buy. Now that I've started this house flipping thing, I kind of like it."

Joe was moving? He'd irritated the snot out of me over the last half a year, but I'd grown used to having him at the next farmhouse over.

"Neely Kate's gonna miss you," I said.

"We'll still spend plenty of time together," he said.

Had Dena factored into that decision? I was happy he was moving on, even if it felt a little like he was rushing things with her. The vision hadn't affected me like I'd expected—in spite of the kissing and Dena's invitation, I wasn't jealous—I mostly felt relieved that Joe wasn't stuck in his unhappiness anymore.

"Well," I said, shooting Joe a look of gratitude before smiling at Dena. "We hate to keep you two."

"Oh, you're not keepin' us," Dena said, somehow oblivious to the tension surrounding us. "We were just about to get something to eat. Can we join you?"

Levi glanced at me, then said, "That would have been great, but we were just leaving. I promised Rose to take her up in the Ferris wheel, seeing how she's never been."

"You've never been on a Ferris wheel?" Dena asked in amazement. "How is that possible?"

"Rose's mother never allowed such frivolities," Joe said. "Rose lived a sheltered life until her mother died last year."

Horror washed through me again. He'd saved my embarrassment over my vision—and I had no doubt he knew what had happened—only to throw me to the wolves.

"Oh, that's right," Dena said. "I forgot your mother was murdered by Daniel Crocker last summer."

Was *all* my dirty laundry getting hung out to dry tonight? "Yes. Memorial Day weekend."

"It's hard to believe that was a year ago," Dena said. "And then with your sister and Mason . . . you've had quite a year."

She didn't even know the half of it.

"Rose is a resilient woman," Levi said, picking up our trash. "And I admire her all the more for it." He put his free hand around my lower back. "Now, if you'll excuse us, we have a date with that Ferris wheel."

He didn't wait for an answer, just ushered me back toward the carnival crowd, only pausing to toss the trash in a can.

I expected Levi to ask for some kind of explanation, but he kept guiding me toward the Ferris wheel at the opposite end of the carnival. "Levi, I owe you an explanation."

He stopped and looked at me in disbelief. "You don't owe me *anything*."

"But after what Joe said . . . and Dena."

"Those weren't their secrets to tell," Levi said, his eyes filling with fire.

I stared up at him in shock. Was he mad he'd heard it from them first? "I know I should have told you . . ."

"No." He shook his head, looking frustrated. "No. You shouldn't have."

My mouth gaped. "You didn't want to know?"

"Of course I want to know, but I wanted *you* to tell me . . . when *you* were ready. I know you've been hurt, Rose, and I know that asshole back there was one of the guys who hurt you."

Asshole seemed too harsh, but Levi had no way of knowing Joe had helped keep my visions secret. Or that he was Neely Kate's brother. "How did you know?"

He pressed his lips together. "I'm trained to read body language, just like that sheriff ex of yours. My patients can't speak up for themselves, so I need to know if their owners are telling me the truth." He paused and lowered his voice. "Look, Rose, I can see you've been hurt, and I want to earn your trust. I'm willing to bide my time."

"But why?" I asked, shaking my head. "Why me when you have your pick of half the women in this county?"

A soft smile lifted his mouth. "I'm intrigued."

And so was I. What man heard such secrets and didn't ask for more clarification?

Unless . . .

"You already know," I said in a deadpan voice.

"What?" But the guilty look in his eyes told me that I was onto something.

"You already know about my past."

He didn't answer for a few seconds. "Just as I told you on our first date, this town likes to talk. I've heard bits and pieces, but I have no idea what's true or not."

"And you didn't ask?"

"If someone told you that I like to run around naked with Mr. O'Brien's cattle, would you ask me if it was true?"

I could see his point. I offered him a tiny grin. "Neely Kate probably would."

He laughed. "And that's why I'm dating you and not Neely Kate. That woman scares me." But the grin on his face suggested he was joking. Mostly. "Rose, I keep telling you, your history is yours to share . . . or not. You may kick me to the curb before you want to tell me any of it, although I truly hope not." He stepped closer. "But let me make something perfectly clear—your past means nothing to me other than how you feel about it. I don't need to know anything about it to know I like you. I'm enjoying getting to know the woman in front of me."

His words meant more than he probably realized. "Thank you."

"Now let's go ride a Ferris wheel."

We'd used all our tickets, so Levi bought more. He refused to consider letting me buy the next strip, even though I'd put some cash and my phone into my skirt pocket. The line to the Ferris wheel had gotten longer since everyone was wanting to ride close to sunset. Several of Levi's clients saw him and said hello, and Levi always introduced me as his friend Rose. One little girl who looked to be five or six years old gave me a shy smile and said to Levi, "She's pretty."

Levi squatted down in front of her. "I think so too."

"Is she your girlfriend?"

He glanced up at me and grinned, then turned back to her. "Not yet. I'm trying to convince her I'm a nice guy."

She looked up at me with big eyes. "Dr. Levi really is nice. My puppy, Pebbles, was sick, and he made her all better again."

I couldn't help being charmed by her. "Dr. Levi is a good vet, isn't he?"

She nodded. "So will you be his girlfriend?"

The little girl's mother put a hand on her head. "Aubrey, you can't ask her that." She gave me an apologetic look. "I'm so sorry."

I laughed and glanced at Levi. "It's okay." I looked down at Aubrey. "Dr. Levi seems like a really great guy. I'll think about it."

Levi stood as the mother hurried the little girl off.

"You're playin' dirty," I said.

He laughed. "Just gathering character witnesses."

I laughed too.

"So are you really thinking about it?" he asked.

"Levi . . ."

"Sorry. I know I promised to take it slow." He paused and looked at me in earnest. "It's just that I've never liked someone so much and been so unsure about where I stood."

I cocked my eyebrows. "So you're tryin' to lock it in?"

He cringed. "When you put it like that, it sounds terrible."

"Can't we just keep taking it one date at a time? I'm having fun, but all this pressure . . ."

"Of course, Rose. I'm sorry. I'll back off."

But I could see it wasn't enough for him, and I couldn't help thinking it would be better to end it now for his benefit.

Several minutes later, it was our turn to board the Ferris wheel. I got into the seat first, and he sat next to me before pushing down the bar that locked us in. There was one more empty seat after us, and the ride started as soon as the next pair was seated.

Levi snagged my hand between both of his. "Rose, I'm sorry. I shouldn't have pushed my own insecurities onto you. Can we erase the last ten minutes?"

I really did like him. I just didn't like him as much as I'd hoped I would. As long as I was honest with him, I didn't see the harm in the two of us continuing to get to know each other. "Sure."

He continued to hold my hand with one of his as we looked out over Henryetta. He pointed in front of us. "There's downtown. Where's your farm from there?"

I pointed to the left. "About fifteen minutes north of town. Off County Road 24. If it's too far to take me home, I can—"

"It's not too far. I want to see your farm."

I grinned. "It'll be too dark to see the farm. But you'll see the farmhouse." I instantly regretted my words. What if he expected to come in?

"Then maybe I can come back when it's daylight, and you can give me the tour."

"I'd like that."

I was quiet for the rest of the ride, and I had to agree with Neely Kate. Riding the Ferris wheel with the right guy could be very romantic. Unfortunately, the one guy who came to mind wouldn't be caught dead here. Joe had been right. Momma had always considered the carnival frivolous, and there was nothing soft or frivolous about James Malcolm. I couldn't see him willingly going on rides at a carnival. I had to consider that. Despite the turmoil of Levi wanting me to make more of a commitment, I'd had fun tonight, and I needed more fun in my life.

When we got off the ride, I said, "I've had a long day, and I'm tired. Do you mind if we call it a night?"

He gave me a worried look. "No. Of course not."

We headed out to the parking lot, which had only partially cleared out. As we got closer to our row, a mangy looking dog ran past us toward the street. Levi dropped my hand and took several steps in pursuit of the dog, leaning to glance around a car to see where the stray was going. Seconds later, we heard screeching tires and the sounds of a dog yelping in pain. Levi took off running as several people started screaming.

I ran after Levi, but a small crowd of teens had already gathered around the scene by the time I reached him, blocking him from sight. Through the mass of people, I saw Levi on the ground next to the dog, who lay on his side and was now unnervingly silent. A car sped out of the parking lot, presumably the one that'd hit the poor dog.

Levi saw me and asked me in an urgent tone, "Rose?"

"Yes?" I said as I edged closer.

"Can you get my bag out of the back of my truck?" He dug into his jeans pocket, pulled out his keys, and then tossed them to me. "And get a blanket too."

"Of course." I caught the keys and took off running to Levi's truck. The black leather bag was in the backseat, along with several blankets. I grabbed them and ran back, pushing my way through the teenagers.

Levi took the bag and immediately dug out his stethoscope and listened to the dog's chest and stomach. The dog, who'd started coming to his senses and was no doubt terrified out of his mind, released a low growl and snapped. Levi snatched his hand out of the way and reached into his bag, pulling out a vial and a syringe. He ripped the syringe out of its package more quickly than I would have thought possible and jabbed it into the bottle, pulling out some of the liquid. Then, without flinching, he turned back to the dog and immediately injected the syringe into the animal's hip. The dog's head bobbed, and he stopped growling within seconds.

As soon as the dog was out cold, Levi quickly wrapped him in the blanket and stood. "I'm sure he has internal injuries. I have to take him to my clinic right away."

"Of course," I said as I leaned down and picked up his bag.

"Show's over," a man said to the teens. "Time to get on the bus."

There were a few groans, but they followed him to the waiting bus on the back row.

"I'm not sure how long I'll be," Levi said as he hurried to his truck with me at his side. "I suspect he needs emergency surgery."

"It's okay," I insisted. "You do what you need to do."

"But I'm your ride home."

We had reached his truck, and I opened the back door. Levi put the dog on the backseat and took the bag from me. "Ride to the clinic with me, and I can either take you home later—although I have no idea how long I'll be—or have someone pick you up."

"I'll stay here and have Neely Kate or Maeve pick me up. This is closer."

He shut the back door and cringed when he looked at me. "This was supposed to be my night off, but I don't feel right pawning this guy off on Dr. Anderson."

"Of course you don't. You go. I'll be fine. *I promise.*"

He opened the front driver's side door. "Rose, I feel absolutely *terrible* about this."

"Please don't." I gave him a grin, but I was still shaken up after seeing the injured dog. "I got to see you at work, Dr. Romano, and I'm impressed. You were very take-charge. I like that in a man."

He grinned.

"So don't worry about leavin', okay? I'll talk to you later."

He leaned over and gave me a quick kiss. "I'll make it up to you, Rose. I promise."

"I know."

He got inside and backed up, giving me a wave as he pulled away.

I was standing in the road, so I walked back to Levi's empty parking spot, realizing I'd left my purse in his truck. I could call him back, but he'd already left the parking lot. I'd just get it tomorrow. Besides, I had my phone, which was the important item. Who should I call? Maeve was closer, but I didn't want her to have to take me all the way out to the farm. Maybe I could have her take me to her house and Neely Kate could pick me up there. It had been a few weeks since Maeve and I had had a good chat. She'd probably be happy to hear from me even if it was after nine.

Decision made, I started to pull my phone out of my pocket . . . but I didn't get very far. Someone had moved up behind me, and there was something hard and narrow pointed between my shoulder blades.

I'd had enough experience to know it was a gun.

HydraFacial MD®

SKIN HEALTH FOR LIFE™

DETOXIFY • **REJUVENATE** • PROTECT

Name: _____

Skin Type: _____

- [ ] Antiox-6™ Daily   AM / PM
- [ ] DermaBuilder™ Daily   AM / PM
- [ ] Beta-HD™ Daily   AM / PM
- [ ] ETX™ Daily   AM / PM
- [ ] Pur Moist™ Daily   AM / PM
- [ ] UV Smart® Daily   AM / PM

Recommendations _____

_____

_____

Next Treatment Date: _____ Time: _____

CHAPTER 9

"Do as I say and you won't get hurt," a man said behind me.

"I only have twenty dollars." I slowly pulled out the folded-up bill I'd stuffed into my pocket and held it up to show him.

The man behind me jabbed the gun harder into my back. "Put your hands down."

He wasn't here to rob me. The thought sent a wave of panic through my head. "I think there's been a misunderstanding, so how about I head over to the carnival, and we'll forget this ever happened?"

"There's been no misunderstanding." He jabbed me again. "*Lady.*"

A cold sweat broke out over my body. He knew I was the Lady in Black. This was bad.

I cast a glance toward the carnival. Most of the crowd had dispersed, and the parking lot was nearly empty. I hadn't seen Brett since we'd gotten in line at the tilt-a-whirl, and I'd been looking. Had I been right about him being sent to watch me? Either way, it was obvious that *he* wasn't going to save me—if Jed were watching me, he probably would have tackled the guy behind me by now—which meant I needed to save myself.

"I'm not sure what you want, but I'm not the person to help you." As I scrambled for a plan, I realized my pepper spray and Taser were in my purse in Levi's truck.

The suspicious car that I'd seen parked outside my childhood home was approaching from my right, and there was a terrible sinking feeling in the pit of my stomach.

I took a step forward to make a run for it, risky since the kidnapper had a gun pointed at my back, but the man grabbed my upper arm and tugged me back and into his chest, dragging me behind a van. It did a great job of hiding us from the bus of teenagers and the other people walking to their cars. "Oh, no, sweetheart. You're not goin' anywhere."

I opened my mouth to scream, but his grimy hand clamped over my mouth and nose, cutting off my air supply.

Terror shot through me, and I reacted out of instinct, chomping down on his meaty palm with my teeth. He cursed but didn't let go, instead tightening his grip over my face.

I swung my heel backward into his shin as I reached up for his arm, but other than releasing a new wave of curses, that didn't seem to faze him either.

Struggling to take a breath, I dug my nails into his arm, frantically pulling down as my vision began to fade. The sedan had pulled to a stop in front of us, and a man hopped out and opened the trunk.

There was no way I was getting in there without a fight.

I reached up toward my captor's face, digging my nails into whatever parts I could reach. He cursed again and released me. Gasping for breath, I was faint enough I nearly fell to my knees, but I knew if I did that I'd be a goner. I got two steps before the driver of the car blocked my path. By the time I saw his fist, it was too late to react. He swung into the side of my head, and after the initial burst of pain, everything went black.

～

WHEN I CAME TO, I was lying on my side with my hands bound in front of me at the wrists and my ankles secured together with duct tape. Something nasty was stuffed in my mouth, and a cloth had been tied around my face, holding it in place. My head pounded on the left side, and I struggled not to panic as I tried to figure out where I'd been taken.

Then I remembered. I was in some kidnapper's trunk.

Why had they taken me? What did they plan to do with me?

They knew I was Lady. Had the guys who'd taken Scooter kidnapped me too as part of a revenge scheme against James? I tried not to let my imagination run wild, but I was terrified. I suspected Brett had no idea I'd been taken, and it would likely be hours before anyone knew I was missing.

The car came to a stop and the brake lights lit up the interior of the trunk right before the car engine turned off. We'd reached our destination, which meant I needed to come up with some kind of plan to get out of this. Only, my brain wasn't cooperating.

The car engine turned off, and my breath stuck in my chest with anticipation and fear.

Breathe, Rose. Now was not the time to lose it. *Think.*

The trunk lid opened, and the sudden transition from the pitch-black trunk to the bright fluorescent lights of wherever they'd brought me made me squint. Two sets of hands grabbed my upper arms and pulled me out, scraping my legs on the lip of the trunk. One of them was the man who had hit me, and I presumed the other one, a guy with a tattooed arm, was my initial kidnapper based on the scratch marks on his face. I suspected he was going to hold that against me.

They set me down on my now shoeless feet, but the way I was bound made it impossible to stand. They hooked hands around my upper arms and started to drag me across the concrete floor of what I realized was an empty warehouse.

I forced myself to stay calm. I needed to keep my wits about me, and the first order of business was to figure out where I was. If I found a way to make a break for it, I needed to know where to go. But there was nothing around that hinted at our location, and even if I broke free from their hold, there was no way I could run with my legs taped together.

I was in deep crap.

They stopped in front of a door next to a dark room with a window facing toward us, then opened the door and shoved me inside. I fell to the floor face first. My bound hands broke my fall, and I rolled to the side, my shoulder hitting a sharp piece of metal. I released a cry through the fabric in my mouth, but the door had already been shut behind me.

I had several things to my advantage. One, even though the room was dark, the light from the warehouse streamed through the window, giving me enough light to see I was in an office. Two, my hands were bound in front of me, which meant I could use them. Three, I was pissed as hell, and I was fighting my way out of here.

I had no idea how long I had until someone came back, so I got to work right away, ignoring the pain in my shoulder and head. I yanked the cloth wrapped around my mouth down over my chin and pulled the nasty rag out of my mouth. Then I crawled across the room to the desk, got to my knees, and opened the closest drawer. I could barely see the contents, but I felt around and found paper clips, ink pens, Post-it notes . . . scissors.

I nearly cried with relief as I pulled them out. Sitting on the floor, I turned the scissors so they were pointing toward me, but my hands were too shaky to get a good hold on them. I closed my eyes and forced myself to take a breath and calm down. I needed to be level-headed. The panic wasn't helping.

After several cleansing breaths, I opened my eyes and focused on the task at hand, cutting through the tape with agonizing slowness. They must have been given an impressive budget for the tape, judging by how much they'd used to bind my hands and feet. As soon as I made it halfway through, I slammed my hands down several times on my upright knees to break through the rest. I didn't waste any time before snagging the scissors again and cutting through the tape at my ankles. Once I was free, I scrambled to my feet and reached for the doorknob. Locked.

Now what?

There was only one answer, really. Call James.

I grabbed my phone out of my pocket and pressed his speed dial number. Hopefully the single bar of service on my screen would be enough.

"Malcolm," he barked in a harsh voice, obviously still pissed at me since he had my number programmed into his phone.

To my irritation, I started to cry when I heard his voice. "James."

"Rose?" His anger instantly gave way to panic. "Are you in trouble?"

"Two guys knocked me out and stuffed me in a trunk. And now I'm in an office in a warehouse." I was babbling like a fool, and I needed to pull myself together. Just because I'd gotten a hold of James didn't mean I was safe. "They know I'm Lady."

"Who? What warehouse?"

"I don't know." I looked around the room, but there were no hints as to my location.

"You're breaking up."

I glanced at my phone. "I only have one bar."

"Try to pull up your map app. If it will open, we can figure out where you are."

Why hadn't I thought of that? I opened the app, frustrated by the spinning wheel. "The page won't load. I don't have enough service."

"That's okay," he said in a deceptively calm voice. "We can still figure it out. Tell me what you see."

"I'm locked in an office with a window overlooking the interior of the empty warehouse."

"There's nothing in it at all?"

"No. Nothing other than the car they brought me in. It's some kind of dark sedan, older. The warehouse doesn't look brand new; it's not all that old either."

"Jed," he barked. "An empty warehouse in Fenton County that's in decent shape. Nothin' stored in it."

Jed? What was Jed doing there? Why wasn't he with Neely Kate?

There was silence for a second; then I heard Jed's muffled voice. "There's nothin' like that in Fenton County."

I wasn't in Fenton County. *Where was I?* Fear swamped my head.

"Rose," James said in his cool-as-a-cucumber voice. "You said they put you in the trunk of a car. How long were you in there?"

"I don't know," I said, trying to catch my breath. "They knocked me out. I didn't come to until I was almost here."

"Okay. Listen to me. We're gonna come get you, but you have to look around and tell me what you see."

I sucked in a breath, willing myself to stay calm, and did as he'd asked. "There's a desk in front of a window, but there's no chair. The calendar on the bulletin board is two years old."

"That's good. The warehouse hasn't been used in two years. What else do you see? Is there writing at the top of the calendar?"

Having James' calm voice in my ear was settling me down. "Farmer's Bank and Trust."

"Farmer's Bank and Trust," he repeated.

"That doesn't narrow it down," I heard Jed say. "They have branches in Louisiana *and* all over Arkansas."

"Tell me more, Rose," James said. "Look for envelopes with addresses on them."

I got to my knees. "There's nothing on the top of the desk, but there were supplies in one of the drawers. That's where I got the scissors to cut the duct tape."

Keeping down, I glanced out the window, looking for my abductors again, but the only thing out there was the car they'd brought me in. Where were the men?

I searched the open drawer, finding nothing, then moved to the next one.

"Rose, talk to me." Tension strangled his voice.

"I'm lookin' through the next drawer." I found a single envelope inside, but just as I was about to inspect it for markings, I heard gunshots from the main part of the warehouse.

"What's happening?" James demanded, his voice tight. "Is that gunfire?"

My heart pounded into my ribcage. "Yeah, but I can't see what's goin' on." I rose up on my shaking knees. "Three men just burst through a loading dock door shootin' guns. And there are gunshots comin' from outside the office door."

But where were they hiding? Because from what I'd seen earlier, the car was the only thing they had to hide behind.

"Stay down!" he said. "Is there anywhere to take cover?"

"The metal desk. I'm getting under there. The wall is made of concrete blocks."

"Good. Now stay down and keep hidden. Let them have their shootout, and when the coast is clear, we'll figure out how to get you."

There were multiple rounds of gunshots, and I hated that I felt so defenseless. Why had I left my purse in Levi's truck? Not that I'd been carrying my gun lately. While I didn't like carrying it, I'd been given it for self-defense—a precaution I clearly needed given the fact that this was not my first kidnapping. If I got out of this alive, I would start carrying it more regularly. No. *When* I got out of here.

"What's happening now?" he asked.

"There are lots more gunshots. Some are still close, so I'm guessin' at least one of the guys who took me is still alive."

"And you didn't recognize the guys who took you?"

"No. I've never seen them before."

"What did they look like?"

"In their thirties. Average looking."

"Tattoos?"

I hadn't given it much thought, but now I remembered seeing a flash of something. "One had some kind of bird on his arm, but I didn't see much of either of them."

The gunshots abruptly stopped.

"Has the gunfire ended?"

"Yeah." My breath was coming in rapid pants.

After several seconds, James asked, "Do you hear anything?"

"No."

"Stay there. We have no idea why those guys busted in, but we're gonna let them do their business and be on their way."

I didn't answer, my ears straining to listen.

James and I were silent for nearly ten seconds before he said, "Rose. I'm sorry." The fear in his voice scared me.

My heart skipped a beat. "What are you sorry for?"

"I had Brett watchin' you, and when he saw you were with that vet, I called him off. This is my fault."

"This isn't your fault," I whispered. "You're not responsible for me."

James paused, then said, "Your voice hasn't been breaking up. See if you can pull up your map."

I glanced down at my phone—there were two bars, but the app still wouldn't load. I scooted out from under the desk and pulled a solid three bars.

The app had finally started to load when I heard the door-knob jiggling. I glanced up in panic, about to dive for the desk, but there wasn't any time. The door opened, and I saw a man I recognized standing in the doorway. He'd been at the parley three weeks ago. He was one of Buck Reynolds' men. Tim Dermot.

He reached a hand toward me. "Give me the phone."

I wanted to protest, but the gun pointed at my chest helped me change my mind. Still on my knees, I handed it to him. He snatched it from me and promptly dropped it on the ground behind him. If it had been a living entity, the three shots he pumped into it would certainly have killed it.

I jumped and let out a gasp before he turned back to me. "Who were you talkin' to?"

Should I lie? The truth seemed better in this instance. "Skeeter Malcolm. He knows where I am, and he's comin' to get me."

Okay, semi-truth.

A small smile spread across his face. "That's what we're countin' on."

Well, crappy doodles.

"If you're countin' on him comin' for me, then why shoot my phone? Why not just offer him a polite invitation to join us?"

"Because we're not stayin' here." He leaned over and grabbed my upper arm, tugging me to my feet. "Time to go."

"I think I'd rather just stay here and wait for James." *Dammit.* I'd used his real name.

Dermot's eyes lit up. "James, huh? So Buck's right. You two *are* screwin'."

I jerked free of his hold. "My personal life is none of your business."

"Everything to do with *James* Malcolm's life is our business. If you're part of it, then it *is* our business."

I could continue arguing that we hadn't slept together, but that meant nothing. It was obvious James found me valuable—the hows and whys didn't much matter.

The more details I gave Buck Reynolds, the more leverage he would have.

"I won't be any part of tryin' to hurt him."

His only answer was to grab my arm and drag me out of the office.

My head swam when I saw the bodies of the two guys who'd captured me lying on the floor in puddles of blood that soaked their clothes. Tim continued to drag me toward the loading dock doors.

"What do you want?" I asked. Instinct told me to resist, but from the looks of it, Tim Dermot and his two buddies had just busted in to rescue me. Or take me hostage themselves.

Again, he stayed silent as he marched out the door with me in tow. I saw two guys standing next to a car. The one facing me was wearing a grim expression, probably because his arm was bleeding. The other guy was wrapping a piece of gauze around it for pressure. He tied a knot and then pivoted to face me.

Standing in front of me was none other than Buck Reynolds.

I'd just jumped out of the frying pan and into the fire.

"I take it you're here to kidnap me too," I said, sounding sassier than I felt. I was about to pee my pants with fear, but I didn't want *them* to know that.

A grim smile twisted his lips. "Hardly. I'm here to hire you."

CHAPTER 10

I lifted my chin and gave him a hard stare, hoping he didn't see my shaking hands. "If you wanted me to landscape your yard, all you had to do was call my office for an appointment."

He laughed. "You're funny."

"Strange," I said, getting ticked. "Because I'm not feelin' very funny right now."

He held up a hand. "Now calm down, Lady."

Lady. There it was again, but then Buck had learned my identity at the parley. "I'm not for hire."

"See, I think you are . . . for the right price."

I balled my hands at my sides. "Are you *threatenin'* me?"

He pulled a pocket knife out of his jeans pocket and flicked it open. He gave me a cold stare as he advanced toward me with the four-inch blade pointed at my chest. Everything in me screamed to run, but I was barefoot and wouldn't make it three feet before he caught me. I'd rather piss him off for standing up to him without flinching.

But that was easier said than done when he brought the blade to rest on my throat.

My breath was coming in rapid pants, and I was worried the blade would be jarred by my jerky movement. But he surprised me by hooking the knife under the cloth that had been tied around my head and giving it a jerk, cutting the gag in two.

Buck leaned close enough for me to smell his bad breath. "You seem pretty ungrateful considerin' we just saved your life," he said in a dry tone.

Maybe he had a point, but I wasn't about to let on how much he intimidated me. "How do I know you didn't orchestrate this whole scheme to convince me to trust you?"

Wearing a smug smile, he stepped back, stuffed the knife back into his pocket, then held out his hands. "The only thing I arranged was your safe rescue."

"And yet you knew exactly where I was when Skeeter Malcolm had no idea."

Tim Dermot laughed. "So, he's Skeeter now. And that's sayin' a whole helluva lot about him if he lets *two* different groups snatch you. Malcolm's getting sloppy."

"So you're not denying you were part of this?" No matter how he answered, I didn't trust him one iota. I needed to focus on getting myself out of here. Buck had two men with him, but maybe I could get to the car that had been used in my kidnapping. It would be foolhardy to try it, and they would definitely chase me down. Was it worth the risk?

"I would have had to sacrifice two of my men to stage this," Buck said with a shake of his head. "Malcolm may find *his* men expendable, but I can assure you that I'd not be so careless with *mine*."

There was no good way to answer. To defend James would hint that I had a special relationship with him. To remain silent would suggest I was condoning the actions Buck was accusing him of. I chose to ignore it. "If you had nothing to do with this, then how did you find me so quickly?"

"The how of it was simple enough. We've been watching you,

bidin' our time. You're a very popular woman, Lady. You're almost constantly with someone, and when you were finally alone, you were snatched out from under our noses."

If Buck hadn't staged my kidnapping, then who had? "For the sake of argument, let's say I buy that you followed me and dispensed with the two men who took me. Who were they?"

"We're about to find out." He walked a couple of feet past me before glancing over his shoulder. "Well, come on. You want to know as much as I do."

I grabbed the cloth still looped around the back of my neck and tossed it onto the ground as I followed him. I was halfway tempted to head for the kidnappers' car after all, but I suspected the keys were in one of the dead men's pants.

Buck had longer legs than I did, and he wasn't waiting for me. Dermot, on the other hand, was sticking close, probably to make sure I didn't run off. So much for escaping in the car.

Dammit.

I didn't like this one bit. Buck had said he wanted to hire me, but he hadn't so much as hinted at what he wanted me to do, although calling me Lady indicated it was criminal in nature. Did he know about my visions?

Buck was standing in front of the two dead men when I caught up to him.

"Do you recognize them?" he grunted.

Was he talking to me or to his buddy?

When Dermot didn't answer, I said, "No." But then I took another look at the driver and said, "Wait. Yes. That one." I pointed to him. "I saw him this afternoon in that car." I gestured behind me.

"Any idea about who he might work for?"

I shook my head, resisting the urge to wrap my arms across my chest even though I felt close to falling apart. I needed to look strong. "None."

"Dermot?" he asked.

"No." Dermot squatted next to the driver and fished the guy's wallet out of his pants pocket. He opened it as he stood. "Elijah Landry. His license says he lives in Shreveport."

Buck turned to me. "Why would a guy from Shreveport want you?"

That surprised me too, but this was almost certainly about James, not me. Still, the hint of condescension in Buck's voice pissed me off.

"Any truth to you being from Louisiana?" he asked. "My own research suggests you've always lived here except for the six months you went to Southern Arkansas University before you dropped out and came home."

He'd researched me, and while I wasn't exactly surprised, I was beyond pissed. "You want to know why someone from Shreveport wants me? How about you tell me why a nobody Fenton County guy would want me?"

"I guess you'll have to ask Malcolm that yourself." Buck grinned, looking plenty pleased with himself.

I was done with this nonsense. "Then I'll be on my way to go *ask him.*" I spun around and started walking toward Elijah Landry's car, praying he'd left the keys in the ignition after all.

Of course I never made it that far.

But I did get about ten feet before Buck said, "You ain't goin' nowhere, Lady."

I ignored him and kept walking.

"I said stop!"

I considered arguing the point—he'd never *said* stop—but the silent treatment seemed to be far more effective.

I heard a gunshot behind me, and a bullet ricocheted off the concrete floor about ten feet to my left. I flinched, but anger quickly overtook the rush of terror. I kept walking. I'd won James over by hiding my fear and refusing to let him intimidate me, and I'd be damned if I'd kowtow to Buck, who was nowhere near the man James Malcolm was.

I could hear Buck's footsteps behind me, but I didn't even slow down. Another gunshot took out the back tire of the car.

"You plannin' on walkin' all the way back to Henryetta?" Buck shouted.

I stopped and slowly turned around to face him, wearing my Lady persona like a cape of courage. "If that's what it takes."

"I already told you I'm not lettin' you go."

"Then I guess you'll have to shoot me." I turned around and headed for the door.

This was insanity, and we all knew it. I was barefoot, and the minute or so we'd spent outside hadn't given me any clue as to where we were. But dammit, I refused to beg Buck Reynolds for anything. He would treat me with respect . . . even if I had to die to get it.

I heard another gunshot, and this time the bullet hit the metal door. My right thigh felt like it was on fire, and for a second I was sure he'd shot me, but the pain was on the outside of my leg. Something had bounced off the door and grazed me. However I'd gotten the wound, it was bad enough that I felt blood running down my leg.

"Shit!" Buck shouted, leading me to believe he hadn't meant to hurt me. Which told me he really did need me, and he'd been trying to intimidate me into submission.

I'd come to a halt already, so I turned around again. "You have a very interesting way of interviewing people for a job, Mr. Reynolds. So let me save us both time: *Not interested.*"

Tim Dermot's eyes widened when he saw the trickle of blood running down my calf and seeping through the side of my skirt. "Malcolm's gonna kill you."

The look on Buck's face betrayed his panic, which I knew wouldn't work to my advantage. If he thought James would kill him, he was likely to kill me first and hide my body where it couldn't be found.

"Let me make this perfectly clear, gentlemen," I said, trying to keep my voice steady, but the burning in my leg was becoming overwhelming. "Skeeter Malcolm knows I've been taken, and if I don't check in with him relatively soon, he will presume *you* killed me. I can assure you that he *will* come after you, and he will exact a very painful and most likely drawn-out death from all three of you. Doing away with me at this point would be a *very* bad idea."

"She's right," Dermot said.

"Shut up!" Buck shouted.

"In fact," I added, "if you return Scooter along with me, you might be able to work out some sort of lesser punishment."

"I didn't take Scooter Malcolm!" Buck shouted.

I didn't believe that for a second, especially not now. "You've already kept me hostage and shot at me numerous times. You're pretty much a dead man walking, but if you return Scooter, you might have a chance."

"Are you deaf?" Buck yelled. "I didn't take Scooter Malcolm!"

"Then where is he?"

"The hell if I know," he said, sounding defeated. "That's why I wanted to hire you. To find him."

My mouth nearly dropped open. "If you can't find him, how in Hades did you think *I* can?"

"You found my necklace, didn't you?"

I put my hand on my hip. "Why would you ask me to find him when you're so damn certain I work for Skeeter?"

"Because I was pinning my hopes on the fact that you didn't. You claimed to be working to help the county; then you gave me the necklace when I know Malcolm wanted it. But now I think you were bullshittin' us. Why would Malcolm care so much if you're not screwing him? So you're either sleepin' with him or on his payroll."

"I am *not* on his payroll. I provide services that help him ferret out turncoats, and before you ask, *no*, I will not be offering those services to *you*. The only reason I helped Skeeter in the first place was for the good of the county."

"And to save your D.A. boyfriend," he said with a sneer.

I shook my head in disgust. "Keep it up, Mr. Reynolds, and you'll be diggin' your own grave. Literally."

"If I'm dead anyway," he said, "why don't I just take you with me?"

I shot him a deadly glare even though my courage was starting to wane. Nevertheless, I wasn't going to beg this man for my life.

"Buck, think this through, man," Dermot said. "This is goin' all wrong."

"No fuckin' shit!" Buck shouted as he started to pace the warehouse.

Dermot walked around him and approached me. "Look, Lady. We didn't take Scooter. We've got nothin' against Scooter. He's like Switzerland. No one wants to touch him, and if Malcolm was thinkin' straight, he'd know we didn't do it."

I snorted. "And he probably thinks Mr. Reynolds isn't stupid enough to shoot me, and yet here we are with a puddle of blood poolin' at my feet."

"Goddammit, Buck!" Dermot shouted, turning around to face his boss. "Why'd you have to go and throw a damn fit!"

"She wouldn't listen to me!"

"We knew she wouldn't, you damn fool! You were supposed to reason with her!"

"Let's make this perfectly clear: *I'm* in charge here," I said. "I'm making the rules, and if you can't deal with that, shoot me dead right now." It was a huge risk—a very stupid one—but I needed their respect, and this was the only way I could see to get it.

Neither man said anything. I'd just lived two seconds longer than expected.

I reached out my hand. "I need your phone so I can call Mr. Malcolm and have him send someone to pick me up. And if you're respectful until his representative shows up, I'll try to convince him not to kill you."

Buck stopped pacing and shook his head. "No. We'll take you to him."

"If you think I'm stupid enough to get into a car with you—"

"We're not in Fenton County. We're in Louisiana. It will be faster if we take you."

Louisiana? But our location was neither here nor there at that immediate moment. "If you think I'm gonna get in a car with three men who are carryin' guns when I don't have a weapon, let alone a pair of shoes, then you must be addled in the head."

"How about we give you something to make you trust us?" Dermot asked.

I didn't think that was possible, but I found myself saying, "I'm listening."

"We'll promise to lay low," Dermot said.

"You can promise me the moon, but there's nothing to stop you from shooting me before we get to the end of the road."

"If we wanted to shoot you, we would have done it by now!" Buck shouted.

"And who's to say you won't take me back to Fenton County and then hold me hostage there?"

Buck took several steps toward me and stopped. "We could just toss you in the damn trunk like Landry did. But we haven't. I need you, and even though we've gotten off to a rocky start, I think we can still salvage this."

I released a sharp laugh. "You call this a rocky start? I'll let you take me back, but I want your phone. I'm calling Mr. Malcolm before we leave. If I don't return home safe and sound, I want him fully aware that *you* are responsible. Then *and only* then will I get in your car."

"No," he barked.

I turned around and nearly fell when pain shot through my leg.

"Dammit, Buck!" Dermot shouted. "We're supposed to be savin' our asses, not puttin' the stamp on our death warrants! Give her the damn phone!"

"Why in the hell would you trust her to make this call?"

"We don't have a choice thanks to your trigger-happy finger."

I'd taken several steps, trying my best not to limp, silently chanting *I'm as badass as Neely Kate* over and over in an effort to suck it up and ignore my pain, when Buck said, "Fine. Take it."

I turned around and saw Buck holding out his phone to me. He approached slowly, his gun still hanging at his side.

"If you're trying to make me feel better, that's not doin' it." I pointed to his gun.

He shoved it in his pants, and I took the phone and started to punch in the number, thankful I'd committed James' number to memory in case I ever needed it.

"Where the fuck is Rose?" James snapped into the phone with plenty of venom in his words. "If you've hurt her, I swear to God I'll make you suffer until you're begging me for mercy."

I hid my shock. James had Buck Reynolds' number programmed into his phone.

"James," I said, trying to keep my voice from shaking. "I'm okay."

"You stole Reynolds' phone?"

"No . . ." I looked into Buck's face. "He gave it to me."

"This is a ransom call." His hard edge was back.

"No. It's a long story, but the two men who kidnapped me are dead, and Buck and two of his guys freed me."

"They're the guys who showed up?"

"Yeah, but like I said, I'll explain it all to you when I get back to Henryetta."

"Where are you?"

"Buck says Louisiana, but I don't know any more details. He and his men are bringing me home."

"Don't get in a car with them, Rose. Give me the location, and we'll come get you."

"That's what this call is about—their guarantee to deliver me safely. Because now you know that my well-being is in their hands."

"Put me on speakerphone," he snarled.

I pushed the button, and James' voice was amplified. "Reynolds, you listen to me and you listen good. If she comes back with so much as a paper cut, you're a goddamned dead man."

Buck's gaze lifted to me, and I could see he was about to back out of the deal. James was going to flip his lid when he saw me.

"James," I said, putting a lot of force into my tone. "I have a few scrapes and bruises. He can't be held accountable for those."

"I'll deliver her nearly the way we found her." Then Buck snagged the phone from my hand and ended the call. "Let's go."

Dermot headed for the car and grabbed a bag off the hood. "Before we go anywhere, I need to clean that wound up," he said.

We all knew why.

"Gary," Buck shouted to the third guy, who'd been leaning against the car and cradling his injured arm. "Stay with Tim and clean up the mess."

"What?" I said. "It's just gonna be you and me?"

Buck wrapped my arm around his neck, offering no preliminaries, then half-dragged and half-carried me to his car. "Open the back door."

I wasn't sure who he was talking to, but Dermot opened the door. Buck practically dumped me onto the seat. "Dermot. Take care of it."

"Let me look," Dermot said as he dropped to his knees in front of me.

I pulled up my skirt, exposing my upper thigh. Dermot grabbed a flashlight and shone it on my leg.

He studied it for a moment with a serious expression. "It

looks like a flesh wound—the bullet grazed you—but you're gonna need antibiotics all the same."

Dermot opened the bag and grabbed a towel, doused it with water from a bottle, then patted the area around the wound. I tried not to flinch, but it hurt like Hades.

"It looks like it's nearly stopped bleeding. I can stitch it if you want."

I shot him a look of surprise.

Buck started pacing. "Tim was a nurse before he came to work for me. He's good."

That was shocking. Nurses were supposed to be nurturing people, not killing men in gunfights, but the careful way Dermot wiped my leg told me that deep down he was a healer.

"Okay," I said. Better to get as patched up as possible before I showed up on James' doorstep.

Ten minutes later, Dermot had given me two stitches and cleaned the wound as much as possible given our situation. Buck had gone back into the warehouse, leaving Dermot and me alone together. He taped some gauze over my stitches and said, "What are you gonna tell Malcolm?"

"Honestly, I don't know." Part of me wanted to tell James everything, but if I did, all hell would break loose.

Dermot frowned. "Look, I know that Buck did this to you, but he's freakin' out. He knows he's number one on the suspect list, and we have no idea where Scooter could be. You are literally his last hope."

My back stiffened. "Why should I give two figs about Buck Reynolds? He is *not* a nice person, so what in the Sam Hill are you doing hangin' out with the likes of him?"

He gave me a wry grin. "Maybe I'm not a nice person either."

"You're bein' nice to me now."

"And you're smart enough to know that part of me is doin' it in the hopes of savin' our skins."

I held his gaze. "But part of you is doin' it because that's who you are deep down," I said softly. "You're a healer. So how did you get mixed up in this?"

He was quiet for a moment, in a way that told me he was thinking it through. "Sometimes you make a simple choice that starts you down a path you hadn't planned on takin' . . . and then you find there's no turnin' back." He put on the last piece of tape and looked up at me. "How'd *you* get mixed up with Skeeter Malcolm?"

I glanced down at my leg. "That was one of those paths I'd never intended to take."

"It might not be too late to get out of it, Rose," he said gently. "Buck was willing to take a chance that you might be neutral, but if you keep turnin' to Malcolm to bail you out, that won't hold water for long."

I could see the truth in what he said, but I wasn't sure where that left me. I suspected I'd already fallen down the rabbit hole. The question was if I wanted to crawl out.

CHAPTER 11

*D*ermot dropped the tape into his bag and pulled out a
pill bottle and placed it in my hand.

"This is antibiotic. Be sure to take it. It's not uncommon for
bullet wounds to get infected." He pulled out another bottle and
uncapped it, tapping several pills into his palm. "These are pain
pills. Take one every four to six hours for pain. If you run out and
need more, let me know and I'll bring you some." He dropped all
but one of the pills back inside.

"I don't think I should take that before I meet James. If I'm
acting off, he'll know and start askin' questions."

"He's gonna know you were hurt. There's blood all over your
skirt."

"I know, which means I'll need my wits about me if I'm gonna
handle this."

"Then let's numb your leg more so you're not flinching
from pain."

"Okay."

He injected enough lidocaine to ensure I wouldn't feel a thing
for several hours, then grabbed a gauze package from his bag.
After he wrote something on the package, he handed it to me.

"My number's on the back. Like I said, call me if this gives you any trouble."

I'd just stuffed it into my pocket when Buck came back out.

"We need to get goin'," he said in a grunt. "Malcolm's gonna have my hide." He pushed Dermot out of the way, shoved my legs inside the vehicle—which didn't hurt at all thanks to Dermot's numbing injection—and closed the door.

He and Dermot got into another argument; then Buck stalked to the driver's door.

I tried to open the door and found it locked. When I tried to unlock it, I discovered it had been child-proofed.

"I want Dermot to take me back," I said in a short tone.

Buck's eyes met mine in the rearview mirror. "Why? He say some pretty words to get on your good side? Well, my job for the next forty minutes is to convince you to find Scooter."

"If I find Scooter, it's sure as hell not gonna be to help you."

"I just saved your life."

"Yeah, and then you shot me."

"It was an accident!"

"Save your breath, Mr. Reynolds. I only help people I trust. You would be one of the last people to end up on that list."

"Then it's gonna be a long damn car ride," he grunted.

"So be it."

He was right. It was a long drive, and it gave me plenty of time to think about everything that had happened tonight. I had a name and address for one of the kidnappers. I needed more information about the other guy, and Buck had it.

Then there was the matter of Scooter. If Buck *had* taken Scooter, then why would he go to so much trouble to ask me to look for him? It seemed likely he was innocent—of *this*—which left a big question mark as to what had happened to James' brother. And that meant plenty of upheaval in the county—not just because James was on a warpath, but because someone had stolen one of his loved ones. It was the kind of thing that made someone in that world look weak.

Of course, if I helped Buck, there was a chance I'd be asked to help others in the criminal world. Aside from all the other implications, none of them knew about my visions, and it would be dangerous for anyone to find out. Still . . .

What if I had the opportunity to make this county safer?

I couldn't ignore the fact that looking for Scooter would help the county, not to mention James. He had to be worried sick.

"What do you know about Scooter's disappearance?" I asked in a direct tone.

Buck sat up in his seat as though I'd startled him. "I know he worked his shift at Walmart last Wednesday and didn't show up the next day." He caught my gaze in the rearview mirror. "When I caught wind that Scooter was missin', I knew right away that I'd be at the top of the suspect list. We didn't waste any time before diggin' around ourselves, but we came up with a whole lot of nothin'. Everyone likes Scooter. He dabbled in Skeeter's businesses years ago, but for the last five years or so, he's stayed out of it."

"Which explains why he's working at Walmart," I said.

"Exactly. But the thing about Scooter is he never wanted much."

His words piqued my interest. "Wait. It sounds like you know Scooter personally."

Buck shifted in his seat again. "I may have befriended him in an attempt to get some secrets about his brother, but that was a couple of years ago."

"I presume everyone knows Scooter is Skeeter's brother," I said. "And it's no coincidence that someone took me so soon after he went missing. I need the name of the other guy who snatched me. And all the information you have about both of them."

"Why would I give you that?" he asked in a bitter tone.

"I'm gonna need everything you know about Scooter's disappearance and my kidnapping if I'm gonna look for him. There's no sense in me duplicating the work you've already done."

"You're gonna look for him?"

"I'm not doin' it to save your sorry butt. I'm doin' it to keep peace in this county."

"I still expect you to report your results to me."

That seemed fair, but it also felt traitorous. "I'll keep you in the loop."

"What's your price?"

That caught me slack-jawed. "You plan to pay me?"

"I said I was hiring you, didn't I?"

I knew we were on the south side of the county—we'd passed several familiar landmarks—but I was surprised when he flipped on his turn signal as we approached the old fertilizer plant.

"What are you doin'?"

"I'm sure as hell not gonna risk taking you any further into town and runnin' into Malcolm's men. You'll be safe here until Malcolm comes to get you."

He drove onto the abandoned complex and stopped in front of the office. This place had seen a lot of criminal activity in the past, so I wasn't sure how safe it would be, but beggars couldn't be choosers. I wanted out of Buck's car.

I opened the door and scrambled out, ignoring the gravel poking the soles of my feet. Thank God my leg was still numb.

Buck rolled down his window.

"And how is anyone supposed to find me here?"

He held up his phone. "You're gonna make a call. But first we need to work out your price."

I was about to tell him I wouldn't take a cent from him, but then I realized he had something more valuable to offer than money. "I want a favor."

"What do you want?"

"I don't know yet, but if I call in my favor, you have to do it, no questions asked."

He remained silent.

"Let's be honest, Mr. Reynolds," I said in a dry tone. "You want me to find Scooter to save your butt, yet you can't deny that you're also tryin' to get one over on Skeeter. You seem to think I'm his girlfriend, so it would be quite the feather in your cap if you got Skeeter Malcolm's girlfriend to do your biddin'."

His mouth pinched into a flat line.

"But I am *not* Skeeter Malcolm's girlfriend. Neely Kate and I investigate things. *On our own.* So I'll do this, but when the time comes, you will do a favor of my choosing, no questions asked."

"Only if you prove I didn't take him."

"Done. I'll start lookin' tomorrow." I held out my hand. "Now I need to make that call."

Buck handed me his unlocked phone, and I pressed Skeeter's number in the list of recent calls.

"Malcolm," he grunted.

"James. I need someone to come get me."

"Where are you?"

"I'm at the fertilizer plant."

"Since you're using Reynolds' phone, I take it he's there with you."

"Mr. Reynolds is just about to leave."

"Sit tight." Then he hung up.

I handed the phone back to Buck, but rather than let go of it, I grabbed his wrist and held on. This was my opportunity to get some answers, and I'd be a fool not to take advantage of it.

I closed my eyes and focused hard, asking, *Does Buck have information on Scooter?* The vision didn't come immediately, and Buck tried to pull away, but I dug my fingers in until a vision burst into my head.

I was in a living room with Tim Dermot and Kip Wagner, holding a beer bottle in my hand.

"You think she's gonna do it?" Kip asked.

"Yeah," I said in Buck's voice, then took a sip of beer. "She's too damn cozy with Malcolm to suit me, but I think she'll find his brother, if for no other reason than to make Skeeter happy. And it'll save our skins in the process. Win-win."

The vision faded and I said, "You think I'm too cozy with Skeeter." Then I released his hand and took a step back.

After opening and closing his mouth a couple of times like a guppy, he said, "That may be true, but I expect results sooner rather than later."

I gave him an indignant look. "You still don't get it, do you? You asked for *my* help. That makes me the person calling the shots. Don't get too big for your britches."

"And the same could be said for you. I just saved your life."

"We're gonna call that a gesture of good faith." I pointed to his hand. "I could have kept your phone and given it to Skeeter so he could go through all your contacts, but I didn't—*my* gesture of good faith."

He looked pissed but kept his mouth shut and drove off. I was surprised he'd stuck around so long, truth be told. He risked getting caught by James' men.

I didn't have to wait long for someone to arrive. Less than ten minutes later, I was sitting on the curb in front of the office part of the plant when I saw James' car speed around the corner. He skidded to a stop in front of me and was out of his car faster than I could get to my feet.

He took one look at my bloody skirt and his face twisted with rage.

"I'm going to kill the fucking bastard."

I shook my head, unable to speak past the burning lump in my throat. Everything that had happened over the last couple of hours hit me at once. Now that James was here, I could let my guard down because I knew in my heart he'd die before he let anything happen to me. It only drove home how much I'd missed him. I hadn't seen or talked to him in three weeks, and every day had been agony.

I took a step forward and reached for him. He was there within seconds, and I flung my arms around his neck, collapsing into his chest as I started to cry.

He wrapped me up in his arms, holding me as I sobbed.

Some brave woman I'd turned out to be.

"Are you hurt?" His voice sounded strangled. "What did they do?"

"I'm okay," I choked out. "Just hold me."

He cupped the back of my head and pressed my cheek to his chest as I cried my heart out. The reality that I'd almost been murdered multiple times tonight was sinking in. I had to be strong with everyone else, but I could let my guard down around James. I knew *he* wouldn't take it as a sign that I was weak or incapable of taking care of myself . . . and I was fairly certain he felt the same way about me.

He stroked my back, whispering in my ear, "You're okay. I won't let anything happen to you again."

But he couldn't promise that unless he locked me away somewhere, and I refused to agree to that.

I let myself have a good cry, then made myself settle down. I tried to take a step back, but James' arms were like a vise.

"I'm okay now," I reassured him.

"I'm not." He pulled me close again, resting his cheek on the top of my head. "Give me a minute."

We stood like that for another half minute before he looked down at me with worry in his eyes.

"Your leg . . . Is that your blood?"

"I'm okay."

He broke loose and started to lead me to his car, only to stop and pick me up with my hurt thigh on the outside. He set me down on the trunk and checked the bottoms of my bare feet. "Where are your shoes?"

"I lost them somewhere between when I was kidnapped and the warehouse in Louisiana."

His gaze jerked up to mine as he gently lowered my uninjured leg. "You sure it was Louisiana?"

I gave him a half-shrug. "That's where Buck Reynolds said we were, and the road signs on the way back confirmed it."

"I need to know exactly where they took you."

"I paid attention as we were driving back. I can tell you how to get there, although I'm not sure what'll be left. Tim Dermot and some other guy stayed behind to clean up."

He gave a nod and placed his hands on my knees. "What happened to your leg?" His question was direct.

"James, it doesn't matter."

"It sure as hell matters to me. I want to see it." I knew he was warning me that he was about to push up my skirt. I expected him to do it matter-of-factly, like Dermot had done, but he grabbed the hem with his left hand and slowly slid it up, the knuckles of his hand lightly brushing the inside of my thigh. A fire ignited inside me, and I sucked in a breath of surprise.

He ignored my reaction as his right hand followed the left, skimming my outer thigh, and I released a low moan before I realized what I was doing.

His gaze lifted to mine, full of a fire that had nothing to do with anger, but he glanced down when he reached the edge of my bandage. He pulled off the gauze, then stiffened. "What happened that made you need stitches?"

"It doesn't matter."

"The hell it doesn't." He used his phone to shine more light on the wound, and his gaze jerked up to mine. "A gunshot wound?" His voice sounded strangled.

I cupped the sides of his face with both of my hands. "I'm okay."

"Who stitched this?"

"Tim Dermot. He gave me antibiotics and some painkillers too."

His eyes hardened, but he didn't pull away. "Like hell you'll take those. I'll get you some myself."

"He wouldn't give me anything to hurt me. They saved me, James." My voice cracked.

He stood between my spread legs and rested his hands on my hips. "It could have been a setup."

"I wondered that too, but Buck and Tim were just as curious about the men who took me as I was."

"And who were they?"

"I only IDed one of them—a man named Elijah Landry. I saw him outside of Momma's house this afternoon. He must have been looking for an opportunity to snatch me. But the big surprise is that he was from Shreveport."

"*Shreveport?*" He shook his head, lifting his hand to my face. "When your call cut off . . . I've never been so scared in my life, Rose."

His admission shocked me. "I was pretty scared too."

He paused; then his face hardened. "Do you think they planned to kill you?"

"I don't know. They were apparently guarding the office door after they shut me in there. If they were going to kill me, then wouldn't they have just done it?"

"I don't know," he said. "Maybe not."

I knew what he wasn't saying—not if they'd planned to torture me or interrogate me first. Not if someone else had been on their way to the warehouse to do those things.

"Listen, I know you think Buck took Scooter, but he didn't. I suspect the guys who kidnapped me did. And if they were waiting on someone to join them, then we can still find whoever took Scooter. I think there's a good chance he's alive."

His eyes widened.

I wondered why he looked so surprised, and then it occurred to me that we'd never discussed his brother's disappearance. "I know about Scooter. Why didn't you tell me?"

He didn't answer. We both knew why.

I decided to be honest. "You hurt me at the parley, James."

He swallowed. "I know."

"I know what you were doing. You were trying to push me away."

Pain filled his eyes. "I know," he whispered. "I'm so sorry."

I moved my hand from his cheek and slid it into his dark hair. "I've missed you."

He didn't answer for a few seconds. "I don't know what to do about you, Rose. You drive me crazy. I can't think straight. You're dangerous for me, and God knows I'm dangerous for you."

I sucked in a breath, but I couldn't bring myself to say I was sorry.

"You called me a coward for trying to ignore what's going on between us. Maybe you were right."

"Did you just admit that I'm right?"

He quirked his brow. "I said *maybe*." He took a step closer, and there were only inches between us now. "I thought I'd lost you, Rose. And I couldn't handle it."

He softly pressed his lips to mine, as though giving me a chance to back out. I tugged him closer instead.

His kiss became demanding and his tongue explored my mouth. I released another moan as he slid his hand behind me, cupping my butt cheek and tugging me firmly against him. I wrapped my legs around him and locked my ankles together, thankful I didn't feel any pain from my wound.

He groaned and his hand slid up and under my shirt. The sensation of his warm fingers on my bare skin sent a shiver through my body.

"You are the sexiest woman I've ever known," he growled into my ear. Then he leaned in even closer and nipped my earlobe. A shot of lust shot through me, but he pulled back and looked me in the eyes. His gaze was tortured. "And you have no idea how much I want you, but we still can't."

"Buck Reynolds thinks I'm your girlfriend," I said, my hand still holding the back of his head. "I assured him multiple times that I'm not, but I know he thinks you find me valuable, which makes me valuable to use against you."

"He's right."

"About which part?"

"All of it. You *are* valuable to me. My most valuable asset. Why do you think I had Jed following you all the time? He's the only man I trust." He lifted a hand to my cheek again and gave me a soft caress. "I've been careless with your life. For that I'm sorry."

"Asset? You mean for my visions?" I couldn't hide my disappointment.

"You really believe that?" His thumb lightly brushed my neck.

No, but I wanted to hear him say it. I leaned into his touch. "We've been at odds, and someone still took me," I murmured. "Your plan didn't work. Maybe there's no need for us to keep away from each other."

"Three weeks isn't long enough, Rose. We need to give it more time."

I pulled him close and rested my head on his shoulder. He was probably right. If we allowed more time to elapse, people would eventually forget. They'd think James, who was notorious for keeping company with a lot of women, would move on. Three weeks hadn't been long enough.

He'd betrayed me over the necklace to make me stay away. Well, if we needed to put distance between us, it was time for me to step up and help carry the burden. And it was time for me to try and protect him like he'd always protected me.

I lifted my head and looked into his face again. "Dermot found me on the phone with you. He said they'd been counting on me callin' you." I paused. "I gave them more proof that there was a connection between us because I *did* call you. You were the first person I thought of." I shook my head. I felt like my heart was ripping in two, but I forced myself to keep talking. "I can't call you when I get into trouble anymore. From here on out, I need to rely on myself."

The truth had hit me as I said the words. The thought of not having him there to save me made me feel naked and terrified . . . which was exactly why I needed to learn to do without him.

Despite the pained look on his face, he didn't argue.

I put my hands on his chest and pushed him slightly, not enough to really move him, but enough to get my point across. I felt nauseous, not in my stomach but deep in my soul.

We couldn't do this, whatever *this* was. I couldn't have an open relationship with the king of the Fenton County crime world. A secret fling might be exciting in the beginning, but eventually I'd want more. Because this was James, and my feelings for him would only grow. They'd already grown too large for me to put in any box.

Even if we started a relationship, it wouldn't be anything like the one I'd had with Mason—going to bed together every night, date nights at Jaspers and Little Italy, dropping by each other's offices just to say hello. We'd be stuck in the shadows, sneaking around like we were cheating. And yet . . . while I'd always wanted marriage, kids, and a simple life, that kind of existence seemed too quiet for me now. Maybe there was nothing wrong with something more nontraditional . . .

The sticking point was that James was firmly on the wrong side of the law. It didn't matter how moral he appeared to be. And while I'd skirted over the line a few times, I was still seen as a law-abiding citizen. I had two businesses. I had friends and my family to consider. I had a lot to lose, and if word got out that I was sleeping with Skeeter Malcolm, I could set fire to my entire world.

It was a lot to risk.

"Take me to the office," I said, my voice heavy with unshed tears. "I'll figure out a way home."

"No. I'll take you home."

He started to lift me off the trunk, but I put a hand on his. "There's something I need to tell you first."

His gaze lifted to mine, waiting.

"Buck Reynolds hired me to perform a task for him. That's how he found me. He saw Landry and the other guy snatch me."

His anger was back. "What's the job? And tell me you said no."

"At your parley, I said that I was there to broker peace for the county. That I didn't work just for you." He remained silent. "If we really want to sell this—that I'm not connected to you—then we need to prove it. Which means I have to go through with it. I need to look like a free agent."

His body stiffened and his eyes narrowed. "He knows about your visions?"

"No. Only that I've completed tasks for you and found his necklace when he couldn't."

"What does he want to hire you to do?"

My chin quivered and I took a deep breath. It was time to be strong. If I told him the truth, he'd either figure out a way to stop me or demand to take an active role in helping me find his brother. "If Buck asked me what you'd hired me to do, would you want me tellin' him?"

"That's bullshit, Rose!"

I slowly shook my head. "It's not, and you know it. I've already agreed to do it . . . and like I said, I can't keep callin' you to be my backup. Not if I want to convince everyone I'm neutral. That means no more Brett. No more Jed following me around. After you take me home, we have to cease all communication."

"No."

"We can't have it both ways, James. I'm in this world now as a mediator. I freely accept it. I made that decision when I set up the parley. I can do good for the county. I can help you keep peace. But that means I need to do this on my own."

He spun away from me and ran his hands over his head. "You'll be dead before the month's out."

127

"I'd like to think not," I said with a hint of teasing. "I'm kind of scrappy."

He turned around, anguish washing over his face. "Why in God's name are you *doin'* this, Rose? Go back to bein' a landscaper. Marry that vet and have a family. Leave all this shit behind you and let *me* deal with it."

A tear rolled down my face. "Some things are worth fightin' for. Even if they don't belong to you."

He stalked over and pulled me to him, fisting the hair at the back of my neck. He tilted my head back to look up at him. "Don't be so sure it doesn't belong to you."

More tears rolled down my face, and he kissed my cheeks. I closed my eyes and savored in his kisses, each of them both a gift and a curse.

His mouth found mine, possessive and wild, one hand still holding my hair while the other roamed over my butt and then moved to my breast. I clung to him and kissed him back, just as wild, just as feral.

His lips moved over my cheek up to my ear, leaving a path of burning desire. "God, I want you. I'm not sure I can give you up."

I wasn't sure I could give him up either, but I knew I could help him so much more behind the scenes than I could sneaking around with him in the dark.

"Give me one night," he said in a raspy voice. "God, I want you. And I'm sure one night won't be enough, but I'm asking for it anyway."

After everything I'd told myself, I knew what my answer had to be, and yet I found myself saying, "One night."

I'd become neutral Lady tomorrow. Tonight I belonged to James Malcolm.

CHAPTER 12

*T*he drive was agonizingly long. After all his twists and turns to make sure we weren't being followed, he finally turned down the partially hidden driveway to his house. We'd both stayed on our side of the car, as though we knew that touching each other before we got to his house was dangerous.

But he practically leapt out of the car after he parked in the garage and circled around to meet me as I got out. He shut the door and pushed my back against it, kissing me, soft and leisurely this time. Then he broke loose and smiled—the soft smile that warmed up his eyes.

The smile he saved for me.

He grabbed my hand, tugging me up a couple of steps and then through a door into his kitchen. Pulling me against his chest, he stroked my hair from my face. "Are you thirsty? Hungry?"

"I only want you."

He took my hand again, more gently this time, and led me around the corner into his living room and up the stairs.

I stopped in my tracks when we reached the top. "Neely Kate." How could I have forgotten that she had no idea of anything that had happened? She'd be worried sick when she realized I hadn't come home.

"Jed took care of it. He knows I have you."

"Took care of it?"

"Told her you're with me. He's with her now."

"You know about them?"

"Since the day they left town."

I frowned. Jed had told him before Neely Kate had told me?

"No talk about Jed and Neely Kate," he grunted, pushing my back to the wall and covering my body with his. His hand came to rest on the side of my neck, and my body burned with desire just from the feel of him against me. "You're mine tonight. There's no one else. Just you and me."

He kissed me again, and I pressed myself into him. Maybe if I tried hard enough, I could seep under his skin and into his soul. Then we could fuse together, and I'd still have a piece of him with me after I left.

His hands grabbed my hips, and he pressed himself into my abdomen, proving how much he already wanted me. I wrapped my arms around his neck, my knees weak. He lifted me, cradling my butt in his hands as my legs wrapped around his waist, still kissing me as he carried me into his room.

He set my feet on the ground, then took a small step back, his eyes skimming over me.

"Are you on the pill?" he asked.

"Yes."

"I can still wear a condom."

"Do you always wear one?" I asked.

"Always."

"Then I trust you not to wear one tonight."

He kissed me again, soft and gentle, as his hands lightly cupped my face and then skimmed down my neck and my nearly bare shoulders.

"You are so damned beautiful," he said breathlessly as he lifted his head. His hands reached for the hem of my shirt and slowly lifted it, tugging it over my head, then tossed it onto the floor. He was already reaching for the button at the back of my skirt, and the zipper came next. Pushing the fabric over my hips, he let the fabric pool at my feet.

He took a step back and stared at me, taking in the view. I'd worn a strapless nude-colored bra and panties today—boring— but at least they matched and both had a hint of lace. "I would have dressed up more underneath had I known this was happening."

He grinned the sly grin I was used to. "I'm not complaining."

"I want to see you," I said, closing the distance between us and reaching for the hem of his T-shirt. I lifted it, and he helped me pull it over his head and arms. I traced the scars on his side and his shoulder. He'd shown them to me a few weeks before, trying to convince me how dangerous his life was. They were wounds from past skirmishes with men who'd wanted what he had. It had only made me more intrigued.

His upper chest and arms were covered with elaborate tattoos. I'd seen them before but hadn't paid much attention. Multiple images that appeared to tell a story—the story of his life, I assumed. I had no idea what most of them meant. Probably no one did other than James, and possibly Jed. I traced the largest piece with my finger, a tree that covered the left side of his chest, the branches reaching up to the base of his neck and over his shoulder. Multiple leaves lay at the base of the trunk, but something else caught my attention—a tiny daisy at the base of the tree, a fragile-looking thing with a single petal falling and caught in midair as if blowing away.

I looked up into his eyes and the way he watched me now . . .

I knew he would tell me the meaning of each and every tattoo if he had time. But time wasn't on our side. It was after one in the morning. We only had hours.

I placed a kiss on the daisy, because the story behind it was what had convinced me James was a good man beneath it all. It was a symbol of his shame for failing to save Jed's little sister from drowning when they were kids—a shame James would carry to his grave.

James carried so much regret and shame, more than anyone knew. It was a secret I would guard with all my heart.

He sucked in a breath as my lips caressed his skin, his hands digging into my hips. He leaned down and kissed me again, more urgent now. Feeling that same urgency, I fumbled with his belt and then the button on his jeans. He released a groan of frustration and grabbed my hands, moving them to his chest so he could dispense with his zipper.

As he worked off his shoes and jeans, I slid my hands over his hard pecs, up to his shoulders and then down his arms. How many times had I imagined touching him like this?

I looked down and realized he was fully naked, having removed his underwear with his jeans. I wrapped my hand around him, but he covered my fingers with his and made me stop. "No. I'm tryin' not to just throw you on the bed and take you. Don't make it more difficult than it already is."

"I'm ready," I said, freeing my hand and guiding his under the edge of my panties. "See?"

His eyes widened in surprise at both my boldness and the proof.

"Take me right now," I said. "We'll do this slower next time."

"Next time," he grunted.

"There better be a next time tonight. If you think you can get away with only one—"

He kissed me into silence as he slid his thumb under the edge of the top of my panties and slid them over my hips—being gentle with my leg as he let them drop to my feet.

"How tired are you?" he asked, leaning into my ear as he reached around and unhooked my bra and tossed it aside. "Because I assure you that we can do this all night."

"Promises, promises," I teased.

His eyes darkened as they scanned my now-naked body. "Lady, you have no idea."

A shiver of desire washed over me. He noticed, and his grin turned predatory. He kissed me again, a kiss so consuming I lost myself in him.

His hands found my breasts, and then one moved lower. I moaned into his mouth as desperation filled me. I needed this man. I had no idea how I would walk away from him, but at least we had this. At least we had tonight.

I wasn't going to waste a single minute.

And as if sensing my need, he pushed me down on the bed, scooting me up so my head was on his pillows. He knelt between my spread legs as he watched me with a gaze so intense I wondered how I didn't combust. Naked and spread open to him, I was the most vulnerable I'd ever been with James, but I'd never felt more connected with him either.

He leaned over me, his mouth covering mine, and I hooked a leg around his lower back, rising up to meet him as he entered me. He released a guttural sound as he filled me, and I gasped— some tiny part of me reveled in how right it felt, but I already needed more.

His mouth lowered, kissing and nipping a trail down my neck and chest to my breast. A jolt shot through me when he found my nipple.

"James," I moaned as I climbed higher, tightly wound.

I could tell his restraint was tenuous. I wanted him uninhibited. I wanted to make James Malcolm come undone. I lifted my pelvis and, grasping his butt cheeks, invited him to go deeper.

"I'm not fragile," I said, my chest rising and falling. "Don't hold back. I want all of you."

He grabbed my wrists and pinned them over my head with one hand. He stared down at me, his eyes burning with lust and desire. "I've wanted you for so long."

"Then claim me."

My words unleashed him. Grunting, he kissed me again, losing control and leaving me at his mercy. I reveled in it as I climbed higher and higher until I shattered into pieces, crying out as wave after wave of pleasure washed over me.

He let go of my hands and grabbed my hips, pumping as though he couldn't get deep enough. "Oh, God, Rose." After one last drive, he released a groan and collapsed on top of me.

This was so perfect it broke my heart.

Rolling to his side, he gathered me in his arms and kissed me slowly and leisurely, and then with growing hunger as his hand roamed over my cheek, through my hair, and down my neck.

He leaned back and looked down at me with a mixture of awe and sorrow. "I have a feeling you'll be my ruin, Rose Gardner."

And I was certain he would be mine.

CHAPTER 13

$\mathcal{T}$he throbbing in my thigh awoke me. James was curled up behind me, his arm slung over my side and holding me close.

I couldn't help smiling. He was possessive even when he slept.

I needed to get up and take something for the pain, but I wasn't ready to leave him yet. The clock on the nightstand table read 6:42. I didn't have much time left, and I'd already wasted a couple hours of it sleeping.

Rolling onto my back, I stared into his face, unable to resist the urge to touch him. He looked so at ease right now—all the tension I was accustomed to seeing was gone. I lifted my hand and let my fingertips trail over his face, the stubble on his chin scratching them.

His eyes cracked open and a lazy, satisfied smile stretched across his face. "I could have sworn I dreamed you were in my bed last night."

"I'm here," I said, but sorrow crept into my words.

He shifted so he was leaning over me. "We don't have to make this a one-night thing," he said, searching my face.

I stilled. "So you're proposin' we have random hookups?"

He continued to study me as though trying to determine whether I thought that was a good thing or a bad one.

"The agreement was one night, James."

"You can't tell me that you want to walk away after last night?" he asked in disbelief.

"The agreement was one night," I said with more heat. "What about distancin' myself from you?"

"You're crazy if you think I'm going to let you walk away from me now."

"That's not what we agreed to!" I sat up and tried to get out of bed, but he pulled me back down.

"Rose."

I tried to push his arm away, but who was I kidding? The only way I was getting out of this bed was if he let me. "You're bein' unreasonable, James."

"Unreasonable?" he said, getting irritated. "You're the one who wanted this so damn bad!"

I worked loose and sat up, the sheet falling to my waist. "And you're the one who said my life is in danger if people think I'm tied to you!"

"I'll claim you. Just like I did last night, over and over and *over.*" His voice turned husky as his gaze fell to my breasts.

"Braggart," I said as I pulled the sheet up to cover my breasts since I wanted him to actually hear me. "And we both know that won't work. You tried to tell me, but I was too stubborn to listen."

He sat up too and placed a kiss on my shoulder. "Your stubbornness is one of my many favorite traits."

"Only when it works in your favor. When it doesn't, you hate it."

He tilted his head to look into my eyes. "There's not a single part of you I hate."

I grinned. "I'm gonna remind you of that the next time you're pissed at me."

"We can figure out a way to make this work, Rose."

"I don't want to sneak around. I don't want to hide us, but I can't be with you either. You're a criminal."

Thankfully, he didn't take offense. "Not a single charge has stuck."

"But we both know you've done illegal things. And everyone else knows it too." I started to slide out of bed, but he stopped me again. "Let me go. I have to get some ibuprofen and take my antibiotic."

"I'll get it. Promise me you'll stay there."

"Okay, but not for much longer. I have to go soon."

He pushed me back down and kissed me until I was mindless and boneless. He grinned down at me. "Wait there."

As he got out of bed, he pulled off the sheet and tossed it onto the floor.

"Is your plan to keep me naked so I can't leave your house?" I asked as he disappeared into his bathroom.

"Not originally," he said, his voice muffled. I heard a cabinet open and then running water. "But it's not a bad idea."

He was back out a few seconds later with a glass of water and two bottles in his hand. He sat down next to me as I sat up, then handed me the water as he opened the first pill bottle.

"Who would believe that big bad Skeeter Malcolm would be playing naked nurse with me?"

He grinned and handed me two pills. "I'll play naked nurse with you any day of the week."

I swallowed the over-the-counter pain killer while he unscrewed a prescription bottle and dumped a pill into my palm.

"That's not the bottle Tim Dermot gave me."

His eyebrows shot up. "I thought I made it clear that I was going to supply your antibiotics. You can't trust him, Rose."

I popped the pill into my mouth and took a sip of the water.

"You know you're not leavin' until you tell me every detail of what happened last night, right?"

And things had been going so well.

"I don't think that's a good idea," I said. "I'm supposed to be neutral, remember? No more runnin' to you with my problems."

"You've absolutely lost your mind if you think I'll ever agree to that, so start talkin'."

I shot him a glare, but I figured he had a right to know since there was a chance the same guys had taken Scooter. "I'm not having this conversation stark naked."

He took the glass of water from me and put it on the nightstand. "If you're sitting there telling me this is my last chance to see you naked, then you definitely are."

"James . . ."

I tried to lean forward to get the sheet he'd tossed onto the floor, but he snaked an arm around my waist and hauled me back, pinning me down on the bed. "Start talking . . . unless you plan to spend all day here with me." He leaned over and started to kiss my neck. "Although I'm likin' that plan."

I had to admit it was tempting, much too tempting, but I had actual work to do, not to mention a parrot to find along with the task of looking for James' brother. "They kidnapped me in the carnival parking lot."

His head rose and his jaw clenched as he searched my face. "And where *the hell* was that vet?"

"He had to leave for an emergency."

"And he just left you in the damned parking lot?"

"Calm down, James," I said, trying to sit up, but he held me down.

"Calm down? Any asshole who allows his date to get kidnapped doesn't deserve her." An ornery look filled his eyes. "But I'm noticin' a trend, Lady. How many boyfriends have let you get kidnapped?"

I scowled. "Levi's not my boyfriend."

"No shit. He dumped you in a parking lot."

I pushed out a sigh. "He *didn't* dump me. I was about to call Maeve." I told him about the kidnapping—how one of the guys had surprised me from behind while the other drove up. "They knocked me unconscious, and when I woke up, I was in the trunk of the car and we were at the warehouse."

He listened silently while I told him about cutting myself free and calling him.

"Someone burst into the office and took your phone. Who was it?"

"Tim Dermot."

"What happened to your phone?"

I cringed. This part was tricky. "He shot it. Then he took me out to see Buck, who was wrapping some other guy's arm. I never heard his name. Wait . . . later they called him Gary."

His eyes narrowed. "So when did *you* get shot?"

I lifted my shoulder into a half-shrug. "I wasn't exactly shot, James."

"The two stitches on your leg say different."

I tried to get up again, but he held me in place. "I think I should keep the rest to myself. It falls within that neutral zone."

"Like hell it does."

"I'll tell you this part: they pulled out the wallet of the driver. He's the guy from Shreveport."

"Elijah Landry?" After I nodded, he said, "So who was the other one?"

"I don't know. They didn't get his wallet."

"That you saw," he said. "You can bet they got it. So I still need to know two things: One, what did Reynolds hire you to do, and two, when and how did you get shot?"

"Technically that's three things."

He gave me a look.

Groaning, I pushed his arm hard enough that he let me loose. I got out of bed and walked over to pick up my skirt. It was stiff with dried blood, and there was no way in Hades I was putting it back on.

James got up and followed me. "I'm not lettin' you leave until I find out what happened."

I groaned and squatted to pick up my shirt, which was dirty enough to have turned a dingy gray. I dumped it and the skirt on top of the dresser, then opened a drawer, looking for something to wear.

"Rose."

"I told him I wasn't working for him, especially after he insulted me, and we had a disagreement."

He stomped toward me and grabbed my arm, turning me to face him. "He shot you because you refused to work for him?" His face turned red. "I'm going to kill him with my bare hands."

I patted his arm. "Calm down. I handled it."

"How the hell is getting shot *handling* it?"

I gave him a glare. "He was trying to intimidate me, James. I had to stand up to him, and I *did*. He pissed me off, so I told him I was leaving and I started walking out. He shouted at me to stop. When I didn't, he shot around me a few times—never *at* me. The last bullet ricocheted off the door when I was walking out and hit me. It was an accident. He nearly pooped his pants when he realized he'd hit me, which confirmed he was only trying to intimidate me. I demanded his respect and insisted that I was in charge of the situation, and he ultimately caved."

He didn't answer at first. "You could have been killed," he finally said. "You need backup."

I shook my head.

"You have to be smart. Jed and I would never do something on our own. Things can go sideways too fast. I want Jed to stick with you."

"First of all, you don't get a say. As of this morning, you and I are no longer associates in any way. And second, last I heard, Jed Carlisle doesn't work for you anymore."

He cringed and rubbed his chin. "You heard about that, huh?"

"Yeah. So what was he doin' with you last night?"

"We got a lead on Scooter."

That caught my attention. "What kind of lead?"

"Someone at Walmart said they saw him get into a dark sedan last Wednesday afternoon. The driver was a guy with dark, shaggy hair."

"Average height and build?" I asked.

"And a tattoo of a bird on his arm."

My eyes widened. "That was the guy who grabbed me from behind."

"So there *is* a connection between your kidnapping and Scooter's disappearance."

"Yeah . . . looks like it." I wasn't sure if that made me feel better or worse, especially since Buck and his men had killed the two men who probably could have told us where to find Scooter. Had they done it on purpose so they couldn't talk? I turned back around and snagged a T-shirt from James' drawer, then walked into his en suite bathroom.

"What did Reynolds hire you to do?" he asked, following me inside.

I ignored him as I went into his water closet to pee. He was waiting for me when I came out, still standing there in all his naked glory, which was very hard to ignore.

I lifted my eyes to his face. "I'm gonna take a shower, but I need to wash my hair and I don't want to smell like you."

One side of his mouth lifted into a smirk. "I kind of like the idea of you smellin' like me."

"So you can leave your mark on me? I expected better from you, James Malcolm."

He laughed. "Get in, and I'll be back."

I'd soaked all my hair when he joined me in the marble tile shower, carrying several bottles I recognized from the night I'd stayed at his house several weeks ago. He'd taken them out of the guest shower. Before I could stop him, he started washing my hair. I closed my eyes and pressed my chest to his as he worked in the shampoo and then grabbed the shower head and rinsed out the lather.

"What did Reynolds hire you to do?" he asked quietly as he worked in the conditioner next.

I ignored the question, and after he rinsed out my hair, I leaned to the side to pick up a bottle of his body wash. I squirted it into my hand and began to spread it over his broad, solid chest.

"How much do you have to work out to maintain this?" I asked with a grin.

He grinned back. "Enough."

"What kind of answer is that?" I asked, sliding my hands down his abdomen.

"A better one than the answer you're givin' me." His voice was tight, and his body tensed as I moved down between his legs. After I made sure he was well-washed and completely turned on, I slid my hands down to his butt cheeks and pulled him against me.

He growled and pushed my back against the tile wall, spending several minutes letting his mouth roam over my body until I was panting.

"What do you want, Rose?" he asked in a husky, commanding voice.

"You," I said, tugging him to his feet. "Now."

He grabbed my uninjured thigh and hooked it around his hip as he entered me.

I released a loud moan and wrapped my arms around his neck to hang on as he lifted me off the ground.

He kissed me while he worked his magic until I was begging him for more. He gave it to me—and then some—until I was spent and satiated and in desperate need of a nap. He still had me pinned to the wall, his face buried in the curve of my neck.

I played with a damp piece of his hair that stuck out, over-come with sadness. Part of me desperately wanted to continue this, but I couldn't—and deep down I knew that. "James, we have to talk, and I need you to be sensible and honest."

He stayed like that a few seconds, nestled against me, before he finally lifted his head. I worried he'd shut down to protect himself, but emotion swirled in his eyes.

I tightened my hold around his neck. "This conversation might be more manageable if we weren't so . . . intimate right now."

He held my gaze, not budging. "It seems to me it's the best time to have it if you want honesty. It's the only time we're truly honest with each other. If you're more concerned about me being sensible, then we should get dressed. For us, the two don't seem to go hand in hand."

I stared into his eyes, torn, but I finally said, "I need your honesty more." I hoped good sense would follow for both of us.

A soft smile lit up his face. He thought he'd already won this conversation.

"Let's say we keep doin' this," I said. "How do you see that happenin'?"

"We used to meet on Tuesday nights. We'll just change the location."

"We met for an hour. That's enough for you?"

His face lowered to my neck, and he began to kiss and nip. "I'll need way more than an hour."

I pushed his face back up to look at me. "So for how long? And where would we meet?"

He turned serious. "We can meet here. It's the safest place. And I want you all night." He practically growled the last part and a thrill shivered through me.

His eyes lit up. He'd noticed.

"So once a week? That would be enough?" I asked matter-of-factly.

"Hell, no, it's not enough. I'd have you in my bed every damn night if I could."

"But you can't, can you? You're not even here every night. When you brought me here before, you said you only come twice a week."

"Then you should do the same."

"Until this has run its course?"

"How soon do you think it will take for this to run its course, Lady?" There was an edge to his voice that I couldn't interpret.

I made a slight gesture toward him. "We're here for honesty. Are you sure you can handle it?"

"What's that supposed to mean?"

"It means I'm about to lay my heart bare for you, James Malcolm, and I need you to do the same."

Some of the softness left his eyes. I knew where this path would lead, yet I had to travel it anyway. My self-respect demanded it.

"I'm not the kind of woman who has flings. I thought I could try it with you, but maybe we have too much history. Too much respect for each other. I'm fallin' for you. Hard. When I tried to convince you to start something, you told me that I was the kind of woman who needed a family and kids. Part of me isn't so sure anymore. How can I go back to a quiet life after seeing the things I've seen, doing the things I've done? The thing is, deep down, *I still want those things*. Not right now, but down the road that's what I want—*what I need*. But it's not just me here, James. You're an equal part of this, and I need you to be honest with me and tell me what *you* want."

"You want to hear me say that I want to get married and have kids and put a picket fence around this place so we can play house?" he said with an undercurrent of anger. "Because I already told you that's not me."

"*No.* I want you to tell me the *truth*. What do you want for your life? Where do you see yourself in ten years? Twenty?"

"This is the only life I've ever known."

"I know. I know." I ran my fingertips down the side of his face. "But is it what you want for the rest of your life?"

"What I want is irrelevant. Wheels have been set in motion that can't be stopped."

I shook my head. "I don't believe that's true."

"Then you're livin' in fairyland. There's no walkin' away from the kind of life I've chosen, Rose. I keep tellin' Jed that, but he's got his head up in the clouds over Neely Kate. Love makes people stupid. It makes them believe the impossible."

That caught me off guard. "You think Jed's in love with Neely Kate?"

"*That's* what you pick up on?"

He tried to set me down, but I clung to him like a monkey to a tree, and pain shot through my thigh from tensing my leg.

His face softened. "You shouldn't be in the water this long. It's not good for your stitches."

"No. We're finishing this conversation."

A scowl covered his face.

"I know this is unfair. We've had one night together, and I'm that stereotypical woman who's already demanding more, but my heart's on the line, James. Either way, I'm probably gettin' hurt—I know that. But I need to know what you see for us. Do you see us meetin' twice a week for six months? A year? Five?"

"Honestly, Rose, I don't know." He sounded defeated. "I've never wanted anyone like I want you. I've never needed anyone until you, and I don't know what to do with it. I thought if I stayed away from you, I'd get over you, but it didn't work. Last night, I told myself that if I had just one night with you, I could burn you out of my system and we could go back to normal. But I was stupid. So stupid." He lifted his hand to my face, smoothing the wet hair from my cheek. "I'm addicted to you, and now that I've had a taste, I want you even more. And that makes you dangerous." Instead of sounding harsh, he sounded resigned.

"And yet you still want to keep seein' me?"

"Everyone has a weakness. Turns out mine is you. Like you said, I'm hopin' this will just run its course."

"Wow," I said sarcastically. "*That's* romantic."

His gaze held a hint of challenge. "You said you wanted honesty."

"Yeah," I said softly. "I did." I'd known going into this conversation that there could be no good outcome, so why was I so disappointed? Maybe James was right. Maybe being in love made you believe in the impossible. Only, I wasn't in love . . . right?

"I want to keep seein' you," he said, fondling my breast. His tone was dark and commanding. Last night, he'd discovered that tone turned me on, and he was using it to his advantage.

I squirmed, but I saw right through what he was doing. He wanted to get me all hot and bothered so I'd agree to whatever he wanted. And damned if he wasn't close to succeeding. "You want to burn me out of your system hard and fast."

He instantly stopped caressing me, his eyes dark. "That's how you see this?"

I held his gaze. "Isn't it?" I could see that there was probably some truth to it.

"Dammit, Rose." He buried his face in my neck again. "I don't know what to do with you."

"Do you really think I'm like a drug?" I asked softly. "If you use me enough, you'll get your fill and be ready to move on?"

He shook his head. "I told you love makes people stupid." Then he put me down, grabbed a towel, and walked out of the bathroom.

I was pretty sure that was the closest I'd ever get to hearing James Malcolm say he loved me.

CHAPTER 14

*A*fter I got dressed, I found him downstairs in the kitchen, standing in front of his open laptop with a coffee cup in his hand. He was wearing a pair of jeans and a dark gray T-shirt that clung to every muscle, reminding me of what I was giving up.

I, on the other hand, was dressed like a hobo. He'd left me a pair of his shorts that had a drawstring, and the T-shirt I'd picked out practically came to my knees. I looked like I was playing dress-up, but I sure wasn't putting my old clothes back on. I couldn't help thinking that he'd strategically planned for me to look as unsexy as possible.

He cast a sad glance at me. "I have coffee. I can make us some eggs and bacon."

"Only if you want it." We were delaying the inevitable, and it was hurting even more than I'd expected.

He reached for his phone and tapped on the screen, then set it down again and looked at me. "Now that we're dressed, it's time for the sensible conversation."

He gestured to one of the bar stools at his counter, and I sat down while he grabbed a coffee cup and filled it up, adding cream and sugar. A hint of a grin lit up his eyes. "Sensible conversations this early require coffee."

I accepted it and gave him a tiny smile back even though my heart was breaking.

"I need to know what Reynolds asked you to do."

I groaned. "Not that again."

He leaned forward, resting his hands on the counter. "You asked me where I saw myself in the future, but your dream of a nuclear family aside, where do you see yourself? How does the Lady in Black play into it?"

I sat up straighter. "I don't know."

He stood. "Do you want to do errands for men like Buck Reynolds?" His tone was strained, and I could see he was trying to understand my motivations instead of just barking orders at me . . . which he knew from experience never worked.

I set the mug on the counter. "No . . . I don't know." I looked into his eyes. "I returned that necklace to Buck to help the county. You know that. What he's asked me to do could help the county even more."

"What if I told you that I'm certain he took Scooter? And that the kidnapping was his elaborate ploy to get you to do his dirty work?" His tone was more emphatic, but he was still restraining himself.

"I had a vision, James. Buck Reynolds isn't behind either of them."

"Forced or spontaneous vision?"

"Forced. But I was careful." Mostly.

"What did you blurt out?"

I grimaced. "It doesn't matter. He had no idea what I was doin'."

"You're certain he doesn't know you have visions?"

"Yeah. I'm not sure what he thinks I did for *you*, but he knows that I like investigatin'."

"So he wants you to investigate something?"

I groaned. "*James . . .*"

He took a step closer. "Rose, if you do this, others will ask. You *have* to know that. Especially if you distance yourself from me."

"I would never do anything to hurt you. Never."

"I know!" he said, getting more frustrated. "It's not me that I'm worried about getting hurt!"

"Jed taught me some self-defense. And I'll start carrying my gun. Not in my purse," I said, thinking on the fly. "I'll use the thigh holster he gave me."

"Do you *want* to work for the others?" He sounded incredulous.

I ran a hand through my damp hair. "It depends."

He exploded. "Depends on *what?*"

"On what they want, James. If it's for the good of the county, then maybe I do."

He stalked up, looming over me. "What does Reynolds want you to do?"

I wondered if I should just tell him, but I suspected he'd think it was too dangerous and have Brett or Jed follow me everywhere. "James, you can't keep me from doin' this, just like I can't stop you from bein' the king of Fenton County."

Surprise filled his eyes. "You don't want me to be king?"

I took a deep breath. "I've never made any secret of the fact that I'm constantly worried about you. Being in charge puts a target on your back."

"You don't want me to be king?" he asked more quietly, as though putting things together.

I didn't answer.

"I'm never leavin' this world, Rose. You have to know that. If you have some scheme cooked up to get me out of it—"

"I would never put you in danger. I would *never* try something underhanded."

He put his fingers under my chin and tilted my head up to face him. "I'm never leavin', Rose."

That was the crux of our problems. "I know."

"And yet you're doin' it anyway."

"I'm keepin' you safe."

He dropped his hold on me and took a step back. "I never asked you to keep me safe."

I slid off the stool. "You would do anything to keep me safe. You've proven that time and again. Why do you find it odd that I want to do the same for you?"

"You don't get it, Rose. I've lived in this world for years and done just fine. I. Don't. Need. You." He paused. "Except in my bed. Turns out I need you there."

I shook my head. "You can't have it both ways. All of me or none."

He paused. "And if I asked for all of you, would you give it to me?"

I really wanted to tell him yes, but the things that stood between us might as well be mountains or skyscrapers, and if we weren't going to mow them down, I couldn't see my way toward us being happy. So I didn't say anything at all.

His eyes darkened. "I'm goin' to ask you one more time. What does Buck Reynolds want you to do?"

"And I'm gonna tell you one more time that it's none of your cotton-pickin' business."

His phone vibrated on the counter, and he reached over to pick it up. His face hardened as he tucked it into his pocket. "Time for you to go."

I gasped in disbelief. "So you're kicking me out because I won't tell you?"

"No. I called Jed to pick you up, and he's here."

"*What?*"

"People are watchin' you. It's better if we're not seen together."

He was right, but I was still surprised and a little hurt. I'd thought we would have more time together.

"So you want me to go? Just like that?" My voice broke. *Dammit.* I didn't want to cry, but my stupid eyes didn't care what I wanted.

"No. God. No. I don't want you to go. You know that." He slipped his arms around my back and pulled me close. "But you're right—this is what we agreed to, and you don't seem inclined to change your mind. As much as I want this, I have to respect your decision." His hold tightened. "I assume Reynolds has asked you to do something that relates to my brother. I don't know what it is, but you have to know this is dangerous."

I didn't confirm or deny. Instead, I closed my eyes and tried to memorize the feel of him. His solid chest and arms. I never felt safer than when I was with him, and I was losing this. Probably forever.

"This was a mistake," he said, his voice rough. "I've only made it worse for you. I'm a selfish asshole. See? I don't deserve you."

I tilted my head back to look up at him. "You deserve love, James. And whether you believe that or not, there are people who love you all the same." *I love you.* But I couldn't bring myself to say it. It wouldn't help anything. "And this wasn't a mistake. I'm grateful."

"*Grateful.*" He nearly spat the word as he wrapped his arm around my back and led me to the front door. Sure enough, Jed's car was idling in the circular driveway, and he was pacing the length of the car on the driver's side.

The two men locked eyes silently, and a new tension filled the space between them, which made me even more worried about James. His brother had been kidnapped. He'd lost Jed. And now he was losing me. Panic set in.

James led me down the steps and reached for the back passenger-side door, but I grabbed his arm. "*Wait.*"

He stooped down and waited.

"You've lost everyone," I whispered. "Scooter. Jed. Me. You don't have anyone."

He smiled at me with sad eyes. "I have Merv. I have people you don't even know about. Don't worry about me, Rose. I'm fine. You need to be worryin' about yourself." He paused. "If you get into trouble, I want you to call me."

"You know I can't."

"That's bullshit, and we both know it. Bein' free of my name doesn't mean jack shit if you're dead." His fingers dug into my arm and desperation filled his words. *"Promise me."*

"I promise."

He kissed me, hard and possessive, as though he couldn't get enough of me. Then, just as abruptly, he released me and took a step back. He opened the door to the backseat.

I threw my arms around his neck and clung to him for several moments before I finally relented and got in the car. James shut the door behind me, turned around, and walked into the house without saying a word.

Jed got into the car and started to drive while I leaned my head against the back window.

"How'd you get roped into comin' to get me?" I finally asked, trying to take my mind off the fact that I was driving away from the man I loved.

I was cursed. Maybe I needed to give up on men altogether.

"I didn't get roped into it," he said. "I came of my own free will."

"But James called you, and you don't work for him anymore."

"You and I are friends. And me and Neely Kate . . ."

"Are *good* friends," I finished with a halfhearted grin.

He caught my eye in the rearview mirror. "Neely Kate is worried."

"Does she know anything about what happened?"

"She knows that you had a run-in and James picked you up

and took you home with him. She's goin' to kill me when she finds out I knew more and didn't tell her."

"So why didn't you?"

"Because she would have wanted to call you, and honestly, Skeeter needed you more."

I sat up at that. "What?"

"He's been a mess since your fight at the parley, and when your call got disconnected last night . . . It wasn't pretty." He paused. "I have no idea what he would have done if something had happened to you."

"You mean he would have been upset?"

"No, I mean there would have been a massacre. There was no way he was going to let Buck Reynolds hurt you and live to talk about it. Especially after Scooter."

I laid my head on the back of the seat. "Buck Reynolds didn't take Scooter."

"The fact that he took *you* strongly hints otherwise."

"Buck Reynolds saved me." I told him what I'd told James, again leaving out what Buck had hired me to do.

"And you're sure your vision proves he didn't do it?"

"Positive. Does James have any enemies in Shreveport?"

"None that I know of, but he might have made some while he was working for J.R. Simmons."

"I don't think so. He seemed just as surprised by the Shreveport connection as I was." I decided to try to ask him questions about Scooter, hoping I could play it off in a way that wouldn't rouse his suspicions. Maybe it didn't much matter either way. James already suspected something. "James said you got a lead on Scooter. Someone saw him get taken at Walmart. Was it another employee?"

"It was his girlfriend."

"And she just came forward with that information?" I asked in disbelief.

Jed didn't say anything for several seconds. "She says she was scared."

"But you don't believe her?"

"I'm not sure."

Thanks to Bruce Wayne, I already had Scooter's girlfriend's name. I made a mental note to stop by Walmart to see if Jeanne Putnam was working today. Maybe Bruce Wayne would have some more information about her too. "Joe knows Scooter's missin', but he says there's no missing person report."

"We take care of our own," Jed said.

"Even though you're not working for James?"

"We all go back further than me working for Skeeter. We've known each other since we were kids. Scooter's my friend. I'm tryin' to find him."

"So what have you found?"

"A whole lot of nothin'. No one knows anything. This was the first solid lead we had."

"Y'all were so certain Buck took him. How much effort were you puttin' into pinnin' it on Buck versus findin' out who actually took him?"

Jed didn't say anything, which was an answer in itself.

"Did James really fire you?"

"I told him that I was takin' Neely Kate to Oklahoma, and he told me to come back or I was fired. There was no way I was leavin' Neely Kate to deal with her past alone, so he fired me by default. He's done this before, but this time I decided enough is enough."

I wasn't sure what to make of James leaving Neely Kate unprotected. Maybe he'd figured she'd come back with Jed. I'd probably never know now that I wouldn't be talking to him anymore. The realization that our weekly talks were officially over left a gaping hole in my heart.

"You really don't want to work for him anymore?" I asked.

"He's treated you more like a partner than he's ever treated me." He tried to hide the pain in his voice, but I heard it just the same. "I think it's time to move on."

"Will you still be his friend?" I asked.

"I'm not sure Skeeter can be friends with someone who's not an associate."

"He and I have been friends since last winter," I said.

He cast a dubious glance at me in the rearview mirror. "I'm worried about who's got his ear. If you and I aren't there talkin' sense into him, I'm not sure anyone else will. Merv isn't to be trusted."

"Neely Kate said he got physical with her last week and that you intervened."

Jed hesitated. "He hasn't been right since he got shot last winter. He's been hotheaded and argumentative. He was chompin' at the bit to string Reynolds up for Scooter, and I barely got back from Oklahoma in time to stop him."

"He really would have killed Buck Reynolds with no proof?"

"He'd already decided he was guilty and was well on his way to convincin' Skeeter."

"James would have fallen for it?"

"Merv can be persuasive, and Skeeter was already out of sorts over you. Add in Scooter's disappearance and the fact that he was pissed at me . . ."

It was a recipe for disaster.

Jed found my gaze in the mirror. "Merv's never been a fan of yours. Ever since the parley, Merv's been usin' the situation to his advantage, tryin' to poison Skeeter against you."

There was no love lost between Merv and me, so that didn't come as much of a surprise.

"You need protection, Rose," Jed said. "What's to stop the person behind the kidnapping from tryin' again?"

"That's presumin' those two guys were workin' with someone else." I paused. I'd already figured as much.

"I think we should make that assumption. I'm gonna stick tight to you and Neely Kate until this is resolved."

I shook my head. "I understand why you want to watch over Neely Kate, but you can't be watchin' over me. I'm tryin' to distance myself from James, and you're too closely tied to him."

"You think you're goin' around town without a bodyguard?"

"No," I said, thinking of an impromptu plan that wasn't half bad. "I know someone who would be perfect."

CHAPTER 15

*J*ed dropped me off at the office and said he'd call and check on Neely Kate in an hour or so. He wanted to give me time to talk to Neely Kate about the night before.

It was still early, but she was already sitting at her desk. Her face lit up when she saw me, and she jumped out of her chair. "Are you all right? Other than your clothes."

Ignoring her question—I was definitely not all right, but I was trying to feel like I was—I walked over and gave her a long hug. I was grateful James' shorts were long enough to cover not only my stitches, but most of my bruises and scrapes.

Neely Kate had brought my dog to the office with her, and Muffy jumped up on my legs, wagging her tail like a wind-up dog.

Neely Kate's arms wrapped around me, holding me tight. "What happened?"

Tears filled my eyes. I wondered how much I should tell her— then remembered the vow I'd made to stop keeping secrets. "I was kidnapped."

"*What?* Oh, my word!"

I picked up Muffy and sat down in my office chair, cradling my little dog in my lap and rubbing her head. Then I told Neely Kate the whole story about the kidnapping, this time including the bit about Buck Reynolds wanting to hire me to look for Scooter.

"Do you want to investigate Scooter's disappearance?" she asked.

"Yeah. I know Jed and Merv have been lookin', but don't you think those two burly guys are more likely to intimidate people into silence? Scooter's girlfriend saw someone drive away with him on Wednesday, and she only came forward yesterday. I think *we* might be able to get more answers. People tend not to take us seriously." She started to get worked up, but I held up my hand. "I say we use that to our advantage. They'll be more likely to talk."

"So you want to put Squawker on hold?"

"No. We only have a handful of appointments today. Let's see if we can move some to the end of the week so we can focus on our two cases today."

"I can't believe you're saying that," she said, jumping up and down a little.

I shrugged. "I have good reason to look for Scooter. As for the parrot, we'll see how he fits in with the rest of our day. Obviously he's second priority." But then again, when I thought about the circumstances of Squawker's disappearance, I wondered if there was more to it. I stood and said, "But first I need to go home and change clothes."

"I brought you clothes and shoes. Jed suggested it. He said you were spending the night with Skeeter." She gave me a narrow-eyed look. "I thought you were pissed at him."

"Turns out nearly gettin' murdered makes you see things a bit differently."

"So you forgave him?"

"Yeah."

"And what does that mean exactly? Are you two together? What about Levi?"

Oh crap. Levi.

"I don't know about Levi. I really like him, but there's no spark, you know? I kept hopin' it would show up, but instead I got kidnapped and then went home with the king of the Fenton County crime world and hardly spent any time sleeping." I hadn't really intended to say quite so much, but the words all came out in a rush.

Her eyes widened and her mouth dropped open. "You and Skeeter . . . ?"

I nodded.

She still looked shocked. "And you hadn't slept together before?"

Of course, it was at that exact moment that Joe decided to walk into the office with a takeout tray stacked with three coffee cups. Muffy jumped off my lap and took off running for him.

"I think I've interrupted something," he said, looking uncomfortable.

"No," Neely Kate gushed. "Going by what's in your drink carrier, you're here in the nick of time."

Muffy continued to jump up on his legs, and he glanced down at her with a grin. "Just a minute, Muff."

I sure hoped one of those cups literally had my name on it because I was about to pass out from exhaustion . . . and maybe die of embarrassment.

Joe handed a cup to Neely Kate, then wandered over to my desk and handed one to me. "A peace offering."

"Oh!" Neely Kate gushed. "I want to hear the details of what prompted this!"

Joe took out the last cup and set the empty tray on Neely Kate's desk. He squatted to rub Muffy's head, his gaze squarely on her, and said, "Based on the conversation I walked in on, I thought you two were discussing Rose's date."

Neither of us said anything. No reason to open *that* kettle of worms.

"You were sayin' something about a peace offerin,'" Neely Kate prodded.

"Uh, yeah." Joe stood and turned toward me, and Muffy pranced over to her dog bed under my desk. "I want to apologize for my behavior last night. I have no idea why I got so antagonistic, especially since I had a great time with Dena." He grinned.

"Oh, my word!" Neely Kate said. "You slept with her already."

"So?" Joe asked, looking guilty despite his protest. "We're consenting adults, and it had been a while for both of us."

Neely Kate stuck her fingers in her ears and began to hum off-key. "I don't want to hear about my brother's sex life."

Joe laughed. "Fair enough. But I plan on seeing her again, so that might tell you something about how my evening went."

Neely Kate gave me a sideways glance, appraising my reaction, but I gave her a tiny smile. Sure, our encounter at the fair had been a little weird, but the thought of Joe dating Dena didn't bother me. If anything, it made me feel happy for him.

Joe gave me a strange look. "I take it you spent the night with Levi, but I'm a little surprised you didn't go home to change." His gaze landed on the Harley-Davidson logo on my black T-shirt, something Levi probably wouldn't be prone to wearing. I crossed my hands over my chest on impulse.

Neely Kate reached under her desk and pulled out a small bag. "Here you go."

I got up and snagged it from her before heading back to the small bathroom. Neely Kate had packed me another dress, which surprised me. It was nothing like my typical work uniform, but then again, I only had that handful of consultation appointments on my schedule. Maybe she'd picked the dress because we were investigating . . . or maybe she was trying to set me up with Levi again.

Levi.

We definitely hadn't been exclusive, but it seemed beyond tacky to go on a date with one man and then spend most of the night fornicating with another. Of course, most people didn't get held hostage by two different bad guys between dates either . . . not that I was going to allow myself that excuse. While there would be no repeat performance, I was in love with James Malcolm. The thought of going out with Levi to make myself forget James didn't sit right. I'd been stringing him along for three weeks, and look where it had gotten me. So I'd gone from two men to none.

I had the worst luck at love.

Neely Kate had included my makeup bag. Since I usually wore very little, it only took me five minutes to apply a little bit of makeup and to French braid my barely damp hair.

To my surprise, Joe was still telling Neely Kate about his date. He was sitting on her desk with Muffy curled up on his lap.

"We're goin' out again on Thursday night," Joe said. His gaze lifted to me as though testing me out.

"That's great Joe," I said. "I'm happy for you. Truly."

His head bobbed forward and a look of acceptance covered his face. "And I'm happy for you and Levi."

If only it were Levi who'd stolen my heart . . . I'd certainly have a lot fewer problems. But I couldn't tell him any of that, so all I said was thanks.

"You still playin' bingo tonight?" Joe asked his sister.

"It's Tuesday night. Granny's got bells on. Literally. She heard tiny bells would make her lucky, so she's sewn them into her underwear."

Joe started to laugh.

"You should come," Neely Kate teased. "You'll be a hit with all the ladies."

A sly grin spread across his face. "I think I'll stick with the one I went out with last night. Which reminds me." He turned to face me. "I'd like to apologize to Levi for acting like an asshole."

I shook my head. "Oh, that's not necessary."

"Yeah. It is," Joe said. "Levi's new to town, and I tried to intimidate the crap out of him. His office is just out of city limits, which means he uses the sheriff's department. I don't want him to be worried about calling if he has a problem."

The bell on the front door rang, and my stomach sunk when Levi walked in with my purse in his hand.

Well, crap on a cracker.

"Speak of the devil," Joe said. He stood and put Muffy on the floor. "Just the man I planned to go see."

Muffy stood halfway between the desks, watching Levi with open curiosity.

Levi gave Joe a wary look. "Deputy Simmons."

Joe grimaced and held out his hand. "Call me Joe. I need to apologize for the way I acted last night. I'm not usually so—"

Levi shook his hand and gave him a smile. "Water under the bridge, Deputy."

"Glad to hear it," Joe said.

Levi turned his attention toward me and gave me a warm smile. "Good morning, Rose. I wasn't sure you'd be here this early, but I decided to take a chance. Your phone was going straight to voicemail, and I figured you'd need your purse."

"We got an early start," I said, grateful that Joe was standing behind him, because the expression of utter shock on his face would surely have made Levi start asking questions. I walked over and took the bag from him. "You didn't have to do this. I could have come and picked it up."

Levi squatted on the floor and held out a hand toward Muffy. "Hey, Muffy. Remember me?"

She came over and sniffed his hand, and he began to rub behind her ears.

Levi looked up at me. "It was no bother. Besides, I wanted to apologize again for leaving you like that last night."

A noxious smell suddenly wafted up, and Levi stood abruptly, coughing a little as he waved his hand in front of his face. "We could see about experimenting with Muffy's diet."

"We've already tried that," Neely Kate said. "But we're sure open to ideas."

"How's that poor dog that got hit by a car?" I asked.

"Doing much better, but his surgery took a while, so it's a good thing you didn't come to the clinic with me after all." He glanced at Neely Kate and then back to me. "I've got a late start today, so I was wondering if you could get away and walk over to Dena's for breakfast."

I grimaced. "I really wish I could, but Neely Kate and I are about to head out with Muffy."

"Yep." Neely Kate nodded. "We've got a busy day planned."

Levi stood and gave my legs an appreciative glance. "You wore a dress again today."

I shrugged. "Neely Kate's influence." Literally.

Levi moved closer and lowered his voice. "Are you sure you're not mad? You're not acting like yourself."

"Of course not. I'm sorry," I said, feeling terrible. He was such a nice guy. Why couldn't I have feelings for him? "I'm fine. I just have a headache." I needed to end this, but I certainly couldn't do it in front of Joe and Neely Kate. Levi deserved better than that.

"Did you take something for it?"

It was actually my leg that was throbbing, and I wasn't supposed to take anything else for a good two hours. "Yeah, but it's starting to wear off. Don't worry about me. I'll be fine."

"The Presbyterian church is having a string quartet come in tomorrow night. They're playing Vivaldi's 'The Four Seasons,' and I was wondering if you'd like to go," he said, looking nervous. "The quartet is from Little Rock, not from Magnolia like the one I hear they hosted last year." He made an exaggerated grimace, then grinned. "I've been told it made cats within a half-mile radius howl. When they gave me complimentary tickets, I figured it was because they wanted me there in a professional capacity . . . just in case."

I forced a smile. He really was great company, and the invitation sounded fun. Still, this wasn't fair to him. I knew I would have been upset if the situation were reversed—if I'd been seeking out a commitment from him, and he'd left our date to have hours of sex with another woman.

I opened my mouth to decline, but Neely Kate said, "She'd love to. Do you want to pick her up from the office again?"

He shot Neely Kate a surprised glance before turning back to me. "I'd planned to drop her off at the farmhouse last night, and since I've never seen it, I was thinking I could pick you up from there. The concert doesn't start until eight."

"How about you come early for dinner?" Neely Kate suggested. "Rose is a great cook."

I was going to kill Neely Kate.

Levi gave us both curious glances. I hated putting him in this position, but it would be rude to tell him no after the fuss Neely Kate had made. Besides, I did like his company, and maybe I could convince him to just be friends. It seemed highly unlikely, but maybe it was worth a try . . .

In the meantime, Levi was waiting for a response, and I couldn't leave him hanging. "That's a great idea," I said with a smile I hoped didn't look forced. "Besides, after all the dinners you've insisted on payin' for, it's the least I could do."

"You don't owe me anything. I just enjoy the pleasure of your company." He leaned over and gave me a kiss on the cheek. "I really am sorry about last night."

"I know, Levi. Please don't give it another thought."

"Okay. I'll text you later."

"Okay." I watched him walk out the door and gave him a little wave as he walked past the windows.

"Who were you sleeping with last night?" Joe asked as soon as Levi was out of view.

"That's none of your business," I said with a scowl.

"So you *were* sleepin' with someone else."

I was tired and off my game. "I *never* said that." I picked up my coffee and took a sip to stall for time.

"You didn't have to." He walked over to my desk. "Is Mason in town?"

I started to choke on hot coffee.

Joe shot a glance to Neely Kate. "Is he?"

"Who Rose is sleepin' with is none of your concern, Joe."

I grabbed a handful of tissues and began to wipe the coffee off my desk.

He started to open his mouth, then shut it. Then a dark look filled his eyes. "There are rumors goin' around."

That pissed me off enough to stop my halfhearted cleanup job. "And what exactly have you been hearin'?" I said, putting a hand on my hip.

"That you've been hooking up with Skeeter Malcolm. I'd dismissed them because I knew you were seein' Levi, not to mention you're a helluva lot smarter than that. Or so I thought."

"I have *not* been sleepin' with Skeeter Malcolm." I told myself that last night was a fluke and couldn't be included. "But I did help him resolve that incident a few weeks ago."

"With the necklace."

"But we hadn't seen each other since." I hoped he didn't notice I'd used past tense, something that technically kept it from being a lie.

"Then whose clothes were you wearin'?"

Neely Kate came to my defense. "That's none of your cotton-pickin' business, Joe!"

I decided to try to use this situation to my advantage. "What do you know about Scooter's disappearance?"

He blinked hard. "What?"

"I want to know everything you know about Scooter Malcolm's disappearance."

"Are you investigatin' it?" He shot a dark look at his sister before shifting his gaze to me. "You know interferin' with a case is illegal."

"Well, first it would have to be a case, right?" I asked in a defiant tone. "Otherwise, it wouldn't be interferin'. And second, it's perfectly legal if we're apprenticin' with a real P.I."

His eyebrows nearly shot up to the twelve-foot ceiling. "*Excuse me?*"

"Oh," Neely Kate said, sending a scowl my way. "Did I not mention that we started working with Kermit Cooper?"

"Kermit the Hermit?" he asked in disbelief.

That name explained so much.

"How in God's name did this come about?" he shouted.

"Funny you mention the Lord's name," Neely Kate said. "Because it was definitely the work of divine intervention."

"Kermit Cooper is one of the sloppiest, laziest private investigators in southern Arkansas."

"Really?" Neely Kate asked in a sweet voice. "He's been so helpful to us."

Joe took a step closer and leaned forward, alternating his gaze between the two of us, probably trying to determine which one was likely to crack first. "Is Kermit working Scooter's case?"

Neely Kate lifted her chin. "I'm not at liberty to say."

"Actually," Joe said in a dry tone, "you *are*. Who hired him? Malcolm?" Then he turned his attention on me. "Were you with Skeeter Malcolm last night?"

His question caught me so off guard I could only stare at him wide-eyed. How did I answer? Tell him I was wearing James' clothes because mine had been ruined during my kidnapping? Or admit that I'd slept with James?

I was going with neither.

"Excuse me?" I finally said. "Did you just hear yourself?"

"Yeah, and the words came out exactly as I'd intended. Did

you leave your date with Levi Romano and go sleep with the head of the crime syndicate in this county?"

An *oh crap* look filled Neely Kate's eyes.

I sucked in a deep breath and gave him a deadly glare. "Who I sleep with is none of your business, and why do you automatically assume I slept with someone? Levi left me high and dry in the carnival parking lot. If you *must* know, something happened to my clothes."

That caught his attention. "What?"

I scowled. Me and my big mouth. "It's none of your concern, and I didn't mean that about Levi."

"He didn't leave you? Because he came in here acting like he did."

I shook my head, then took a long sip of my coffee. "He did leave me, but he had a good reason. I told him to go." I frowned, feeling terrible. "I shouldn't have painted him in a bad light. I didn't mean that."

"What happened after he left?" Joe was picking up on far too much.

"Nothing. Let it go."

"Who took you home?"

I opened my mouth, still trying to figure out what to tell him, when Neely Kate said, "Me. I came and got her."

"I still don't understand why she was wearing men's clothes when I walked in. Because from where I'm standing, it doesn't look like she went home with you last night."

"That'll just have to remain one of those mysteries of life," Neely Kate said, starting to push her brother toward the door.

"You know this only makes you two look more suspicious, right?"

Neely Kate chuckled. "Sounds like you're needin' a good case to work on if you're lookin' for a mystery in Rose's choice of clothing."

Joe let her continue to push him, but he stopped at the door.

"Rose, you can call me if you ever get into trouble. Once upon a time, I used to be that person for you. I still can be."

"You were on a date, Joe. How was it gonna look to Dena if your ex called you to take her home?" I shook my head. "I'm fine. You're makin' too big a deal out of this."

"Somehow I don't think I am." He paused. "I don't want you two gettin' mixed up in Scooter Malcolm's disappearance. I'm certain this is a power play, and the last thing I want is for you two to get stuck in the middle of it."

Little did he know.

"We hear you, Joe," Neely Kate said with a bright smile as she opened the door.

"Oh, I *know* you *hear* me. It's the *listening* part you seem to have trouble with."

He walked out the door, and Muffy started to whine.

Neely Kate spun around to face me. "What in Sam Hill were you thinkin'? What possessed you to ask him about Scooter?"

"I don't know," I said with a shrug. "My lack of sleep. My desperation to find Scooter. The deficit of clues. Joe was the one to tell me he was missin'. I thought maybe he might tell me more. Obviously I misjudged."

She gave me a coy look. "How much sleep did you actually get last night?"

A blush rose to my cheeks. "It doesn't matter. It's not happening again. It was a one-time thing."

"How can you be so sure about that?"

"Because we both agreed to that."

Neely Kate snorted. "That's a crock of malarkey. That man's stupid in love with you."

I gasped and turned to her. "Neely Kate."

"Which part are you protesting? The part about him being stupid, or being in love with you?"

"Neither," I grumbled.

"He might love you, but it's in his own possessive way. Bottom line is that Skeeter Malcolm thinks of Skeeter Malcolm and no one else."

That wasn't true. I'd seen James put the needs of the county above his own. Staying in his role was a sacrifice—one he continued to pay for dearly and daily—but James truly believed he was stuck. That if he left, he'd be responsible for the actions of whoever took over next. Of course, if I confessed this to Neely Kate, she'd likely dismiss it as a lie, not that I blamed her. The man James showed the world didn't care about anyone.

"We both know a relationship with James won't work," I said with a sigh. "But I still keep thinkin' about him. Last night was probably a mistake."

"Which is why you're going to give Levi another chance."

I grimaced. "I can't do that to Levi. It's not fair."

She was quiet for a moment. "If you didn't like Levi and were just using him, then I'd tell you to end it. But you *do* like him. You're just used to fallin' fast for guys, and look where that's landed you in the past. Sometimes slow is okay."

"Do you really believe that?"

She gave me a sad smile. "You know what? I'm the absolute worst person to be askin' for love or life advice."

"But you're much more experienced than me," I said—and immediately regretted it when she stiffened. "I didn't mean anything bad by that."

Neely Kate put her hand on my shoulder. "I know, but you're right. I've been dating since high school. You only started dating last year, but I'm pretty doggone sure you know more about love than I do. You've had real love *twice*. I don't think I've ever had it at all, so maybe you should be the one givin' *me* advice."

"Don't be silly. What about Ronnie?" I asked.

She shook her head and turned quiet. "I realized some things last week in Oklahoma, and one of them was that I married Ronnie for all the wrong reasons. Turns out love wasn't one of them."

"Oh, Neely Kate, I'm sorry."

She shrugged. "Now I just need to find him to serve him the divorce papers so we can both get on with our lives."

I felt badly for her. Ronnie had disappeared soon after her miscarriage. She'd discovered he had some ties to the criminal world, so she'd presumed he was dead. But Joe had tracked her wayward husband to New Orleans, only to see Ronnie boarding a bus to Memphis with another woman. And the wedding ring on his hand hadn't been the one Neely Kate had given him.

"Maybe I should give up on love for now," I said.

"Nope. That's your fear talkin'. If Skeeter Malcolm wasn't in the picture, would you still be this unsure about Levi?"

"Good question." I tried to picture James out of my life. It filled me with profound sadness, but he was *already* out of my life, so wasn't that a moot point? "No," I said. "I think I'd worry that I wasn't fallin' for Levi yet, but I'd probably keep goin' out with him."

"Well, there you go. Case closed."

Cased closed. Only, it wasn't closed the way she thought. I was going to end things with Levi.

"Movin' on to *important* things . . ." I said. "If we're gonna try to look neutral, we have to distance ourselves from James as much as possible." I gave her a direct look. "Which means no more calling James when I get into trouble like I did last night. No more Jed following us around."

The look on her face was equally relieved and terrified. "We're gonna do this on our own?"

"No, I have someone else in mind. The person who trained you."

"Kermit?" she snorted. "You think we can count on *him*?"

At least she was being realistic about our mentor. "No. Not present tense. Past. I'm talkin' about your cousin. Witt."

CHAPTER 16

"*W*itt?" she asked in surprise.

"He's the one who taught you self-defense and how to shoot, right?"

"Him and Alan Jackson."

"He lost his job and he's lookin' for work."

"He wants to open a garage, not be a bodyguard."

"But he needs money, right?" I cocked my head. "Why don't you seem more excited about this?"

"Because it's dangerous."

My mouth parted in surprise. "You don't think he can handle it?"

"I *know* he can." She paused. "He's been in trouble with the law before, Rose."

"Oh." Did she think that would prejudice me? "You of all people know I won't hold that against him. Look at Bruce Wayne."

"But we're not askin' Bruce Wayne to do anything illegal, are we?"

I blinked. "I wasn't plannin' on askin' him to rob a bank."

"He can't legally carry a gun, Rose. If he shoots someone while defendin' us, he could get tossed in jail and they'd throw away the key."

"I didn't know."

She sighed and sat down at her desk. "I know."

"We can't do this alone, Neely Kate. It's too dangerous. And we can't use Jed. He might not be workin' for James anymore, but his loyalty lies there, and everyone knows it. We have to look like we're free agents." I paused. "But I understand if you don't want to work this case because it's too dangerous or because of Jed. I can focus on it while you work on the parrot."

She put her hands on her hips. "We're working both cases together, so get *that* thought right out of your head. Jed Carlisle doesn't get a say in this, and no one has connected the two of us with the exception of when he's shown up to help you and me in the past. It's a whole different story when it comes to you and Skeeter."

I groaned. "You've heard rumors?" If Joe had heard them, then of course *she* had.

"After the parley, Buck's been tellin' everyone that you're Skeeter's woman."

"Even though we took his side?" I narrowed my eyes. "Why didn't you tell me?"

"What good would it have done? You were done with him. Or so I thought."

I sat on the edge of my desk. "It made me a target." If I'd known, I would have done a better job of looking out for myself. "Well, that's neither here nor there. We need a bodyguard."

She pressed her lips together. "I suppose Jed rarely sees any gun action with us, and when he got into a gunfight helpin' you, he took off before the sheriff deputies showed up. Besides, Jed usually hangs in the background. If we used Witt, we wouldn't need to hide that he's with us. We're likely to be safer that way."

"Are you sure? We can try to think of someone else."

"No. Let's go see him and make the offer." She pulled out her phone and called him. After nearly ten seconds, she sighed and hung up. "He's probably still sleepin'. I say we just head over there."

"I need to get a new phone first," I said. When she opened her mouth to ask me what had happened to the old one, I added, "You don't want to know."

~

A HALF HOUR LATER, I was sitting in my truck with coffee number two in my hand and my brand-new cell phone on the seat next to me. Muffy's tail looked like it was about to fall off from wagging so hard. Muffy had stayed in the truck with Neely Kate, who'd taken the opportunity to cancel our few appointments for the day. She'd spent an awfully long time on the phone with one of them, judging from what I could see from inside the store. (Most likely to Jed, although she refused to admit it.)

"I think we should go to Walmart next," I said while we were still in the cell phone store parking lot. "It's bound to be safe in public, and even if we had a bodyguard with us, he'd be more likely to tackle someone than shoot at them."

"True," Neely Kate said. "And I can handle that part."

I shot her a glance out of the corner of my eye. "Beatin' up Merv seems to have empowered you."

A grin lit up her eyes. "You have no idea."

Since Bruce Wayne had never told me what department Scooter's girlfriend worked in, I decided to call him and find out. It seemed better than aimlessly wandering the store and drawing attention to ourselves by asking around.

"Hey, Bruce Wayne," I said when he answered, putting him on speaker. "Can I ask you a few questions about Scooter? I have Neely Kate with me."

"Still not investigating?" he asked in a dry tone.

"Okay . . ." I conceded. "You know me too well."

"You're good at it, Rose. You and Neely Kate are a force to be reckoned with. If you two are looking, I feel a whole helluva lot better. You'll both find him . . . one way or another."

That caught me off guard. "Do you think he might be dead?"

He was quiet for a moment, and when he finally spoke, he sounded subdued. "There are only three reasons someone would have snatched him. One, to get back at Skeeter, and that one could go either way. Two, if he heard or saw something he shouldn't have, and someone felt threatened. He spends time at the Trading Post and One Eyed Joes, and everyone knows he's Skeeter's brother."

"I can't imagine that would have a good outcome," I said.

"It wouldn't." He sounded guarded. "The third possibility is that it has nothing to do with Skeeter at all. Maybe Scooter pissed someone off. He's runnin' a few side deals of his own."

"Wait." I held up a hand even though he couldn't see it. "I thought Scooter wasn't mixed up in that anymore."

"He's not with Skeeter."

"What's he doin' then?" Neely Kate asked.

"Selling pot. He's growin' it in his field."

"Well, crap," I said. "That puts a whole new spin on it, doesn't it?"

Neely Kate didn't say anything.

"What are the chances he pissed someone off?" I asked.

"Everything's a mess right now," Bruce Wayne said. "So I'd say fifty-fifty." He paused. "The fact you're askin' questions must mean you don't think Buck Reynolds snatched him. That's what everyone else is sayin'."

"I'm certain of it," I said. "Which means we need to be lookin' in other places because nobody else is. Would Scooter's girlfriend know details about his pot dealing?"

"She's likely to know more than me," he said. "Now that I'm travelin' down the straight and narrow, he won't tell me anything."

"It's safer for you that way. He's bein' a good friend," Neely Kate said.

"But we're not as close as we used to be," he said, sounding sad.

"Maybe Scooter should have taken the straight and narrow too," I said. "Sounds like James gave him the chance when he cut him off from his world."

"Sure, it sounds good," Neely Kate said. "But it's not so easy to do on a Walmart paycheck." Then she added, "Besides, his brother does far worse."

While she had a point, she definitely sounded judgey. Was she trying to make a point about James? I'd already told her it was over.

"You're right," I said. "And I obviously wasn't thinkin' things through." Probably in more ways than one.

"I know Scooter's made a few new friends since last fall," Bruce Wayne said. "Jeanne will know who they are better than I would."

"Okay," Neely Kate said. "We'll ask her. Do you know what department she works in?"

"She's a cashier."

That would certainly make it harder to talk to her. If she'd worked the floor, we would have been able to hide in an aisle.

"Anything else you can think of?" I asked.

He paused for a moment. "Not off the top of my head, but if I think of something, I'll let you know."

"Thanks, Bruce Wayne," I said. "We'll let you know something as soon as we can."

"Rose, I . . . thank you. You too, Neely Kate. Scooter was there for me when I needed help. I just want him safe."

"Just doin' our job, Bruce Wayne," Neely Kate said.

Except this case was personal to all three of us, for a variety of reasons, and we all knew it.

I hung up and turned to Neely Kate. "I want to have a vision of you."

She went stock-still. "Why?"

"I want to see if I can force a vision of where Scooter is."

"Oh, my stars and garters. That's a great idea."

"But . . ." I said hesitantly. "I'm not positive what I'll see."

"You're worried about finding me in a compromising situation," she said. When I nodded, she reached over and grabbed my hand. "Now that you know about me and Jed, I'm fine with it."

I cringed. "I really don't want to see you in bed with Jed."

She squeezed my hand. "You won't. We haven't slept together."

"What?"

She shrugged and gave me a shy smile. "He wants to take it slow."

As soon as I picked up my jaw, I gave her a warm smile. "That's great, Neely Kate. I think he really likes you."

"I think he does too. So go ahead and have the vision."

I closed my eyes and focused on us finding Scooter. An unchanging gray void surrounded me. I consoled myself with the fact that it wasn't black, which signified death. Gray meant the future was yet to be determined. I changed the question slightly, thinking instead about what would happen after we found Scooter, and the vision changed.

It was nighttime and I was standing next to Neely Kate's beater car on the side of an empty road. I was frantically calling Jed on my cell phone, but I couldn't get any service.

"I'm comin'," I said. "I promise I'm comin'!"

The vision ended and I said, "You're still comin'."

Neely Kate's face blushed. "Oh, my word. I'm scared to ask what you saw."

I grinned. "Not what you seem to be thinking." Then I explained the vision to her.

"What does it mean?"

"Heck if I know. I could try to have another, but they usually turn out the same."

"Why was I alone?"

"I don't know, but you were calling Jed. Maybe you were goin' to meet him."

"What does that have to do with findin' Scooter?" she asked.

"I couldn't see anything about findin' Scooter, so I asked what happened after we found him. Maybe you're gonna go straight to see Jed."

"Maybe . . ."

We couldn't figure it out, so I started to drive to Walmart. Muffy made a contented sound as she snuggled up with Neely Kate, drawing my attention to her. "I think it's too hot to leave Muffy in the truck, but I think both of us should go in."

"Do you want to drop her off with Maeve at the nursery?"

"I know I *should*, but I'm still reeling from Mike's insistence that we sell Momma's house. I'm not sure I'm ready to talk to Violet about it yet." I didn't necessarily mind selling Momma's house. I had very few fond memories of the place. It was the way it was being handled, like Mike wanted to sell it out from under Violet. Something was off. Especially since he'd asked me to keep it a secret. I wanted to talk to Violet, but we needed to discuss this alone.

"I doubt she's gonna be there anyway," Neely Kate said. "She's still settlin' in."

I thought about it for a moment. "Let's try to keep Muffy with us. I didn't get to see her at all yesterday." Truth was I missed her.

"How are we gonna take her in?"

"How about we make her a purse dog?"

Neely Kate snorted. "Your brand-new purse? She's barely gonna fit."

She was right. While Muffy wasn't that big, she was nearly ten pounds and about a foot and a half long. But my new purse was a lot larger than my old one, mostly because I'd started carrying assorted self-defense items. "I'll take everything out." I reached down and rubbed Muffy's head. "I want to keep her with me."

A couple of minutes later, we were walking across the parking lot, me with my bag slung over my shoulder and a dubious Muffy stuffed inside. Her head stuck out under my armpit, making me wish Neely Kate had remembered to pack deodorant in my cosmetics bag. But Muffy didn't seem to mind that part—it was the lack of anything hard to sit on in the bottom of the bag that was making her anxious. She was trying to stand and couldn't get her footing.

Then a nasty smell hit my nose, and I realized my BO was nothing compared to the smells my little dog was producing.

"I'm not sure this is gonna work," I mused as we walked through the automatic entrance doors.

"I'll make it work. We're gonna sneak you right in," Neely Kate said, walking in with her head held high like she owned the place. We started to walk past the greeter, and Neely Kate squealed as she rushed over to him. "Oh, my goodness! Ben! Is that you?"

The gray-haired man looked confused, not that I was surprised. I was part of this operation, and *I* was confused, but Neely Kate subtly waved me past her. As soon as I was a good ways past them, I edged into an aisle and looked back.

The elderly gentleman squinted at Neely Kate. "Sarah Beth? You sure have gotten big. And prettier."

"I'm so sorry," she said. "I thought you were my granny's old beau. My mistake."

A smile lit up his face. "If your granny looks anything like you, I'll be happy to be her new one."

Neely Kate gave him an ornery grin. "Isn't that a wedding ring on your hand?"

He laughed and winked. "What Carol don't know won't hurt her. Especially since she ran off to Florida with the yard boy. I can't get this damn thing off."

"You should get it cut off," Neely Kate told him. "Get you a fresh start."

"And ruin a perfectly good gold ring? I'll just save it for my next wife."

She laughed and leaned closer. "My granny plays bingo every Tuesday night." With a wink and a wave, she said, "I'll be there too."

He waved back as she walked toward me.

"Did you really just try to set up your granny?"

"It's never too late for love, Rose. Besides, Granny's frugal enough to appreciate not havin' to buy him a weddin' ring." Then she grabbed my purse arm, getting a lick from Muffy in the process, and led me down to the checkout lanes.

I wished we'd thought to ask Bruce Wayne what Jeanne looked like. It would have been easier to find her . . . if she was working. There was no guarantee of that.

We walked down the line, trying to read the name tags of the four cashiers we could see, but two of the women were turned away from us.

"I think we can eliminate the older woman," I said as we passed a woman with gray hair who looked to be in her sixties.

"Not necessarily," Neely Kate said. "Maybe she's a cougar. You never know these days. Wait here." Bold as could be, she strode up the aisle and looked over an endcap display of sunscreen. Then she wandered down a few more aisles, checking out the candy selection in the lane of the other cashier we hadn't identified. A few seconds later, she returned.

"The second woman is her. I say we do a little shoppin'," Neely Kate said. "Then I can ask Jeanne questions while we check out."

"Good idea. I need to stock up on a few things while we're here."

Neely Kate grabbed a cart. "Let's do it."

After I picked up some deodorant, I headed to the sporting goods section.

"You plannin' on going camping?"

"Nope." I picked up a small pocket knife, two rolls of duct tape, some zip ties, and two five-pound dumbbells.

"Do I want to know what you're plannin' on doin' with all that?" Neely Kate asked.

"A little extra self-defense preparation." When she looked at me, I added, "I plan on carrying one in my purse to pull out and smack someone in the head if I need to. Then I'll keep the other one under the driver's seat of my truck as backup."

I started to roll the cart away, but she put her hand on my arm to stop me. Muffy leaned over and nuzzled her hand, and Neely Kate absently rubbed her head.

"None of that would have helped you last night, Rose," she said in a quiet voice. "You didn't have your purse with you. Levi had it."

I looked her in the eye. "I need to be more prepared. I'm going to start wearing my gun, and I need to figure out a way to wear a pocket knife too." My anxiety increased. "What if I hadn't found a pair of scissors to cut myself loose last night?"

Muffy released a small whine and reached out to lick my hand holding the purse strap.

"Then Buck Reynolds' guys would have freed you," Neely Kate said.

"What if they hadn't shown up? I sure as Pete don't want to depend on someone like Buck Reynolds to save me. I need to learn how to save myself."

"You already do save yourself."

"Not all the time."

"Sometimes you're the one doin' the savin'. Mason. Joe. Have you forgotten about that?"

"I almost got killed last night, Neely Kate. I need to be able to help myself *every* time."

She gave me a sad smile. "Then we'll figure it out together. And Witt too. Let's go check out and find him."

There were two people ahead of us in Jeanne's checkout lane, both with a lot more things than we had, but Jeanne was so efficient, she had them checked out in no time.

"We don't have enough stuff," I said.

Neely Kate studied the cashier as she handed a receipt to the woman in front of us. "I don't feel like buying a bunch of junk just to ask questions." Her eyes lit up. "I have an idea."

"The way you said that has me worried."

Neely Kate grinned. "Oh, ye of little faith." She grabbed the pocket knife and peeled off the sticker, then plopped the knife onto the conveyor belt.

I squatted to grab one of the dumbbells while Neely Kate unloaded the rest. It was awkward bending over with a dog in my purse, and Muffy was getting more nervous. She wasn't used to being cooped up in such tight confines. She started moving around in the bag, releasing little whines. I was rubbing her head comfortingly when Jeanne turned her attention to me.

Everything about Jeanne Putnam was thin and brittle—from her stringy, dull brown hair to her spindly arms and rail-thin body. She looked like she was in her thirties and had been living hard.

She gave me a long, cold stare. "You ain't supposed to have a dog in here."

This did not bode well. "I know," I said, giving her a bright smile "But I haven't let her out of the bag, and I'm checkin' out, so we'll be out of here in no time."

She gave a slow shake of her head and started scanning things. She picked up the package of zip ties. "This is an odd assortment of things. Whatcha plannin' on doin' with it?"

I hadn't formed a plan to ease her into questioning, so I decided to be honest. "Protectin' myself the next time someone tries to kidnap me."

Her head jerked up and her eyes held mine. "Is that some kind of sick *joke?*"

"No. Jeanne. I think the same guys who kidnapped Scooter kidnapped me last night."

Her body stiffened and she took a step back. "You're full of shit," she said, then flung an arm toward me. "You're standin' in front of me now."

"I'm not foolin' you. I promise. I was wondering if we could ask you some questions about Scooter."

A wild look filled her eyes.

I took a step closer and lowered my voice. "I'm friends with Skeeter Malcolm. I'm lookin' for his brother." Sure, I was trying to distance myself from him, but Jeanne had to know Scooter's brother would want to find him. It seemed like it would buy me some credibility.

"He didn't say nothin' about you," she sneered.

"You've talked to him?"

"'Course I talked to him. He had me dragged down to the pool hall."

"When?"

"The day after it happened. Some guy showed up and took me over there."

"But you didn't tell them that you saw Scooter taken until last night. Why?"

Jeanne shook her head and picked up one of the dumbbells and scanned it.

"Jeanne," Neely Kate said, "we want to help you."

Jeanne's face jerked up with an angry glare. "You don't want to help me. You're just like that asshole in the pool hall."

"Skeeter?" she asked.

"No, the other one."

She gasped. "*Jed?*"

I understood her surprise. I'd never seen Jed be rude to a woman.

"No, that big guy. The one who looks like a tank. The one who took me over there."

"Merv?" Neely Kate asked, her eyes narrowing.

Fear filled Jeanne's eyes. "I don't want to talk about it no more."

"Jeanne," I pleaded. "We want the same thing you do. We want to find Scooter and bring him home safe."

When she didn't say anything, Neely Kate said, "I had a run-in with Merv last week. When you saw him, did he have a bruised face from his busted nose?"

She gave a quick nod as she picked up the pocket knife.

"I'm the one who gave it to him."

Jeanne jerked her gaze up again, giving her a skeptical look.

"It's true. He and I had a disagreement. He shoved me against the wall and tried to choke me, but I fought him off. I busted his nose and broke his hand."

"So?" she said with a sneer.

"I'm not scared to stand up to Merv, and I'll stand up to him for you. Just tell us what you know."

"He called me a liar! He thinks I'm working with some guy named Reynolds." Tears filled her eyes. "He thinks I let that man take my Scooter."

"What did he say?"

She twisted the pocket knife around in her hand. "There's no price tag on this."

"Jeanne," I said. "What did Merv say?"

She shook her head. "I can't talk about this here."

"Can we talk to you when you get off?" I asked.

She pressed her lips together.

"Please?" I asked. "I know other people are hurtin' over Scooter too. Skeeter. Bruce Wayne."

She glanced up at Bruce Wayne's name.

"He said Scooter has made some new friends that he doesn't know. He thought you might be able to help us."

Hope filled her eyes, but it quickly fled. "How do I know I can trust you?"

"I guess you don't," Neely Kate said. "But all three of us want to find Scooter, and none of us trust Merv. That last one alone should make me and Rose more trustworthy."

She looked into Neely Kate's eyes. "Okay."

Neely Kate reached over and grabbed her hand. "We'll help you. I promise."

The two women exchanged glances for several seconds before Neely Kate released her and dug a card out of her purse. "I'm Neely Kate and this is my business card. Text me when you get off, and we'll meet somewhere. Okay?"

Jeanne glanced down at the pink card in her hand and nodded. "Okay, Neely Kate."

Pink? Our landscaping business cards were white with blue lettering, which meant she'd had her own cards made.

I shot a glare to my best friend. There was no way in Hades I was going with that name. Besides, we were supposed to be working under Kermit the Hermit. But then again, with this case we weren't.

Jeanne waved the pocket knife. "I need to get a price check on this."

Neely Kate waved. "That's okay. We don't need it."

"What? Yes, I do," I said, practically lunging over the conveyor belt. "Get a price check!"

Jeanne looked less than thrilled, but she picked up her phone and called Sporting Goods.

Muffy was already agitated, and she saw her chance for escape when I leaned forward. She hopped onto the conveyor belt, which suddenly turned into a treadmill for my dog. Her little legs ran to keep up, and she looked at me with a desperate expression that clearly telegraphed *Help!* But my cart was in the way. I gave it a good shove, ramming it into the endcap in the process, and sent a hundred plastic bobble heads of President Bill

Clinton and Governor Mike Huckabee, which had both been clearance-priced to forty-nine cents, flying all over the floor.

"Oh, my word!" I shouted as I scooped Muffy into my arms. "I'm so sorry!"

But Muffy wasn't having any part of being cuddled. She released a huge stinker of a fart and took advantage of my gagging to try to wiggle free.

"No, Muffy!" I tried to put her back into my purse, but she'd had enough. She leapt out of my arms onto the floor and took off running, veering toward the next aisle.

Well, crappy doodles.

"Muffy!" I shimmied between the cart and the candy display and stood at the back of the aisle, looking left—the direction she'd run.

"Oh, my stars and garters!" Neely Kate said. "Where'd she go?"

I shook my head. "I don't know."

Then I saw her furry butt as she backed out of an aisle with her teeth clamped on someone's pants. She dug her back feet in and tugged, but whoever she had a grip on dragged her back out of sight. My mouth dropped in shock. Surely that wasn't Muffy. She'd never do such a thing, but how many little white, wiry-haired dogs were hanging out in Walmart?

"Muffy's attackin' someone!"

"*What?*" Neely Kate shouted.

I took off running, trying to figure out a logical reason for Muffy to do such a thing. She'd only ever reacted that way with bad guys.

"Get off me!" an elderly woman shouted, waving at Muffy with a baguette. "Go away."

I froze, certain I recognized the voice. "*Miss Mildred?*"

CHAPTER 17

She stood upright but kept her back to me. "You must be mistaken. Would you please remove your dog?" Her voice had an odd high pitch to it, which seemed unnatural, and there was a scarf tied around her head and neck.

Muffy continued tugging at her leg.

Neely Kate came to a skidding stop at the end of the aisle and her eyes widened. "*Miss Mildred?* What in heaven's name are you doin' with all those baked goods?"

Sure enough, her cart was half full of cakes, packages of cookies, a half dozen cupcakes, two pies, and a few loaves of bread. "Are you opening a bakery?"

She turned around and glared at me . . . or at least I thought so based on the set of her jaw. She was wearing sunglasses that completely concealed her eyes.

What in the world was she up to?

She turned around and grabbed hold of the cart. "That's none of your daggum business."

"Are you wearing *a disguise?*" Neely Kate asked.

She didn't answer, but I realized Neely Kate was right. How else could she go out and buy all these prepackaged baked goods? If anyone in the garden club caught her, she'd likely be expelled.

"What are you *really* up to?" I asked.

"None of your business."

I caught Neely Kate's eye, and she looked just as worried as I felt. I bent down and pried Muffy off Miss Mildred's pant leg. When I stood, Muffy released a soft whine.

"Miss Mildred," I said. "Are you okay?"

"I was okay until your dog attacked me! How'd that mongrel get inside this store? I'm going to call security."

I ran my hand over Muffy's head as she intently stared at my elderly neighbor. Muffy knew something was up too.

A woman wearing a blue vest walked over, shooting a glare at Muffy. "Dogs aren't allowed in the store."

Miss Mildred turned to the manager. "Her flea-infested dog attacked me."

"Muffy does not have fleas," I protested, holding her closer.

The manager frowned. "We're gonna need you to leave."

"I'll pay for my things and go."

The manager gave me a grim look. "Just don't cause any more trouble."

"Yes, ma'am."

Jeanne was still holding the pocket knife, staring in wide-eyed disbelief when I carried Muffy back to the checkout lane.

"Still no price," she said, sounding rattled. I wasn't surprised. There were four carts backing up behind my empty one, not to mention there was a huge cleanup needed at the end of her aisle.

"Let's just pay for the rest of these things and go," Neely Kate said.

"No. The pocket knife was the most important thing," I protested.

"I'm sure Witt has one you can use."

Which meant I would once again be relying on someone else to take care of me. *"No.* I'm buying *this* one." But before I'd finished my sentence, Muffy started growling and wiggling in my arms. "Muffy. It's okay, gir—"

She jumped out of my arms again, growling as she bolted toward the front door.

"Muffy!"

I took off after her and heard Neely Kate say, "Sorry, Jeanne. We won't be needin' any of that!" before she sprinted after me.

I burst through the automatic doors and shouted, "Muffy!"

She'd made it halfway across the parking lot when a car door slammed. Seconds later, a car peeled out of a parking space and headed toward the back of the parking lot with Muffy in fast pursuit.

"*Muffy!*" I shouted in a stern voice. "*Come!*"

She stopped in her tracks and glanced back at me before turning to watch the speeding car.

She was growling, and I was scared she was going to take off after it again, but she just released a loud bark before trotting back to me and Neely Kate.

"What do you make of that?" Neely Kate asked.

"She didn't like something about him."

"Did you see who it was?"

I shook my head. "He was a blur, but it was definitely a guy— dark hair, dark T-shirt, jeans . . ."

"You just described half the men in the county," she said in a dry tone. "But Muffy sure didn't like him."

That was exactly what had me worried. "I need to get my gun."

Neely Kate shot me a look of surprise.

"For all we know that guy was here to kidnap me again. I need to be prepared." I turned around and started to head back inside. "I need that pocket knife."

She grabbed my arm and stopped me. "Rose. Maybe you should hide out for a few days. Maybe stay with Skeeter or even leave town."

I stared at her in disbelief. "One minute you're pushin' me on Levi, and the next you're shovin' me back toward James. We can't have it both ways, Neely Kate."

"I know," she said with fear in her eyes. "I'm scared."

"I'm not hidin'. I spent the first twenty-four years of my life hidin', and I'm done." I took a breath. I needed to focus on the task at hand. "Someone tried to kidnap me last night, and I can't help thinking they were about to try it again."

"Maybe we should tell Joe."

I considered it for a moment before shaking my head. "He'd lock me up and throw away the key to hide me. I need to keep lookin' for Scooter. And the parrot . . ." My voice dropped off when I saw Miss Mildred walk out with her cart full of pastries. "What in the world do you think she's up to?"

Neely Kate followed my gaze. "Committing suicide by sugar overload?"

"No. She's too ornery for that."

"Maybe we should follow her and make sure she's okay," Neely Kate said. "If she's as out of it as she's acting, she's liable to drive to New Orleans before she figures out she took a wrong turn."

She had a point. "Okay, but then I want to go home and get my gun." Too bad we hadn't found out when Jeanne got off work.

"Deal."

Miss Mildred tossed her multiple bags into the trunk of her car and pushed her shopping cart into the corral.

"What is she *doin'*?" Neely Kate asked in disbelief. "She tossed those cakes and pies and everything in her trunk like they were dirty laundry."

"Maybe she's on a medication that makes her confused."

"That's the only explanation I can think of that makes sense."

We got in the truck and followed her from far enough away that she wouldn't notice unless she was looking.

When she turned down her street, I stayed on the cross street

—there were no other cars, thankfully—and watched her park in the driveway. Miss Mildred grabbed the bags out of the trunk and headed straight to her backyard instead of the front door, something else that was uncharacteristic of her.

Now I knew something weird was going on.

"Maybe we should call Joe and have him take her to get a psych evaluation," I said.

"Let's see what she's up to first."

I turned down her street and parked one house away.

"No need to sneak around," Neely Kate said. "I'm flat-out worried enough to risk tickin' her off."

"Agreed." I hooked up Muffy's leash to make sure she didn't run away again. After we got out, Neely Kate, Muffy, and I circled around the side of Miss Mildred's house.

I gasped when I saw the heavily landscaped yard. I hadn't been back here in years, and while I knew that Miss Mildred's position as president of the Henryetta Garden Club had inspired her to always try and one-up her friends, I was shocked it had gone this far. The yard was broken up into segments and bursting with roses and hydrangeas and other flowers. The only places not festooned with flowers were the stepping stone paths leading through the flower beds and the fountain of a man and a dog in the middle of the yard. There was no sign of Miss Mildred, but she'd set the Walmart bags down on the back porch.

I started to turn to Neely Kate to see what she made of that when I realized the fountain statue looked remarkably like Miss Mildred's deceased husband. He was standing next to his old hunting dog and holding a welding torch close to his leg. Water shot out of the end where the flame would have been, then collected in the basin he was standing in. Two things grabbed my attention: One, the unfortunate placement of the torch made it look like he was peeing, and two, the stream of water was falling short and landing on the dog's head.

Miss Mildred emerged from her back door with an armload

of plates and hobbled down the steps, still wearing the scarf and sunglasses. I grabbed Neely Kate's arm and dragged her behind a large bush closer to the corner of the house.

Miss Mildred set the plates out on her small patio table. I counted ten before she had them all laid out.

"Do you think she's havin' a garden party?" Neely Kate whispered.

"No way. She'd cut off her arm before servin' her guests Walmart baked goods."

The elderly woman grabbed one of the bags and dumped the contents in the middle of the table, one of the cakes landing upside down in its container.

"She's lost it," Neely Kate murmured.

I'd been reserving my final judgment, but then I heard her mumbling, "I didn't know what you liked, so I got you all kinds of goodies."

Who was she talking to?

She kept talking as she put a small serving of everything she'd bought on the plates, looking up in the sky every so often while she held a hand to her forehead to shield her eyes.

When she finished, she clapped her hands together once and said, "Okay, come and get it."

I glanced back at Neely Kate and pushed out a sigh. "I think we should call Joe and have her evaluated."

She'd pulled out her phone, presumably about to make the call, when Muffy released a bark.

I squatted next to her. "Shh!"

But it was too late. Miss Mildred turned in our direction holding a cake knife in her hand. "Who's over there?"

I stood and walked out, holding Muffy's leash in my hand. "Hey, Miss Mildred."

She took a step backward, bumping into the table. "You here to finish the job?"

"No, Miss Mildred," Neely Kate said. "We're just worried about you."

"Well, you've got no reason to be. Now get!"

"But Miss Mildred," Neely Kate said, gesturing to the spread of subpar baked goods on the table. "You're clearly confused."

"I'm not confused. Now get out, or I'm gonna call—"

Suddenly, Muffy strained against the leash and started barking at the trees. I bent down and scooped her up, and she instantly stopped barking.

"Go away, you wild dog!" Miss Mildred shouted, waving her arm in wild arcs. "You're gonna scare him away!"

I was about to ask who when I saw a flash of green in the trees and heard a voice say, "Give me more cake."

I shot a glance at Neely Kate, whose whole face had lit up. "You found him, Miss Mildred!"

The parrot flew out of the trees and landed on the back of one of the patio chairs. "Cake is good."

"I wasn't sure which kind you liked," Miss Mildred said, clasping her hands in front of her as she talked to the bird. "I got chocolate and vanilla cupcakes, and red velvet and carrot cakes."

"Carrots!" the bird said.

"I knew you liked the carrot cake I had out, so that's why I got you another one."

"He likes carrots," I said.

Miss Mildred spun at the waist to face me. "How would you know?"

"His owner hired Kermit Cooper to find him. He belongs to Mr. Whipple a few blocks over."

"*Kermit the Hermit?*" Miss Mildred asked. "Then what are you two doin' here? Being nosy?"

I shook my head. "We were worried about you. But now we know why you were buying all that cake." Well, sort of. It could hardly be a healthy diet for a parrot.

"We're helpin' Kermit," Neely Kate said. "He's teaching us how to be P.I.s, and our first case is finding Squawker."

"Squawker!" the bird said.

Miss Mildred's face fell.

"Why are you feedin' him all those cakes?" Neely Kate asked.

"That's none of your daggum business." But she looked like she was about to cry.

"How long has Squawker been hangin' out here?" I asked.

She frowned. "Since Sunday afternoon. I'd set out my carrot cake to cool so I could frost it for the church dinner, and I found that parrot eatin' it. I was hotter than a hornet at first, but then he started talkin' and thankin' me for the cake. I couldn't get mad at a bird with such good manners. So I fed him the rest of the cake, and he stuck around."

"And the cupcakes from yesterday," I said.

"They were goin' to waste anyway," she said defensively.

"You were gonna keep him," Neely Kate said.

"Not for a pet," Miss Mildred grumped. "I was keepin' him outside. He was entertaining." She waved her hand. "He talks."

"Someone broke into Mr. Whipple's home last Thursday night," I said. "And Squawker got loose in the mess. Mr. Whipple hasn't seen him since. He really misses him. We need to bring him home."

"Well . . . there ain't nobody stoppin' ya." She gave the bird a longing look, then turned around and went in the house.

"Bye," the parrot squawked.

"How do we catch a parrot?" I asked.

"Well, if Alan Jackson were here—"

"We want the parrot alive, Neely Kate."

"Good point."

"Let's call Mr. Whipple."

Neely Kate tried his number but got no answer. In the meantime, Squawker watched us like we were the Fenton County High

School Saturday matinee performance of *Our Town*—slightly interested but mostly bored.

"Now what?" I asked.

Neely Kate gave me a grimace. "I know someone else we can call."

I released a long groan. "You call him."

"It's gonna be weird if I do it instead of you."

I dug my phone out of my pocket, thankful my cloud had transferred all my numbers to my new phone, and called Levi's cell phone.

"Rose!" he said, sounding pleased. "I thought you'd text me the details of dinner tomorrow night."

"Actually, that's not what I'm callin' about. It's more work-related. Maybe I should have called the office."

"Don't be silly. Is Muffy okay?"

"This call's about Squawker. Neely Kate and I found him."

"Really? That's great . . . but I take it there's a problem."

"Hopefully not a big one. We don't know how to catch him. We called Mr. Whipple, but he's not home."

"Do you have a bird cage to put him in?"

"No."

"Then you might be better off waiting until Mr. Whipple gets home. If you let him loose in your truck, he might hurt himself."

"But if we leave him here, won't he fly off?" That was a stupid question. Squawker was hopping around on the table, pecking at the cakes. "Say . . . I suspect it's bad for parrots to have cake."

"You're not feeding him cake, are you?"

"No," I said, grabbing a cupcake out of Squawker's reach.

"Parrots don't fly all that much. If he's flown recently, he'll probably just sit there awhile. Your best bet is to wait for Mr. Whipple. He'd probably be the best draw. But if you think Squawker's in danger, or you're worried about him flying away, you can lure him with some type of food he likes."

"Carrots."

"Yep. That will work."

"Thanks, Levi."

"Please feel free to call me anytime, Rose."

I hung up and relayed what he'd told me, but Neely Kate made a face. "We don't have time to sit around waiting for Mr. Whipple to show up."

"It sounds like he's been in Miss Mildred's backyard since Sunday afternoon. We could probably leave him here and ask Miss Mildred to keep an eye on him."

She frowned. "I'd rather try to catch him. We could take him to Mr. Whipple's house and put him in the aviary in the back."

I didn't think it was a great idea, but now that we'd found the parrot, I was hesitant to walk away.

Neely Kate knocked on the back door and asked Miss Mildred for a carrot while I stood several feet from the bird.

"Hi, Squawker. Are you missing your . . ." What did he call Mr. Whipple? ". . . Daddy?"

"Daddy go bye-bye."

Since parrots merely "parroted" back what they heard, that meant Mr. Whipple likely said that to him whenever he left the house. "Your daddy is missing you."

"Go bye-bye, Scooter."

I blinked hard, sure I must have heard him wrong.

Neely Kate emerged from the back door with a carrot in her hand.

"Neely Kate," I said in a tight voice. "Listen to this."

"Squawker. Who went bye-bye?" I asked.

The bird shifted his weight on the back of the chair and remained quiet.

"Do you miss your daddy?" I repeated.

"Go bye-bye, Scooter."

Neely Kate's mouth fell open. "What?"

"Scooter's not a very common name," I said, getting excited.

Neely Kate's eyes rounded, but then she shook her head. "I'm not sure that helps. He's been loose for days. He could have heard it anywhere."

"True, but what if that's why someone broke in? To keep Squawker from spreading his secrets?" I hurried to Miss Mildred's back door and knocked.

She opened the door, shooting me an angry look. "What are you still doin' here?"

"Have you heard Squawker talk much since he showed up?"

She looked surprised, then glared at me. "Maybe."

"Did he say anything out of the ordinary?"

"No. Other than he talked a lot about a scooter."

Neely Kate rushed up behind me. "What did he say?"

"I don't know . . . something about wanting to go bye-bye with a scooter. I don't have one, but I told him I could maybe get him one once I get my Social Security check on the first."

Miss Mildred was clearly attached to him.

"Anything else?" Neely Kate asked.

"Something profane and about blood."

I gasped and turned to Neely Kate. Mr. Whipple had mentioned that earlier, but he'd written it off as something the parrot had heard on a TV show . . . Except what if it wasn't?

"This is important," Neely Kate said slowly. "We need to know *exactly* what he said."

"He said something like . . ." Her eyes narrowed. "*Shut up, you assholes, and clean up the blood.*"

CHAPTER 18

*W*e needed to talk to Mr. Whipple again. And soon. The phrase Squawker had been repeating was the same one the older man remembered from Wednesday night—and it matched Anita's memories too. If it was about Scooter's blood, it didn't bode well for his safety.

We decided to leave the parrot in Miss Mildred's backyard until we could reach Mr. Whipple—who unfortunately didn't have an answering machine. Miss Mildred agreed to keep an eye on him as long as we gave her part of the reward money.

"We don't know if we're even gettin' reward money," I said as we got back into the truck. "Any money goes to Kermit, and I doubt he's payin' us. I can't believe you agreed to share it."

"Exactly," Neely Kate said, strapping in her seatbelt. "If we get nothin', then she gets thirty percent of it."

"She's gonna be steamed."

She gave me a smug look. "I think I know something she'll like better than a reward."

I couldn't imagine what that could be, and she refused to tell me.

We headed out to the farm next, and Neely Kate sent a text when she thought I wasn't looking. Probably to Jed.

"Well, we need to talk to Mr. Whipple and Jeanne," I said, "but we can't reach him, and we have no clue when she's off work."

"Look on the bright side," she said, "we'll have time to talk to Witt. And grab some lunch." She turned in her seat, wearing a satisfied grin. "Rose, we solved our first official P.I. intern case!"

"Well . . ." I said. "We found Squawker, but we still haven't handed him over to Mr. Whipple."

"Don't jinx it," she said. "Next time we look for a bird, let's bring a cage."

"Let's hope there isn't a next time."

Muffy was glad to get home after her eventful morning, and after the Walmart incident, Neely Kate and I agreed to leave her home the next time we headed out.

After letting Muffy roam and sniff around for a few minutes, we headed inside. I started a pot of coffee, then went upstairs to find my gun and holster.

I'd tucked them in a drawer with my yoga pants and leggings several months ago. The self-defense and shooting lessons Jed had given us a few weeks ago hadn't been enough. I wasn't close to being ready to defend myself.

I heard a car coming down the drive from the county road to the house, and I quickly loaded my gun with the clip and hurried down the hall to Neely Kate's room, which overlooked the front yard. My farmhouse had a great view of any cars driving in, but it was also secluded and hidden from the county road by a thick hedge of trees. Considering I might have someone after me, being on guard seemed like a good idea.

"Neely Kate," I called out from her doorway. "We've got company."

"I know. It's Witt."

Witt? That must have been who she was texting on the way home.

The smell of bacon drifted up to me. Had she bribed him with breakfast? Whatever it took.

I went back to my room to get more clips, strapped on the holster, then grabbed a backpack out of my closet. For all the supplies I wanted to carry, a Walmart purse wasn't going to cut it.

I came down the stairs and found Witt sitting at the kitchen table with a coffee cup in his hand. The table was already set for breakfast.

Witt turned his gaze toward me with half-open eyes. "I hear you have a job for me."

Nothing like cutting to the chase.

I dropped my backpack on the floor and grabbed a cup of coffee, wondering how long it would take to get used to wearing a gun on my thigh. "I hear you're lookin' for one."

He lifted his shoulder into a half-shrug, then took a sip from his mug.

I sat down across from him, realizing Witt looked pretty rough, like he'd been on an all-night bender. "How're you doin', Witt?"

"I've been better." He set his cup down. "You got some kind of pity job for me at the landscaping business?"

I sat up a bit in surprise. "No. I hadn't even considered it."

His shoulders lost some of their stiffness. "Good. I hate digging holes."

Neely Kate seemed to freeze in front of the stove at that but quickly resumed her work as if nothing had happened. She'd finished with the bacon and started in on some pancakes.

I rested my forearm on the table. "Look. I know you want to start your own business, so this is just a temporary thing that will help you earn some money in the meantime. It might not take more than a couple of days."

"I'm listening."

"I know you taught Neely Kate how to shoot and defend herself, but have you ever worked as a bodyguard?"

He started laughing. "Is this for real?"

"Totally for real."

"No, but it seems easy enough."

"Someone tried to kidnap me last night."

His eyes finally opened all the way.

Neely Kate snorted. "*Tried?* They succeeded in the attempt. You just got away."

"Who was it?" Witt asked, concern filling his eyes.

"I'm not sure." I shook my head. "I mean, I know the name of one of the men, but I'm not sure why he did it, although I have strong suspicions."

"You're wanting me to find out?" he asked, sounding confused.

"No. Neely Kate and I are figuring out that part. We just need you around to help protect us."

He laughed again. "Neely Kate can take care of herself and you to boot. You don't need me."

"Neely Kate's not always with me," I said, feeling frustrated. He was right. Neely Kate could likely defend herself and me. But me . . . I'd gotten out of a few scrapes, but I sure as Pete didn't feel comfortable walking around alone, knowing that someone might try to snatch me at any moment. I needed to change that, but I wasn't going to figure it out over the next hour or so.

"So I would be *your* bodyguard?" He took a sip of coffee. "I thought that was Jed Carlisle's job."

"Jed works for Skeeter Malcolm," I said, figuring Witt wouldn't know about the recent change in his employment status. "And I'm trying to distance myself from him."

"Why? *Malcolm's* your real protection," Witt said. He turned serious and set his cup on the table. "After you and Neely Kate found that necklace, word's gotten out that *you're* the Lady in Black. You know that, right?"

"I'm quickly discovering it," I said.

"But there's been some confusion about how you sided with Reynolds. It's creating a . . . stir."

"What does that mean?"

He pushed out a breath and leaned closer. "It means people aren't sure which side you're really on."

"They think I'm on Buck Reynolds' side?"

"No. Some of them think you're neutral."

I cast a glance back to Neely Kate, but she was focused on turning the bacon.

"What I'm about to tell you is confidential," I said to Witt. "It can't leave this room."

He stuck out his hand toward me, pinky finger extended. "I pinky swear."

"Oh," Neely Kate said from behind me. "That's the ultimate Rivers swear. It's how you know he means it."

I wasn't above a pinky swear. It sure beat spitting in each other's hands and shaking.

I hooked my pinky finger with his. "Consider anything you hear from me or Neely Kate having to do with Lady, or Skeeter Malcolm, or anything to do with the crime world confidential."

He shook our hooked fingers. "Deal."

We dropped our hands, and I said, "The people who took Scooter tried to take me too."

"They got you," Neely Kate said again. "You just got away."

Witt held my gaze. "So you're lookin' at someone who has a grudge against Skeeter."

Witt seemed like a jovial, somewhat lazy kind of guy, but when I looked in his eyes, I could see it was a façade. He wanted people to underestimate him. I didn't need to read between the lines for him.

"We figured as much," I said.

"Not professional—although it might be that too—I'm talkin' personal. He wants to take Skeeter Malcolm out at the knees. He wants him to hurt. The logical person is Buck Reynolds or Kip Wagner. Maybe both. But you know that."

"Well, it's not Buck. He hired me to find Scooter." I felt like a traitor telling Witt when I still hadn't confirmed what I was up to with James or Jed, but he needed to know everything if he was going to help us. Besides, he'd just pinky sworn to keep my secrets.

Based on the look on Witt's face, I'd finally managed to catch him by surprise. "Maybe he's tryin' to throw Malcolm off."

"Buck Reynolds and his guys busted in and saved me from the kidnappers. The whole thing's suspicious, but I'm going to come out right now and tell you they didn't snatch Scooter. James—"

"*James?*"

Crap.

His eyes bugged out. "You call Skeeter Malcolm *James?* Does Buck Reynolds know that?"

"He does now."

He made a face and leaned back in his chair. "That's not good, Rose."

"Tell me about it."

"I'm confused. Are you and Malcolm a thing?"

"No," I said as firmly as I could muster. "We are not a thing. We became friends when I worked with him last winter."

The look in Witt's eyes suggested he wasn't convinced. "We need to do damage control. If you're really not with Malcolm, we have to get the word out fast, or you won't just be a target for whoever kidnapped you."

"Whose side are you on, Witt?"

He cocked his head. "Who says I'm on a side?"

"Everybody in the criminal world took a side last winter," I said. "Whose side did you take?"

"No one's. Sure, most of the guys from the shop turned on Skeeter last winter and pledged themselves to Gentry, but I made it clear that while I didn't have a beef with Malcolm, I wasn't loyal to him either." He shifted in his chair. "I don't want back in that world. I did my time. That was enough. But I still hear plenty of things. How can you be so sure Reynolds isn't behind all of this?"

Witt didn't know about my visions, so this could get tricky.

"Tell him," Neely Kate said, setting the pancakes and the bacon down on the table. I glanced up at her, and she nodded with a knowing smile. "He'll understand. Remember Granny?"

Alarm covered Witt's face. "What about Granny?"

"Nothin's wrong with Granny," she said, grabbing syrup from a cabinet. "But knowin' Granny will make you more receptive."

He looked on edge.

"Now, this is something else you can't tell anyone, Witt," I said. Up until a year ago, my gift had been a carefully hidden secret. My momma had convinced me that only an evil soul could see visions. I'd slowly let people in—Joe and Neely Kate and Mason and James and Jed—and they'd convinced me that my visions were nothing to be ashamed of. That they were useful, sometimes even lifesaving. Even so, I'd still kept them a secret. Now I couldn't help thinking they should stay that way. If I was straddling two worlds, the fewer people who knew about my ability to suss out the truth, the better.

Witt gave me an impatient look, but he nodded his agreement.

"I have visions of the future. Sometimes they're spontaneous. But sometimes I can force them. That's what I did for Skeeter Malcolm last winter—I interviewed people he suspected of bein' turncoats and looked for the truth."

His eyes lit up. "You've gotta be shittin' me."

Neely Kate sat down and grabbed a pancake off the plate.

"I got information for him, and in return, he helped me protect Mason from whoever was trying to kill him," I said, hoping to stave off his questions.

"Damn . . ." He shook his head, then stabbed two pancakes and transferred them to his plate. "And with everything goin' on last winter . . ."

"I saved his hide a few times," I said.

"No wonder he thinks you're valuable." If he'd dropped the theory that we were personally involved, all the better.

"I hadn't done anything for him since last February, but he got involved in the whole mess around Reynolds' necklace." I paused, then added, "I forced a vision of Buck Reynolds, which is how I know he's not the one who took Scooter."

He gave a short nod and picked up the syrup bottle. "How much does this bodyguard gig pay?"

"Not much, but more than nothing. A hundred dollars a day. I'll probably need you twenty-four seven until this is resolved. You'll stay here with us. Is that okay?"

"And you can work on my car," Neely Kate tossed in. "It's makin' that weird noise again."

Witt shot her a mock grimace before he turned his attention to me. "I can't legally carry a gun, you know."

"I know."

"So what good am I?"

"I have no doubt that if Neely Kate gets into trouble, you'd do anything to help her. I'd like to think you'll do the same for me." I stabbed a pancake and put it on my plate. "And maybe you can teach me more about defending myself."

He was silent for a moment. "You're neutral? You're really not tied to Malcolm?"

I cast a glance to Neely Kate, then said, "It's complicated."

"Oh boy . . ." Witt groaned. "Here we go."

"We've had ties to Skeeter in the past," Neely Kate said in a steady voice. "But we're free of them now."

"And how does Malcolm feel about that?" Witt asked, cutting off a small wedge of the pancakes.

Witt deserved honesty. At least as much as I could give him. "He agrees with the principle of distancing himself, and he tried it after the parley over the necklace." I hesitated. "He finds it difficult in practice. While I didn't tell him what Buck hired me to do, he guessed it involves his brother. He's smart enough to know he can't stop me, but he asked that I use Jed as a bodyguard. I refused."

"So we don't have to worry about Skeeter Malcolm getting mixed up in the middle of this?"

I made a face. "I think they'll leave me and Neely Kate to our own devices as long as they know we're well-protected. But seein' how Scooter's wrapped up in this, I suspect he'll be part of it any way you slice it. Do I plan on keeping him updated on what we find? No. I plan on having absolutely no contact with him at all."

Witt looked only half convinced.

"If you're worried about lookin' like you've aligned yourself with Skeeter Malcolm," I said, catching his gaze, "then I will do my utmost to make sure that doesn't happen. Can I guarantee it? Not any more than I can guarantee you won't look like you've aligned yourself with Buck Reynolds. I hope to look like an impartial party, which is why I need you and not Jed."

He still looked unsure, so I reached across the table. "Give me your hand."

A grin spread across his face. "I knew you couldn't resist the Rivers-boy charms."

I nearly snorted. Tall, good-looking, and charming, Witt was the exception to the typical Rivers-boy genes. "I'm gonna have a vision. Give me your hand."

His smile faded. "Why?"

"I'm gonna see if you're aligned with anyone when this is done."

His head jerked to face Neely Kate. "Can she do that?"

"She can try," she answered around a bite of pancakes. "She doesn't always see everything she asks for."

"She asks for it?"

Neely Kate rolled her eyes. "Just give her your hand."

He slowly reached across the table, and I put my hand over his, looping my fingers around the side. Closing my eyes, I focused on finding Scooter. My vision filled with a dark gray haze like before, something that alarmed me, especially in light of Squawker's new favorite phrase, but I changed the question. This time I asked if Witt would appear neutral when we were finished looking for Scooter.

The scene was dark, but it was nighttime. Sheriff cars with flashing lights were parked outside a gas station. I could see Neely Kate standing next to Witt's car, and she was wringing her hands with a worried look on her face.

"She told you that you'd stay neutral," she said. "And she delivered."

"But what did she do to make that happen?"

I was back in the kitchen and I blurted out, "She said you'd stay neutral."

Was *she* me? And what was I going to do to make *that happen*?

CHAPTER 19

Both Neely Kate and Witt obviously wanted to know about my vision, so I told them as much as I could. In truth, I was worried—she'd seemed out of sorts in the vision, and the situation had clearly involved the sheriff. I couldn't help worrying that I kept seeing the same murky gray haze every time I asked anything about finding Scooter.

We started to clean up the kitchen, and my phone vibrated with a text from Buck's number.

I HAVE INFO. COME SEE ME.

I glanced over at Witt. "Buck Reynolds says he has some info and wants me to meet with him. If you don't want to do this, I understand."

He was quiet for a moment. "So if I'm stayin' here with you two, does that mean I'm getting breakfasts like that every day?"

Neely Kate threw a dish towel at him. "You're a mooch, Witt Rivers!"

"I'm a Rivers, ain't I?" He grinned and tossed the towel back at her. "And you better wrap up the cleanin' if we're goin' to meet Reynolds."

"Where are we meetin' him?" Neely Kate asked.

"I don't know," I said.

WHEN AND WHERE?

He texted back seconds later, and I read his response out loud.

THE FERTILIZER PLANT. THIRTY MINUTES.

"Okay," Neely Kate said, putting a clean dish in the cabinet. "I bet Buck Reynolds is gonna be excited to see me."

"I'm not sure 'excited' is the word I'd use," I said.

"Do I want to know what that's about?" Witt asked.

I laughed. "Let's just say Buck Reynolds doesn't want Neely Kate anywhere near any more of his jewels."

I locked an upset Muffy in the house, and as I walked down the porch steps, I took a long look at Witt's car. It didn't look much newer than Neely Kate's car, and it was a clunker. "How well does your car run?"

"You're seriously asking a mechanic that question?" he asked in disbelief.

I gave him a pointed look. "Well?"

He shrugged. "It's decent."

"Then we're takin' your car. My truck's too conspicuous."

He grinned. "Well, all right. I guess I'm on the clock."

Witt drove, Neely Kate took shotgun, and I sat in the back. My lack of sleep caught up to me despite my nerves over meeting Buck, and I found myself drifting off. I woke up when we were about five minutes away, roused by a combination of Neely Kate calling my name and the throbbing in my leg. I'd transferred the important items from my purse to my backpack, including a bottle of ibuprofen. I fished it out and wished I'd thought to bring a bottle of water too.

"I thought maybe we should come up with some sort of plan," Neely Kate said. "You still have a headache? Have you had too many visions in a row?"

That sometimes happened when I first started forcing one on top of the other, and sometimes after particularly intense visions. "No, I'm fine." I popped the pill in my mouth and swallowed it dry, praying it didn't get stuck on the way down. "Neely Kate, you can stay in the car if you want."

Neely Kate snorted. "You can't be serious."

I sighed. "It was worth a shot."

"You really want to do this without me?" I could hear the hurt in her voice.

I reached over the seat and put my hand on her shoulder. "Of course not. If I did, you wouldn't be with me right now, but we haven't talked about what happens if we *don't* find Scooter. There's bound to be a penalty. It doesn't make sense for all three of us to pay it. So I'll go in and be the front person, and then I'll come out and tell you what he said."

Neely Kate gave me a hard stare. "We're all going. It's settled."

I didn't have much time to give it more thought because Witt was already driving into the plant's parking lot. I tried not to think about meeting James here the night before . . . and everything else that came afterward. My skin flushed at the memory of going home with him, and I squelched the sudden urge to call or text him. He was off-limits, and I'd do well to remember that.

Buck's car was already there, along with a couple of other cars, which meant we were outnumbered.

"Neely Kate," I said. "Do you have your gun?"

"Yeah, in my purse."

"Got anywhere to hide it on you?"

She jerked her head around to face me.

"We're playin' with the big boys, and we don't have Jed and Merv here to protect us. We need to be ready because I'm *not* getting snatched up again."

She gave one slow nod and pulled her gun out of her purse, then stuffed it down the back of her capris and under her blousy shirt.

"Witt," I said. "Your job is to observe everything. I'm gonna be focused on Buck, so you and Neely Kate need to pay attention to everything else. If either of you thinks something's off, then use a code word to clue me in that it's time to leave."

"So the only one goin' into this meeting wearing a gun is NK?" Witt asked.

"Nope." I said. "I'm wearing mine under my dress."

"I still need a gun," he said with a frown.

"Not today you don't," I said. "The code word is bananas." I reached for the door handle—we were certainly being watched, and the longer we took, the more suspicious we'd look. "Let's go."

I was out of the car first, but Neely Kate got out and stepped in front of me, wearing her Lady in Black sidekick face—the one that said, *Mess with me, and I'm not responsible for the consequences.* Witt took the rear, following close, and I was in full-on Lady mode, surprised I could so easily make the transformation without the hat and the dress.

I quickly scanned the roofs of the buildings around us and realized Buck had at least two men up there with rifles. Good to know if we needed to make a hasty retreat.

We entered the semi-dark office and found Buck sitting on a beat-up metal desk in the small reception area—the only piece of furniture in the space—surrounded by three of his men, including Tim Dermot and the other guy from the night before. Buck was lounging with his arm braced to the side, but the posture looked forced, and I suspected the sweat on his forehead wasn't completely due to the rising summer heat.

"Lady," he said, sitting up as we entered. "I see you brought your friend. And a new bodyguard."

"Lone wolves don't survive in this world," I said in a curt tone. "And I told you I'm neutral, hence the new guy. So, what do you have for me?"

He kept his gaze on Witt behind me. "Not so fast. I wanna know who your new bodyguard is."

"That's neither here nor there," I said, putting my left leg in front of me. It made me look prepared to take on anything, but it would also make it easier for me to reach my gun if the situation called for it. "He's not affiliated with anyone, which makes him mine. Now what do you have?"

"He's a Rivers." The speaker was the man I hadn't seen before. "He used to work for Crocker before Lady took him out. Did some time for armed robbery. He's not with anyone."

Buck eyed him up and down. "That's not true, now is it? You're aligning yourself with the Lady in Black."

Crap. Why hadn't I seen it that way? Had Witt?

I felt the tension radiating off Witt, who stood behind me and to my left. "I'd rather align myself with someone who's trying to see to the betterment of this county than with someone who would sooner burn it down."

Buck stiffened. "Is that how you see it, boy? That I'm burnin' it all down?"

"Enough, Mr. Reynolds," I said in a firm voice.

My tone carried a reprimand, and he shifted his angry eyes to meet mine.

"Let me make this clear," I said, my words clipped. "I thought we'd had this lesson last night, but you seem to be a slow learner, so let me spell it out *one more time*: If I do a consultation job for you, you will treat me with respect. You will treat my associates with respect. If you are incapable of that, then we are walking out that door right now."

Anger blazed in his eyes, and he leaned forward, his muscles tightly wound as though he were a wildcat ready to pounce. "I don't know who you think you are—"

He was acting tougher today, but he'd added to his audience, which meant he couldn't afford to look weak. Well, neither could I. And while I wanted whatever information he had, I wasn't going to let it be at the expense of my reputation.

"I think we're done here," I said, then started to turn around to leave. There was a look of confusion in Witt's eyes, but my focus was on the movement I heard behind me. In one fell swoop,

I lifted my dress with my left hand, grabbed the gun out of my holster with my right hand, and spun back around, pointing it at Buck's chest. He was now standing directly behind me, and it was obvious he'd planned on physically dragging me back. The look of surprise on his face sent a rush of power through my veins.

Power plays. This world was full of prancing peacocks, but dammit, I could preen with the best of them.

"That's strike two, Mr. Reynolds," I said in a deadly cold voice. "One more and you're on my blacklist."

His men all had guns pointed at me, while Neely Kate had hers pointed at Dermot. Then I realized Witt had a weapon out too, pointed at Buck.

He'd had one all along. What had I done?

Buck looked like he wanted to rip my head off. "Looks like we're at a stalemate, Lady."

I cocked an eyebrow, forcing myself to take slow, steady breaths even though my heart was racing. I couldn't afford to look scared. "Are we? I have no qualms about pullin' this trigger and finishin' it. Can you say the same?"

He'd added more sweat to his forehead, and the certainty in his eyes wavered. I could let this man try to save face, but I was sick to death of men thinking they could get one up on me. Sure, I was playing in a man's world here, and James may have dragged me into it, but I was good at sniffing out the truth, and Buck Reynolds obviously thought so too since he had come to *me*.

I wasn't going to back down.

"Before we go one step further, let's make this *perfectly* clear," I said in a firm voice. "You *will* treat me and my associates with respect. I have no reason to help you, and I am *more* than willin' to walk away from you entirely. What happens next is completely up to you, Mr. Reynolds."

He glared at me for several more seconds, then cursed under his breath and said, "Put away your guns."

They were slow to respond, but that wasn't too surprising—

Neely Kate and Witt still had their guns trained on Dermot and Buck. Then I realized they were waiting on *me*. I lowered my own gun, keeping it at my side, and Neely Kate and Witt followed suit.

I lifted my chin, pushing past my light-headedness now that the danger had slightly passed. "You told me you have information. That's why we're here. Start talkin'."

"We found out that Elijah Landry has been livin' in Henryetta."

That wasn't all that surprising since he was clearly involved in local criminal politics. "How long?"

"A couple months."

"What's he been doin' here?"

"We haven't found out much. No one knows him, but he's been workin' at Maynard's junkyard, laying low. It recently changed owners."

"How recently?" I asked.

"A few months ago."

"And who's the owner?"

"A corporation in Louisiana. Sandusky Enterprises."

"And who owns that?"

"We can't tell. It's an obvious dummy corporation, and they don't own anything else."

I'd look into that later. "What about the other guy?"

"He didn't have any identification."

I gave him a look of contempt. "You expect me to believe that? I find that coincidental given you searched his pockets *after* I left." When he didn't answer, I said, "If you want me to find Scooter and clear your name, I need every bit of information you have. Otherwise, this is pointless."

He didn't answer.

"Where was I taken last night, and who owns it?"

"Fenway Manufacturing. It went bankrupt a couple of years ago and filed for bankruptcy. It's owned by the bank."

"Fenway Manufacturing. Any connection to Henryetta or Fenton County?"

"None that we know about. They probably picked it because it's been vacant for so long and it's out in the middle of nowhere."

We'd look into that too. "Have you heard anything about a parrot?"

"What?"

"Heard of anyone looking for one or wanting to buy one on the black market?"

Disgust washed over his face. "You using me for your own private purposes? We worked out your payment . . . unless this is it." He lifted his eyebrows.

I gave him a long hard stare. "The deal's off. Let's go."

I turned around and started to walk out, Witt falling in line in front of me and Neely Kate behind. Both of them were still holding their guns at their sides. Buck didn't holler after me, so I kept going.

We'd all opened our car doors by the time Buck appeared in the doorway. "You sure are a touchy bitch."

"And *that* disrespectful remark, Mr. Reynolds," I said, slowly turning to face him, "is strike three." I took a step toward him. "You really are a shortsighted man, aren't you? There's a reason Skeeter Malcolm is running this county, and it has everything to do with his ability to use the brains God gave him."

His face turned red. "I knew you were workin' for him."

"No, Mr. Reynolds, I still stand by my original statement that I'm workin' for the good of the county. It's my belief that Skeeter Malcolm is the better leader."

"I could kill you."

"You could," I conceded dryly. "But it would only be further proof that I'm right."

His chest rose and fell in heavy pants, and he looked like he couldn't decide what to do.

I took a step closer, my gun still at my side. "When I ask a question, it's for a reason, Mr. Reynolds. If you knew where I was going with my questions about the parrot, then you wouldn't need me, would you? Turns out I have information you don't."

I took another step closer. "*You* asked for *me*," I said slowly. "Think about *that* when Skeeter Malcolm finally comes callin' to string you up for killin' his brother."

I turned around again to walk back to the car.

"I didn't do it!" Buck shouted after me. "You know that!"

"No longer my concern."

"You'd let the kidnappers go free?"

"You made sure that didn't happen," I said, although I wasn't as convinced as everyone else seemed to be that they'd killed the two guys to keep them quiet. "As far as I know, there's no more threat and we can presume Scooter's dead." It killed me to say it so cavalierly, but I was beginning to suspect it was true. Especially if Squawker had heard someone talk about cleaning up Scooter's blood.

"There's evidence of a third guy."

I stopped again. I'd suspected as much, but it still pissed me off that he was holding out on me. "And you're just now tellin' me that?" I asked in disbelief. "Seriously?"

"We were gonna see if you could figure it out."

"Did it ever occur to you that time was of the essence?" I asked. "That Skeeter Malcolm is close to gathering his troops and coming for you?"

The look on his face suggested he hadn't. He really was a stupid man, and his stupidity would probably help him meet his maker sooner rather than later, but I wasn't going to let him destroy the county on his way down.

"I'm feelin' generous," I said. "You have two minutes to tell me everything."

"The second guy didn't have ID," Tim Dermot said, pushing past Buck and standing in front of him. "But he had a burner phone in his pocket with one programmed number. We called it and got a liquor store. Henryetta Package Store. They asked if it was Bud."

"Bud?"

"Yeah, the guy said he'd been waiting for Bud's call. We hung up."

I cast a quick glance at Neely Kate before shifting my gaze back to Dermot. "How long ago?"

"A half hour?"

"Any of your men been out there?"

"Not yet."

"Don't send anyone. We'll take care of it."

"So you're still gonna look for Scooter?"

I glanced from Dermot to Buck, then back again. This man had sense—the very opposite of his boss. "I'm answering to you, Dermot."

Buck started to protest, but Dermot elbowed him hard in the stomach, without so much as a glance at his boss. "Done," he said. "You were askin' about a parrot?"

"We think the missing parrot we were looking for might have seen something to do with Scooter's disappearance."

"What the hell?" Buck scoffed. "My dog might have seen me knock Johnny Bueller's lights out, but he's not tellin' anyone."

Dermot looked like he wanted to punch his associate. "Parrots talk, Buck." Then he shook his head. "We haven't heard anything about a parrot. Are you tryin' to find him so he'll tell you what he heard?"

"We've already found him," Neely Kate said. "He won't stop talking about Scooter going bye-bye, and we're tryin' to figure out what he witnessed and where."

Dermot shifted his gaze to my best friend, and his eyes widened slightly. It was like he was noticing her for the first time —and very much liking what he saw. "You don't say."

"We think someone tried to steal him from his owner and he

escaped in the process," I said. "We're hoping his owner can shed some light on the situation. Do you know anything else?"

"No, we're trying to find out more about Landry. The car was registered in his name, but that's as far as we got. If we find out anything else, I'll let you know."

I nodded, then ducked into the car, and Neely Kate and Witt followed.

Witt didn't waste any time leaving the property, and he let out a loud whoop as soon as he turned onto the main road. "What the hell just happened back there?"

"That was Rose in action," Neely Kate said. "I told you she was good."

He glanced over his shoulder at me. "You realize what you did back there, right?"

"Stood up to Buck Reynolds? The man's dumber than a door-nail. The fool was so anxious to one-up me last night, he shot me in the leg. And here he was today trying to do it again."

"Shot you?" Neely Kate asked, her voice going up an octave.

"It was barely a scratch," I said in dismissal.

"I wasn't talkin' about you standin' up to him," Witt said. "Sure, that too, but I'm talking about the power shift that just happened."

"What are you talkin' about?"

"Dermot just usurped Buck Reynolds."

"*What?* No . . ."

"Yeah. I'm tellin' you, Dermot's in charge. Otherwise, Reynolds' men would have stopped him. You did that."

CHAPTER 20

J was still reeling from Witt's announcement when he asked, "What now?"

"The Henryetta Package Store, don't you think?" I asked Neely Kate. "One of us is gonna have to go undercover. Maybe we should both do it."

She shook her head. "I'll pretend to be Bud's girlfriend looking for him."

"You think that will work? It's dangerous."

She rolled her eyes. "Please."

Nevertheless, I couldn't help worrying.

I'd never been there before, but Witt knew where it was. He parked in the laundromat parking lot next door. "I've been in there a time or two," he said. "I think it's best if I stay out of sight."

Neely Kate was out of the car before I could give her any last-minute instructions.

Witt chuckled as we watched her strut across the parking lot. "That's Neely Kate. Headstrong."

"Has she always been like that?" I asked, realizing I had access to a treasure trove of insights on my best friend.

"Mostly. When Jenny Lynn dropped her off when she was

twelve, she was scared but bold, determined to take life by the horns. She fit in better than most people expected. I'm two years older than her, so I took her under my wing, but she didn't need me for long. She found her way, and most everyone loved her in school. Then I got in trouble after graduation and ended up in lockup for a few years. When I came home, she'd graduated and taken off for Oklahoma. Granny was upset because she'd stopped hearin' from NK."

"She'd stopped callin'?"

"Yeah. Abrupt. Granny said she knew things weren't as rosy as Neely Kate let on. She'd started talkin' to Granny about comin' home, and then she practically vanished."

My gaze followed Neely Kate into the store, and my stomach twisted with worry. "What happened to her there, Witt?"

"I don't know. I was fixin' to find her and bring her home when she showed up lookin' like the walkin' dead."

"What? What does that mean? She was hurt?"

"She had some bruises for certain, makin' it obvious she'd been through somethin', but it was more than that. She went straight to her room and barely left, just slept and cried and wouldn't talk to anyone."

My heart broke. "What happened to her there?" I asked again.

"Damned if I know. She never told a soul, but it was obvious someone had hurt her bad and she needed to get control back. Alan Jackson and I made sure our little cousin could kick the ass of any man who tried to hurt her again."

"And you never figured out what happened?" I asked, still watching the door.

"No. I told her I was there to listen if she needed to talk. Instead, she bottled it all up, and before I knew it, she was back to her normal self . . . only something was different in her eyes. Something was off."

"She went to Oklahoma last week," I said quietly.

Witt sat up straighter. "What?"

I sighed. "She just took off and left me a note."

"What for?"

"To face her past. She came back looking better, but . . ."

"She's still broken."

"Yeah."

"That asshole husband of hers . . ." He shook his head. "I had no idea he was gonna hurt her, Rose. Otherwise, I would have literally kicked his ass before she walked down the aisle."

"I know." I grinned. "Neely Kate's lucky to have you."

"You can be our honorary cousin," Witt said. "We'll stand up for you too."

"You already did," I said, looking him in the eye. "What were you doin' with a gun back there?"

"Do you know how it would have looked if I hadn't had one? No one would have taken me seriously. But now that we've established you aren't takin' shit, I'm hopin' we won't have to pull 'em out again."

Witt had a point. "If we ever get in a situation where you have a gun and the police are comin', you give it to me. I'll deal with it."

"Rose . . ."

"I'm serious, Witt."

"I know you are. Thanks."

Neely Kate walked out of the liquor store, and I took it as a good sign that she wasn't being chased. She climbed into the front passenger seat and shook her head. "There's good news and there's bad news."

"What happened?" I asked.

"There was only one guy working in the shop, and when I told him I wanted to talk to the guy who'd been there an hour ago, he told me he wasn't sellin' whatever I'd been smokin'. Said he was the only one who'd been there all morning and he didn't remember me."

"Is that the bad news or good news?"

"Neither. Then I told him I was Bud's girlfriend, and I was

lookin' for him. He said he was too, and he'd appreciate it if I had Bud call him pronto.'"

I cringed. "Unless Bud becomes a ghost, that's not likely to happen."

"I asked him for his name and number if I needed to give him an update about Bud, and he said the number for the liquor store's in the phone book . . . as if people used those anymore."

"So, he was an old fart?" Witt asked.

"I guess," Neely Kate said. "His name tag said Gene, but I don't know if that's his real name. But he mentioned something about Bud workin' at the junkyard on the side, so now we know two of them worked there. Maybe that's where they met."

"Okay, short of following Gene around, there's nothin' more to do here," I said. "Let's head back to the office and see what we can find out about Elijah Landry and Sandusky Enterprises."

⁓

AN HOUR LATER, we didn't know much more. Witt and I had taken on the task of looking up Elijah Landry, and we hadn't found anything interesting. Apparently he'd lived in Shreveport all his thirty-six years, and there was no record of the time he'd spent in Henryetta.

Witt was sitting at Bruce Wayne's desk searching the *Henryetta Gazette* when he shouted, "Hot damn!"

"What?" Neely Kate and I asked simultaneously.

"There's an Elijah Landry in the paper about fifteen years ago. He attended his grandparents' golden wedding anniversary at the Henryetta Baptist Church." He looked up and grinned. "It's him—says he's from Shreveport."

I hopped up and rushed over to his computer. "Is there a photo?"

"A few, and a long list of the relatives who attended. Half are from Louisiana, and the rest are from Arkansas."

"Anyone you recognize from Fenton County?" I asked.

"A Mr. and Mrs. Timothy Beagle and Mr. and Mrs. Elwood Landry."

"You've got to be kiddin' me," Neely Kate said. "Those women don't get first names?"

"Now Neely Kate," Witt groaned, giving me a conspiratorial wink, "what do those women need names for when their husbands' names work perfectly well?"

She shot him a glare.

He laughed. "Okay. Further down it says that Mrs. Pam Beagle and Mrs. Priscilla Landry are the daughters of Seymour and Mary Ellen Constant, the happy couple who didn't kill each other after livin' together for fifty years. Priscilla's son Mike was in attendance. Pam had two sons, but only her son Paul was there. Merlin was in the state pen."

That caught my attention. "The state penitentiary? We should look into that. Let me see the photo." I leaned over Witt's shoulder and studied the grainy photos—there were several. One of the happy couple. One large group photo, and one with the couple, their two daughters and sons-in-law, and their grandsons—two young men in their twenties by the look of them. And although the photo was fifteen years old, I had no trouble recognizing Elijah Landry. "That's him."

We were all silent for a moment.

"So Elijah had family here. Does it give their address?" I asked.

"No," Neely Kate said, "but I'll call my friend in the property tax department, see if she can find out where they lived."

I nodded. "Good idea. Witt, print off that photo so we can show it around."

"On it."

"You used to go to Henryetta Baptist Church, Rose," Neely Kate said. "Do you remember Seymour and Mary Ellen Constant?"

"No, but I know someone who will." I gave her a look. "Miss Mildred."

"We have to go back there anyway," Neely Kate said with a slight shrug. "We can ask her then."

"Yippee," I said sarcastically.

Neely Kate's phone buzzed and she answered, saying, "Sparkle Investigations."

There it was again. *"Neely Kate."*

She ignored me. "Do you want to come by our office?" she asked. After a pause, she said, "Sure, we can do lunch. How about Merilee's on the square? In about fifteen minutes? . . . Okay. See you then." She hung up and swiveled her office chair to face us. "That was Jeanne. She just got off and wants us to feed her lunch."

"We just had breakfast about an hour ago," I said.

"I could eat," Witt said.

"I guess that's a small price to pay for answers. But *once again,* we need to talk about the name of our nonexistent company."

Neely Kate twisted her mouth to the side. "It's not set in stone."

"That's good because you'd be chiselin' it out."

Witt looked like he was choking back laughter as he handed me the printed photo. It had been zoomed out to fill the page and was kind of grainy, but it was clear enough to show around.

Neely Kate frowned. "Y'all may have hit pay dirt with Elijah Landry, but the only thing I found out about Sandusky Enterprises is that they were incorporated a year ago and bought Maynard's junkyard back in March."

"We'll figure it out," I said, folding the photo over once and stuffing it into my backpack. "In the meantime, why don't we head over to Merilee's and make sure we get a table? You know they can get pretty crowded around noon."

Witt shot out of his chair. "You don't have to tell me twice."

As we walked across the square—Witt already nearly to the restaurant—Neely Kate called her friend in the records department and asked for her help. When she hung up, she said, "June's really busy, but she says she hopes to get something to us later this afternoon."

"Why don't we try Mr. Whipple one more time?"

She nodded. "Good idea." But once again the phone rang and there was no answer. I was starting to get worried. "Maybe we should go over and check on him after lunch."

Neely Kate looked worried too.

It was a good thing we got there early because the place was already packed. We'd just been seated at a table when Jeanne showed up, still wearing her Walmart vest. She took one look at Witt and took a step backward. "What's he doin' here?"

"This is Neely Kate's cousin, Witt, and he's helpin' us look for Scooter," I said. "Have a seat. You must be starving after workin' all morning."

"Well . . ." She glanced at Witt again.

"We're payin'," I said.

When she still hesitated, Witt stood. "I'm not feelin' very hungry. I think I'll go sit outside." He gave us a wave and headed out the front door.

Jeanne watched him leave, then took his seat even though there was an open chair across from Neely Kate. She grabbed the laminated menu in the middle of the table, flagged the waitress down, and ordered a club sandwich and fries, plus a cheeseburger to go.

Neely Kate and I ordered our own lunches and a to-go sandwich for Witt. As the waitress walked away, Neely Kate folded her hands on the table and looked at Jeanne dead-on. "We'd like to ask you some questions about Scooter."

"That's why I'm here, ain't it?" The hostility in her voice surprised me, and Neely Kate's flinch told me she noticed it too.

Neely Kate took a moment, then asked, "When did you see him taken?"

"Wednesday afternoon behind Walmart. Just like I told ya."

I took a breath and turned my upper body to face her. "Jeanne, what's goin' on?"

"Whaddaya mean?"

"I mean, this morning you wanted us to help you find Scooter, now you don't. What happened?" Then it hit me— Muffy had chased someone out of Walmart. What if that someone had seen Jeanne talking to us? What if they'd scared her off?

"I don't know what you're talkin' about," she said, but her eyes darted to the side.

I lowered my voice. "Jeanne. Someone was there when we were talkin' to you this mornin'. My dog chased him away, but he came back, didn't he?"

Tears filled her eyes.

Neely Kate reached out and snagged Jeanne's frail fingers in her hand. "We can help you, Jeanne."

"I don't care about me. I only care about Scooter." Her voice broke and a tear tracked down her cheek.

"We care about Scooter too," Neely Kate said. "Who came to talk to you? And what did he threaten?"

Jeanne wiped a tear from her cheek with the back of her hand. "He was a big guy. Looked to be in his thirties. He told me if I told y'all anything, he'd kill Scooter."

I blinked. "Was it someone you know?"

She shook her head. "No, but I've seen him before." She paused. "He was one of the guys who took Scooter."

"There were two of them?" I asked, then felt stupid. Of course there were. How could one guy kidnap a grown man? They'd used two men to kidnap me. But why was this the first time we were hearing of it?

"Did you tell Skeeter Malcolm about both guys?"

She nodded. "His henchman interviewed me first. Then I talked to Skeeter, but he got a phone call and they sent me on my way." She licked her lips. "The guy today said he knew I'd talked to Skeeter's guys. He was pissed . . . and he said I was lucky they hadn't killed Scooter yet."

Suddenly, I knew why she'd waited for nearly a week to tell Skeeter what she knew. The kidnappers had already issued a warning.

Neely Kate was still holding her hand, so I grabbed the other one and held tight. "We're gonna help you, Jeanne, but you have to tell us everything."

Panic filled her eyes. "You can't tell Scooter's brother. You have to swear." I cast a glance at Neely Kate, and Jeanne added, "Or any of his men. They'll kill Scooter if you do." Her breath came in rapid pants. "Swear to me you won't tell them."

Well, crap on a cracker. But we had to know what she could tell us, what she wouldn't tell James and the others. "Okay," I said. "I swear."

Neely Kate nodded. "Your secret is safe with us."

Jeanne wiped another tear and lowered her voice. "Scooter was out of sorts for a few days before they . . . took him. He thought someone was watchin' him. Sometimes his brother had him watched—" Her eyes widened. "Not because he was after him. More like they were bodyguards, keepin' an eye on him to make sure he was safe. Sometimes his brother just sent someone and didn't tell him."

That didn't surprise me. James had done the same with me.

"But Scooter said this time was different. He started insistin' on driving a different way home, and he was paranoid about lockin' the doors. He thought maybe he'd pissed off one of the guys who bought pot from him, though he said they all seemed happy." She paused and licked her upper lip. "When I finished my shift on Wednesday, I went back to see Scooter. We were ridin' together, and he had to work a half hour longer than me. So I was hangin' out with him in the back while he was movin' bags of potting soil." She blushed. "I like watchin' him move heavy things like that."

Neely Kate squeezed her hand. "Who doesn't love watchin' their man be all manly?"

Jeanne nodded and another tear rolled down her cheek. She pulled both her hands free and swiped it away. "It was just me and him, which was unusual. There was usually someone else with him. And I wasn't supposed to be there, so I was tucked in behind piles of bagged mulch. They probably thought he was alone." She wiped a tear. "A four-door car pulled up, and at first Scooter thought they were picking up some mulch or potting soil."

"Was the car a dark sedan?" I asked.

She looked surprised. "Yeah."

"I bet it's the same car they used to snatch me."

She blinked and seemed to be more interested.

"I told you—they took me and I got away."

Hope filled her eyes and she grabbed my arm. "Did you see Scooter?"

I shook my head. "No. I didn't, and I'm sure he wasn't there. Three other men came and saved me. They killed the guys who'd snatched me, so we couldn't ask them questions, but there was no sign of Scooter."

But was that right? What if he'd been there and I just hadn't known it? It still bugged me that Reynolds' guys had killed Elijah Landry and Bud. But they'd saved my life. It felt ungrateful to judge.

Jeanne wiped away more tears. Our food came, and she looked embarrassed when the waitress also handed her and Neely Kate to-go bags. "I shouldn't have ordered that. But Scooter wasn't here to cash his paycheck and money's tight . . ."

"Don't you worry about it," Neely Kate said in a cheerful voice. "Our treat."

I let Jeanne take a bite of her sandwich before I said, "What happened after the guys pulled up in the car?"

"Both of them got out and grabbed Scooter by the arms. They

started to drag him to the back of the car, but Scooter was having none of it. He tried to break loose, then yelled, 'Run, Jeanne!' That caught the guys' attention. The bigger one—the one who came to see me this morning—whacked Scooter in the back of the head, and I screamed. Scooter slumped to the ground, and the big guy lunged for me and put a hand over my mouth to stop my screaming. The other guy wanted to take me too—he said there weren't supposed to be any witnesses—but the big guy insisted his brother had only told him to take Scooter. He said they could use me to their advantage. Then he told me not to tell anyone or Scooter was a dead man." Tears filled her eyes. "They dumped him in the back of the trunk and took off."

"What made you decide to tell Skeeter?" Neely Kate asked.

"They came to get me, and when I saw how powerful they were, I thought maybe they could save him."

"And you have no idea who the men were?" I asked. "Had you ever seen them before?"

"No."

I pulled the folded photo of Elijah Landry out of my backpack. "Do you recognize either of these guys?" I asked, pointing to the two young men in the picture.

She sat stock-still, and I was sure she was going to say yes—so when she shook her head, my heart sank. Were we dealing with two different sets of kidnappers after all?

"I don't recognize one of them," she said. "I recognize both."

CHAPTER 21

∽

"*Y*ou're certain?" Neely Kate asked.

She nodded.

"Was this the guy you saw this morning?" I asked, pointing to Paul Beagle.

She nodded.

I turned to Neely Kate. This was huge. "We need to look for Paul Beagle." I glanced out the window and saw Witt sitting on a bench across the street, pretending to be ogling a young woman as she walked by. Or at least I told myself he was pretending. "I'm gonna take Witt his lunch and tell him about this new lead."

I turned my gaze to Jeanne, making sure she was comfortable with that.

"Do you really think you can find Scooter?" she asked, looking hopeful.

"We're one step closer thanks to you." I grabbed Witt's bag and stepped out into the sunshine, sweat already beading on my forehead. I scanned the street before crossing it and caught a glimpse of Jed in the distance. If Witt saw him, he was going to be pissed. I pulled out my phone and sent Jed a message.

If you're gonna follow us, you can't let Witt see you. We promised him we're working independent of James.

He read my text, then pocketed his phone.

Butthead.

I headed across the street and sat next to Witt on the shaded bench. "We got you something," I said, handing him the bag. "You found a spot with a good breeze."

He opened the bag and pulled out his sandwich, then took a bite. "Good place to observe things too," he said through a mouthful of food. "I can see you girls if you leave Merilee's. If I turn a bit, I can see your office to the side. And if I turn the other way, I can see Jed Carlisle bidin' his time until you girls leave." He took another bite, as nonchalant as he pleased.

How did I respond to that?

He chewed, watching me and waiting for a response. Finally, I said, "It's not exactly what you think."

"And how's that?" he asked good-naturedly and took another bite.

"I don't think he's here on Skeeter's behalf."

"Why else would he be here?"

"I suspect it's more personal in nature."

He lowered his hand to his lap and narrowed his eyes. "Personal how?"

"I'm not at liberty to say."

"Then I may not be at liberty to help you." I would have expected anger behind those words, but I heard resignation instead. "Look, you're just foolin' yourself if you think you can work independently of Skeeter Malcolm. No one's ever gonna trust you, and even if you could, you'd be a sittin' duck."

I didn't say anything. How would I answer? I was pretty sure he was right.

"There's no denying you pulled off a nifty trick with Buck and Dermot, but you probably gained a new enemy too. It's a rough world, Lady. I suspect Malcolm's done a good job of shieldin' you from a lot of the ugliness, but it's there, bobbin' below the surface, just waitin' for the right moment to snatch you and drag you under."

"You think I'll end up dead if I continue this?"

He sat up straighter. "I like you, Rose. A lot. You've made Neely Kate's life so much better. She's never had a friend like you —someone good—but even if you don't end up dead, you'll lose your goodness. Once you wallow in pig shit, it's hard to lose the stench."

I nodded and folded my hands in my lap. I could see the truth in his words. It wasn't so different from what James had told me. "But I can make a difference, Witt. I have the power to help people."

"Did you ever think that the people you're tryin' to help might not deserve it?"

He shoved the last half of his sandwich into his mouth, probably to signal he was ready to end the discussion. Too bad I wasn't done.

"I'm committed to findin' Scooter," I said.

"And I'll help you with that, because you're right—if Scooter Malcolm turns up dead with no clear-cut answer as to who did it, this county will become a war zone. But after that, I'm done, and I'm gonna do my best to convince Neely Kate to leave it behind too. And if that means distancing herself from you, so be it."

I gasped.

"It's not personal, Rose, as stupid as that sounds. But NK's been through way too much. I just stood back and let it happen in the past, but this time I'm steppin' up."

I nodded. "I understand." And I did. "She's lucky to have you."

"Rose, I want you to—"

I held up my hand and cut him off. "Let's just stick to the task at hand, okay?"

He looked a little hurt by that, but he'd hurt me too. "I showed

Jeanne the photo, and she recognized Elijah Landry *and* Paul Beagle. We have a connection."

His eyes widened.

"We're fine in the café, and as you pointed out, someone else is watchin' us. So why don't you head back to the office and look him up? With Neely Kate's friend looking for addresses for their parents and grandparents, and you looking for something on Paul, we'll have plenty to go on."

"You want to head out to the junkyard where Landry worked?"

I shook my head. "Not yet. It seems like we should check it out, but I feel like we need to be armed with more information first."

He nodded and stood. "Thanks for lunch."

"A deal's a deal."

"Rose," he said in a pleading voice.

I stood and lifted my gaze to his. "You're right. I'm bein' careless with my best friend's life."

"I know you would never intentionally hurt her."

But I could hurt her all the same. Was that what my vision of Witt was about? Would the situation get too risky for me to continue to involve Neely Kate?

I went back into the diner and found the waitress handing Neely Kate the bill. I snagged it as I sat down, pulled my wallet out of my purse, and laid some cash on the table.

"Before you go," I said softly to Jeanne, "I'd like to say a prayer for you. Would you mind?" It felt like sacrilege, but I was using the gift the good Lord had given me, and I was praying that we'd find Scooter safe and sound, so surely He wouldn't smite me.

Neely Kate shifted in her seat next to me.

"Yeah . . ." Jeanne said, sounding surprised. "Sure."

I grabbed her hand and closed my eyes. How many visions could I get away with? There was only one way to find out . . .

"It's a silent prayer," Neely Kate said, explaining my silence.

I focused and asked, *Does Jeanne see Scooter?* I was met with a familiar gray fog. I switched the question to *Will Jeanne see Paul again?*

This vision burst forth. I was in Jeanne's head, staring at a gun pointed at my chest. I was sobbing out, "I didn't mean to tell them, I swear." The gun went off and my chest burned as I fell to the ground, something sharp poking me in the side. I struggled to breathe, my chest rising to suck in air, but pain radiated through my chest. I heard gurgling blood, and panic flooded me when I realized I was dying.

Paul's face leaned over me, wearing a crocodile smile. "I gave you fair warning."

"Finish her," another man said.

Paul aimed his gun at my head, and I heard the explosion before everything went dark and I was shoved into the icy darkness of death.

The vision ended, and the abrupt change from the horrific scene to the noisy, chaotic diner was beyond jarring.

"He gave you fair warnin'," I said in a robotic voice. Then the icy coldness I often felt when I had a vision of someone's death set in.

"Amen," Neely Kate said in a cheerful tone.

"Thanks for lunch," Jeanne said, starting to stand. "Could you let me know if you hear something?"

I tugged her back down. "Can you wait just a moment? I need to talk to Neely Kate before you go."

"Okay . . ."

I grabbed Neely Kate's arm, pulling her from her chair and toward the hall to the bathrooms.

"Why is your hand so cold?" she asked, then started rubbing it. "It's like ice. What did you see?"

"Paul's gonna kill Jeanne for talkin' to us."

Neely Kate gasped. "What are we gonna do?"

"I don't know, but we can't let her go. We have to protect her."

"How are we gonna do that?"

"Do you have any suggestions? She needs to be guarded."

Neely Kate pushed out a breath. "Maybe we should turn to Skeeter. Scooter *is* his brother."

"We promised her that we wouldn't, Neely Kate."

"I know, but we're out of our league, Rose." She paused for a moment, looking past me toward Jeanne. "Maybe we should call Joe."

I gave that one some consideration. "She could tell Joe about the kidnapping, and I can tell him she's in danger. They can protect her . . ." I said, thinking out loud. "What's the downside?"

"The sheriff would get involved in the investigation," Neely Kate said. "Our paths could cross, and we'd no longer have the excuse that it's not an open case."

"Do you have any other ideas?"

She shook her head.

"Then let's hope we can convince her."

All the luck in the world wouldn't have helped us.

"No. No way," Jeanne said in a panic, pushing her chair back. "I ain't talkin' to no police."

"You're in danger, Jeanne," I said. "You need protection."

"The police aren't gonna help me. I'm better off on my own."

"Do you have any family out of town?" Neely Kate asked. "Anyone you can go stay with?"

"My sister lives in El Dorado."

"Go stay with her," I said. "Don't even pack. Just leave here and go."

She released a harsh laugh. "And where am I gonna get gas money when I can't even buy my own lunch?"

I pulled my wallet out and handed her the rest of my cash. "It's only sixty dollars, but it will get you to El Dorado. Call us when you get there so we know you're safe."

She took the money and gave me a look of disbelief. "Why are you doin' this?"

"Because we care about you," I said. "We want you to be safe."

"Why?"

"Because people have helped me," I said. "I'm just payin' it forward. Now go to your sister, and we'll let you know when it's safe to come home. But if you feel unsafe at any point, you need to call the police, okay?"

"Yeah." She lurched over the table and threw her arms around me. "God bless you girls." Then she jumped up, grabbed her purse and to-go bag, and ran out the door.

And I couldn't shake the feeling that I'd just screwed up.

CHAPTER 22

*W*e went back to the office, and we tried Mr. Whipple again with no response. We decided to go check on him, but first I told Neely Kate and Witt all the details about my vision.

"So there's at least two of them left," Neely Kate murmured.

"Let's look at what we know," I said, sitting on the edge of my desk so I could face them both. "We know there are at least four men. Elijah Landry, who lived in Shreveport and had grandparents in Henryetta. He was part of both my kidnapping and Scooter's."

Neely Kate nodded.

"Then there's Paul Beagle. According to the newspaper article, he lived here in Henryetta fifteen years ago, and we know he was also part of Scooter's kidnapping. Based on my vision, his brother is involved. Then there's the guy who was in on my kidnapping attempt. The man at the liquor store called him Bud —if he was even the same guy. For all we know, he could have taken the burner phone from someone else."

"So the fourth guy is Merlin Beagle," Neely Kate said. "The one you heard in your vision telling Paul to finish off Jeanne."

I glanced over at Witt. "Any luck finding information on Paul Beagle?"

"Not a single thing. It's like he doesn't exist."

I frowned. Neely Kate and I were pretty new to investigating, but people usually left some kind of footprint online. "How many search pages did you go back?"

"I know what you're gettin' at," he said. "But I promise you that I searched every which way I could, and the only thing I found was that article in the *Henryetta Gazette*. The other Paul Beagles I found were in other parts of the country, and they were all too old to be him."

Neely Kate's phone rang, and she glanced at the screen and smiled. "Hello, Miss Mildred," she answered. "Why yes, I *am* surprised you tracked Mr. Whipple down." She looked amused. "You don't have to do that, Miss Mildred. We really don't mind takin' Squawker home . . . Uh-huh . . . Okay, we're coming over right now. Don't leave, all right?"

She hung up and said, "Miss Mildred not only figured out who Mr. Whipple was, but took it upon herself to track him down. He's on his way home, and she says she's takin' the parrot to him."

"That bird's gonna fly away if she doesn't wait for Mr. Whipple to come over," I said in disbelief. "She needs to leave him be."

Her eyebrow lifted. "Do you think she's gonna listen to me? She says she's gonna keep him on her shoulder by feeding him a carrot."

"Oh, mercy," I grumbled, grabbing my backpack as I stood. "Let's get over there before she loses Squawker. We need to talk to that bird." That was something I'd never expected to hear myself say.

We all piled into Witt's car, and we were halfway to my old neighborhood when I got a call from Dermot's number. "Hey, Dermot."

"I'm checking on your progress." He sounded tense.

"We're making some headway," I said, "but we still have a ways to go."

"Malcolm's demanded that Buck return his brother by eight p.m., or he's gonna start a war."

I resisted the urge to release a groan. "Who made that call?"

"Malcolm himself only a few minutes ago. Buck's shittin' his pants, demandin' to know what you're doin'."

"We have a name for the third kidnapper, and we're trying to find out more about him. We've also verified there's a fourth guy, but we know next to nothin' about *him*."

"The third guy. Who is he?"

I wondered if I should tell him, but giving updates was part of our agreement. "We figured out that Elijah Landry had ties to Henryetta through his grandparents. We found a photo of him with his grandparents, parents, and his cousin. We showed the photo to a witness, and she recognized both Landry and his cousin as the guys who kidnapped Scooter."

"Witness? What witness?"

I didn't want to give up Jeanne, so I said, "It doesn't matter. It's reliable."

"And how do you know about the fourth guy?"

"That's a professional secret. We're about to see if we can find out more from the parrot. I'll let you know what we learn." I hung up before he could answer. Turning to Neely Kate, I said, "I need to call James."

"I knew it!" Witt said. "You swore you weren't gonna be involved with him anymore, but here you are—"

"He's given Buck Reynolds an ultimatum: return Scooter by eight or he's declaring war. If this were between Buck and anyone else, I'd be callin' them too. I have to stop this." I thought about the guilt James lived with. He didn't need any more. "James is about to do something he's gonna regret."

Neely Kate turned to Witt. "She's right. She has to call him."

"Dammit."

I hated this. I hated putting Witt in the middle of something he didn't want any part of, but we had to keep the peace.

Neely Kate gave me an expectant look, but I put the phone in my lap. "I'll wait until we get to Miss Mildred's." I wanted to talk to him without an audience.

She nodded and her eyes filled with sympathy, but Witt's hands tightened on the steering wheel. I was going to have to split off from them at some point. Witt was uncomfortable with my continual name-dropping of James—even though we were looking for James' brother—and he'd made it clear he'd protect Neely Kate at any cost. Neely Kate would refuse to stay behind and take a stand. The whole situation was going to cause a rift between two cousins who were close. I couldn't let that happen.

This had to be the reason Witt and Neely Kate had been alone in my vision.

We drove past Miss Mildred a block away from her house. She was wearing a house dress and a church hat, and Squawker was perched on her shoulder. The hat had a long carrot attached to the top, and the parrot was eyeing it while Miss Mildred hobbled down the street with her cane.

"Oh, my word . . ." Neely Kate gushed when we saw her. "Have you ever seen such a thing?"

"I've gotta get a picture of that," Witt said. "No one's ever gonna believe it otherwise."

"You will not," Neely Kate said, swatting his arm. "You're driving."

"She's definitely losin' it," I said, feeling sorry for her. "The Miss Mildred I knew growing up would never have tied a carrot to her church hat."

Witt parked the car about twenty feet in front of Miss Mildred, and Neely Kate and I both got out and waited for her to reach us on the sidewalk.

"I told you we'd help, Miss Mildred," Neely Kate said.

"I can walk a damn parrot home just as well as you can," she muttered.

"We were actually gonna drive," I said.

"Well, there you go," the older woman grumbled. "You were gonna drive." Only, she made it sound akin to killing baby bunnies.

"How about we walk with you?" Neely Kate asked, falling into step beside her.

"I'm capable of walkin' on my own," Miss Mildred snapped.

"Of course you are," Neely Kate said, "but we really need to talk to Squawker."

"You're gonna talk to him?" she asked in disbelief.

"He does talk . . ."

Miss Mildred lifted her shoulders in a barely perceptible shrug. "Suit yourself. But you're gonna look like a damn fool."

Says the woman walking down the street with a carrot tied to her hat.

Neely Kate shot me a look that said, *How do we interview a parrot?* Maybe we should have given that part more thought in the car.

"Squawker," I said. "Did you see something bad?"

"Something bad," he repeated.

Neely Kate gave me a sidelong grimace.

"Maybe we should try saying the phrases he used before," I suggested. "But only parts of them. That way we'll know if he's just mimicking us or really saying what he heard."

"Good idea," Neely Kate said.

"Squawker," I said. "Blood?"

He remained quiet.

"Did you see Scooter?" Neely Kate asked.

He stayed silent again.

"He doesn't want to talk to you," Miss Mildred sneered. "He wants to enjoy our stroll."

The only problem was that we didn't have time for a stroll.

"You three go on ahead," I said. "I'm going to hang back and make a call."

"Okay." Neely Kate continued walking with Miss Mildred, asking her more questions about the bird and her interactions with him. Witt drove the car all the way to the end of the street and parked at the stop sign to wait for us.

When Neely Kate and Miss Mildred were out of earshot, I pulled my phone out of my pocket and called James.

"I was hopin' you'd change your mind," he said in a sexy voice.

I tried to ignore the immediate rush of heat flowing through my veins. Just as I was about to chastise him for giving an ultimatum to Buck, I realized I'd never confirmed what Buck had hired me to do, and I wasn't sure now was the time to reveal it. Which meant I had to change tactics. "I've been thinkin' about Scooter," I said. "I never asked you how you were doin' with him missin'. I'm sorry."

"Don't you worry about Scooter. I'm takin' care of things."

"How exactly are you doin' that?" I asked.

"It's not your concern anymore."

"Did you get another lead? Because I told you that Buck Reynolds isn't responsible."

"I don't want to talk about Buck Reynolds," he said in a low tone. "I want to talk about when I can see you again."

"James. This is serious."

"Rose." He sounded exasperated. "You want to put distance between us publicly, but you were only partially right. You need to stay the hell away from the *entire* crime world. So tell Reynolds you're retiring, and I'll hire a real bodyguard—one without any ties to me—to watch you until the message gets around that you're no longer workin' for me or anyone else."

"You'd hire a bodyguard for me?" I asked in disbelief.

"I can't very well have Brett or Merv watchin' you if we're claimin' you're free of me."

But he'd do everything in his power to make sure I was safe. "I thought you wanted to see me again."

"I do. We can meet at my house. No one knows where I live, and they'll be none the wiser."

I was tempted, but there were more urgent matters at hand. "How about we meet to discuss it?" I asked. "Let's say tonight behind the Sinclair station. At eight."

He was quiet for several seconds. "I can't. Not tonight. In fact, I need you and Neely Kate to stay home tonight."

"Why?"

"Not your problem anymore," he said.

Dammit. "What are you doin', James Malcolm? This is about Buck Reynolds, isn't it?"

"Rose . . ."

"I told you he wasn't involved. What are you doin'?"

I heard voices in the background, and he said, "Hang tight, Merv."

"Merv?" I asked. "Are you takin' advice from that hothead?"

"This is none of your concern, Rose," he said in a tight voice.

"You're about to start a war, so yes, it is my concern."

"I have proof that Reynolds took my brother, and that's all you need to know."

"What proof?"

"Once again, Rose, it's not your concern. Now I have to go." Then he hung up.

What proof had he gotten? I pulled up Jed's number and called him.

"Rose? Everything okay?"

"Neely Kate and I are fine, if that's what you're askin', but James is about to do something stupid. I need to know what supposed proof he has that Buck Reynolds is behind Scooter's disappearance."

"Proof? I don't know anything about proof."

"He just told me that he has some, and he says he's takin' care of it tonight. He told me that Neely Kate and I need to stay inside."

He was quiet for a moment. "They've cut me out of the loop."

"What? I thought you were helpin' look for Scooter."

"I was. But Merv and I had another run-in last night, and Merv convinced Skeeter to let me loose for good. Merv said it isn't good business to involve me since I've decided not to return to the fold. He claims I'm no better than those turncoats you exposed last winter."

"And James believes that?"

"He wants blood, and Merv seems to be offering it to him. What good is his leadership if he can't keep his brother safe? His reputation is on the line. He needs to make a show of force."

"So Merv has taken your place?"

"Looks like it."

"Can you keep a secret from James?" I asked.

"Depends on what it is."

"But you're not even workin' for him anymore."

"We go way back, Rose. Workin' for him or not, I'm still loyal."

Miss Mildred and Neely Kate had stopped on the sidewalk. Miss Mildred was pulling a handful of lettuce out of her pocket and adding it to the top of her head. Squawker pecked at her head and snatched up a piece of lettuce, flinging it at Neely Kate, then squawked in a piercing voice, "Salad!"

I shook my head. *Focus.* "Buck Reynolds hired me to find Scooter."

"What?"

"I'm pretty sure we know things that James doesn't. We're makin' progress, but Tim Dermot called to tell me that James issued an ultimatum. Either Buck returns Scooter by eight tonight or he's declarin' war. Unless there's a miracle, or we get a breakthrough in the next few hours, that's not gonna happen."

"Shit."

"I'm not sure what to do, Jed. I have to stop this from happenin'."

"Tell him what you're up to. Tell him what you found."

"Do you think he'll listen?"

Jed paused. "Not if he thinks he has solid proof. You don't know what it is?"

And if James didn't believe me, he'd probably try to figure out a way to stop me from looking into it. So then I'd be dodging Merv and Brett while trying to investigate. "No."

"He's gonna think Reynolds played you."

"There's something else," I said.

"What?"

"Reynolds may not be in charge anymore."

"What does that mean?"

"I met with Buck Reynolds this morning. He let his idiocy show through again, and I took a stand. When I was about to walk away, Dermot stepped forward and took charge. And nobody stopped him. Witt says Dermot usurped his power."

"Well, shit. Did Dermot kick you off the case?"

"No. He gave me more information to keep lookin'."

"Then Reynolds really didn't take him," Jed said, sounding surprised.

"What do you know about Maynard's junkyard?"

He hesitated, then said, "I know it changed ownership a few months back. Why?"

"Dermot says Elijah Landry—one of the deceased kidnappers—worked there, along with his dead buddy named Bud. Landry just showed up in town a few months ago. We haven't been out there yet. We're still collectin' more information, but we're runnin' out of time, Jed."

"Don't go out there, Rose. I don't know much about who took over, and the timing seems too coincidental."

"There's more."

"Okay . . ."

"We've figured out there are at least four guys involved in this. Two are dead. The other two are Paul Beagle, Elijah Landry's cousin, and his brother Merlin. Ever heard of them?"

"Paul Beagle? Doesn't ring a bell. Don't know any Beagles."

"Are you sure?"

"Positive."

"What if he just got out of prison?"

"Unless he was in lockup for a couple of decades, I'm sure I would have heard of him."

"That doesn't make any sense. Jeanne identified him out of a fifteen-year-old picture we found online. He was living here in Henryetta, but his brother Merlin was in jail. We're pretty sure he's the fourth guy."

"What was the brother in jail for?"

"Don't know. That's all it said in the article with the picture. We haven't had time to investigate that either. Right now, we're interviewing a parrot."

Neely Kate was singing "Row, Row, Row Your Boat," and the bird had started singing with her. Miss Mildred had attempted to join in with what I could only guess was supposed to be the harmony . . . or maybe she was singing it in a round, just *really* off key.

"*What?*" Jed asked.

I sure hoped he hadn't heard the commotion. "Long story, but bottom line, we think he saw something happen to Scooter."

"Good luck with that. I'm gonna do some digging into the junkyard. Let me know if you find out anything more significant."

"You too."

By the time we hung up, Neely Kate and Miss Mildred had made it to the corner and were headed toward Mr. Whipple's house. Squawker must have recognized it because he let out a squawk and started saying, "Daddy. Daddy."

"Oh, that's so sweet," Neely Kate gushed. "He missed his

daddy." She stopped and let Miss Mildred continue for a few feet before she asked, "Well?"

I frowned. "No luck. In fact, James says he has proof Buck took Scooter."

"Where in the world did he get that?"

"He wouldn't say, and Jed doesn't know either." When her eyes widened, I lowered my voice. "Yeah, I called him. Don't tell Witt."

She nodded.

"Jed says he's been cut out of the loop. Merv convinced James not to trust him."

"*What?*"

"Short of goin' over there myself, I'm not sure what to do to stop him. And trust me, I'm willing to resort to that, but it would only be a temporary reprieve at best. In the meantime, we'll keep lookin' and hopin' we find him first."

She nodded, but there was a worried look in her eyes. "I think you should have a vision."

"Of what?"

"We've found out more things. Maybe it's enough to make a difference. Why don't you see if we find him?"

"Okay."

I grabbed her hand and closed my eyes, concentrating on whether we'd find Scooter.

The vision was slow to come, but it finally consumed my field of vision. It was dusk and my phone was ringing. I answered it and said in Neely Kate's voice, "Rose. I was gettin' worried."

"I know where he is, Neely Kate," Vision Rose said with tears in her voice. "I found him."

The vision ended and I found myself staring into Neely Kate's anxious face.

"She found him," I said.

"She?"

"Me," I said, overcome with a wave of exhaustion. "I called you and told you that I found him."

"So we *are* making a difference," she said.

"Looks like it." But why was I crying? Were they happy tears or sorrowful ones?

CHAPTER 23

J wasn't sure who was more excited—Mr. Whipple or Squawker. The bird instantly flapped off his perch on Miss Mildred's shoulder and flew to his owner, while the elderly man had tears in his eyes.

"You found him," Mr. Whipple said. "You actually found him."

"*I* found him," Miss Mildred snapped.

"This morning?" Mr. Whipple asked as he stroked his parrot's head.

"No. Back on Sunday."

"You didn't see the signs? Why didn't you call?"

"I wasn't sure," Miss Mildred hedged. "I didn't want to get your hopes up."

More like she hadn't planned to give him back. Also not like her. Now I was *really* worried.

"The important thing is that he's home," Neely Kate said. "Maybe we should get him inside before he flies away."

"Good idea," Mr. Whipple said.

Miss Mildred stared at the front door and shook her head. "I need to get back to the house. I left a carrot cake in the oven."

"That's Squawker's favorite," Mr. Whipple said in surprise.

"Is it?" she asked.

The thought of the carrot cake, now for one instead of two, made me a little sad. "Why don't we have Witt take you home, Miss Mildred," I said. "It's mighty hot out here."

She gave his car a long look, then said, "Okay."

"I'll go with her and make sure she gets home okay," Neely Kate said, knowing there was no way Miss Mildred would let me help her.

"I don't need any help," Miss Mildred protested weakly.

"Of course you don't, but I need to give Witt some special directions about what to do after he drops you off." Turning toward me, Neely Kate said, "Why don't you get started, and I'll meet you inside."

Mr. Whipple was already walking through the door, so I followed him in. He sat in his chair, still stroking the bird's head. "I can't believe he's back. Where did you find him?"

"Miss Mildred's backyard. Neely Kate and I found out this morning. I think he's been living in the trees."

"Thank you," he said. "You'll never know how much I appreciate it."

"Well, I was wondering if I could ask you a few questions."

"Of course."

"You mentioned that Squawker had said some things before your break-in. Could you tell me more about what he said?"

He stilled. "Which part?"

"The *shut up and clean up the blood* line. You claimed he probably heard it on TV, but what if he didn't?"

The bird squawked and said, "Shut up, you stupid asshole, and clean up the blood before mer—"

"Squawker!" Mr. Whipple shouted; then his eyes widened. "Sorry. I'm trying to keep him from saying those things."

And yet it seemed like he'd interrupted the parrot for another reason. I wasn't sure what to make of that. "I'd really like to hear it," I said with a half-smile. "I've never been around a parrot before."

"I'm trying to keep him from cursin'," the elderly man said, his hand and voice shaking. "And sayin' lewd things. He hears my neighbor say . . ." His voice trailed off, and a panicked look stole over his face.

"Did Squawker hear your neighbor say that line about the blood?" I asked in a soothing voice.

"You have to go." He jerked to his feet, the sudden movement startling the bird, who clung to his shoulder with his claws and flapped wildly.

"Did someone warn you not to talk about it?" I asked as he shoved my arm.

"No. I've just had a long day, and I need to get Squawker settled." He continued to push me toward the door. I let him, because it was his house and we'd done our job—or I guess Miss Mildred had done a lot of it. I turned to face him. "Mr. Whipple. A man's been kidnapped, and I have reason to believe Squawker might know something about it."

I also couldn't help remembering my vision about Jeanne, and what had almost happened to her for talking. It also reminded me that she hadn't called us yet.

He shook his head. "I don't know nothin' about that. You need to go." Then he pushed me out the door and closed it, the bird nearly escaping again in the process.

Witt and Neely Kate pulled up as I hit the sidewalk. She rolled down the window and rested her elbow in the opening. "You're done already?" she asked in surprise. "I thought we were gonna ask him questions."

"That's just it. Squawker said the line about the blood. Only, he was startin' to say more and Mr. Whipple cut him off."

"What did he add?"

"He said, 'Shut up, you stupid asshole, and clean up the blood before mer—' Then Mr. Whipple cut him off. It sounded like it was mid-word."

"Before mer . . ." Neely Kate said. "What could it be? Mercury?"

"Before 'merica becomes great again?" Witt supplied.

"Before Merlin gets back?" I said as it hit me. "Paul's brother."

Neely Kate's eyes widened.

"Have you heard back from your friend at the courthouse?" I asked.

"No." She pulled her phone out of her pocket. "I'm gonna check in with her."

"Maybe we should see if the neighbor on the corner is home. The one who saw Squawker at the park. I'd like to talk to him." I started walking before either of them said anything.

I cut across the street and headed for the house that was in desperate need of new paint and my landscaping services. I knocked on the front door, and a guy in his early to mid-forties opened the door wearing a sleeveless shirt that looked like he'd used it as a napkin for the chicken wing in his hand. "Whaddaya want?"

"I heard that you spotted Mr. Whipple's bird at the park last Saturday morning."

"So?" His eyebrows rose to an exaggerated height. "What of it?"

"I was wonderin' if you could tell me what time and where exactly."

"I see that damn bird there all the time," he said. "And he was doin' what he always does—annoying the shit out of me."

"Do you know of anyone who'd want to steal Mr. Whipple's parrot?"

He lifted his hands in a surrender-like gesture, and some of the grease from his wing started to run down his wrist. "I never stole that bird."

"We found the bird, Mr. . . . ?"

His shoulders slumped in what looked like relief. "That bird annoys the shit outta everyone. Anyone could have took him, but it wasn't me. If *I'd* took him . . ." He held up his chicken wing with a huge grin, then licked the grease off his arm and slammed the door shut.

I headed back to Witt's car, which was now parked directly across the street. "I don't think he was involved," I said as I climbed in the back.

"Did you have a vision?" Witt asked.

"No," I said. "He slammed the door in my face before I could even think about havin' one."

Neely Kate still had the phone pressed to her ear. "I'm on hold. Oh, and I already called Kermit and told him we'd returned Squawker to Mr. Whipple. Boy . . . did he sound surprised."

I bet. "If only he knew everything." I took a breath. "Squawker saw something," I said. "I'm certain of it. Just like I'm certain someone scared Mr. Whipple to keep quiet."

"Who?" Neely Kate asked. Then her eyes lit up. "Hey, June," she said into her phone. "That's okay. I didn't mind waiting. That's right. Seymour and Mary Ellen Constant." She wrote something down on a piece of paper. "You don't say? Okay. Thanks."

I rested my hand on the side of Witt's seat.

"You're never gonna believe it. Elijah Landry's grandparents lived on the street behind Mr. Whipple's. And his aunt and uncle own the house now."

Witt pulled away from the curb, drove to the end of the street, and turned the corner. "What number?"

"2500 Spring Street."

"You were back quick enough that I guess you didn't have a chance to ask Miss Mildred anything about the Beagles," I asked her.

"She refused to discuss anything," Neely Kate said. "I think she's depressed over losin' that bird."

I nodded. "Maybe we can ask someone from the church."

"That's it," Witt said, pointing to a pale-yellow house that looked well-kept. "And check it out. It looks like the corner of its backyard touches Mr. Whipple's."

"I'm not sure it's a good idea to march up to the door," I said. "Maybe we should ask the neighbors what they know about the house." Again, I remembered my vision with Jeanne.

"Good idea," Neely Kate said as Witt put the car in park. "You stay in the car, Witt. It'll be better if it's just me and Rose."

"I'll be watchin'."

We got out and Neely Kate walked up to the house to the right of the Beagles' place. She knocked on the door, and about ten seconds later, an elderly woman answered the door.

"Hi," Neely Kate said. "I'm Nancy and this is Beth Ann, and we're looking for Mary Ellen Constant. We were told she lived here."

"Oh, honey," the woman said, putting a hand on her chest. "You're one house off and ten years too late."

"I'm sorry?" Neely Kate asked.

"She died," the woman said.

"Oh." Neely Kate turned back to me. "Now we'll never find our cousins."

"Which cousins?" the woman asked. "Her daughter bought the place after Seymour died. She's rentin' it out, but she gave me a contact number in case there were any issues that needed addressin'."

"And have there been?" I asked. When the woman gave me a strange look, I said, "I've been thinkin' about getting rental property, but it seems kind of like a nightmare, what with cranky tenants and such."

"There haven't been many problems." Her face scrunched up. "At least until last week. Things were a little noisy then, but the boys said they were havin' a get-together."

"The boys?" Neely Kate asked.

"Pam's sons. They're between renters, and Paul and his cousin Elijah are repainting the place and sprucin' it up."

"You said they had a get-together?"

"Yeah, it was early in the day, so it seemed odd."

"Do you remember what day?" Neely Kate asked.

"It was Wednesday," the woman said. "They were makin' a ruckus when I left early for Wednesday night church. It was late afternoon because I was helping make the dinner. Then they were at it again on Thursday morning. I was out hangin' my sheets on the line."

"What did you hear?"

"A bunch of yellin'."

"Did you see anything?"

She shook her head. "They said they were havin' a painting party. A few of their friends came over to help." She leaned closer and lowered her voice. "I suspect they were drinkin'. Pam's boys are kinda rough."

"Do you know who any of their friends are?" Neely Kate asked.

The woman gave her a wary look. Neely Kate was asking questions that didn't pertain to rental houses *or* her supposed cousins.

Neely Kate laughed. "There I go again. My momma always told me I was as nosy as a squirrel lookin' for banana bread."

The elderly woman continued to give her an odd look. "I need to be gettin' back to my talk show," she said. "If you want Pam's number, I can get it for you."

"That would be great. I'd love to see if she has any of their family tree plotted out."

She left us on the porch with her front door partially open.

"We need to check out that house," Neely Kate said under her breath. "I don't see any cars out front, and we know that Elijah Landry and his friend are dead."

"But Paul and Merlin aren't. I saw them both in my vision with Jeanne at lunch."

"Yeah," she conceded with a nod.

"The strange thing is how these guys all seemed to come out of nowhere. You would think at least one of them would have a foot in the crime world here. What have they got against James?"

"Maybe it has to do with J.R. Simmons," she said. "Maybe some of his allies are lookin' for revenge."

She was right. "We should start lookin' in that direction, but I have no idea where to start."

The elderly woman reappeared in the doorway with a piece of paper. "Here's Pam's number. How did you say you're related to her?"

"Her momma's sister."

The woman's eyes narrowed. "Mary Ellen didn't have a sister."

"Oh! Silly me," Neely Kate chuckled. "I meant her grandmother's sister. Those family trees get so confusing. Thanks for your help."

Neely Kate spun around and went down the steps, and I followed her as she got into the car.

"Well?" Witt asked.

"She's still watchin'," Neely Kate said. "We're gonna have to come back."

"We can try to find out more about Paul Beagle. Let's go by the church. The church secretary's been there forever and is a gossip to boot. She'll be liable to remember not only the Constants and the Beagles, but everything about the anniversary party, including if the cake was too dry."

"So why didn't we go there first?" Witt asked.

I grimaced. "Because I'm not one of her favorite people." She'd heard enough of the phrases I'd blurted out after visions to hold my nosiness—the way many people dismissed my knowledge of the intimate details of their lives—against me *and* my mother.

"Well, it's still a good idea," Neely Kate said. "Do you know how to get there, Witt?"

"Yeah."

It was a ten-minute drive to the church, but the parking lot was empty when we pulled in. "Let me check," Neely Kate said, hopping out of the car and walking up to the front doors. She gave them a good jerk before shaking her head and returning to the car. "Locked up tight as a drum."

"What time is it?" I asked as I dug out my phone and groaned. "It's already three thirty. They always did close their offices early."

"So now what?" Neely Kate asked.

"I have an idea," I said. "But I need to do this one alone."

It was time to see my sister.

CHAPTER 24

*N*eely Kate and Witt weren't happy about my plan, but they agreed in the end. When I called Violet, Mike answered, and he told me I could come over but only for an hour. I nearly asked when he'd become my sister's keeper, but it seemed like a question better saved for Violet.

The plan was for the Rivers cousins to drop me off and pick me up in a half hour.

Neely Kate squeezed my hand when Witt pulled into Mike's driveway. "Good luck."

Why did I feel like I'd need it?

Witt waited until Mike answered the door, and seconds later my niece and nephew were hugging my legs. "Aunt Rose!"

"It's my favorite niece and nephew!"

"We're your only niece and nephew!" Ashley shouted. We'd played this more times than I could count, but this time I said my lines under the scrutiny of my brother-in-law.

"Who dropped you off?" he asked.

I blinked. "What? Neely Kate's cousin Witt."

"Why don't you have your truck?"

"I didn't need it today. What's this all about?"

"I don't like the company you keep."

I gasped.

"I read the papers. I hear people talk. I know you were associating with Skeeter Malcolm to get J.R. Simmons arrested last winter. Your business partner has a record."

I didn't say anything. I definitely couldn't deny it.

"I can't have my wife and children around criminals, Rose. No matter how much I like you."

"Rose?" Violet's voice came from down the short hall where we were standing. I turned my back on Mike, trying to stuff down my hurt feelings. He and I had always been allies. His disapproval was hard to stomach. But shouldn't I have expected this? I had known there would be a price to pay . . .

"I'll take the kids to get some ice cream," Mike said. His words had shaken me so much, I barely registered the sound of his jingling keys and the kids' excited voices before the front door shut behind them.

"Hey, Vi," I said when I finally pulled myself together and walked into the living room. She looked thin and frail, huddled up on the sofa and surrounded by pillows and covered with a blanket. "How are you feeling?"

"I'm tired but so grateful to be home."

Of course, she *wasn't* home. She and Mike had sold their house after separating, and Mike was renting this house. I worried that she wasn't feeling settled.

"Does it feel like home? You never lived here," I said as I sat on the love seat.

A soft smile lit up her eyes. "Oh, Rose. Home isn't where you live. It's where your loved ones are. And mine are here."

"Is that why you're not moving back into Momma's house?"

Her eyes clouded over. "There's nothing but bad memories there. You felt it too, didn't you? That's why you moved out when you finally saw Dora's farm."

"Yeah." I paused. "So it's true that you want to sell the house?"

"I don't want to go back there, and I didn't think you did either. Unless I was wrong . . ."

I shook my head. "No. I never want to live there again. But what about rentin' it out? It's paid for, so you could make pure profit."

She made a face that hinted she wasn't interested.

"The nursery's about to start makin' a profit," I said. "But there's not enough to bump you back up to full time *and* keep payin' Maeve, and it's obvious you're not ready to be workin' full time. It could be a way to bring in more money for you. I'll even manage it if you'd like."

Surprise filled her eyes. "I hadn't considered that, but Mike was so set on sellin' it."

"What do *you* want, Violet?" I asked, trying to hide my irritation. "It's *your* house."

She gave me a sad smile. "I'll talk to Mike."

Hearing my brother-in-law's name made me think of Elijah Landry. I almost asked her about the Beagles, but I wasn't ready to do that yet. Right now, I just wanted to be Violet's sister.

"I bet the kids are excited to have you back."

"Ashley barely leaves my side, but Mikey's kind of forgotten me," she said with tears in her eyes. "I suppose that's to be expected."

"He'll get used to you being here again," I said. "Just give him time."

She smiled again, and I couldn't help thinking that even her smile looked frail. "Time is a precious commodity, Rose. Don't waste it."

"What are you talkin' about?" I asked, suddenly afraid.

She put her hand on mine. "Stop lookin' so scared. I'm just bein' maudlin. Come sit next to me like you used to when we were kids."

She moved a stack of pillows and I sat next to her, my hip

pressed to hers, thankful I was sitting on her right side since my stitches had started hurting again.

She snagged my hand and laced our fingers together. "I've missed you, Rose."

"I'm just so happy you're back. I promise to make time to see you even when business picks back up this fall."

"I'm not talkin' about just while I was gone. I miss us bein' close. Like we were before Momma died."

She was right. Momma had kept me so cut off from the world. Until Neely Kate came into my life, Violet had been my best friend, my *only* friend. I'd been Violet's best friend too, but it had all been one-sided—just like Momma, Violet had wanted to run my life, only in a different way. Still, she loved me and I loved her, and there was no denying we'd grown apart once I'd started asserting my independence. I wanted to trust that her brush with death had changed her. I *wanted* to be close again. "I'd like to work on that."

She rested her head on my shoulder. "Tell me about your life. How'd your date with that vet go? What was his name?"

"Levi. And he's nice. It was . . . nice."

She was silent.

"There's just something missin'."

"Do you still love Mason?"

"Part of me does, but I'm not as sad. I'm ready to move on." Memories of my night with James filled my head. *Obviously* I was ready to move on, just with the wrong guy.

Violet softly squeezed my hand. "Who is he?"

My body stiffened. "I told you. Levi's the new vet at Henryetta Animal Clinic."

"That's not what I'm talkin' about, and you know it."

I hesitated, then finally said, "Someone I probably have no business bein' with."

"Is he married?" She sat up and turned to face me, her eyes

pleading. "Because Rose, if he is, end it now. I went down that road and nothin' but heartache. For everyone."

I squeezed her hand. "He's not married . . . not to a woman, anyway. He's married to his job."

She pushed out a sigh and sank back into the sofa cushions. "Oh, that's even worse. That means he's giving you up for something that can't love him back. Just like Mason. He ended up leaving you for a new job."

It was nothing like Mason. Mason had left because I'd hurt and betrayed him with my lies. With my life as the Lady in Black.

The woman James had created.

"But you're still seein' the vet anyway?"

"No . . . well, I was. I knew nothing would come of my connection to the other man, and Levi's *so* nice. I *wanted* to feel something more than I did. Last night I did something that wasn't fair to Levi. This morning I'd made up my mind to end it with him, but Neely Kate accepted an invitation from him on my behalf."

"Even though you don't want to go out with him?"

"I suppose this is her way of making sure I end it with the other guy."

"She doesn't approve either?"

"No." I considered listing all the reasons but decided the no was damning enough.

"Then maybe you should listen to both of us—and your own logic."

They were both right, but why did my heart ache so much if being with James was wrong? "You're not gonna ask me who he is?"

"I don't need to know. Unless you want to tell me."

"I don't think you'd understand . . ." I said, which was more than I probably should have told her.

"I'd probably understand more than you think," she said quietly.

We were quiet for a moment before I asked, "Do you still love Mike?"

"There are all kinds of love, Rose."

I didn't like the sound of that. "And which kind is the one you have for Mike?"

"Not the fire and passion I had with Brody. What I have with Mike is more . . . comfortable."

"That doesn't sound fair to you, Vi."

She released a tiny chuckle. "It's more unfair to Mike. He loves me more than I love him. We both know it, and yet he still wants me."

"You could find someone else who gives you what Brody gave you."

She patted our linked hands. "Says the woman who has had two men love her like there's no tomorrow. You're luckier than you know."

I didn't answer. What could I say? The truth was I'd had three men love me, and I'd lost them all. That didn't feel very lucky.

"I'm a realist now, Rose. And I'm grateful. Grateful that Mike still wants me despite all the pain I put him through. I have my family back, and I'll never take it for granted again. And you have your own family too." When I turned to look down at her, she said, "Your friends—Neely Kate, Bruce Wayne, Maeve. All of you are like a family."

"But you're my family too, Vi."

"I know," she said, sounding tired. "But I have Mike and the kids. You need to have other people too. I understand that now." She paused. "Do you mind if I cut our visit short today? The kids are wearin' me out, and I'm about to fall asleep."

"Of course. I'm sorry."

"No, don't be sorry. I miss you so much. I hate that my body is betrayin' me."

"When does Mike go back to work? I can come help with the kids."

"You have a business to run—two of 'em."

"The landscaping business is slowin' down for summer. I'll have slow spells until September. And Neely Kate's learning even faster than I expected. She can fill in for me."

"Mike's goin' back next week, but I'm hopin' to have more energy by then."

"But you know I'm willin' to help. So if you need anything, ask me, okay?"

"Yeah. It might be nice for us to just hang out in the afternoons . . . like we used to sometimes."

"We'll even make cookies," I said. "Only, this time you can be the one watchin', even if it's your own kitchen. Or maybe you and the kids can come out to the farm. They can chase Muffy around and wear themselves out while we sit on the porch drinking lemonade or tea and relaxin'. I'll come pick y'all up."

A soft smile lit up her face. "Okay. Deal."

I stood but stayed next to the sofa because I still hadn't gotten around to the business that had brought me here. "Vi, could I ask you a question about some people from the Henryetta Baptist Church?"

She frowned at my seemingly out-of-nowhere question. "Yeah. Sure . . ."

"Do you remember a Seymour and Mary Ellen Constant?"

Violet's frown deepened. "They sound vaguely familiar. Give me a moment. My memory hasn't been the same since the chemo." She was silent for several seconds; then she smiled. "I do. Mary Ellen was my Sunday school teacher. She used to give us peppermints when we recited our memory verses. She was sweet. I think she stopped teaching right after my grade, so you probably never had her. I haven't thought of her in years."

"What about her daughter and her son-in-law, Pam and Timothy Beagle?"

She nodded. "I remember Miss Pam. Seems like she had two sons who were older than us."

"Yes," I said, trying not to get too excited. "Do you happen to know their names?"

"I remember Paul . . . He was older than me, by about five years. He had an older brother who went to prison. I don't ever remember meeting him. I just heard about him."

"I've tried to look up Paul Beagle, but he doesn't seem to exist."

"That's because he doesn't," Violet said. "Mr. Beagle's not their father. Pam got divorced when Paul was a baby and remarried a few years later."

No wonder we hadn't found any records of him. "So what was *their* last name?"

Her mouth twisted to the side like she was concentrating hard, but then she shook her head. "I can't remember. I'm sorry." She looked close to tears.

I sat on the coffee table and grabbed her hand. "No. Don't be sorry."

"I just feel so stupid when I can't remember things."

"It's a whole lot more than *I* can remember. And I don't have an excuse." I grinned even though I was disappointed. "If it comes to you, will you text me?"

"Sure."

I leaned forward and gave her a kiss on the forehead. "You get some rest, and I'll check on you tomorrow." I paused. "I love you, Violet."

"I love you too, Rose."

I left the house even though I didn't have a car. I started walking, hoping I'd get some brilliant ideas on how to handle this. Witt's vision was prominent in my head, and I knew at some point I'd ditch Neely Kate and her cousin today. What if I had to separate from them so I could find Scooter? Maybe this was the time to do it.

I grabbed my phone and called Jed.

"How do you feel about breakin' into a house with me?"

$\mathcal{I}$ was two blocks away when Jed picked me up. I'd already texted Neely Kate an excuse—saying I was going to visit with Violet longer but I'd found out that Paul and Merlin had a different last name than their mother. I'd asked her to see if she could find out more about Elijah Landry without going to the rental house or the junkyard. We'd do that later.

Jed's car pulled up next to me, and I'd barely shut the door before he drove off. "What's this about?"

"I think I know where Landry and Paul Whatever-his-name-is and his brother took Scooter last Wednesday."

His eyes widened. "And how'd you find that out?"

"The neighbor. She heard a commotion Wednesday when she was leaving for church, and I'm pretty sure the parrot heard them talkin' and was repeatin' what they said." I told him the phrases we'd heard Squawker say. "They broke in and tried to snatch the bird, but Mr. Whipple caught them in the act and the parrot got away."

"Where's Neely Kate and her cousin right now?"

"They dropped me off to see Violet. She tired out before they were supposed to pick me up, so I texted you and sent them on a wild goose chase." When he gave me a questioning look, I said, "It's kind of a long story, but bottom line: Witt wants to appear neutral when this is all over, and when I forced a vision to make sure that happened, I saw that I'd ditched them. It must be because I involved you. Not to mention, in my vision I called Neely Kate to tell her I'd found Scooter. It makes sense that you and I can find him together."

He was silent.

"This is startin' to get dangerous, and right or wrong, I feel like you need to be part of it. Scooter was your friend too."

"Thanks for includin' me. I *do* want to be part of it, especially since Skeeter's shut me out." He was quiet for several seconds. "Where do we need to go?"

I gave him the address and a few directions to the neighborhood. "We have to be careful because we were makin' the neighbor suspicious with all our questions earlier. We can't let her find us snoopin'."

He nodded.

"Neely Kate's liable to be ticked at *both* of us," I said. "I'm used to it, but you . . ."

"I can handle it," he said, but he didn't look one hundred percent sure. "I'd prefer to keep her out of it. You and I both have a stake in this. She just wants to see the 'case' to completion."

"Still, I'll take full responsibility, Jed. You and I haven't discussed what's goin' on between you two—"

He shifted in his seat, looking uncomfortable. "Rose . . ."

"No. Let me finish."

He pulled up to a stop sign and didn't move.

"I'll admit I was worried when I first suspected, but only for a tiny bit. I can't think of two people more perfect for each other, and I know you'll do everything in your power to protect her. This only proves it more. I have no idea what she faced in Oklahoma last week, but I want to thank you for goin' with her."

"I did it for purely selfish reasons."

"And I know you got fired for it. That couldn't have been an easy choice."

"It was surprisingly easy."

That gave me pause. "Well, in any case, you both have my blessing, not that you need it, but you have it all the same."

"Thank you, Rose." He turned to face me and nodded. "That means more than you know." He stepped on the gas and took off. "Now let's go find Scooter, and we can face Neely Kate's wrath together."

~

WE PARKED A FEW HOUSES DOWN, and I kept an eye on the neighbor's house as we approached Pam Beagle's place.

"So far, so good," I said as we walked up to the front door. Jed had suggested it would be better to see if anyone was home before we started sneaking around the house.

I realized I could learn a lot from Jed. Probably more than we were going to learn from Kermit the Hermit. I wanted to ask Jed about setting us up with him, but now didn't seem the time.

He had me stand behind him, on the bottom step, while he knocked on the door.

"I have a gun, Jed," I said quietly, my heart racing. "Strapped to my thigh."

"That's good to know," he said. "Let's hope you don't need it."

When no one had answered after ten seconds or so, Jed knocked again, then tried the doorknob. "Locked."

"Now what?" I asked. "If you weren't here, I'd go around back to see if the back door was open."

"Me too." I followed him around the side of the house and through the chain-link gate into the empty backyard. The back door was locked too, but Jed pulled out some lock-picking tools and had it open in no time. He walked in first and motioned me in, closing the door behind us.

We stepped into a dated kitchen—complete with old Formica counters with metal trim—and I took a moment to catch my breath.

"How're you doin'?" Jed asked.

"Okay. I feel like I'm in the big leagues doin' this with you."

His answer was a half-grin. "Stay behind me in case we find any surprises."

"Okay."

The house was a small bungalow—just like all the homes in my neighborhood—so it didn't take long to make our way through it.

"Nothin'," Jed said, scanning the bathroom. "No signs of a struggle. No blood."

"There's no furniture," I said. "Would there *be* signs of a struggle?"

"There might be scuff marks on the floors or walls. Or even holes in the wall."

Disappointment washed through me. "I was so sure they brought him here."

"Just because we don't see anything doesn't mean they *weren't* here. You said the neighbor told you they were working on the house to get it ready for renters. They might have repaired it already. Or maybe there wasn't any damage at all."

He headed back to the kitchen and stopped in front of a narrow door. "I'll be damned," he said, opening it. "This house has a basement."

He found a light switch and flipped it on, and a dim light appeared at the bottom. "I hope you're not afraid of basements."

"I never used to be—just closed-in spaces—but I might change my mind about basements depending on what we find at the bottom of the stairs."

The staircase was made of two-by-fours with no walls, and two bare light bulbs were attached to the floor joists above, shedding enough light for me to see the cinder block foundation and the dirt floor. But it was the folding chair in the middle of the room and the dark stain in the dirt beneath it that really caught my attention.

"Stay there," Jed said as he made his way to the chair and squatted next to it. He dipped his finger in it and lifted it to his nose. "Blood."

I took comfort in the fact that it was a relatively small puddle. "Do you think they did bring Scooter here?"

"If what the parrot said was true . . ." He glanced over at me, and a hint of a grin lifted his lips. "Words I never thought I'd say."

"No kidding."

"But there was probably blood upstairs if the parrot heard one of them telling another to clean up blood before . . ." He lifted his eyebrows. "It doesn't look like they tried to clean it up down here. And you're sure the bird said Scooter's name?"

"I heard it myself."

He stayed squatted down and scanned the floor.

"What are you lookin' for now?" I asked.

"I'm trying to make out footprints—how many, shoe sizes."

"Can you tell?"

He stood. "They're all blended together. They were movin' around a lot. They may have been interrogatin' him. They were pacin'. See the straight line that's deeper than the others?" He pointed to it. "They walked the same path multiple times."

"But there's no clue as to where they took him," I said.

"I'm pretty sure I know where they took him, and it won't be as easy to get into as this house."

"You think they took him to the junkyard?" I asked.

He nodded. "Yep. I do now thanks to what you've found."

"So why didn't they take me there?"

He turned to look at me. "I wish I knew. Maybe they'd already killed Scooter. We have to face that possibility."

"I haven't had a vision yet that shows him alive. But I haven't had a vision that shows him dead either. There's a gray haze whenever I look."

"And what does that usually mean?"

"That the future's still being decided."

"Then we'll presume that he's still alive . . . and that if he dies, it'll happen tonight."

He made it all sound very matter-of-fact, but I could see the pain in his eyes. "Okay."

His gaze held mine. "Make no mistake about it, Rose. The kidnappers won't be happy to see you if we find him."

"Good. I'm not too thrilled about seeing them, but I'll be happy to get one over on 'em."

"I guess I'm sayin' it's dangerous. Not something I'd involve you in before."

"But I *am* involved. Just tell me what to do. I want to help you, not be a hindrance."

He gave me a sad smile. "You've changed."

"For the worse?"

"No. And I take it back. You haven't changed. You've always been headstrong about doin' what's right. You've rubbed off on Skeeter, whether he wants to admit it or not."

"But not with this," I said. "He's still gonna start this war."

"Not if we find his brother first."

I was trusting in my vision. "Are we done here?"

"Yep. Let's go up."

He didn't have to tell me twice. The thought of them holding Scooter down here and hurting him enough to make a puddle on the floor freaked me out. I made it up several seconds before Jed. "So now we head to the junkyard?"

"Not so fast," he said. "I'd prefer to do this under the cover of darkness, but Merv screwed that up with his eight p.m. meeting time." He paused, then shook his head. "What was he thinkin'? And what was Skeeter thinkin' agreeing to it?"

"Whatever proof he thinks he found must have shaken him up."

"No wonder Merv got me kicked out last night," Jed said, looking out the back window toward Mr. Whipple's aviary. "He knew I'd try to negotiate. Merv's gonna be out for blood."

"And James would listen to Merv?"

"Skeeter wants his brother back, and now that Merv's poisoned Skeeter against me, he's convinced him a show of force is best. Otherwise, he'll look weak."

"He's not poisoned against *me*."

Jed gave me a sad look. "It's only a matter of time."

"I'm gonna call him again," I said. "I have to put a stop to this." I grabbed my phone and placed the call.

James answered right away. "Everything okay?"

"I don't know," I said. "You tell me. You're about to do something you're gonna regret."

"Rose. Enough. I've got proof."

"So you keep sayin', yet you refuse to tell me what it is."

"It's a photo, okay? A photo of Scooter tied to a chair. It was sent from Buck Reynolds' phone, along with a message tellin' me he'll kill Scooter if I don't hand over my kingdom. He demanded a meeting, so we set up a meeting."

Crappy doodles. That did seem pretty bad.

"And what's happenin' at this meetin'?" I asked. "You're not really goin' to discuss handin' it all over, are you?"

"Hell, no. The only thing Reynolds is gonna negotiate tonight is whether or not he'll get to enter the pearly gates. Now I gotta go." And he hung up.

I stared at Jed in disbelief and quickly told him what James had said. "Why would Buck hire me if he did it? Dermot's just as confused as we are."

"Maybe Reynolds hired some outside guys and hid it from his own men. Less chance of what he'd done getting out. And as to why he'd hire *you*? Probably trying to throw Skeeter off track and buy some credibility. If you're lookin' for Scooter and you tell Skeeter, then you've planted some doubt on Reynolds takin' him. And even if he's not claiming responsibility for it, he could sure sow the seeds that Skeeter's too incompetent to run the county if people aren't too intimidated to snatch his brother and his girlfriend."

"I'm not his girlfriend."

"But that's not what some people think."

I resisted the urge to groan. Why was I fighting my pull to James so hard if all these people thought I was with him anyway?

"Reynolds being behind all of this still makes no sense to me . . ."

"You said yourself that Reynolds is a fool."

"But my vision . . ."

"Did you flat-out see proof of his innocence?"

"No, but—"

"Then I think we need to presume Reynolds took him after all. Hell, three weeks ago he was on the verge of a power play. It's not outside the realm of possibility that he did it. In fact, it stands to reason that he did."

It made sense—his behavior had been off all along. And yet . . .

"My gut says he didn't do it," I said, knowing I sounded like a fool.

"Then how do you explain the text with the photo?" Jed demanded.

Good point. "I don't know, but I think I should place a call to Tim Dermot."

After it rang for several seconds, I wasn't sure he was going to answer, but he picked it up just before it went to voicemail. "Lady. Whatcha got?"

"Did Buck Reynolds kidnap Scooter Malcolm or not?" I demanded in a no-nonsense voice.

"Of course he didn't kidnap him," he asked, speaking slowly as if he suspected I might have a head injury. "That's why he hired *you*. What's this all about?"

"Then why did he send Skeeter Malcolm a photo of Scooter tied to a chair?"

"*What?*"

"That's right. He sent him a photo—from his number—and demanded Skeeter show up at a meetin' to discuss handin' over the county. I want to know where they're meeting."

"How could Buck text a photo he has no way of gettin'?"

"Are you sure about that?" I asked. "Maybe Buck's cuttin' you out of the loop."

He paused for several seconds. "Shit."

"Am I chasin' my tail here, Dermot? What was I really hired for?"

"Buck went to a whole lot of trouble to hire you if he did it himself."

"Then how do you explain the photo from his phone?"

His tone turned cold. "How do *you* explain knowin' about Skeeter Malcolm's texts?"

I could have lied, but I wasn't feeling up to it.

"Yeah," Dermot said. "You're not workin' independent. For all I know, you're lying about the photo and settin' us up."

"I called him, just like I called you. I've made no attempt to cover up that I've worked with him, and he knows I'm helpin' Buck with something. I'm usin' all the resources at my disposal to find Scooter, just like I said. But I need to know where Buck is meeting Skeeter."

"I'm tellin' you," Dermot said in a snotty tone. "Buck doesn't know anything about it. All he knows is that he got an ultimatum from Malcolm via text to meet tonight."

"You saw the text yourself?" I asked. "Did you see the photo of Scooter?"

"I saw the damn text, and there was no photo."

"Then how did Skeeter get the photo from Buck's number?"

"How can you be so sure Malcolm's not lyin' to you?" But before I could answer, he said, "But in any case—you're fired. You agreed to keep Malcolm out of the loop, and you disregarded the terms of the contract. We're breaking the terms of the agreement." Then he hung up.

"He's still declaring their innocence," I said, overwhelmed with frustration. "And he claims he saw the text and there was no photo sent to James. Yet James says it came from Buck's number."

"Reynolds sent it and deleted it," Jed said. "It's the logical explanation."

I wanted to argue, but it made the most sense. "We have to stop this. Can you find out where they're meeting?"

Jed shook his head. "No. I'm definitely out of the loop."

"Any ideas where it could be?"

"No. Maybe I would if Skeeter had planned it, but it sounds like someone else set it up."

"Maybe I should try to talk some reason into James in person."

"You've tried twice on the phone. We'd do better to use our time to find Scooter and get the truth from his own mouth."

I mulled it over for a few seconds, then said, "Okay. What do we do next?"

"We scope out the junkyard."

CHAPTER 26

*T*he junkyard was on the west side of town, just outside the city limits. I wasn't sure if that was a good thing or a bad one considering Joe was a whole lot more perceptive than the Henryetta Police Department. It was close to seven, which meant we barely had an hour left before James met Buck Reynolds.

"Do you think they'll really meet?" I asked.

"I think *somebody's* gonna show somewhere."

"Meaning?"

"Meanin' Skeeter will show up to get his brother back, but Reynolds . . . I can see him cuttin' and runnin'. Especially if you're right and he doesn't have him. And Skeeter *will* hunt Reynolds down and demand for him to hand over his brother. Make no mistake of that," Jed said, looking through his binoculars at the junkyard. "Maybe we're scopin' out the wrong place. Maybe we should head down to the warehouse where they took you."

"It'll take over a half hour to get there. Do we really want to take the chance? How about we follow James?"

"He'll notice. And it won't stop him," Jed said. "We need Scooter."

He continued to study the junkyard, but I was nearly jumping out of my skin. "I have a really bad feeling about all of this," I said, a panic attack brewing.

"Me too, but we're trying to fix it."

I shook my head. "No. I'm sure James is walkin' into a trap."

Jed lowered his binoculars and held out his hand to me. "Look."

I grabbed his hand and tried to slow my breathing so I could focus. I closed my eyes and asked if James was being set up. After a few seconds, I saw James lying on the ground in a puddle of blood with multiple gunshot wounds.

My vision ended and I said, "Someone's gonna kill James."

"What did you see?"

Nausea washed over me. "His dead body. He'd been shot multiple times."

"Where was he?"

I tried not to give in to my panic. I needed to focus if I wanted to save him. "I don't remember. All I remember is his body."

"Try it again and pay attention to your surroundings this time."

My eyes burned as I closed them again and focused on whether or not James was walking into a trap. His dead body was there again, but the surroundings were dark, and I couldn't make anything out.

"Someone's goin' to kill James," I repeated when my vision was over.

"Anything this time?" Jed asked.

I shook my head and my voice broke when I said, "No. I couldn't see anything but him."

Jed was silent for a moment. Then he finally said, "I'm goin' in to look for Scooter."

"I'm comin' with you."

"No," he said in a direct tone. "I know you mean well, Rose, but this will go faster if I do it on my own."

I wanted to argue, but I was still shaken up over the visions. "Okay," I said. "But check in, would you? Let me know what's goin' on."

"Okay, I will. I'll be back." Then he got out of the car and strode toward the junkyard like he owned the place. Once he got to the gate, two large, vicious dogs began jumping against the fence, snarling and snapping, but Jed Tased them and they fell to the ground.

He scaled the fence and soon disappeared behind a row of smashed cars.

I was surprised I hadn't heard from Neely Kate, and I knew I needed to let her know what was going on, so I called her.

She answered with, "Rose. I was gettin' worried."

"I know where he is, Neely Kate," I said with tears in my voice. I needed to convince her so she'd let this go, and the only way to do that was to make her think we'd found Scooter. "I found him."

I heard her tell Witt, "She found him." Then she said to me, "Where?"

"I'll explain it all to you later, okay? I need to take care of something first. Just sit tight and wait for me to let you know." As I hung up, I realized I'd reenacted the vision I'd had earlier, even if it had been unintentional. But if that vision came true, I felt even more panicked over my vision of Skeeter dying.

I tried calling James again, but it went straight to voicemail.

Dang it.

I was considering taking Jed's car and driving to the pool hall myself when my phone vibrated with a text from James.

I NEED TO SEE YOU.

I rapidly texted back. I NEED TO SEE YOU TOO. YOU'RE NOT SAFE. I JUST HAD A VISION THAT YOU WERE MURDERED. CALL ME.

There was a pause for nearly ten seconds. CAN'T TALK NOW. I'M SENDING MERV TO GET YOU. WHERE ARE YOU?

I considered telling him, but with Merv and Jed having their dispute, I didn't want to risk it. I'LL HAVE JED BRING ME.

IT WILL DISTRACT MERV. THEY'RE AT ODDS AND I NEED MERV ON TOP OF HIS GAME.

I CAN COME TO YOU.

No. Then seconds later he sent: I'M IN A SECRET LOCATION. I NEED YOU TO COME WITH MERV.

Was he in a safe house? I could see him not wanting to give me directions if that was the case. Bottom line was that I needed to see him, even if I had to endure Merv to do so.

OKAY. TELL MERV TO PICK ME UP AT THE GAS STATION AT THE CORNER OF COUNTY ROADS 5 AND 66. I CAN BE THERE IN FIVE MINUTES.

THANK YOU.

I considered sending Jed a text but decided to wait, figuring he might turn back and try to take me to James himself. What Jed was doing was more important. Finding Scooter was the surest way to end this.

The gas station was a short walk down the road. Thankfully, clouds had filled the sky and the wind had cooled things down. The sun was setting, casting everything in an unearthly orange tone. When I got to the gas station, I was surprised to see Merv already parked in the corner of the lot, his car idling.

I opened the back door but didn't slide in yet. "How'd you get here so fast?"

"I was already on this side of town. Skeeter's not far from here. Climb in so we can go see him."

"Where is he? The pool hall?"

"No. Get in and I'll tell you."

"Why don't you tell me now?"

"Because I think you're workin' with Carlisle, and Skeeter doesn't want him to know."

I called James again, wanting to verify that he'd really asked for me, but it went straight to voicemail. That left me unsettled.

He never turned off his phone. And I would have expected him to keep his phone on in case I texted. There was a lot about this situation that felt wrong, but I needed to get to James, and going with Merv was the surest and fastest way to do that. I felt like a traitor leaving Jed behind, but it made sense to split up in this instance. I climbed into the backseat and shut the door.

"Where is he?" I asked.

"He's at the fertilizer plant."

"That place has seen plenty of action the last few days."

He didn't respond.

My phone vibrated in my hand. I glanced down and saw a text from Violet.

Merv's gaze jerked to the rearview mirror. "No phones."

"Why not? It's just a text from my sister. I haven't even read it yet."

He reached his hand over the seat, palm up. "Skeeter's rules."

I had no intention of giving up my phone before I read Violet's text, but as soon as I read it, I knew I was in deep trouble.

I JUST REMEMBERED PAM'S BOY'S LAST NAME. CHAPMAN. AND HER OLDEST BOY DIDN'T GO BY MERLIN. HE WENT BY MERV.

My jaw dropped as I glanced up into the rearview mirror and held eye contact with Merv Chapman, James' betrayer.

CHAPTER 27

I wasn't sure how to play this, but it seemed inevitable that the look on my face would give me away. I reached for the door handle, only to find it was locked.

"Puttin' it together, I see," he said. "I'm gonna need that phone."

Did he need me dead or alive? I was guessing alive; otherwise, my kidnappers would have killed me the other night. "No."

I turned myself into the corner of the backseat, behind Merv—the furthest I could get from his reach—and immediately switched from Violet to Jed and started typing.

Merv reached into the backseat, grabbing at my clothes and hair in an attempt to get to my phone.

Merv kidnapper. Fertilizer plant.

I hoped Jed understood my gibberish.

Merv was now leaning halfway into the backseat, pulling my arm painfully to get to my phone.

I frantically pressed send, but there was only one bar of service, and I watched in a panic as the send bar crept across the screen. Merv was dangerously close to reaching the phone, so I turned on the lock screen and prayed the message didn't fail.

He snatched it from my hand and looked at the screen. "What did you do?" he growled.

I didn't answer him.

He grabbed a fistful of the front of my dress and pulled me closer. "What did you do?" His eyes looked wild.

I remained silent, staring at him in defiance.

He fisted his hand and punched me in the cheek. His ugly laughter filled the car. "You have no idea how long I've wanted to do that. You're lucky I held back. But the bruise will be a nice touch." He shoved me back in the seat, then grabbed my backpack and searched inside.

Considering the pain shooting through my face, I wasn't feeling very lucky . . . except Merv had underestimated me. He may have taken my backpack with my pepper spray and Taser, but I still had the gun strapped to my thigh. I almost pulled it on him immediately, then thought better of it. If I acted now and Merv refused to talk, my vision could still come true. The cost could be James' life. I would do better to find out more before acting.

James had gotten a texted photo of Scooter from Buck Reynolds, and if Buck was innocent like I suspected, that meant Merv had someone embedded in Buck Reynolds' camp. I aimed to find out who. "One of Buck's men is workin' with you. Which one?"

He dug into my purse. "One of his right-hand men. Someone he trusts. He'll never see it comin'."

Tim Dermot? I'd trusted him too. I felt like I was going to be sick.

"You sent the texts from James," I said.

"I knew you'd come runnin'. You couldn't help yourself. So I stole his phone, which wasn't easy."

Satisfied after his search through my backpack, Merv tossed it onto the passenger side floorboard, then turned his attention back to me. "Where's Carlisle?"

"Do I look like Jed's keeper?"

He grabbed my dress again and slapped me this time, hard enough to make me see stars. "I can do this all night, *Lady*." He spat the name out as though it left a bad taste in his mouth. "And the more battered you look, the more it will piss off Skeeter, so keep on defyin' me."

He was right, and I knew it—even so, I wasn't about to help Merv out. But he grinned at me, and the cruel self-satisfaction in that grin told me he already knew where Jed was. That's how he'd gotten here so fast. Merv was just looking for an excuse to hit me and start wearing me down.

"He's not gonna find Scooter," he said, confirming my suspicions. "If he'd arrived earlier he would have, but we've already moved him."

"So Scooter's alive."

"For the time bein'."

"Until it suits your purpose to kill him," I said in an even voice. I knew that in Merv's eyes, my fate was tied to Scooter's, and it was clear he intended to kill both of us before this was over. "Why are you doin' this?"

"You know why." He backhanded me, this time on the other side of my face, the ring on his hand catching my cheekbone. "You're too sure of yourself. You think you one-upped me with that text?" That same grin flashed across his face. "We're not goin' to the fertilizer plant. You sent Carlisle to the wrong place."

Fear rushed through my blood like a January arctic wind, chilling me to the core, but I tried not to let it show. Still, he must have seen the flicker of fear because his grin spread. "You *should* be afraid. Part of tonight is about teachin' Skeeter Malcolm a lesson about loyalty and consequences, and a good part of that means hittin' him where it hurts him the most."

Hitting James where it hurt the most didn't mean actually hitting *him*, although I was sure Merv had that in mind too.

I had the gun—I could feel it strapped to my leg—but I

panicked anyway, lunging between the two front seats for the front passenger door.

A man was walking from the convenience store to his car parked at the gas pump, and I banged on the window and started screaming, "Help! Help me!"

The man startled and stood in place, clearly torn between helping and running.

Merv wrestled me down to the seat before punching me again. He'd intended to hit me in the face, but I turned my head at the last minute, and the blow hit the side of my head. My vision darkened and I heard a gunshot before I passed out.

≈

WHEN I CAME TO, my head was pounding and Merv was hauling me out of the backseat. He jerked me to my feet, but I was still unsteady and my legs started to buckle. Holding me up with one hand, he pointed a gun to my temple with the other and dragged me around the back of the car.

"Sorry, I don't have your brother," Merv said. "But I brought someone else you seem to be fond of."

I heard James before I saw him. "Rose."

We were in the same warehouse in Louisiana where I'd been taken before, but this time James was standing in the middle of the space. The three wooden chairs arranged to his right were a new addition since my last visit. James had his gun trained on Merv, and he looked furious.

"I'm gonna kill you with my bare hands, Chapman," Skeeter said in a voice so deadly it scared even me.

Merv laughed. "That's not gonna happen, but I'll let you think so for now if it makes you feel better. And you might as well put that gun away. We both know if you shoot me, I'll shoot her too."

"Where's Scooter?" James asked, still holding his gun on Merv. "You said you'd found him."

"He didn't have to find him," I said. "He was one of the men who took him. He's conniving with someone in Buck Reynolds' camp. But Buck's not in on it."

James' eyes hardened. "What's your endgame, Merv?"

"We both know." He took several steps forward, dragging me with him.

I heard a car engine in the distance, and Merv's hold on my arm tightened.

A car pulled through the wide-open warehouse doors and parked next to Merv's sedan. Paul Chapman got out of the driver's door—I recognized him from his photo and Jeanne's vision—then opened the back door and pulled out a man whose face was covered with faded and fresh bruises. One eye was nearly swollen shut. Still, I could see a resemblance to James, although Scooter Malcolm was shorter and heavier.

"Skeeter," the man said when he saw James. "Why'd you come, you fool?"

His words shocked me, but then I remembered he came from the same stock as James. Of course he talked tough.

James remained silent, his gun still trained on Merv.

"Brothers versus brothers," Merv said. "Only, we have the upper hand this time."

"Scooter never wanted any part of this," James said. "And you know I kicked him out five years ago."

"And her?" Merv gave me a shake. "You sure wanted her. And if you dare deny it, I'll shoot her where she stands."

Regret momentarily filled James' eyes, but he didn't deny the truth. His expression hardened, and he snarled, "Cut to the chase, Merv. You were never one for theatrics, so tell me how this is supposed to play out."

"We're waitin' for one more player," Merv said. "And maybe I've warmed up to the idea of a show."

It was the show that worried me. I knew Merv had manhandled Neely Kate just last week. I was certain he'd do the same to me—he already had—but I had no idea how far he'd go. James was going to lose his mind.

And that was exactly what Merv wanted.

He dragged me toward the chairs, turning us to face James as he walked. When we reached them, he said, "Grab one of the chairs, *Lady*." He said the name with even more disgust than before. "You're gonna drag it until I say stop."

I glanced at James before I looped my hand over the back of the chair, but his face had become unreadable. I dragged it as Merv tugged me backward.

He stopped after about twenty feet. "Now sit."

He was no doubt planning to tie me up, so if I was going to use my gun, now was the time. But Merv still had his weapon pointed at my temple. If I made a wrong move, I had no doubt he would shoot me.

I stood behind the chair, still unsure about what to do, but Merv pressed the gun harder into my head. "You'd hate for *James* to have to see your brains splattered on the floor. *Sit.*"

My anger was growing stronger than my fear.

Still holding my arm, Merv dragged me around to the front of the chair and pushed me down until my butt was firmly planted on it.

"Skeeter," Merv said. "Grab that duct tape on the floor and bring it over."

James looked torn, but he wasn't in a position to say no. After a second, he walked over to the roll of tape and squatted to pick it up, never shifting his gaze from Merv.

"Now bring it over like a good *boy*. And drop your gun. I don't like it pointed in this direction. I'd hate for you to accidentally shoot Rose."

James started to put it behind his back, but Merv jammed the gun into the side of my head again. "Good try. Drop it."

James tossed it onto the ground with enough force that it skidded toward Merv's car.

"And the other one," Merv said. "The one on your ankle." He released a short laugh. "It sucks that I know all your tricks, huh?"

James didn't answer, just squatted again with the roll of duct tape in one hand and pulled up his pant leg with his free hand, revealing the gun strapped to his ankle. He pulled it loose and dropped it on the floor.

"And the knife."

James reached around to the other leg and removed a sheathed blade from its strap.

"Okay," Merv said. "Walk over to Rose, and you're gonna tie her up. And make sure it's tight enough, or she'll be the one to pay the consequences."

James walked over and dropped to one knee at my side, still facing me as he set the tape on the floor. His eyes softened as they searched my face.

"Hey," I said quietly. "Fancy meetin' you here."

His mouth twitched.

"Get to tyin' her up," Merv said.

James glanced up at him with hate-filled eyes. "I'll do it, but we both know this is probably the last time you'll let me near her. Let me tell her goodbye."

Uncertainty filled Merv's eyes, but he nodded.

"Step back so I can talk to her."

Merv laughed. "Beg me."

I suspected this was the first of many times tonight he planned to make James beg on my behalf. "Don't do it," I whispered.

James ignored me, looking up at his former friend. "Will you give me half a minute of privacy with Rose? *Please.*"

Merv laughed again. "You have twenty seconds." Then he stepped back several paces.

James cupped the side of my face. His thumb traced below the cut on my cheekbone. "I'm sorry."

I shook my head and threw my arms around his neck, leaning

into his ear and whispered, "I have a gun strapped to my left thigh. Get it and use it."

He whispered back, "Merv will shoot you. I have another plan to get you out of this. But you have to do what I say."

"What about you and Scooter?"

"If you get out, I can take care of the two of us. Cut yourself loose and run out to my car and take off. Keep the gun and defend yourself." Then he leaned back and looked into my eyes. "I'm sorry I dragged you into this. If I could go back and do it all again—"

"Don't you dare tell me you'd do it different," I said with tears in my eyes.

"I wouldn't have fought with you weeks ago." His words were heavy with regret. "Too much wasted time." Then he kissed me, one of his hands holding the back of my head while the other grabbed my left hand. His kiss was hard and demanding and reeked of goodbye.

He didn't plan to get out of this.

But as he pulled back and gave me a tight smile, I realized he'd placed something in my hand.

An open pocket knife.

"Let's get this over with," James barked at Merv. "How do you want me to do it?"

"Hands behind her back, taped to the chair back. Just like you taught me."

I moved my hands behind me, and James gently gathered them together, hiding the knife in my hand and angling it so that I could use it and then wrapping my wrists with tape. After several loops, he tore it off, then ripped off another strip to tape my bound wrists to the center scrolls of the wooden chair. When he finished, he leaned into my left ear and whispered, "I made it thinner on the right side."

"Get up," Merv barked. "What did you tell her?"

"You know how I feel about her. What do you think I told her?"

"Go stand back where you were."

As James walked back over, I realized Scooter was in another chair being tied up by Merv's brother, Paul. James gave him a long look, and Scooter nodded slightly. What had they just silently communicated?

I heard another car engine, and I immediately tensed. Could it be Jed? Had he figured out where we really were? Had my text gone through? Or was it Tim Dermot? I didn't know why it bothered me so much that Dermot was a turncoat. He'd betrayed Buck Reynolds, not James, but he'd shown me kindness. As stupid as I knew it was, it felt like he was betraying me too.

The engine turned off, and the men all turned their attention to the open warehouse doors behind me. Paul grinned, but Merv looked pissed.

"Where the hell is Reynolds?" Merv snapped. "You were supposed to bring him."

"Cool your shit. He's on his way," I heard a man say, but it wasn't Tim Dermot's voice. "Did you take care of the girl?"

I thought he was talking about me, but Paul nodded. "We caught her outside of town, headed toward El Dorado."

I gasped in horror. "Jeanne?"

Paul shot me an evil look. "I told her not to talk to you."

I couldn't stop the sob that rose in my chest. I knew in my gut that he'd killed her. And Merv had egged him on. I'd seen it in my vision.

Scooter began to thrash in his chair. "I told you to leave her alone. I told you she'd keep quiet."

"We left her alone, until she talked to Skeeter's girlfriend. We couldn't risk it."

"But it didn't matter anyway," I said through my tears. "You're gettin' away with whatever you want. Why couldn't you just leave her alone?"

"Did Lady know her?" the guy behind me asked, moving around to face me. I was relieved to see Gary, the guy who'd gotten hurt in the shoot-out, although he seemed to be using his arm just fine now. He gave me an inquisitive look. "Why would you care if she's dead?"

Because I'd convinced her to talk to me. Because she'd wanted to keep quiet, and I'd pressed her for information anyway. Because she'd counted on me, and I'd gotten her killed. My heart shattered into pieces.

But I needed to pull myself together. I didn't deserve to get out of this alive, but I could try to save James and Scooter before I died.

"I thought you said she was badass," said Paul, still standing next to Scooter.

"She is. Or she was," Gary said. "Maybe she's not so tough tied up, but she stared down Reynolds and kept walkin' as he shot at her. No fear whatsoever."

"Don't be stupid," Merv said, moving over and squatting in front of me. "Her weakness is she's soft with other people. She knows she got Scooter's girlfriend killed." He looked into my face. "Am I right?"

He was expecting a response, but I wasn't about to give it to him. I sucked in a breath, willing myself to stop crying.

His hand rested on my left knee and slowly began to slide up, fractions of an inch at a time. Slow enough to make James rabid as he watched, even though he said nothing. I didn't dare look at him.

I held my breath as a wicked smile spread across Merv's face. He slid his hands higher, then shoved my dress up to my lap, revealing my gun.

"What do we have here?" He laughed. "I knew you had it on you. I saw it while you were passed out in the back of the car. I left it there to see what you would do. I was just waiting for Skeeter to snatch it so I could have a good excuse to shoot you."

Terror filled my head and I tasted metal on my tongue.

Surprisingly, Merv left the gun on my thigh. Probably to torment me . . . knowing it was there yet having no way to reach it. "I want you to have a vision."

Merv knew about my visions? But of course he did. He'd been there in the very beginning. When I'd gone to meet James last November. How had I forgotten?

I swallowed, forcing myself to calm down. "Of what?"

"Don't play stupid." He put both hands on my exposed thighs, his right hand just below the gun strapped to my left leg. "You have to be touching me—am I right? Will this work?"

I shot a glance at James, but he was so rigid he looked like a statue.

"Hey!" Merv's fingers dug into my thighs. "I don't want you to have a vision of *him*. I want one of me."

The knife was still in my hand. If I cut myself loose, maybe I could use it to get Merv to let James and his brother go. But Merv would feel the jerky movements of me cutting through the tape if I tried it now.

"I don't know," I answered honestly. "I've always been the one purposefully touchin' the other person."

"Try it," he grunted.

"What do you want to know?" I asked, feeling like I was going to throw up. What if I couldn't see anything? What if I didn't see what he wanted? What if I did?

"I want to know if the transition from Skeeter to me goes as smoothly as planned."

I closed my eyes, terrified of what I'd see, no matter what the result would be. I found it hard to concentrate, and twenty or so seconds later, I still hadn't had a vision.

"Well?" he asked.

I opened my eyes. "I'm tryin'."

He pointed his gun at my chest. "Try harder."

"You stupid son of a bitch," James shouted. "If you'd paid any attention at all last winter, you'd know she doesn't work well under duress."

"And yet she had plenty of visions of your enemies."

"Stop," I said. "Stop shoutin' at him and let me concentrate."

"Do you need me to cut your hands loose?" Merv asked.

Under any other circumstances, I would have said yes. But I didn't dare risk him seeing the knife. "Just be still. Give me a second to calm down."

Come up with a plan, Rose. Save James.

But first I had to sign my death warrant by giving Merv his vision. I'd blurt out whatever I saw, whether he wanted to hear it or not.

Will Merv succeed James?

I saw nothing but gray.

Will James kill Merv?

Nothing.

Will James survive?

Nothing.

Will Merv survive?

Nothing.

I had to tell him something, so I decided to psych him out. But first I came up with a plan of my own.

Several seconds later, I opened my eyes and said, "James is goin' to kill you."

His momentary reaction of fear and surprise was enough—I bucked up my legs and dislodged his hands as I brought the blade against the edge of the tape. It was sharper than I expected, and it sliced through the tape like butter. My plan hadn't included Merv to still be squatting in front of me, but the opportunity was too good to be missed. Going off instinct, I swung my left hand around and buried the blade into Merv's right bicep until it embedded into bone. Merv looked up at me with a stunned expression before I kicked his crotch so hard the top of my foot throbbed. The force of my kick sent him to the floor on his back.

I grabbed my gun and stood, pointing it at Merv's chest, then said in a deadly calm voice, "If you ever touch me again, I'll bury that knife where my foot just was."

"Put the gun down," Paul said in an exasperated tone. "Or I'll shoot you."

Merv lay on his back with the blade still buried to the hilt in his right arm, his knees drawn up to his chest. Confusion and pain waverd in his eyes.

I could see that Gary had his gun trained on me as well.

"Put down your guns, or I'll shoot Merv first," I said.

"Go ahead," Gary said. "I'm second in command. I'll get his place."

Paul looked torn between saving his brother and moving up to second.

So much for loyalty among thieves.

We stood like that for several seconds before a gunshot rang out. I was sure one of Merv's guys had shot me and I just hadn't felt it yet, but to my surprise, Gary fell to the ground. Merv rolled to his right side, away from the shooter, and jarred the knife in his arm. He shouted out in pain.

I shifted my gaze to James, but he was already running for me. He wrapped an arm around my waist and picked me up off the ground, carting me around the front of Merv's car and out of the line of fire.

"That wasn't the plan," he snarled as he snatched my gun from my hand.

"I did the best I could with what I had," I said. I was starting to get light-headed from the adrenaline crash. "Sorry I lost your knife."

He glanced around the bumper. "Don't you worry. I plan on gettin' it back," he said in a menacing tone. He aimed and shot— several rounds rang out, one bullet hitting the hood of the car.

I glanced across the warehouse floor. "Where's Scooter?"

"He's out of sight."

"How?"

He ignored me and got off another couple of rounds.

There was silence for several long seconds before James called out, "Jed?"

"Here." Jed's voice echoed across the space.

"Who's left?"

"Merv. Looks like he went out back. I stayed to make sure you and Rose were covered."

"You take the front. I'll take the back." James grabbed my chin and stared into my eyes with a stern expression. "Swear to me you'll stay put."

"I'll stay. You handle this one."

He took off running for the back door, and a wary silence descended on the warehouse.

Where had Scooter gone?

I glanced around the bumper and saw Paul and Gary lying on the floor in pools of blood, but there were no signs of Merv or Scooter.

What if Merv had taken him hostage?

I heard a sliding sound—metal against metal—followed by a bang. It took me a moment to process it, but I realized someone had slammed the warehouse doors shut and locked them with a bar.

Had James closed me in?

But then I heard footsteps walking toward me, and I knew Merv was still in the warehouse. He'd just locked me inside with him.

And James had my gun.

CHAPTER 28

"Come out, come out, wherever you are," Merv called out in a singsong that sounded wrong in his deep voice.

I stayed quiet, moving around to the passenger side of his car in my effort to hide. I tried to open the car door, but it was locked.

There was banging on the warehouse doors, and James' muffled voice shouted my name.

"I should have made him choose," Merv said, his voice getting closer. "He would have chosen you. It would have been . . . entertaining to watch his brother's face when that happened."

I stayed quiet. How was I going to get away? If I ran for the door, he'd shoot me. Only these two cars provided any cover. Would we circle around and around until he caught me?

James was still banging on the door and shouting threats at Merv.

"Come on, Rose," Merv said. "Don't you want to know how I guessed he'd choose you?"

I didn't care one fig what that man thought, so it showed how stupid he really was to think that would make me bite.

"I'll kill Scooter." He stomped closer, and I crawled back to the front of the car, but he strode toward the office, not even giving his dead brother a spare glance. He disappeared inside, and I noticed James' larger gun ten feet away. I made a run for it and picked it up, thrown off by the weight. Did I have time to get to the door?

But Merv emerged from the office seconds later, dragging Scooter out with him. He held his gun pressed to Scooter's side. Scooter's arms were still tied behind his back, pieces of the broken chair dangling from them, and after seeing Jed do the same thing once, I wondered if James taught a class on how to escape such situations.

That crazy thought passed when I realized I was in the same situation James had been in with *me* less than fifteen minutes ago. The only difference was Merv still had a knife blade jammed into his right arm, but it clearly hadn't stopped him. There was a reason he'd always reminded me of a bull.

"Well, isn't this a purty picture?" Merv asked with a menacing grin. "Skeeter Malcolm's two reasons for livin' in my clutches."

"I'm not in your clutches," I said. "Not anymore. I've got a gun on you, so you could say you're in mine."

He whipped his gun up and pointed it in my face. "Now we're in a standoff."

The banging had stopped, and I heard gunshots and ricocheting metal. James was trying to shoot his way in.

"I'm okay with that." I took a step toward Merv. "Let Scooter go, and let's make this about you and me. It's me you're really pissed at anyway—am I right?" I said, repeating his earlier phrase. "You hate that James needed me last winter. That he used *me* and didn't turn to *you*."

"You're full of shit," he sneered.

"Am I? You hated having to protect me last February. And you hate me even more after you got shot because of me. How dare I usurp your position in Skeeter's life? It's bad enough you had to contend with Jed. But you got rid of him. I was the only one left."

"I'm not some seventeen-year-old girl with a crush," he said in disgust as he moved closer, dragging Scooter with him as an afterthought.

"And neither am I," I said. "I'd be easier to dismiss if I were."

"He relied on you too much. Too fast. I spent years workin' my way up the ranks."

"I know," I said without malice. "And I stole it from you."

"I thought after Skeeter got rid of J.R. he'd be done with you, but he couldn't let you go. He's never been infatuated with a woman like he is with you."

"See? This is about me. So let his brother go."

"Skeeter killed my brother, so now I'll kill his. An eye for an eye, just like the good book says."

"And it also says to love your neighbor as yourself."

He gave me a wry grin. "Well, that's just it. I suspect Skeeter Malcolm doesn't think too much of himself these days."

That caught me by surprise, but I held my tongue.

Scooter stood still, watching me with cautious eyes, but he didn't seem to be jumping into the conversation, so I kept up my badgering. I needed to save him. I'd failed so horribly with Jeanne, and I couldn't do the same with him.

"You don't need Scooter. Besides, you like him. Everyone does. You're liable to piss off half the county if you kill Scooter Malcolm. Nobody gives two cents about me."

"Except for Malcolm."

"That's right," I said, trying to sound self-assured, but my heart was racing and I was struggling to catch my breath. "You have to think this through, plan for the long run, right? Isn't that why you asked me to have a vision? Because you're worried about how Skeeter's men will react to your coup?"

"Most of 'em know he's not himself."

"Then all the better to make your move," I said. "You timed it right, but you can't be a hothead. You have to think about the transition. Killin' Scooter's gonna piss off your new men something fierce. Maybe you can make a deal with Scooter to make him back up your version of how things went down. I can help you cook something up if you'd like."

"I don't need shit from you," Merv spat out.

"Why do you think James kept me around? It wasn't just for the visions. I helped him think things through sometimes. I'm an outsider, so I can think outside of the box, and you need a whole new box, Merv Chapman."

He didn't say anything, so I continued. "The way I see it, you're in deep shit. Skeeter's men are loyal, even when they don't agree with his judgment. So when they find out you killed Scooter and betrayed James . . . it's not goin' to bode well for you."

Panic filled his eyes. "You think I don't know that? But we'll go through the ranks and make them pledge to me or die. We'll make examples of the ones who don't."

"That's downright stupid," I said. "You need every single one of those men. You can't afford to lose any of them."

"I'll be gettin' Reynolds' men too."

"I wouldn't be so sure," I said. "Buck never showed, and Gary's dead."

The look in his eyes told me he hadn't reasoned things through that far.

This was a dangerous game, but the only one I knew to play at the moment. I had to save Scooter, and that meant pushing all of Merv's buttons. He knew my weakness, but I also knew his. He couldn't see further than the power grab in front of him.

"If you send out Scooter, you might still be able to salvage this thing," I lied, and I wasn't sure I should be proud or ashamed that I sounded so convincing. "I'll help you come up with a plan to survive this, but you have to send out Scooter *now*."

"You're only doin' this to save your own ass," Merv sneered, but he didn't look so sure of himself.

"No. I'm as good as dead, and I know it," I said. "You want to make James suffer, and this is the best way to do it. He's sufferin' right now. You heard him out there."

"You're sure as hell not doin' this to help me."

"Not directly, but turns out helpin' you out of this is the best way to save the county. That's always been my goal. To protect the innocent people in the county. I've made no secret of that."

Merv gave Scooter a shove. "Go out the back door."

"What?" Scooter asked in confusion.

"Go," I said. "Tell Skeeter that Merv and I are workin' things through."

Merv looked pissed. "Go before I change my mind. And tell Skeeter and Jed that she's dead if I see either of their faces."

Scooter ran out the back door, and it swung shut behind him. I heard multiple voices shouting, but the clamor outside stopped moments later. Even the banging and gunshots cut off.

"Go on," Merv said, looking dubious. "What's my plan for redemption?"

I couldn't say I blamed his skepticism. I wasn't sure I could help Merv, let alone whether I wanted to. My only goal had been to get Scooter out of the line of fire. "Depends on whether you're still tryin' to stage a coup or not."

He snorted. "Once you start one, you can't just change your mind."

"Maybe not. You can ask for forgiveness."

"Never gonna happen. And even if I felt inclined, there's no stoppin' this now. Besides, you said you saw Skeeter kill me."

"My visions change," I said. Telling Merv I'd lied seemed like a bad idea. "Maybe sendin' Scooter out of here wasn't part of the universe's original plan. Maybe you changed things."

He looked unsure.

"I'll have another." And when he looked unconvinced, I tossed my gun to the floor. "Releasing Scooter was your sign of good faith that you want to stop this madness. Ditchin' my gun is my sign that I'm in this with you." I wasn't sure if I'd just done the stupidest thing in the world or the smartest, but it felt like the best way to get him to listen.

"Okay," he said. His gun was still pointed at me, but he hadn't pulled the trigger, so there was that. "Go on. Have a vision."

"I need to hold your hand," I said, taking a cautious step toward him.

He reached his left hand forward, and I took it between both of my hands, partially because my legs were so rubbery I could barely stand up.

"What do you want to see?" I asked softly, looking up into his eyes.

Some of the hardness fell. "Why are you doin' this . . . really?"

"Partially because of the county," I said. "That part's true."

"And the rest?"

"I don't know." But that was a lie.

Merv had been loyal to his boss—to his friend—for years until I moved into the mix. I had literally been no one to James, worse than no one—I was the girlfriend of the assistant D.A. and definitely not to be trusted. And yet James had trusted me. Again and again and again. Then the next thing Merv knew, I'd inserted myself into James' life with no sign of leaving.

While I didn't condone the choices he had made—he'd hurt and outright killed people—I partially understood them.

"What do you want to see?" I repeated.

He started to say something, then stopped and started again. "How much can you see?"

"Only the future," I said. "Your future."

"Can you see the afterlife?" he asked.

A lump formed in my throat. I had every reason to hate this man. He'd killed people. He'd told his brother to kill Jeanne . . . and yet I could still see his humanity. He needed to pay for what he'd done, but maybe there was still hope for him. "No. Only death itself."

"That's what's in my future," he said as his voice broke.

"Maybe we can change it. I can ask James to hand you over to the sheriff's department. You'll go to prison, maybe for life for your part in killin' Jeanne, but you'll still be alive."

"I've done time. I ain't goin' back."

"Then let's think this through."

His hand squeezed mine, painfully. "Enough talkin'. Have the vision."

I closed my eyes and took a deep breath to try to calm my rattled nerves, then asked, *Will Merv survive this?*

I heard a single gunshot as I leapt into my vision.

Gray surrounded me for milliseconds before plunging me into an icy blackness. It sucked me in and pulled me under, stealing my breath away. I panicked and tried to climb out, but I was trapped. A vise squeezed my chest, and it was impossible to breathe. A warm, thick liquid covered me, pulling me deeper into the darkness.

I was going to die too.

"You're gonna die," I whispered, but I was only semi-alert. The vision was pulling me back in.

The warm stickiness spread across my chest, and I knew it was blood. Lots of blood. Had Merv tricked me and shot me anyway?

"Rose!" I heard James' voice, faint but also near. "Get him off her!"

The sucking blackness lifted just as suddenly as it had fallen, and I could breathe again. I was back in the warehouse, and James was pulling me off the floor and into his arms.

"Jesus. Her body's ice cold, and she's covered in blood. *You shot her.*" He snarled the last part.

"It was a clean shot. I made sure of it." I recognized the voice and turned to see Tim Dermot. Jed was there too, dropping Merv's body onto the floor.

"I'm okay," I pushed out through chattering teeth as I started to violently shake. *I think.*

"She's in shock," Dermot said, kneeling next to me. "Maybe Chapman shot her. Let's get her dress off so I can look her over."

"Like hell you're takin' off her dress." James' arms tightened around me.

"Just hold me . . . warm me up," I said, shaking even more. "I was havin' a vision. The coldness is something I've experienced before when seein' death, but this is different. I've never had a vision of someone while they were bein' killed . . . I got stuck."

Dermot still knelt next to me and gave me an odd look as he took my pulse.

I was vaguely aware that I'd inadvertently exposed my secret, but I was more worried about surviving to worry about it.

Scooter walked up behind Dermot, his hands now free.

"I'm sorry," I said, unsure if he could hear me since I was shaking so hard. "I'm sorry about Jeanne."

He didn't answer, just stared down at me and James.

"Scooter," James said, "I'm sorry. I should have protected her."

He shook his head. "She wouldn't have let you."

Dermot, who was still kneeling beside me, glanced over at James. "Her pulse is weak. We need to get her out of those clothes then wrapped up in something to warm her up. Being covered in Chapman's blood isn't helpin' the situation." He looked toward two men in the doorway. "I need water, towels, and some blankets."

"We're not doin' it here." James got to his feet and strode across the warehouse toward the now-open doors, carrying me like I weighed nothing. "Jed," he barked. "Start my car. Turn the heater on full blast." Then he opened the back door to his car and got inside, cradling me on his lap while I shivered uncontrollably.

"Tell me what to do, Rose," he pleaded.

"It'll pass." At least I hoped. "I just have to warm up. I've never been stuck in death like that before. This time I couldn't breathe. I—I felt like I was drowning in blood."

"Dermot shot Merv from a hole in the roof, and Merv fell on top of you. The blood was his, and you couldn't breathe because he was crushin' you." I continued to shiver, and James started rubbing my arms and my legs. "You were havin' a vision when Dermot shot Merv?"

"I was tryin' to fix it."

"Fix what? *Merv?*" He placed his hand on my head and held my cheek to his chest. "You can't fix everything, Rose. No matter how much you want to. There was no fixin' Merv. He was too far gone."

Yet I had seen a tiny sliver of the decent man I was sure he'd once been . . . and now he was gone. So many people were gone.

I started to cry.

"Shh . . ." he whispered into my ear, then rolled down the window and hollered his brother's name.

Scooter came over to the car door, still looking out of it.

"Get in," James said. "I'll bring you home."

Scooter shook his head. "I'll stay and help clean up. Jed can take me home later. Take care of Rose."

The two men locked eyes for several seconds; then James rolled up the window and said, "Forget cleanin' her up. Drive us home. Then come back and help Dermot with the mess."

I wondered who he was talking to for a moment, but Jed was still in the driver's seat, and he took off like a bat out of hell, dust flying up around the car.

Jed drove us to James' house, and since he lived south of town, we were there in less than twenty minutes. Speeding probably helped.

"Why are we here?" I asked as James got out of the car. Jed had already gotten out and unlocked the door.

"Because I'm not letting you out of my sight."

James stopped in front of Jed with me still in his arms. "Jed . . . I'm sorry."

Jed nodded. "We're good. We'll talk tomorrow. Take care of Rose."

James nodded. Then he bounded up the stairs, still carrying me, and headed straight into his bathroom. He set me down on the side of the tub as he walked into the shower and turned on the water. After stripping off his own bloody clothes, he sat down beside me and approached me like I might break apart if he touched me. "I'm gonna take off your dress, okay?"

I nodded, tears tracking down my cheeks again. In the mirror, I could see I was drenched in Merv's blood as well as my bruised and battered face. I reached up to help James take off my dress, but now that his body heat wasn't next to me, I was shivering uncontrollably again. He must have decided this wasn't the time for gentleness, because he grabbed the neckline of my dress and ripped it down the middle, tugging it down. The dress fell to the floor, and he carried me into the shower, still wearing my bra and panties and the gun holster around my thigh.

After setting me on the tiled bench, he angled the steaming water on me. "Is that too hot?"

I shook my head.

"Do you want it warmer?"

"Yeah."

He adjusted the temperature and then took off my underwear and the holster, tossing them out of the shower and onto the floor. The contrast from last night to now was startling, yet the demanding passion and tender devotion were both part of him.

He washed me with shower gel, his hands gentle, and when he was done, he pulled me to my feet and pressed me to his chest as the water pelted my back. "You've stopped shivering. Are you feeling better?"

"Yeah," I said slowly, but then I decided he deserved the truth. Even if it scared him. "Sort of. I still don't feel quite right."

"What do you need?"

"I don't know. I think maybe I need sleep."

He grabbed a towel and brought it into the shower before he turned off the water. As soon as he had me dry, he got out and grabbed another towel out of a cabinet. I tried to get out too, but he wrapped the fresh towel around me and scooped me up instead. He carried me into his room, tossing down the covers and gently laying me on the sheets. By the time he'd covered me up, I was shivering again.

He sat next to me and studied me with fear in his eyes. "I'm going to make you some hot tea. Maybe you need to be warmed up from the inside."

"Okay."

The tea helped, but it wasn't enough. James climbed into bed with me, pressing his naked front to my back and covering my arms and legs with his own. Within a minute or so, my shivering stopped.

"Are you tired?" he asked.

We were honest when we were naked. "I'm scared to go to sleep." Every time I closed my eyes, that horrible darkness filled my head.

"You're safe, Rose. I swear it. No one's gettin' in here."

I laced my fingers with his. "I know."

"I didn't protect you tonight," he said. "I'm sorry."

"I'm not your responsibility."

"But I want you to be." He leaned over and placed a soft kiss on my temple. "Go to sleep. Let me take care of you. Let me do this so I don't feel so helpless."

"Okay."

He began to lightly stroke my arm, and soon I drifted off into a dreamless sleep. I'd face reality tomorrow.

CHAPTER 29

When I awoke, the room was dark. The drapes had been pulled, but somehow I knew I'd slept late. James was in bed with his laptop, which he quickly put on his bedside table when he saw me stir.

"You're wearing sweatpants and a T-shirt," I murmured as I rolled over to face him.

"I *do* wear clothes sometimes."

I grinned. "What time is it?"

"Eleven thirty."

"*In the morning?*"

"Yeah."

I sat upright, then remembered I was still naked. "Why didn't you wake me?"

"Because you needed to sleep." He tugged me back down, then lay next to me, on top of the covers. He brushed a stray hair from my face.

"What are you doin' here with me? Shouldn't you be workin'?" I asked. "Shouldn't you be takin' care of what happened last night?"

"It's been taken care of."

"Jed took care of it alone?"

"No, Dermot helped. And Scooter. Even if I'd tried to help, Jed wouldn't have let me. He was worried about you. How do you feel?"

"Better."

"You're sure?" he asked, searching my eyes.

"Yeah." I watched him in amazement. If you'd told me a year ago, or even last November, that big, bad, gruff Skeeter Malcolm would be lying on a bed with me one day, worried about me, I would have fallen apart laughing. And yet here he was, a different man from the one I'd first met. He'd been in there all along. I'd just helped find him.

And I wanted him.

"Are you hungry?"

I lifted my mouth to his and murmured against his lips. "Not for food."

A fire filled his eyes, and he leaned over and kissed me as though this was our last time together. As though we didn't have enough time.

I wondered if this was what life with him would be like. Living for the moment and taking what we could get.

But I didn't want to think about the real world right now, or what this might mean. I only wanted to be here in bed with him.

Afterward, we lay in a sweaty, tangled mess of legs and sheets, and I laughed. "If we were together, I wouldn't need to worry about workin' out."

"What if we were together?" he asked quietly.

I froze. Yesterday morning I'd dismissed it. Today, I found that I couldn't.

"You called me a coward," he said, his gaze holding mine. "You said I was afraid to care about someone. You were right."

"James." I lowered my gaze. "I had no right to say that."

He lifted my chin until our gazes met. "You were right. I realized that last night. I was sure Merv was goin' to kill you, and I thought about losin' you, and I realized I've been wasting time. I'm scared of losing you, but it hurts so much more not havin' you at all." He leaned over and kissed me, then searched my face. "I want to try this with you."

"When you say *try this*, what do you mean?"

"A relationship. A commitment."

I tried to rein in my imagination . . . and my expectations. "Sex?"

"Was last night about sex?" he asked, but he wasn't angry. "I was scared shitless. Part of me wants to run from this, hard and fast, but I also see the possibilities . . . I want you in my life, Rose. Both in my bed and out."

"You said I was in danger if I'm linked to you."

"Dermot's takin' over for Reynolds, and now that Merv's gone, there's no direct threat. Not from organized crime, anyway."

"You're sayin' people could know we're together and I wouldn't be in danger?"

"At least for the moment. For the first time in a long while, real peace is on the horizon. Not that it made a difference before. We weren't together, and you were linked to me anyway. You were still in danger." He searched my face. "I'm ready to stop fighting this. But your life is a different story. You have a helluva lot more to lose than I do. That's why I don't want you givin' me an answer yet. I want you to think about it. If we're together, I don't want you havin' any regrets."

I wanted to tell him that I didn't need time. I knew what I wanted, but we still had the same issues we'd had yesterday morning. Or at least most of them. Some of them were too big to ignore. "Okay."

"Two weeks," he said. "I want you to take two weeks to mull it over. If we do this, I'm all in."

I stared at him in disbelief. "You told me you didn't do girl-friends."

"I have no trouble admitting I'm an idiot."

I grinned. "Well, *that's* a step in the right direction."

~

ONCE AGAIN, I didn't have any clothes, so I wore another of James' T-shirts and a pair of sweatpants, but no matter how tight I pulled the string, it wasn't tight enough.

James insisted it didn't matter since he was taking me straight to the farmhouse.

"I haven't asked about Neely Kate," I said. I knew Jed must have let her know I was safe. But what did she know about last night? I asked as much.

"Parts of what happened. The man at the gas station where we think Merv picked you up was shot. Jed got the text you sent and went to the fertilizer plant. He quickly realized no one was there and called Neely Kate lookin' for you. Jed took off for the warehouse—thanks to the directions you gave me yesterday morning. And Neely Kate and Witt heard about the gas station shooting and went to see if you'd been involved since it was so close to the junkyard. Once they heard that the man had seen a brunette in a blue dress wrestling a big guy in a dark sedan, they'd figured out it was you. Neely Kate called me, and I deduced it was Merv."

That explained my vision of Witt with the police cars. "Merv shot that poor man? Because of what I did?" I asked in dismay. "It's my fault. I was shouting for help."

"Merv's aim was off. He barely nicked the guy. He's gonna be fine."

But he was still hurt. Because of me. Not like poor Jeanne who was dead.

A vise tightened around my chest.

"Jed and I weren't sure what you wanted Neely Kate to know, so we decided to let you tell her yourself. She's not mad. Just worried."

"Does she know about Jeanne?"

"Witt found out and told her."

My heart broke even more. "I should have been there for her."

He didn't answer.

After he made me scrambled eggs and bacon for lunch, he took me back to the farmhouse. Then he surprised me by getting out of the car and walking me to the door.

Jed must have recovered my backpack, because James pulled my keys out of his pocket and unlocked the door. He placed them in my palm and closed my fingers around them. "If you need me for anything, call me. Even during the next two weeks. If your answer is no, I still want to be your friend. I don't want to lose you."

Once upon a time, he'd told me he didn't have friends either.

I gave him a sad smile. "I will."

He kissed me then, long and soulful, a kiss that seemed to simultaneously last a hundred years and a few seconds. When he lifted his head, he smiled. "See you in two weeks."

Then he walked back to his car and drove away. I watched him until he was out of sight.

I found Neely Kate in the kitchen making cookies. She glanced up when I walked in, and horror filled her eyes when she saw my face, quickly followed by tears, but I could see she was holding back. She paused. "Oh Rose. What did Merv do to you?"

"I'll be okay. Sorry I worried you to death. Did Witt go home?"

"We figured we didn't need him around anymore since you found Scooter and figured out Merv was behind it. I closed the office today . . . given everything."

"It was the right call. I'm so sorry."

She lifted her shoulder into a half-shrug. James had only been partially right. She wasn't just worried. Her feelings were hurt.

"I want to tell you what happened last night and why I did what I did. No more secrets, remember?"

Her mouth parted. "Really?"

"Really."

She put her last batch of cookies into the oven, then sat down at the table with me. I told her everything. My worry over Violet. The reason I called Jed to help me. The chaos that unfolded in the warehouse. My extreme reaction to being in a vision when Merv was killed.

Then I told her about James.

"I can't believe he wants a relationship with me," I said. "Less than a month ago, he told me he didn't do girlfriends."

"You think that's what he's wanting?" Neely Kate asked. "A girlfriend?"

"He said if I decided to try this, he was all in and committed. That sounds like a relationship."

"What about what *you* want?" she asked me.

"I want to try it, but there's a lot at risk. It's not just me. I have two businesses and employees who are counting on me for a paycheck. You. Maeve and Anna. Bruce Wayne. What if Bruce Wayne inadvertently gets tied to James because of me? I also have to think about Violet and her family." Mike had already expressed concerns about my choice of company.

"So what are you gonna tell him when your two weeks are up?"

"I honestly don't know yet." This was going to be a long two weeks.

"James said Witt told you about Jeanne."

She glanced down at the table. "Yeah."

"We should have called Joe."

Neely Kate lifted her gaze to mine. "She wouldn't let us."

"We should have done it anyway."

"Some people don't want help, Rose, no matter how much you want to help them."

My phone rang, and I dug it out of my backpack, surprised to see Maeve's number come onto the screen. Had she heard any of what happened last night? "Hey, Maeve."

"Rose? Are you at your office or at a client's house?" Her voice sounded shaky.

"I'm at home. What's goin' on? Are you okay?"

"I'm fine. It's Violet. Mike just rushed her to Henryetta Hospital."

My back stiffened. "*What?* What happened?"

"I don't know," she said, sounding like she couldn't catch her breath. "She dropped in at the nursery to say hello. She seemed fine; then she just collapsed. Mike wouldn't wait for the ambulance—he just picked her up and rushed off with her."

"Do you know where the kids are?" I was already halfway up the stairs to change my clothes.

"With Mike's parents. Violet said they came back to town early."

"Thank you, Maeve."

"Let me know if you hear anything."

"I will."

Neely Kate had followed me, and I quickly explained to her what was going on as I threw on a pair of shorts and a T-shirt. "Will you come with me?" I asked. "I'm scared to death."

"Of course." She pulled me into a hug. "I'm here, Rose. I'm always here for you. But first let's put on some makeup to cover up some of those bruises. Your sister's goin' through enough without having to worry about you."

∼

VIOLET WASN'T in the ER when Neely Kate and I got to the hospital. She'd been moved to a room on the second floor.

Neely Kate clasped my hand in hers as we got on the elevator. I knew deep in my gut that this was bad news, and I was pretty sure Neely Kate knew it too.

Violet was lying in a bed with her eyes closed, hooked up to an IV and monitors. Mike sat in a chair next to her. His gaze jerked up when he saw us, and he got up and moved to the door, motioning for us to head back out.

"I don't want to wake her," he said in the hall. His face was pale and drawn under the fluorescent lights. Even though Neely Kate had worked wonders with her makeup, she could only do so much. His eyes lingered on my face, and I knew I'd only added to his list of evidence that I wasn't fit to be around his family.

I nodded, suddenly unable to speak.

"What happened?" Neely Kate asked.

"She's pushin' too hard. She knows—" He cut off his words.

"She knows what?" Neely Kate asked.

But I suddenly knew. Parts of our conversation yesterday came back to me. I was scared.

"How long does she have?" I asked in a whisper.

"When we left Houston, they didn't know. Weeks." Hope filled his eyes. "Months? We were hopin' for months."

I started to cry, then stopped myself. Mike needed me to be strong. Violet needed me to be brave. "What are they sayin' now?"

"If she can get through this infection, the same. She needs to get through the infection."

I nodded. Before thinking it through, I started to reach for his arm. I could have a vision and see if she'd survive this . . .

Then I drew back. We needed to live life the way it was meant to be lived—with surprises, both the good and the bad. I wasn't sure why I had this gift or curse, but it had no place here. Not in this. Not if I could help it.

I pulled my hand back. "I want to see her."

Mike nodded. "She wants to see you too. I'll wait in the hall."

I walked back into the room, and Violet's eyes opened this time, but thankfully she didn't seem to notice my face.

"Rose." She reached her too-thin hand toward me.

I moved closer and took it in mine.

Disappointment filled her eyes. "You know. Mike told you."

"You wanted to keep it from me?"

"I didn't want my last few months filled with people starin' at me and wonderin' if it would be the last time they saw me."

I nodded. "I understand."

Tears filled her eyes. "I'm glad you know though." Her chin trembled. "I'm scared."

I choked back a sob and climbed up onto the bed. I lay down next to her and linked our hands as I buried my own fear. "I'm here, Vi. We'll do this together."

Tears rolled down her cheeks and into the pillow. "Can you have a vision and tell me if Mike will be okay? And the kids?"

"I don't need to have a vision to know they'll be broken. But they'll survive. I'll make sure of it. I'll be there."

She nodded.

"You gave up so much for me . . ." I said, tears flowing down my own cheeks now.

"But I couldn't keep you safe from Momma," she said. "No matter how hard I tried."

"But you made me feel loved," I said. "And that made all the difference." I sucked in a breath and smiled. "Maybe I can't save you from this, but you will never doubt you are loved."

That was the only gift I knew to give.

∾

IN HIGH COTTON
Neely Kate Mystery #2
February 13, 2018

∾

ALSO BY DENISE GROVER SWANK

Rose And Neely Kate reading order:

FAMILY JEWELS

TRAILER TRASH

FOR THE BIRDS

IN HIGH COTTON

Rose Gardner Investigations

FAMILY JEWELS

FOR THE BIRDS

Neely Kate Mystery

TRAILER TRASH

IN HIGH COTTON

(February 13, 2018)

Magnolia Steele Mystery

Center Stage

Act Two

Call Back

Curtain Call

(October 17, 2017)

Darling Investigations

(Humorous mystery romance)

DEADLY SUMMER

January 2018

Rose Gardner Mysteries

Novellas are bonus material

TWENTY-EIGHT AND A HALF WISHES

TWENTY-NINE AND A HALF REASONS

THIRTY AND A HALF EXCUSES

FALLING TO PIECES (novella)

THIRTY-ONE AND A HALF REGRETS

THIRTY-TWO AND A HALF COMPLICATIONS

PICKING UP THE PIECES (novella)

THIRTY-THREE AND A HALF SHENANIGANS

ROSE AND HELENA SAVE CHRISTMAS (novella)

RIPPLE OF SECRETS (novella)

THIRTY-FOUR AND A HALF PREDICAMENTS

THIRTY-FIVE AND A HALF CONSPIRACIES

THIRTY-SIX AND A HALF MOTIVES

SINS OF THE FATHER (novella)

The Wedding Pact

(Humorous contemporary romance)

THE SUBSTITUTE

THE PLAYER

THE GAMBLER

THE VALENTINE (short story)

Bachelor Brotherhood

Spinoff of The Wedding Pact series

ONLY YOU

UNTIL YOU

ALWAYS YOU (November 2017)

Young adult contemporary romance

ONE PARIS SUMMER

Off the Subject Series

(New adult contemporary romance)

AFTER MATH

REDESIGNED

BUSINESS AS USUAL

The Chosen Series

(Adult urban fantasy)

CHOSEN

HUNTED

SACRIFICE

REDEMPTION

Complete CHOSEN Box Set

Emergence (short)

Middle Ground (short)

Homecoming (short)

Curse Keepers Series

(Urban fantasy)

THE CURSE KEEPERS

THE CURSE BREAKERS

THE CURSE DEFIERS

CURSE KEEPERS COLLECTION (box set)

On the Otherside Series

(Young adult sci fi romance)

HERE

THERE

ABOUT THE AUTHOR

Denise Grover Swank was born in Kansas City, Missouri and lived in the area until she was nineteen. Then she became a nomadic gypsy, living in five cities, four states and ten houses over the course of ten years before she moved back to her roots. She speaks English and smattering of Spanish and Chinese which she learned through an intensive Nick Jr. immersion period. Her hobbies include witty Facebook comments (in own her mind) and dancing in her kitchen with her children. (Quite badly if you believe her offspring.) Hidden talents include the gift of justification and the ability to drink massive amounts of caffeine and still fall asleep within two minutes. Her lack of the sense of smell allows her to perform many unspeakable tasks. She has six children and hasn't lost her sanity. Or so she leads you to believe.

denisegroverswank.com

Made in the USA
Lexington, KY
03 August 2017